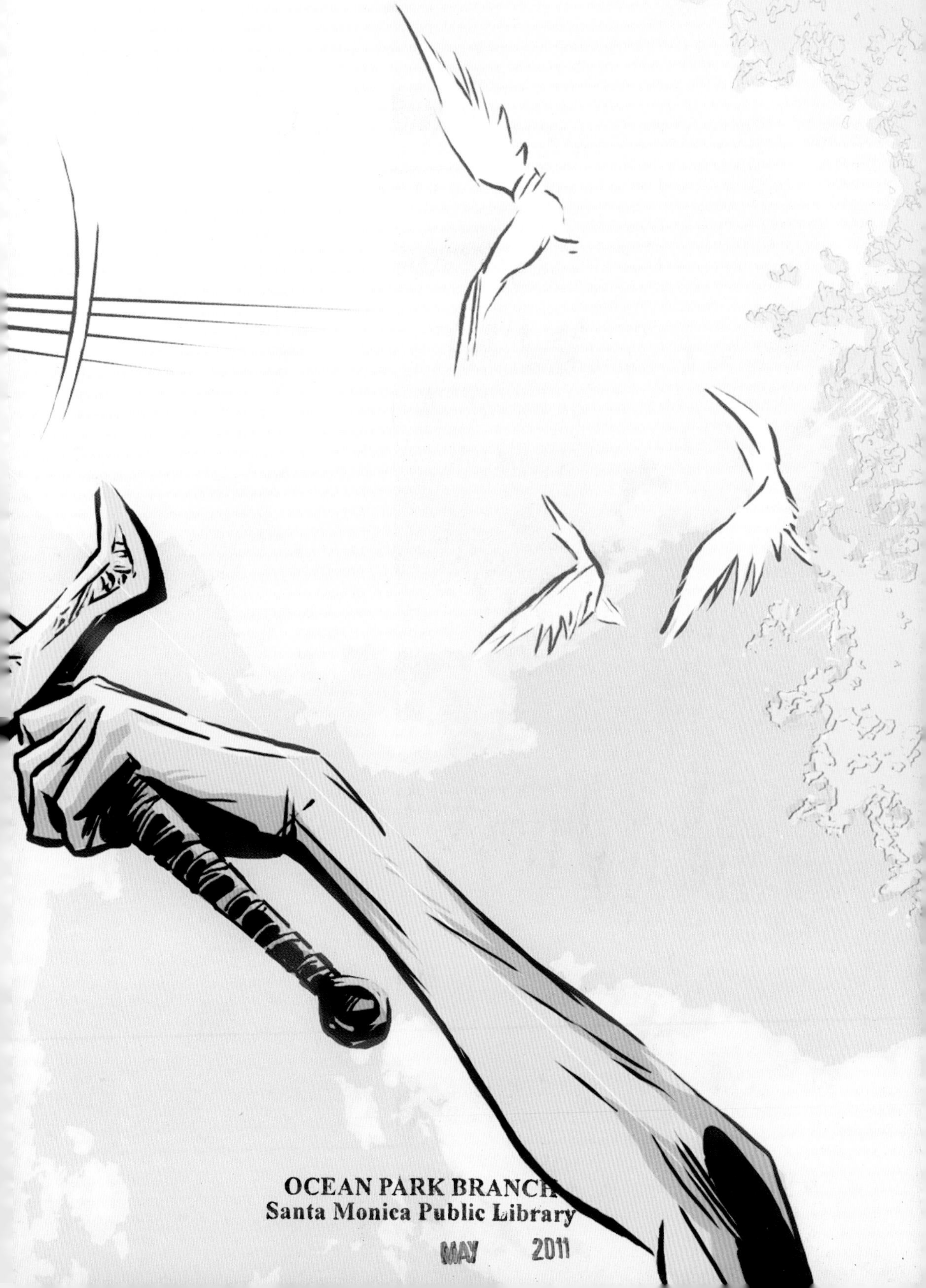

# Excalibur

## The Legend of
## King Arthur

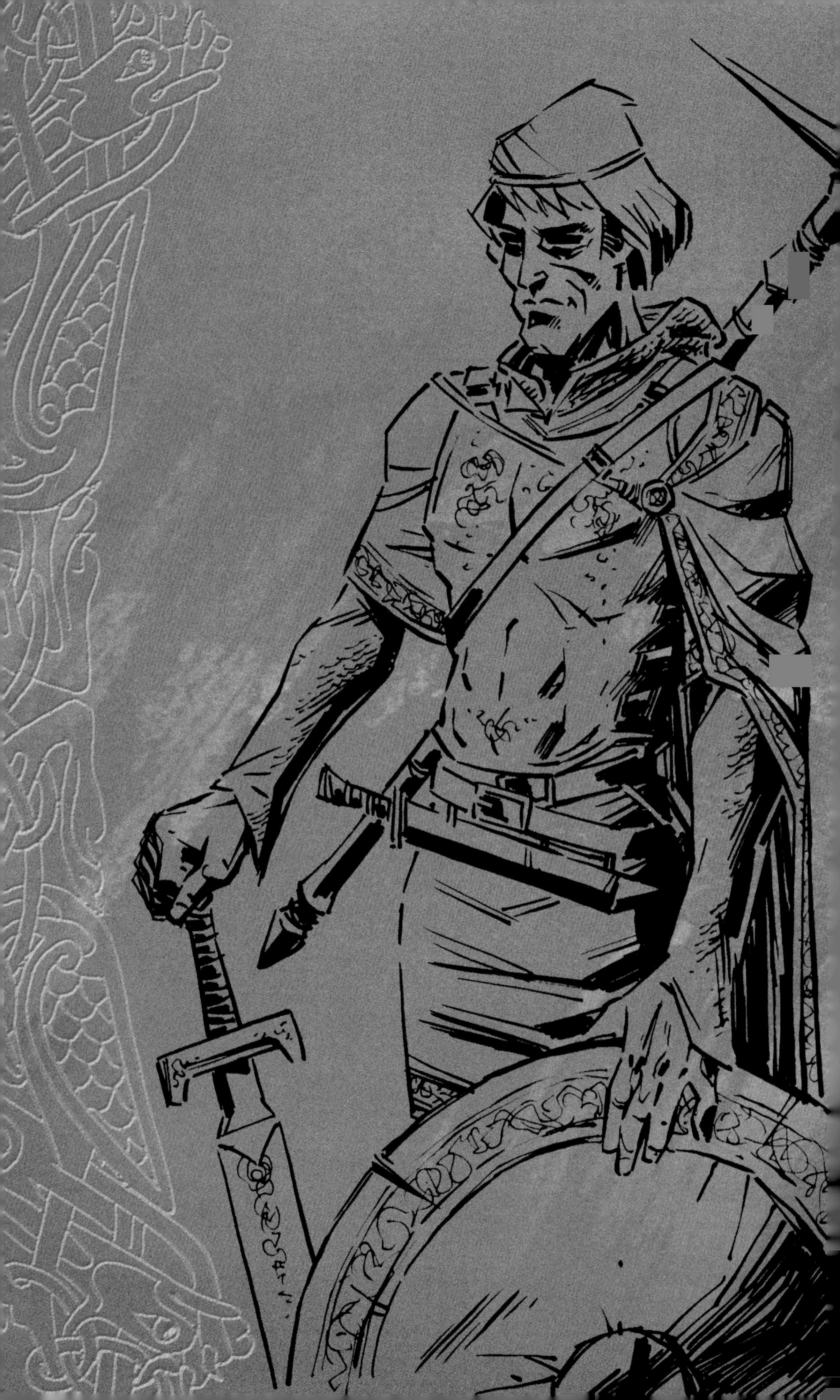

# EXCALIBUR
## THE LEGEND OF
## KING ARTHUR

### A GRAPHIC NOVEL

WRITTEN BY
**TONY LEE**

ILLUSTRATED, COLORED, AND LETTERED
BY **SAM HART**

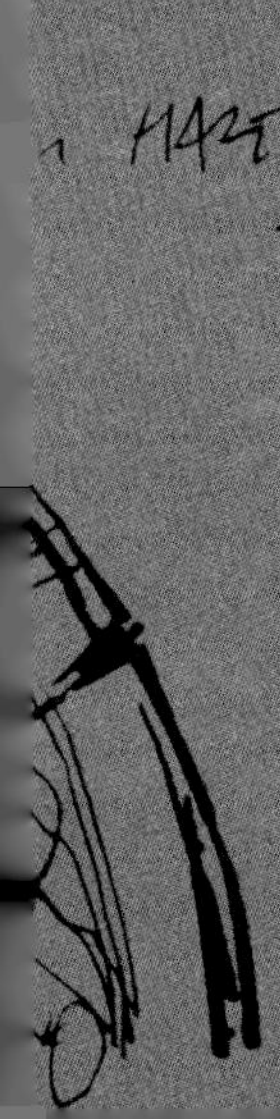

CANDLEWICK PRESS

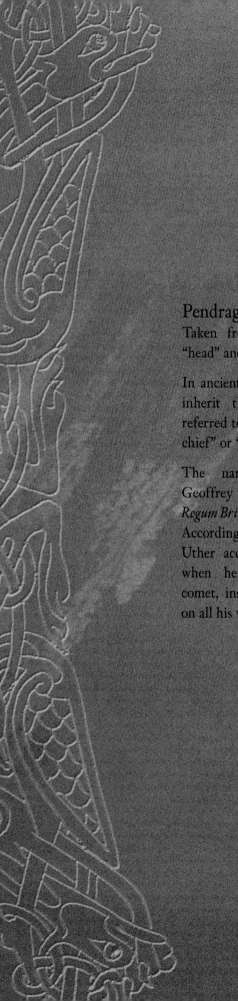

Pendragon (Pen·dra·gən) (n)
Taken from the Welsh *pen*, meaning "head" and *draeg* meaning "dragon."

In ancient times, kings of Britons would inherit the epithet *Pendragon*, which referred to their status as a "supreme war chief" or "head dragon."

The name was misinterpreted by Geoffrey of Monmouth in the *Historia Regum Britanniae* to mean "dragon's head." According to Monmouth's writings, King Uther acquired the title of Pendragon when he witnessed a dragon-shaped comet, inspiring him to display dragons on all his war standards.

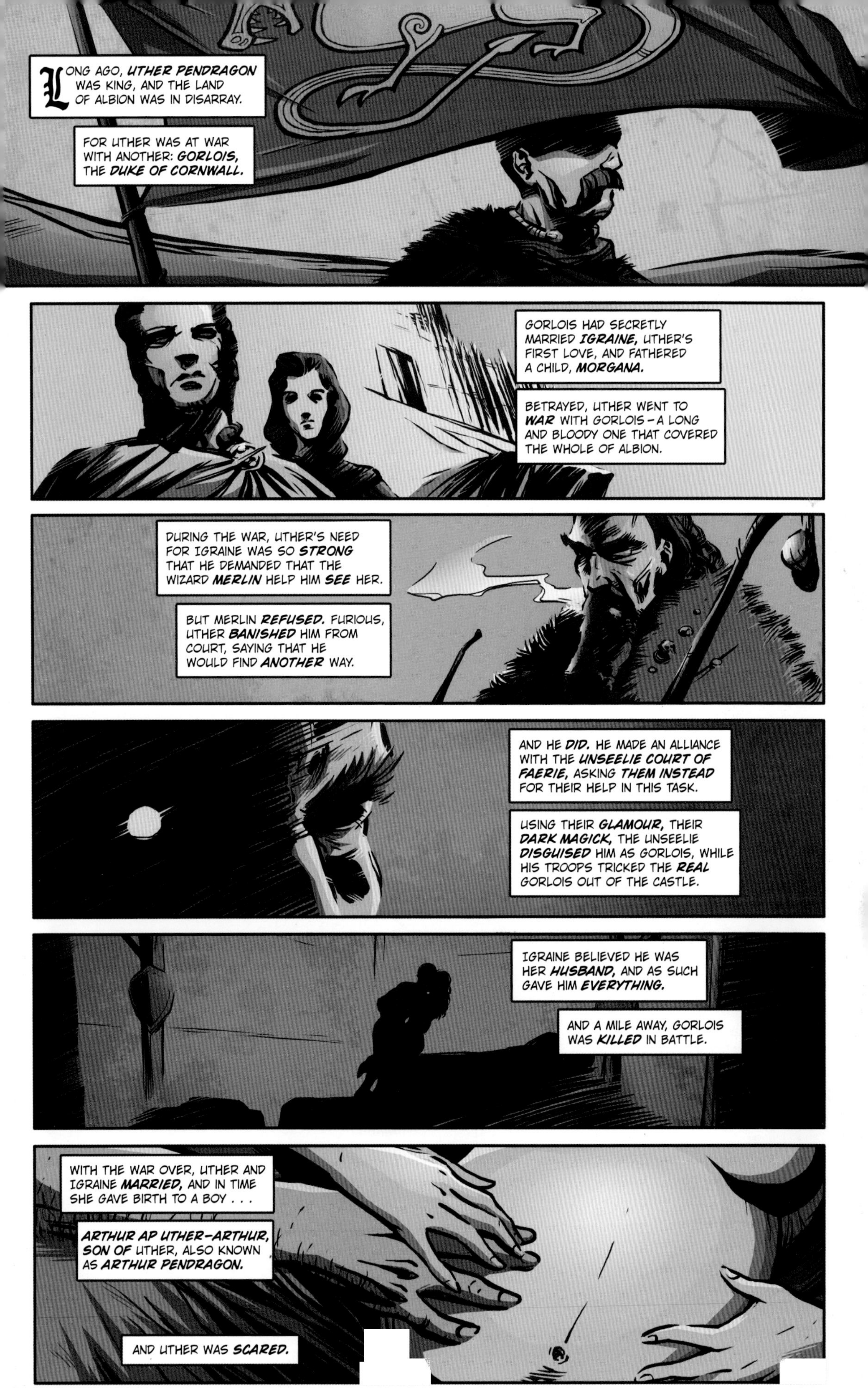
LONG AGO, UTHER PENDRAGON WAS KING, AND THE LAND OF ALBION WAS IN DISARRAY.
FOR UTHER WAS AT WAR WITH ANOTHER: GORLOIS, THE DUKE OF CORNWALL.
GORLOIS HAD SECRETLY MARRIED IGRAINE, UTHER'S FIRST LOVE, AND FATHERED A CHILD, MORGANA.
BETRAYED, UTHER WENT TO WAR WITH GORLOIS – A LONG AND BLOODY ONE THAT COVERED THE WHOLE OF ALBION.
DURING THE WAR, UTHER'S NEED FOR IGRAINE WAS SO STRONG THAT HE DEMANDED THAT THE WIZARD MERLIN HELP HIM SEE HER.
BUT MERLIN REFUSED. FURIOUS, UTHER BANISHED HIM FROM COURT, SAYING THAT HE WOULD FIND ANOTHER WAY.
AND HE DID. HE MADE AN ALLIANCE WITH THE UNSEELIE COURT OF FAERIE, ASKING THEM INSTEAD FOR THEIR HELP IN THIS TASK.
USING THEIR GLAMOUR, THEIR DARK MAGICK, THE UNSEELIE DISGUISED HIM AS GORLOIS, WHILE HIS TROOPS TRICKED THE REAL GORLOIS OUT OF THE CASTLE.
IGRAINE BELIEVED HE WAS HER HUSBAND, AND AS SUCH GAVE HIM EVERYTHING.
AND A MILE AWAY, GORLOIS WAS KILLED IN BATTLE.
WITH THE WAR OVER, UTHER AND IGRAINE MARRIED, AND IN TIME SHE GAVE BIRTH TO A BOY . . .
ARTHUR AP UTHER–ARTHUR, SON OF UTHER, ALSO KNOWN AS ARTHUR PENDRAGON.
AND UTHER WAS SCARED.

FOR THE COST OF THE DEAL HE MADE WITH THE UNSEELIE WAS THE CHILD OF HIS MARRIAGE —*ARTHUR.*

AND SO LITHER CALLED FOR MERLIN ONCE MORE, AND MERLIN *TOOK ARTHUR* FROM LITHER, NEVER TELLING THE KING WHERE THE CHILD WOULD BE HIDDEN.

WITH ARTHUR GONE, THE UNSEELIE COURT CLAIMED THAT LITHER HAD *CHEATED* THEM.

INSTEAD THEY DEMANDED *MORGANA,* LITHER'S STEP-DAUGHTER, TO BE HANDED OVER. AND LITHER RELUCTANTLY AGREED.

BUT THE DAMAGE WAS DONE; THE *TRUST WAS BROKEN* BETWEEN LITHER AND THE UNSEELIE FAE.

IN REVENGE, THE UNSEELIE COURT TURNED TO *LORD ULRIC,* KING LITHER'S CLOSEST FRIEND AND ADVISER, CONVINCING HIM TO *ENVY* HIS KING.

THEY ENCOURAGED ULRIC'S GREED FOR LITHER'S *CROWN,* AND ULRIC FOUGHT AND *DEFEATED* HIS KING AND ONETIME FRIEND.

LITHER DIED—

—BUT NOT BEFORE *THRUSTING HIS SWORD, CALIBURN, INTO A STONE,* STOPPING ULRIC FROM *TAKING IT* FOR HIMSELF.

WITH NO LITHER TO STOP HIM, ULRIC CROWNED HIMSELF *KING OF THE BRITONS.* BUT THE WIZARD MERLIN MADE A *PROPHECY*—

—THAT ONE DAY THE SWORD WOULD BE *PULLED,* AND THE *TRUE* KING OF ALBION WOULD RULE ONCE MORE.

HE WOULD *RULE* THE PEOPLE, HE WOULD *FIGHT* FOR THE PEOPLE...

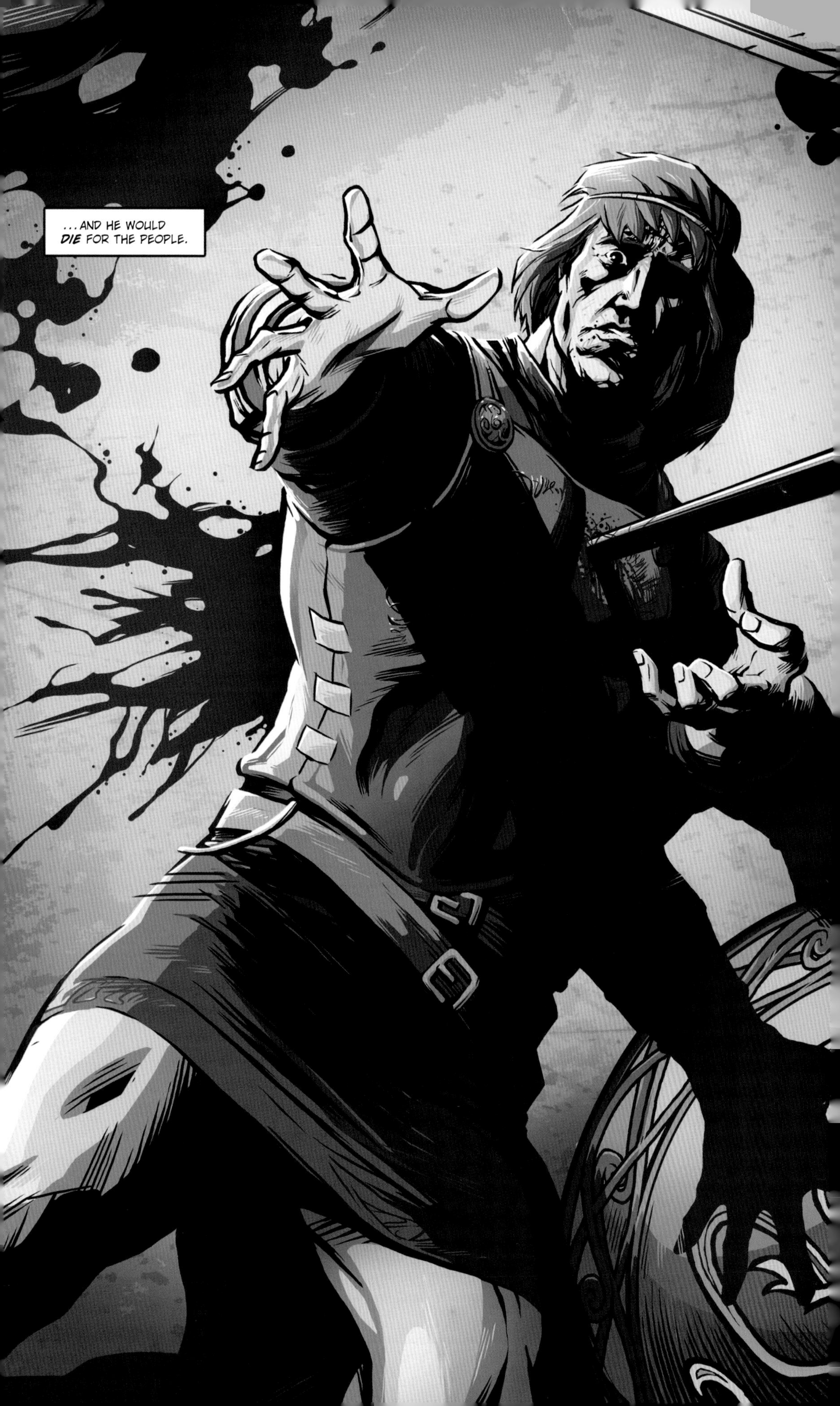
...AND HE WOULD DIE FOR THE PEOPLE.

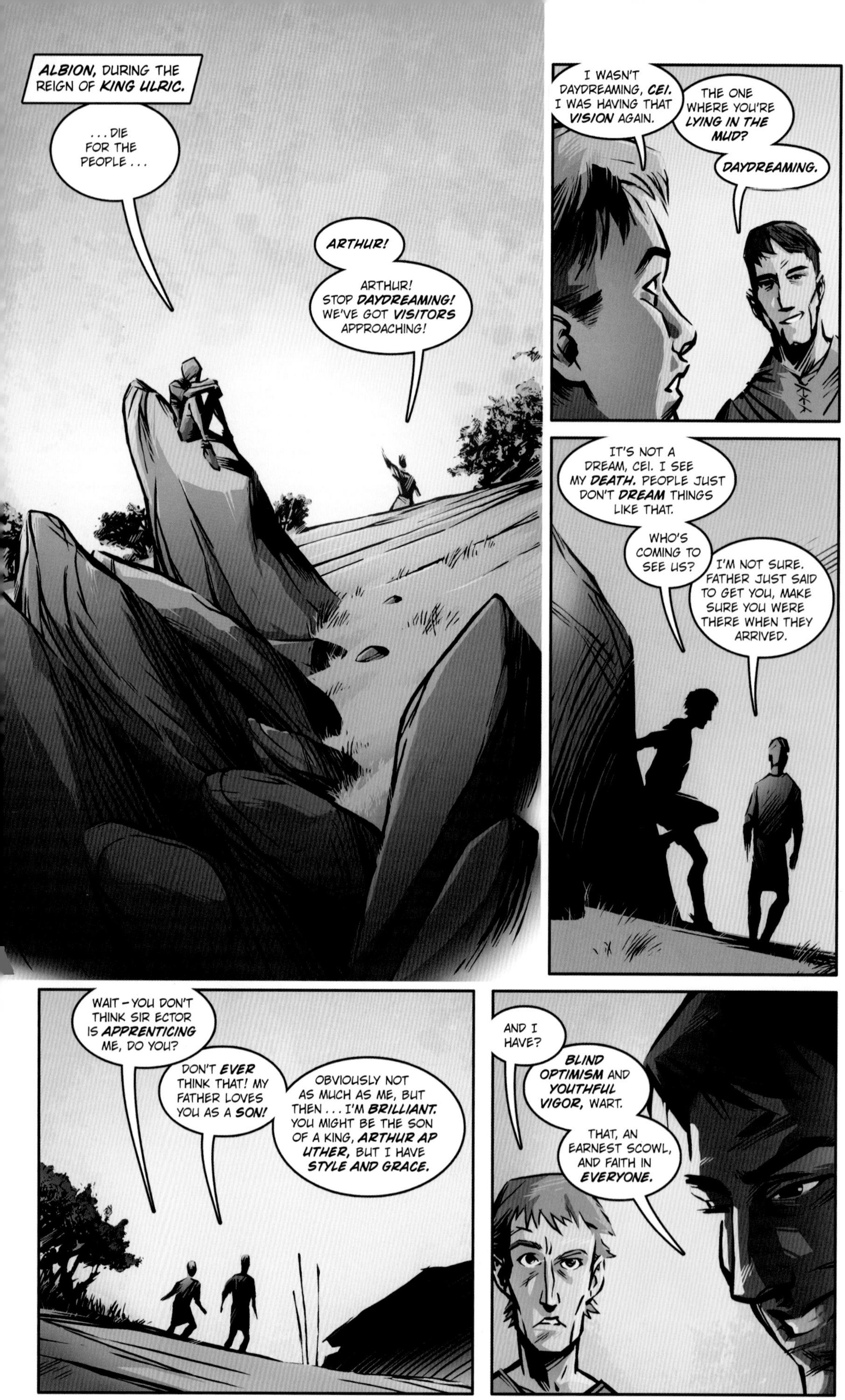
ALBION, DURING THE REIGN OF KING ULRIC.
. . . DIE FOR THE PEOPLE . . .
ARTHUR!
ARTHUR! STOP DAYDREAMING! WE'VE GOT VISITORS APPROACHING!
I WASN'T DAYDREAMING, CEI. I WAS HAVING THAT VISION AGAIN.
THE ONE WHERE YOU'RE LYING IN THE MUD?
DAYDREAMING.
IT'S NOT A DREAM, CEI. I SEE MY DEATH. PEOPLE JUST DON'T DREAM THINGS LIKE THAT.
WHO'S COMING TO SEE US?
I'M NOT SURE. FATHER JUST SAID TO GET YOU, MAKE SURE YOU WERE THERE WHEN THEY ARRIVED.
WAIT – YOU DON'T THINK SIR ECTOR IS APPRENTICING ME, DO YOU?
DON'T EVER THINK THAT! MY FATHER LOVES YOU AS A SON!
OBVIOUSLY NOT AS MUCH AS ME, BUT THEN . . . I'M BRILLIANT. YOU MIGHT BE THE SON OF A KING, ARTHUR AP UTHER, BUT I HAVE STYLE AND GRACE.
AND I HAVE?
BLIND OPTIMISM AND YOUTHFUL VIGOR, WART.
THAT, AN EARNEST SCOWL, AND FAITH IN EVERYONE.

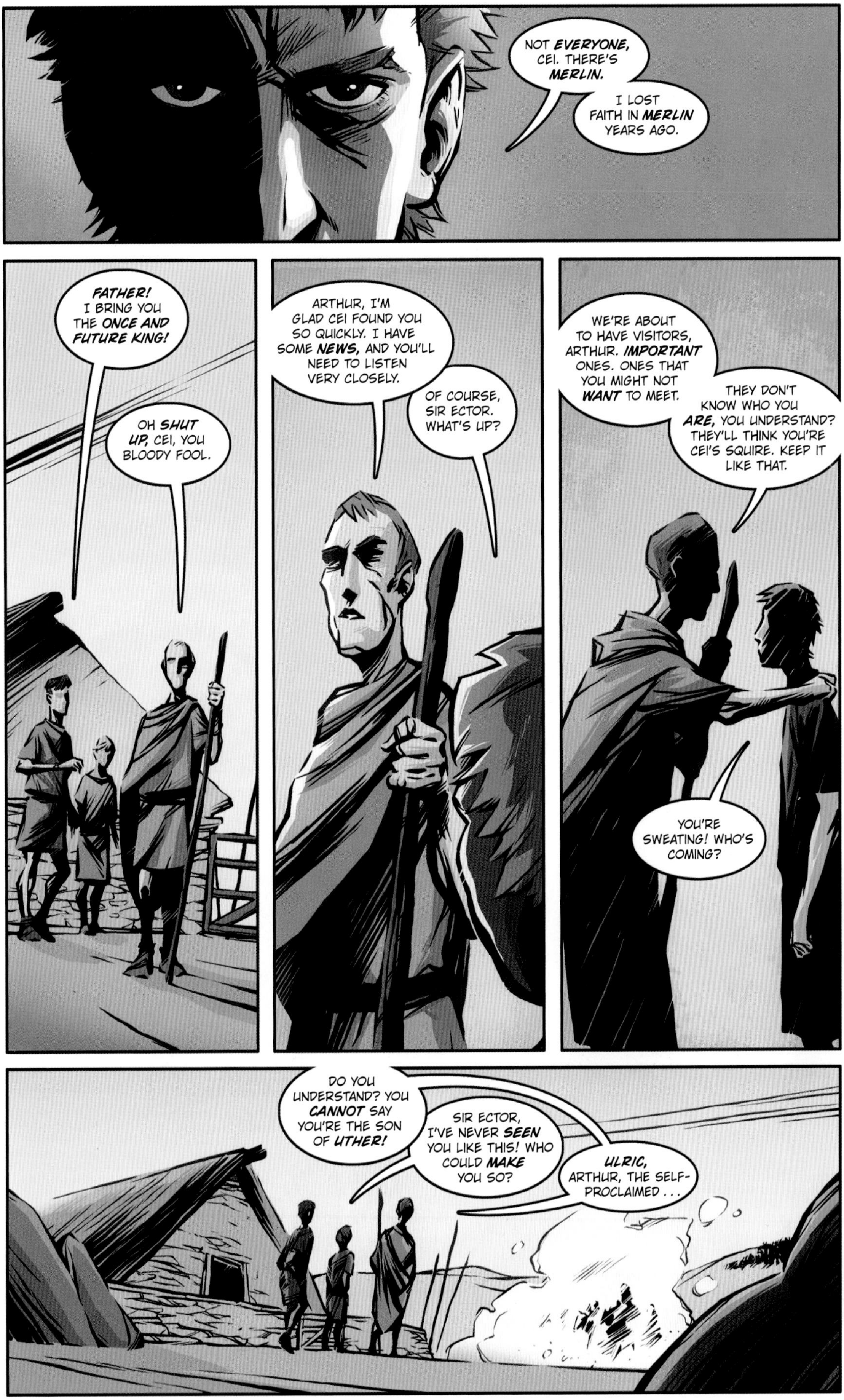
NOT EVERYONE, CEI. THERE'S MERLIN.
I LOST FAITH IN MERLIN YEARS AGO.
FATHER! I BRING YOU THE ONCE AND FUTURE KING!
OH SHUT UP, CEI, YOU BLOODY FOOL.
ARTHUR, I'M GLAD CEI FOUND YOU SO QUICKLY. I HAVE SOME NEWS, AND YOU'LL NEED TO LISTEN VERY CLOSELY.
OF COURSE, SIR ECTOR. WHAT'S UP?
WE'RE ABOUT TO HAVE VISITORS, ARTHUR. IMPORTANT ONES. ONES THAT YOU MIGHT NOT WANT TO MEET.
THEY DON'T KNOW WHO YOU ARE, YOU UNDERSTAND? THEY'LL THINK YOU'RE CEI'S SQUIRE. KEEP IT LIKE THAT.
YOU'RE SWEATING! WHO'S COMING?
DO YOU UNDERSTAND? YOU CANNOT SAY YOU'RE THE SON OF UTHER!
SIR ECTOR, I'VE NEVER SEEN YOU LIKE THIS! WHO COULD MAKE YOU SO?
ULRIC, ARTHUR, THE SELF-PROCLAIMED . . .

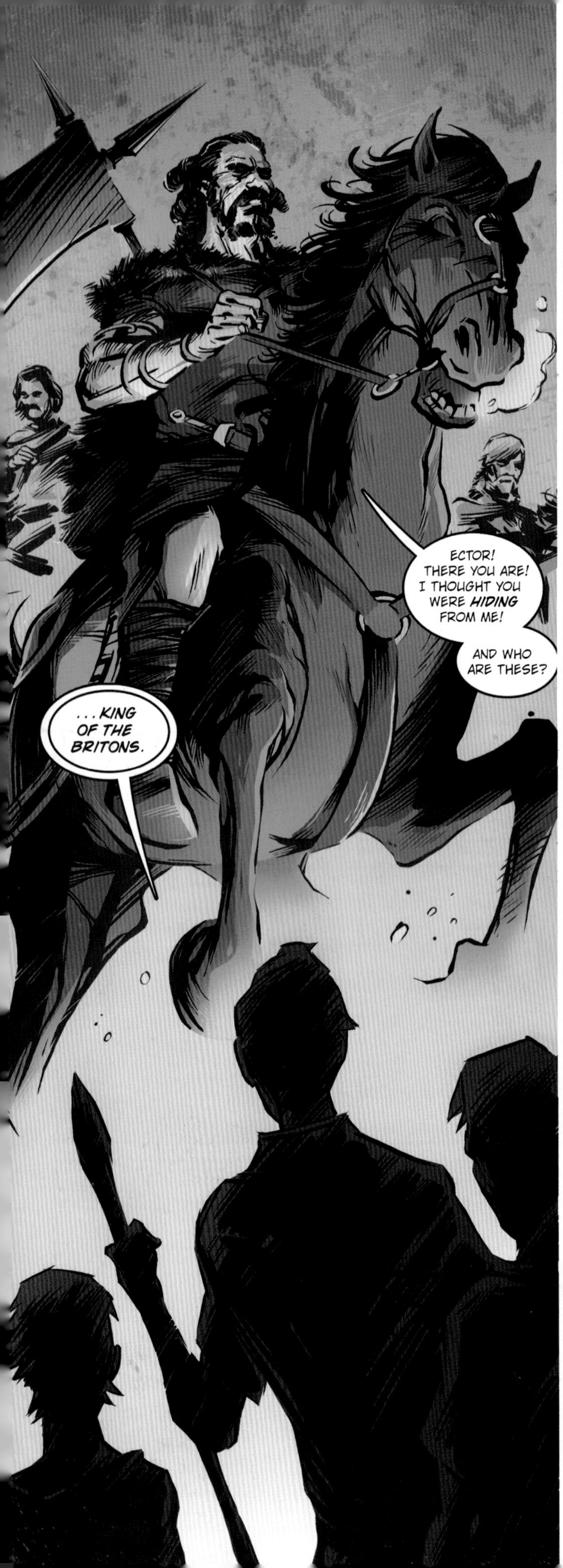
ECTOR! THERE YOU ARE! I THOUGHT YOU WERE HIDING FROM ME!
AND WHO ARE THESE?
. . . KING OF THE BRITONS.

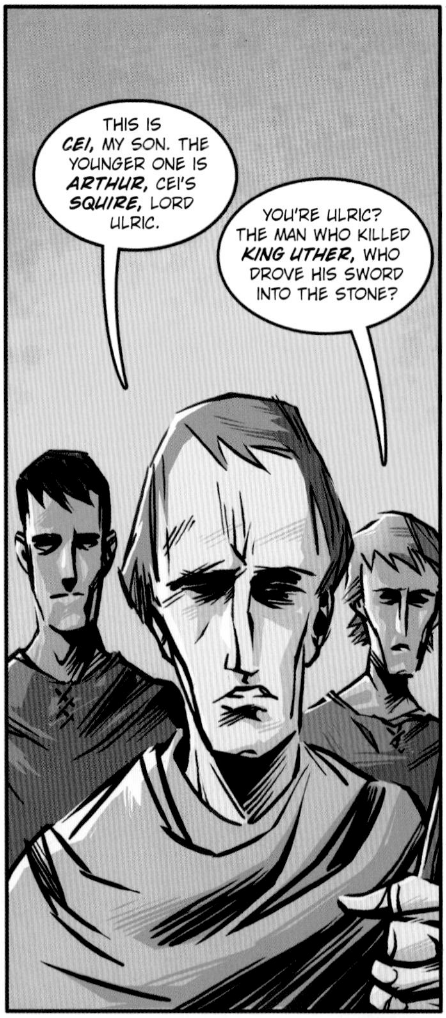
THIS IS CEI, MY SON. THE YOUNGER ONE IS ARTHUR, CEI'S SQUIRE, LORD ULRIC.
YOU'RE ULRIC? THE MAN WHO KILLED KING UTHER, WHO DROVE HIS SWORD INTO THE STONE?

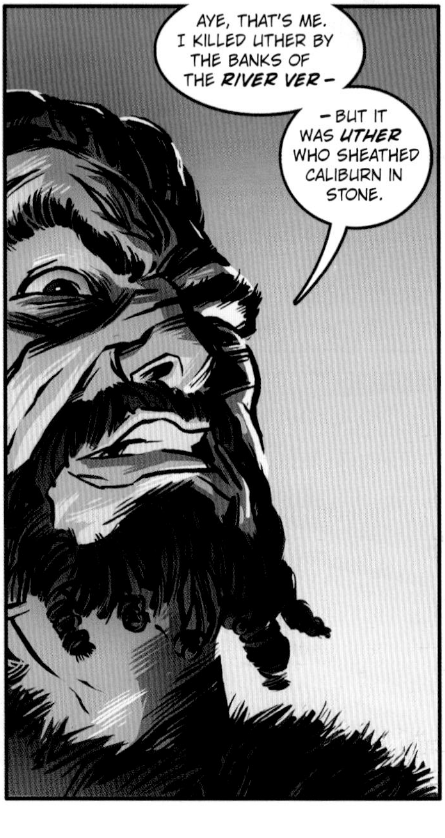
AYE, THAT'S ME. I KILLED UTHER BY THE BANKS OF THE RIVER VER –
– BUT IT WAS UTHER WHO SHEATHED CALIBURN IN STONE.

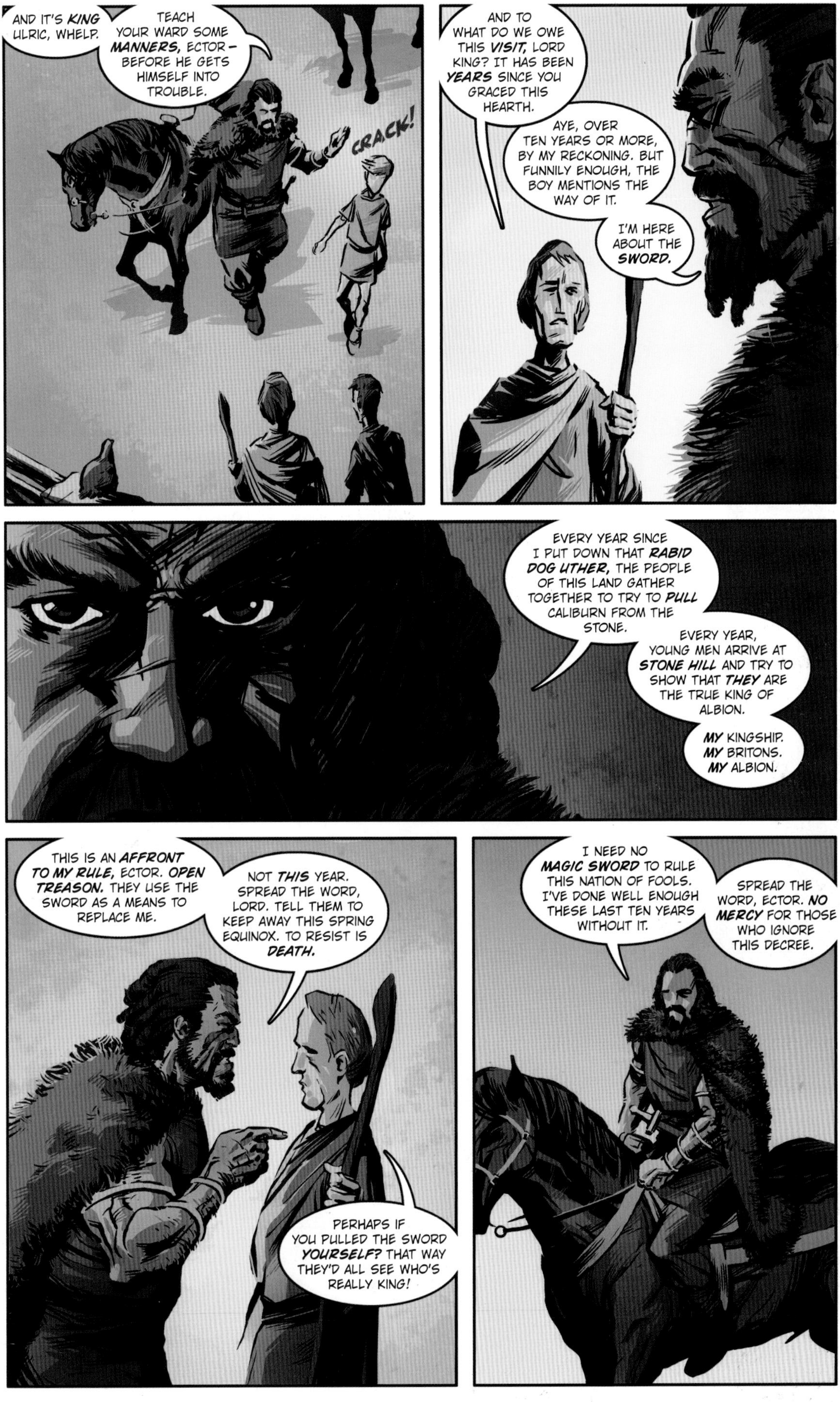
AND IT'S KING ULRIC, WHELP.
TEACH YOUR WARD SOME MANNERS, ECTOR — BEFORE HE GETS HIMSELF INTO TROUBLE.
CRACK!
AND TO WHAT DO WE OWE THIS VISIT, LORD KING? IT HAS BEEN YEARS SINCE YOU GRACED THIS HEARTH.
AYE, OVER TEN YEARS OR MORE, BY MY RECKONING. BUT FUNNILY ENOUGH, THE BOY MENTIONS THE WAY OF IT.
I'M HERE ABOUT THE SWORD.
EVERY YEAR SINCE I PUT DOWN THAT RABID DOG UTHER, THE PEOPLE OF THIS LAND GATHER TOGETHER TO TRY TO PULL CALIBURN FROM THE STONE.
EVERY YEAR, YOUNG MEN ARRIVE AT STONE HILL AND TRY TO SHOW THAT THEY ARE THE TRUE KING OF ALBION.
MY KINGSHIP. MY BRITONS. MY ALBION.
THIS IS AN AFFRONT TO MY RULE, ECTOR. OPEN TREASON. THEY USE THE SWORD AS A MEANS TO REPLACE ME.
NOT THIS YEAR. SPREAD THE WORD, LORD. TELL THEM TO KEEP AWAY THIS SPRING EQUINOX. TO RESIST IS DEATH.
PERHAPS IF YOU PULLED THE SWORD YOURSELF? THAT WAY THEY'D ALL SEE WHO'S REALLY KING!
I NEED NO MAGIC SWORD TO RULE THIS NATION OF FOOLS. I'VE DONE WELL ENOUGH THESE LAST TEN YEARS WITHOUT IT.
SPREAD THE WORD, ECTOR. NO MERCY FOR THOSE WHO IGNORE THIS DECREE.

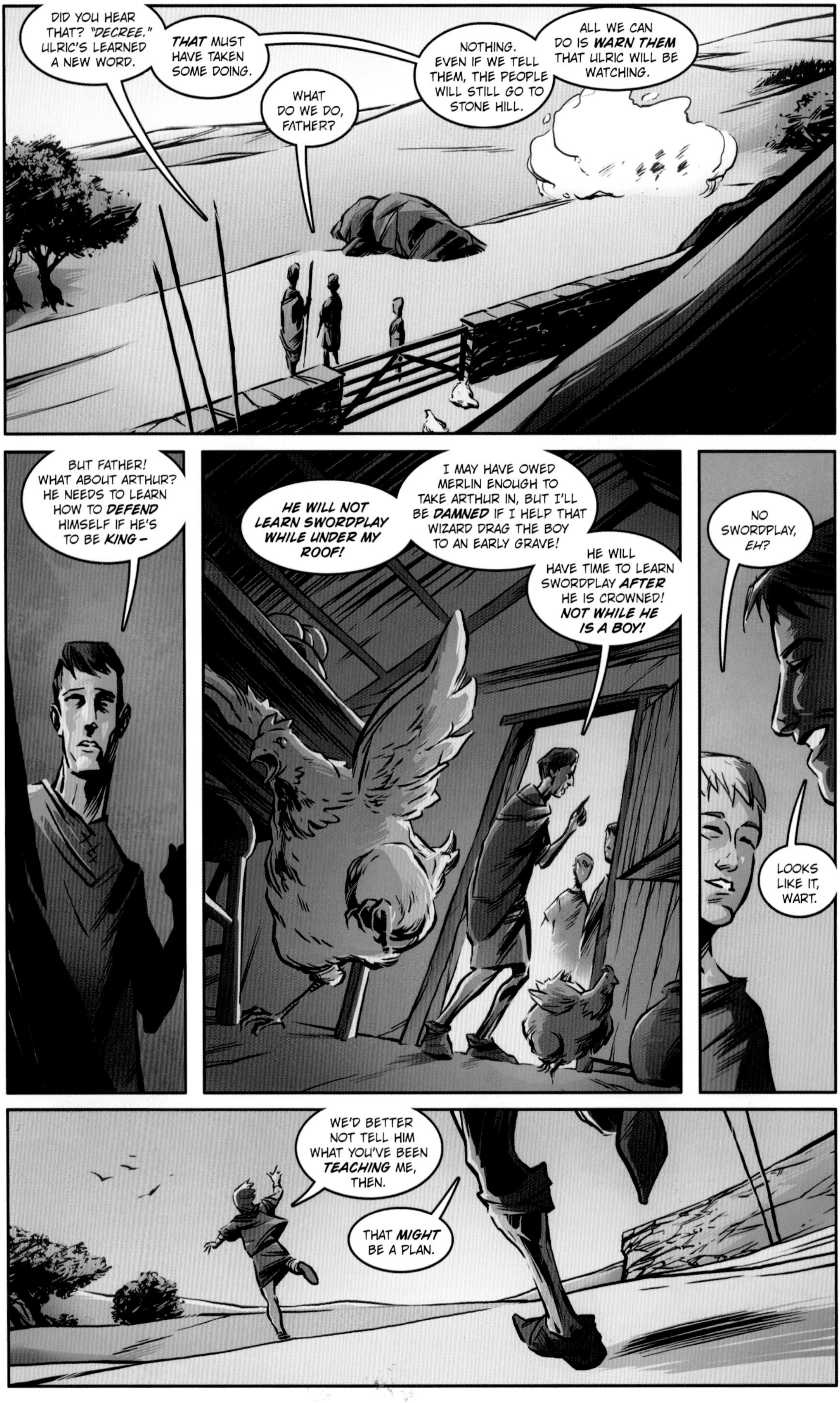

DID YOU HEAR THAT? "DECREE." ULRIC'S LEARNED A NEW WORD.
THAT MUST HAVE TAKEN SOME DOING.
WHAT DO WE DO, FATHER?
NOTHING. EVEN IF WE TELL THEM, THE PEOPLE WILL STILL GO TO STONE HILL.
ALL WE CAN DO IS WARN THEM THAT ULRIC WILL BE WATCHING.
BUT FATHER! WHAT ABOUT ARTHUR? HE NEEDS TO LEARN HOW TO DEFEND HIMSELF IF HE'S TO BE KING –
HE WILL NOT LEARN SWORDPLAY WHILE UNDER MY ROOF!
I MAY HAVE OWED MERLIN ENOUGH TO TAKE ARTHUR IN, BUT I'LL BE DAMNED IF I HELP THAT WIZARD DRAG THE BOY TO AN EARLY GRAVE!
HE WILL HAVE TIME TO LEARN SWORDPLAY AFTER HE IS CROWNED! NOT WHILE HE IS A BOY!
NO SWORDPLAY, EH?
LOOKS LIKE IT, WART.
WE'D BETTER NOT TELL HIM WHAT YOU'VE BEEN TEACHING ME, THEN.
THAT MIGHT BE A PLAN.

CLACK!

DAMN YOU! *STAND STILL!*

CLACK!

WHAT, AND *HIT* ME? UNLIKELY!

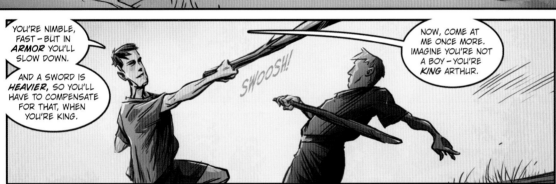

YOU'RE NIMBLE, FAST – BUT IN *ARMOR* YOU'LL SLOW DOWN.

AND A SWORD IS *HEAVIER,* SO YOU'LL HAVE TO COMPENSATE FOR THAT, WHEN YOU'RE KING.

SWOOSH!

NOW, COME AT ME ONCE MORE. IMAGINE YOU'RE NOT A BOY – *YOU'RE KING* ARTHUR.

CLOSE MY EYES...CLEAR MY MIND...

THE KING WOULD DIE FOR THE PEOPLE.

CLACK!

THE KING WOULD DIE FOR THE PEOPLE.

CLACK!

"ARTHUR! *STOP!*"

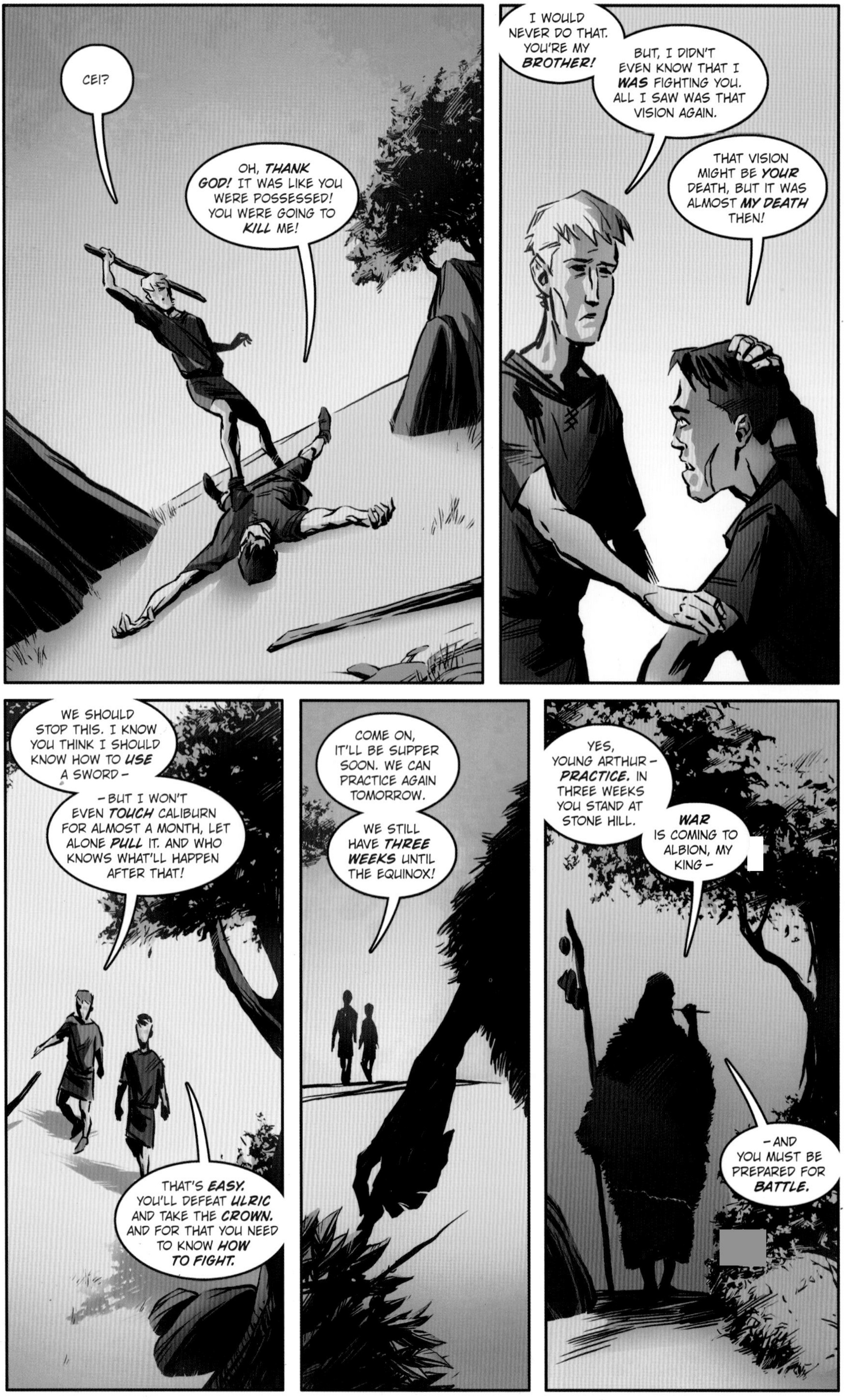
CEI?
OH, THANK GOD! IT WAS LIKE YOU WERE POSSESSED! YOU WERE GOING TO KILL ME!
I WOULD NEVER DO THAT. YOU'RE MY BROTHER!
BUT, I DIDN'T EVEN KNOW THAT I WAS FIGHTING YOU. ALL I SAW WAS THAT VISION AGAIN.
THAT VISION MIGHT BE YOUR DEATH, BUT IT WAS ALMOST MY DEATH THEN!
WE SHOULD STOP THIS. I KNOW YOU THINK I SHOULD KNOW HOW TO USE A SWORD–
–BUT I WON'T EVEN TOUCH CALIBURN FOR ALMOST A MONTH, LET ALONE PULL IT. AND WHO KNOWS WHAT'LL HAPPEN AFTER THAT!
THAT'S EASY. YOU'LL DEFEAT ULRIC AND TAKE THE CROWN. AND FOR THAT YOU NEED TO KNOW HOW TO FIGHT.
COME ON, IT'LL BE SUPPER SOON. WE CAN PRACTICE AGAIN TOMORROW.
WE STILL HAVE THREE WEEKS UNTIL THE EQUINOX!
YES, YOUNG ARTHUR– PRACTICE. IN THREE WEEKS YOU STAND AT STONE HILL.
WAR IS COMING TO ALBION, MY KING–
–AND YOU MUST BE PREPARED FOR BATTLE.

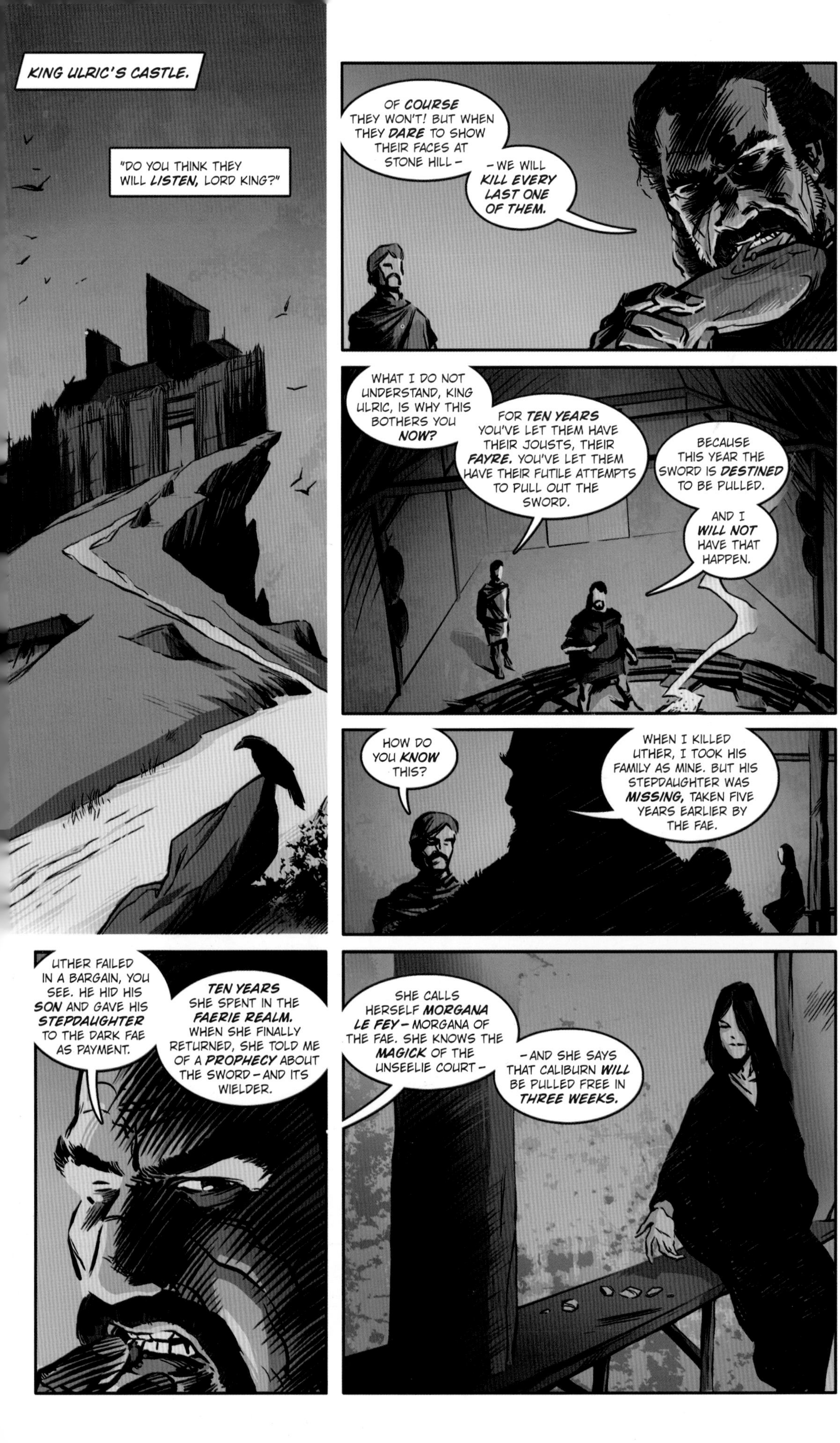
KING ULRIC'S CASTLE.
"DO YOU THINK THEY WILL LISTEN, LORD KING?"
OF COURSE THEY WON'T! BUT WHEN THEY DARE TO SHOW THEIR FACES AT STONE HILL –
– WE WILL KILL EVERY LAST ONE OF THEM.
WHAT I DO NOT UNDERSTAND, KING ULRIC, IS WHY THIS BOTHERS YOU NOW?
FOR TEN YEARS YOU'VE LET THEM HAVE THEIR JOUSTS, THEIR FAYRE. YOU'VE LET THEM HAVE THEIR FUTILE ATTEMPTS TO PULL OUT THE SWORD.
BECAUSE THIS YEAR THE SWORD IS DESTINED TO BE PULLED.
AND I WILL NOT HAVE THAT HAPPEN.
HOW DO YOU KNOW THIS?
WHEN I KILLED UTHER, I TOOK HIS FAMILY AS MINE. BUT HIS STEPDAUGHTER WAS MISSING, TAKEN FIVE YEARS EARLIER BY THE FAE.
UTHER FAILED IN A BARGAIN, YOU SEE. HE HID HIS SON AND GAVE HIS STEPDAUGHTER TO THE DARK FAE AS PAYMENT.
TEN YEARS SHE SPENT IN THE FAERIE REALM. WHEN SHE FINALLY RETURNED, SHE TOLD ME OF A PROPHECY ABOUT THE SWORD – AND ITS WIELDER.
SHE CALLS HERSELF MORGANA LE FEY – MORGANA OF THE FAE. SHE KNOWS THE MAGICK OF THE UNSEELIE COURT –
– AND SHE SAYS THAT CALIBURN WILL BE PULLED FREE IN THREE WEEKS.

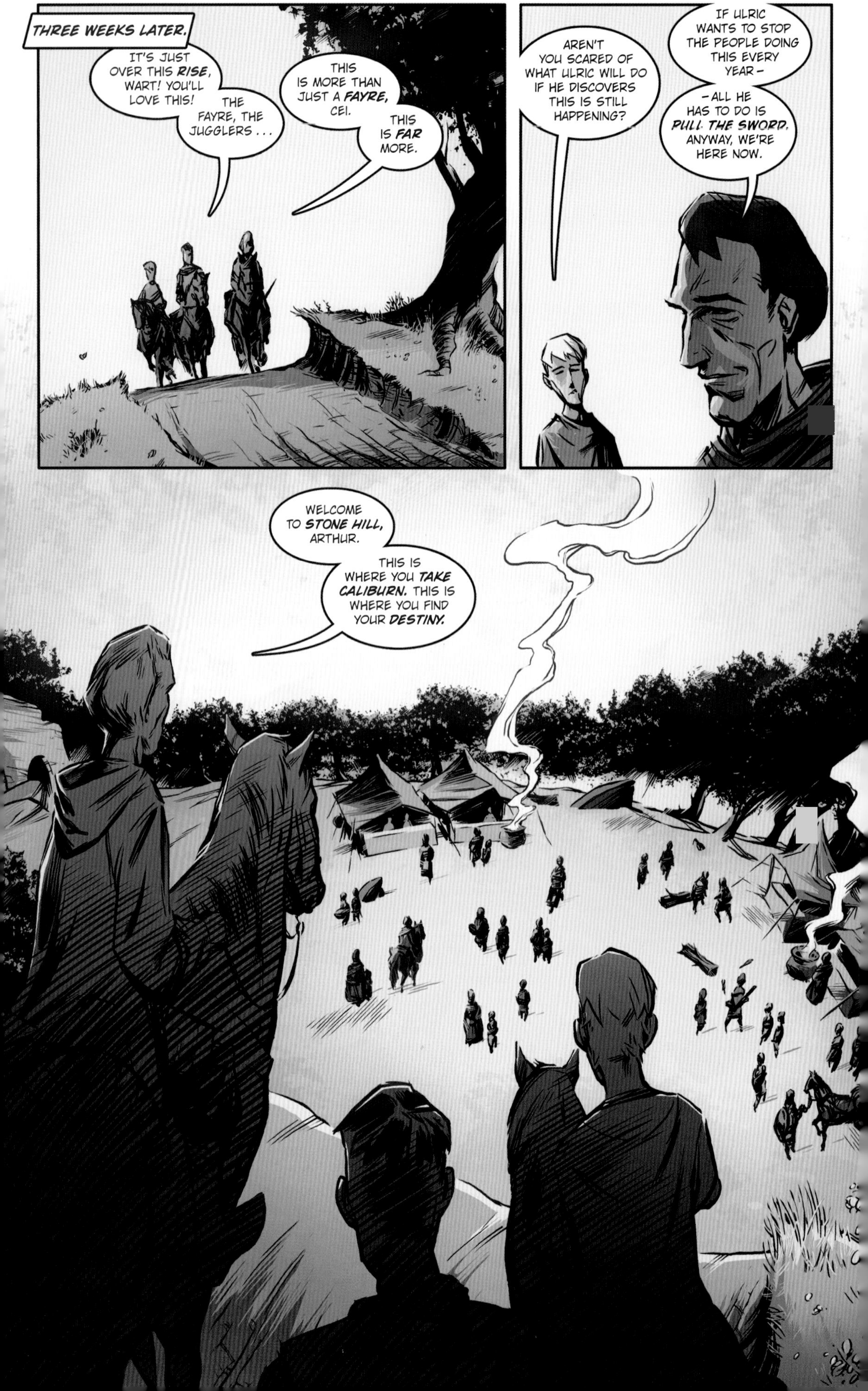
THREE WEEKS LATER.
IT'S JUST OVER THIS RISE, WART! YOU'LL LOVE THIS!
THE FAYRE, THE JUGGLERS . . .
THIS IS MORE THAN JUST A FAYRE, CEI.
THIS IS FAR MORE.
AREN'T YOU SCARED OF WHAT ULRIC WILL DO IF HE DISCOVERS THIS IS STILL HAPPENING?
IF ULRIC WANTS TO STOP THE PEOPLE DOING THIS EVERY YEAR –
– ALL HE HAS TO DO IS PULL THE SWORD. ANYWAY, WE'RE HERE NOW.
WELCOME TO STONE HILL, ARTHUR.
THIS IS WHERE YOU TAKE CALIBURN. THIS IS WHERE YOU FIND YOUR DESTINY.

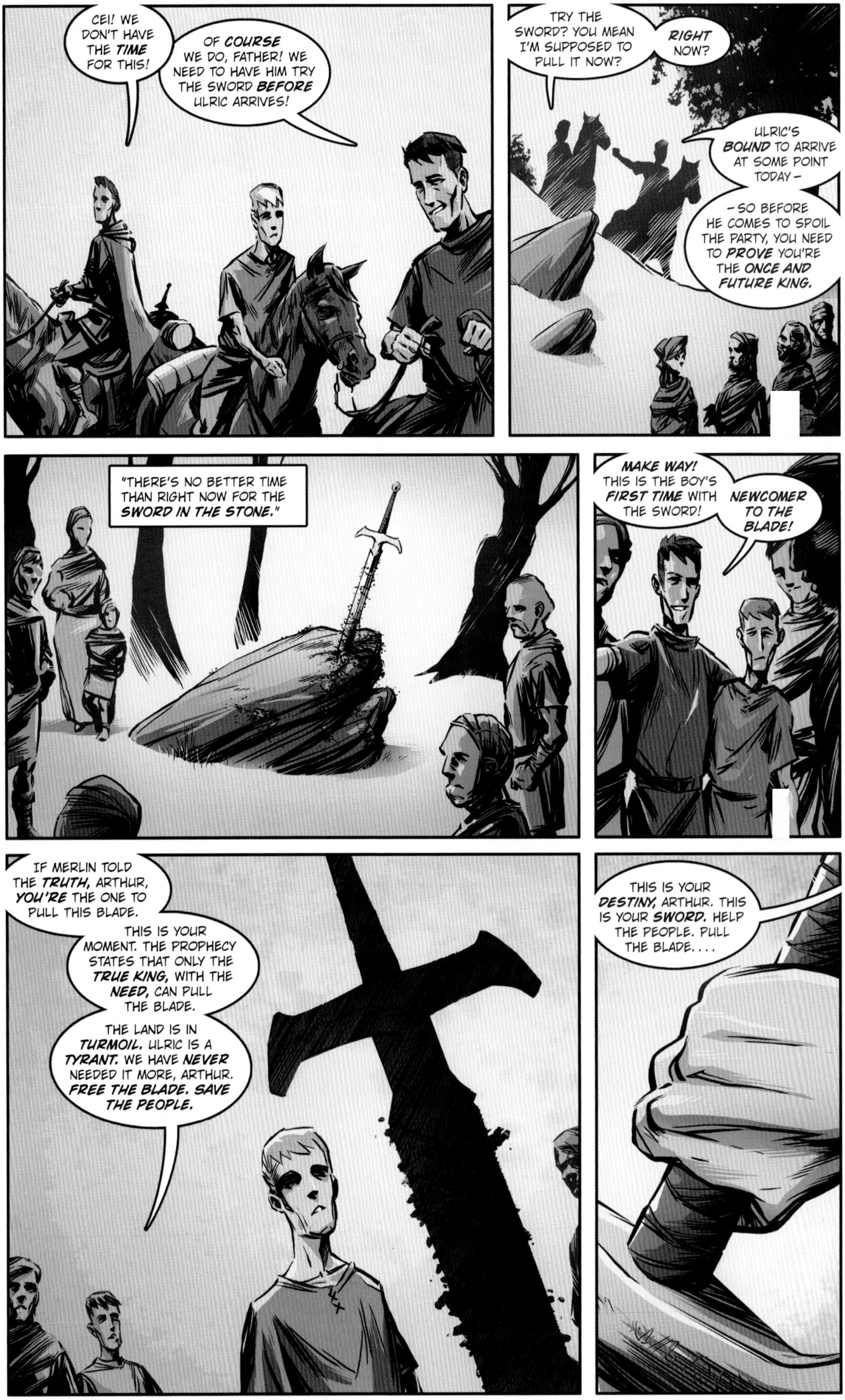
CEI! WE DON'T HAVE THE TIME FOR THIS!
OF COURSE WE DO, FATHER! WE NEED TO HAVE HIM TRY THE SWORD BEFORE ULRIC ARRIVES!
TRY THE SWORD? YOU MEAN I'M SUPPOSED TO PULL IT NOW?
RIGHT NOW?
ULRIC'S BOUND TO ARRIVE AT SOME POINT TODAY –
– SO BEFORE HE COMES TO SPOIL THE PARTY, YOU NEED TO PROVE YOU'RE THE ONCE AND FUTURE KING.
"THERE'S NO BETTER TIME THAN RIGHT NOW FOR THE SWORD IN THE STONE."
MAKE WAY! THIS IS THE BOY'S FIRST TIME WITH THE SWORD!
NEWCOMER TO THE BLADE!
IF MERLIN TOLD THE TRUTH, ARTHUR, YOU'RE THE ONE TO PULL THIS BLADE.
THIS IS YOUR MOMENT. THE PROPHECY STATES THAT ONLY THE TRUE KING, WITH THE NEED, CAN PULL THE BLADE.
THE LAND IS IN TURMOIL. ULRIC IS A TYRANT. WE HAVE NEVER NEEDED IT MORE, ARTHUR. FREE THE BLADE. SAVE THE PEOPLE.
THIS IS YOUR DESTINY, ARTHUR. THIS IS YOUR SWORD. HELP THE PEOPLE. PULL THE BLADE. . . .

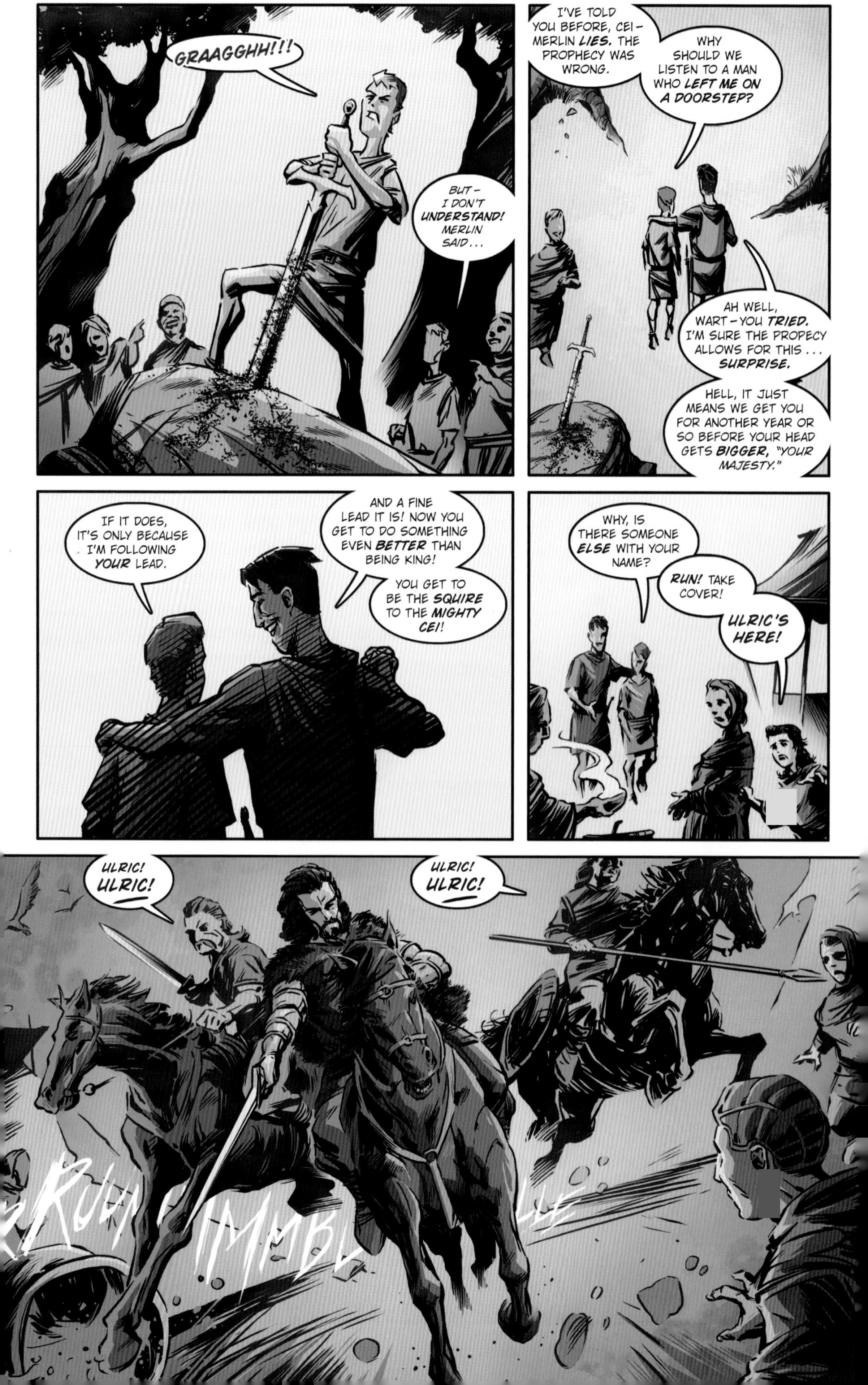

GRAAGGHH!!!
BUT – I DON'T UNDERSTAND! MERLIN SAID . . .
I'VE TOLD YOU BEFORE, CEI – MERLIN LIES. THE PROPHECY WAS WRONG.
WHY SHOULD WE LISTEN TO A MAN WHO LEFT ME ON A DOORSTEP?
AH WELL, WART – YOU TRIED. I'M SURE THE PROPECY ALLOWS FOR THIS . . . SURPRISE.
HELL, IT JUST MEANS WE GET YOU FOR ANOTHER YEAR OR SO BEFORE YOUR HEAD GETS BIGGER, "YOUR MAJESTY."
IF IT DOES, IT'S ONLY BECAUSE I'M FOLLOWING YOUR LEAD.
AND A FINE LEAD IT IS! NOW YOU GET TO DO SOMETHING EVEN BETTER THAN BEING KING!
YOU GET TO BE THE SQUIRE TO THE MIGHTY CEI!
WHY, IS THERE SOMEONE ELSE WITH YOUR NAME?
RUN! TAKE COVER!
ULRIC'S HERE!
ULRIC! ULRIC!
ULRIC! ULRIC!

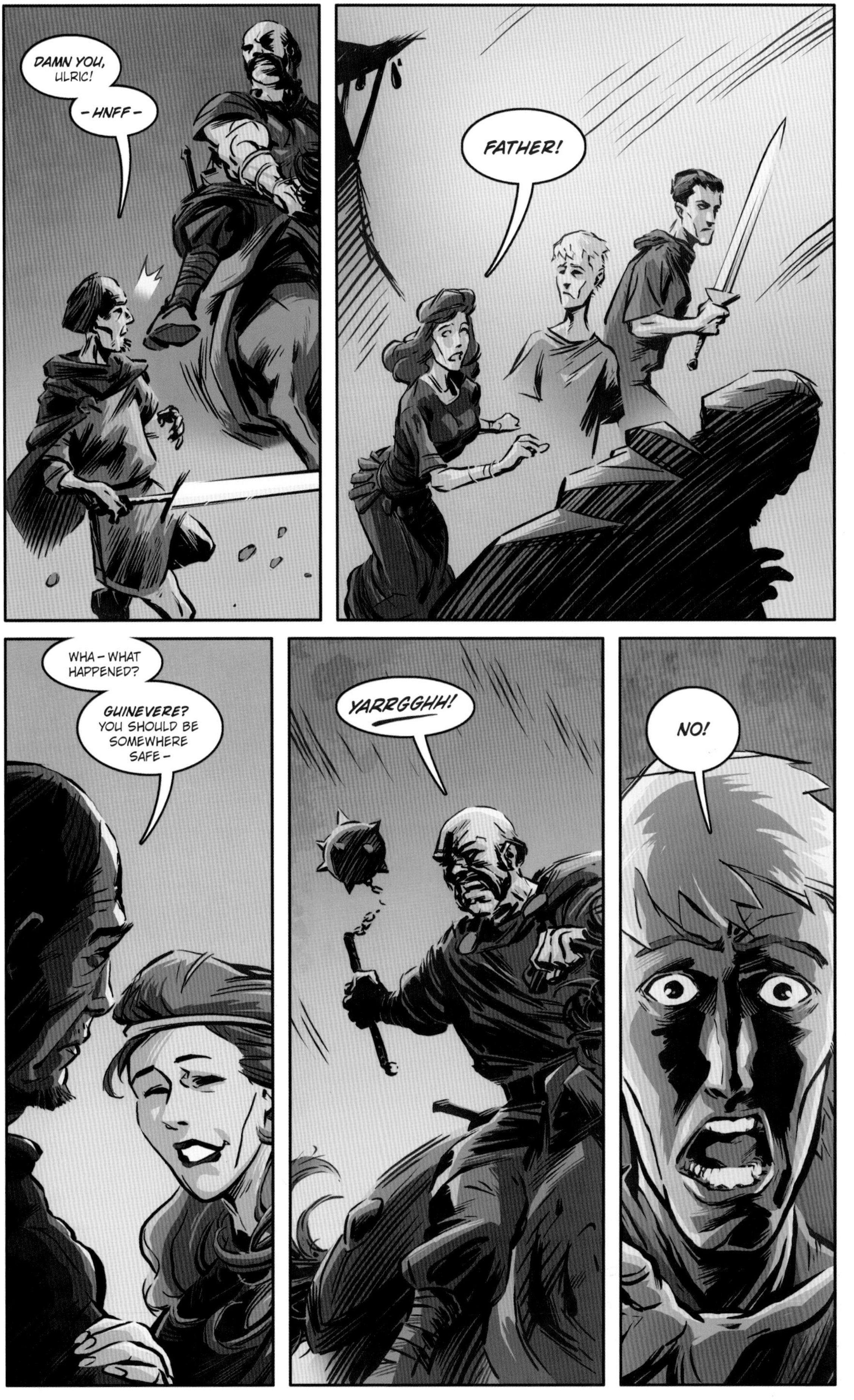
DAMN YOU, ULRIC!
- HNFF -
FATHER!
WHA - WHAT HAPPENED?
GUINEVERE? YOU SHOULD BE SOMEWHERE SAFE -
YARRGGHH!
NO!

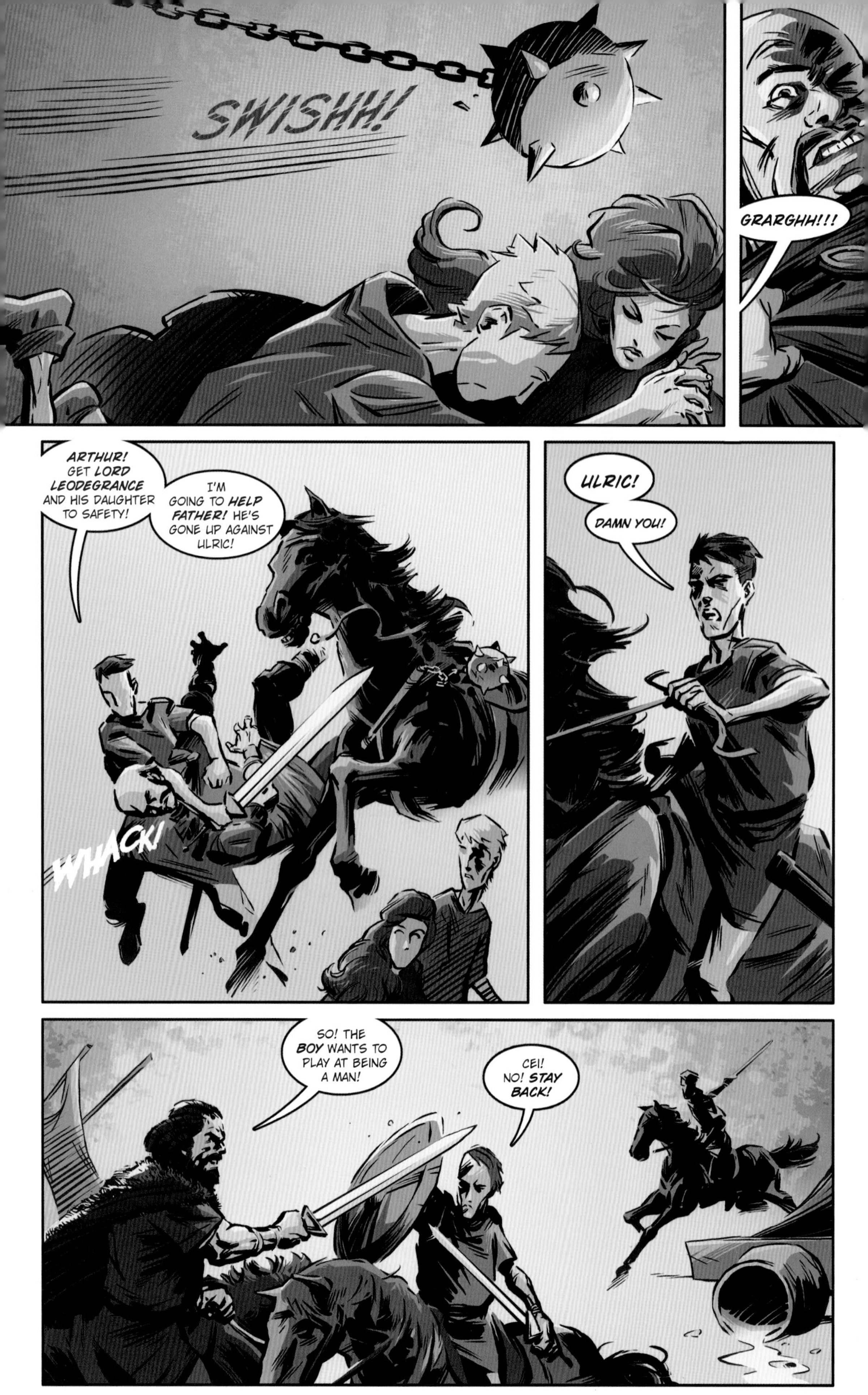
SWISHH!
GRARGHH!!!
ARTHUR! GET LORD LEODEGRANCE AND HIS DAUGHTER TO SAFETY!
I'M GOING TO HELP FATHER! HE'S GONE UP AGAINST ULRIC!
WHACK!
ULRIC!
DAMN YOU!
SO! THE BOY WANTS TO PLAY AT BEING A MAN!
CEI! NO! STAY BACK!

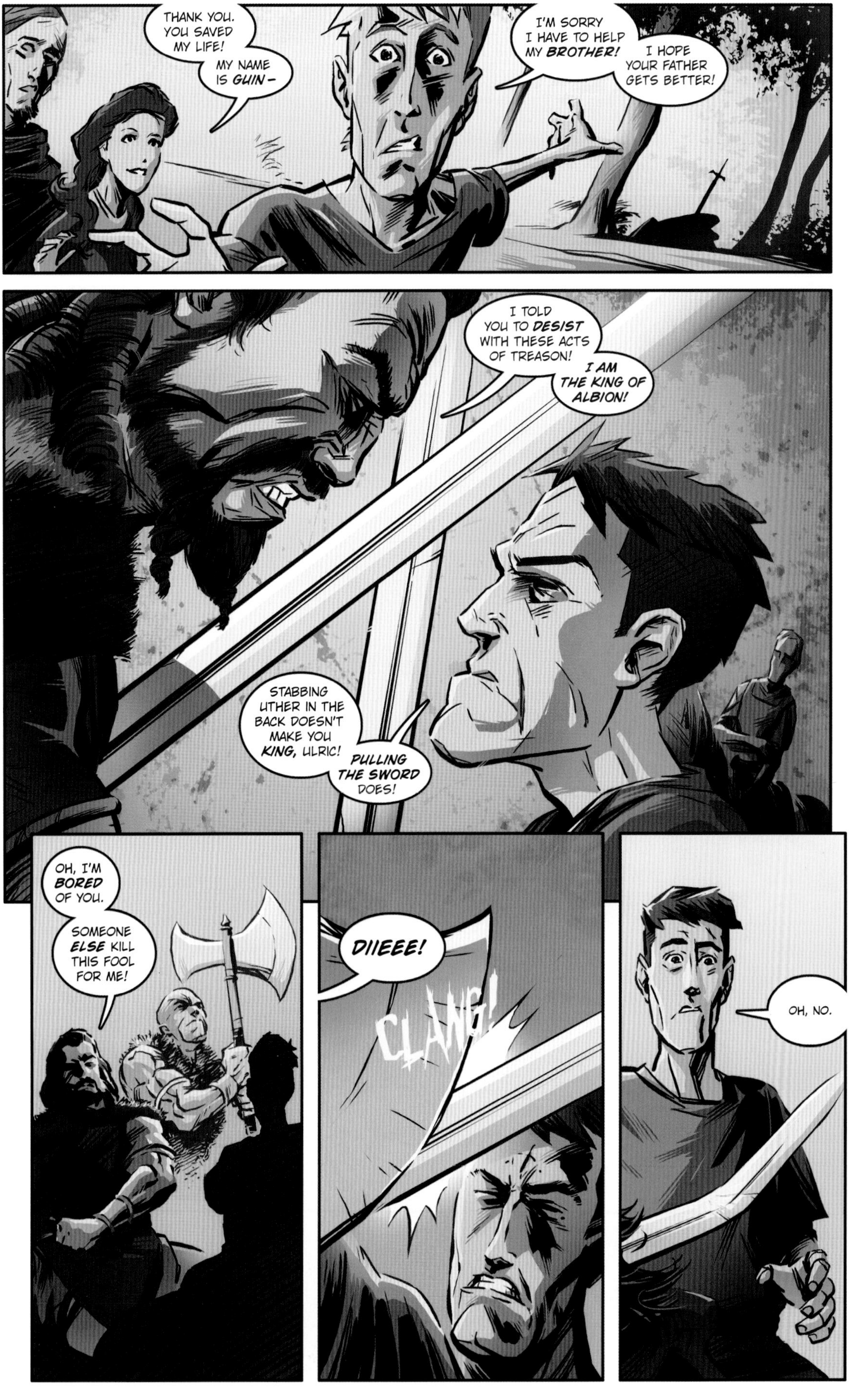
THANK YOU. YOU SAVED MY LIFE!
MY NAME IS GUIN-
I'M SORRY I HAVE TO HELP MY BROTHER!
I HOPE YOUR FATHER GETS BETTER!
I TOLD YOU TO DESIST WITH THESE ACTS OF TREASON!
I AM THE KING OF ALBION!
STABBING UTHER IN THE BACK DOESN'T MAKE YOU KING, ULRIC!
PULLING THE SWORD DOES!
OH, I'M BORED OF YOU.
SOMEONE ELSE KILL THIS FOOL FOR ME!
DIIEEE!
CLANG!
OH, NO.

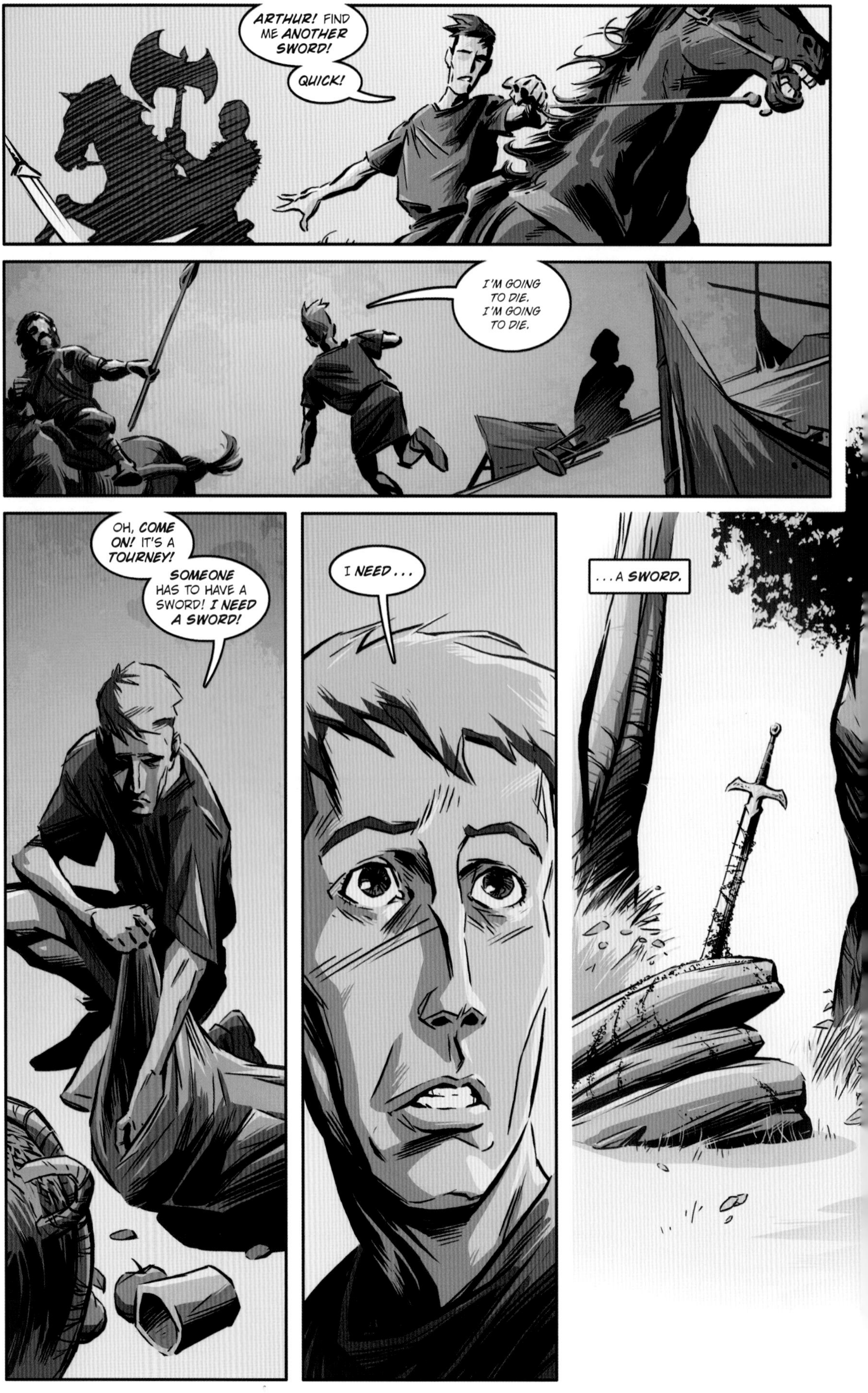

ARTHUR! FIND ME ANOTHER SWORD!
QUICK!
I'M GOING TO DIE. I'M GOING TO DIE.
OH, COME ON! IT'S A TOURNEY!
SOMEONE HAS TO HAVE A SWORD! I NEED A SWORD!
I NEED . . .
. . . A SWORD.

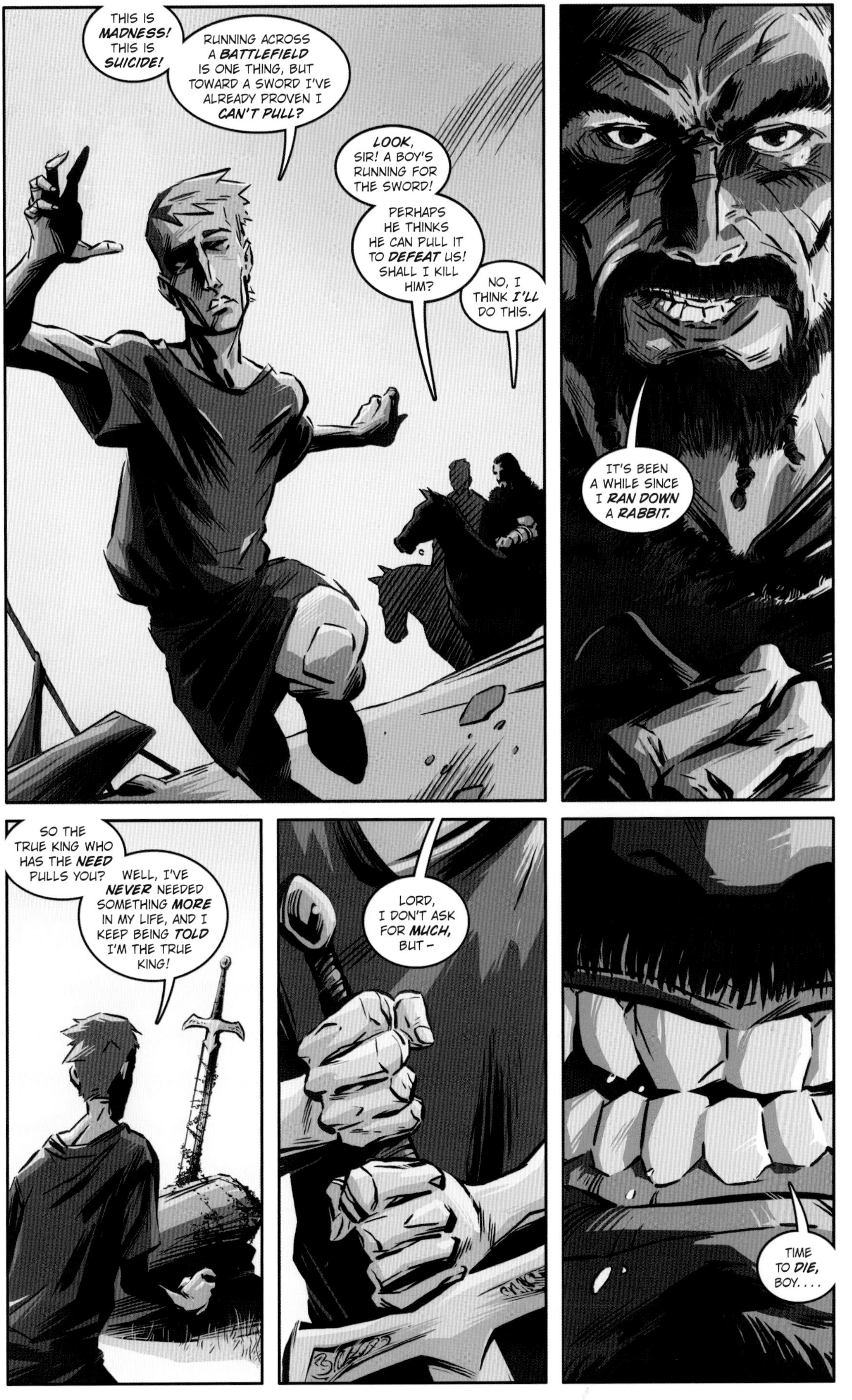
THIS IS MADNESS! THIS IS SUICIDE!
RUNNING ACROSS A BATTLEFIELD IS ONE THING, BUT TOWARD A SWORD I'VE ALREADY PROVEN I CAN'T PULL?
LOOK, SIR! A BOY'S RUNNING FOR THE SWORD!
PERHAPS HE THINKS HE CAN PULL IT TO DEFEAT US! SHALL I KILL HIM?
NO, I THINK I'LL DO THIS.
IT'S BEEN A WHILE SINCE I RAN DOWN A RABBIT.
SO THE TRUE KING WHO HAS THE NEED PULLS YOU?
WELL, I'VE NEVER NEEDED SOMETHING MORE IN MY LIFE, AND I KEEP BEING TOLD I'M THE TRUE KING!
LORD, I DON'T ASK FOR MUCH, BUT –
TIME TO DIE, BOY. . . .

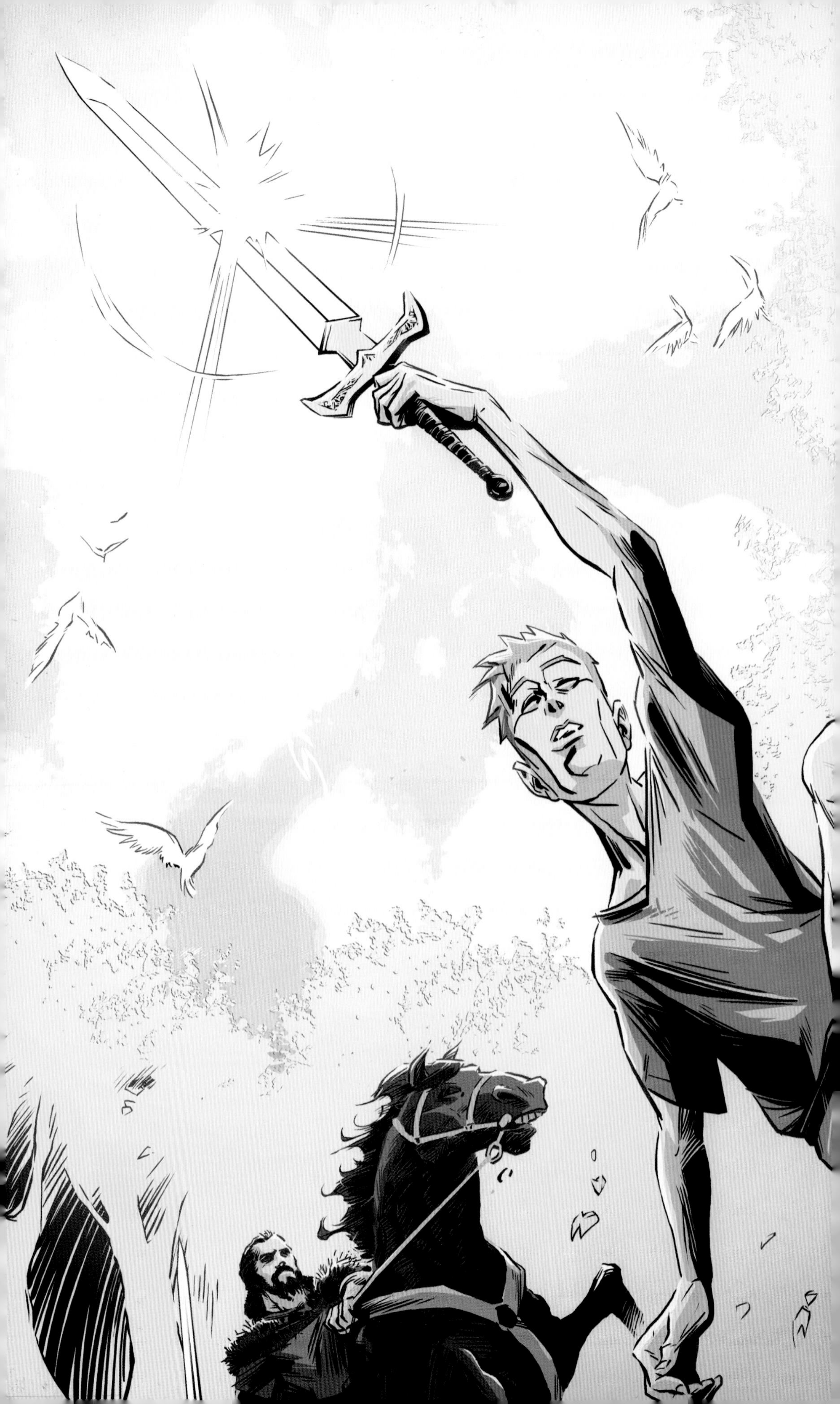

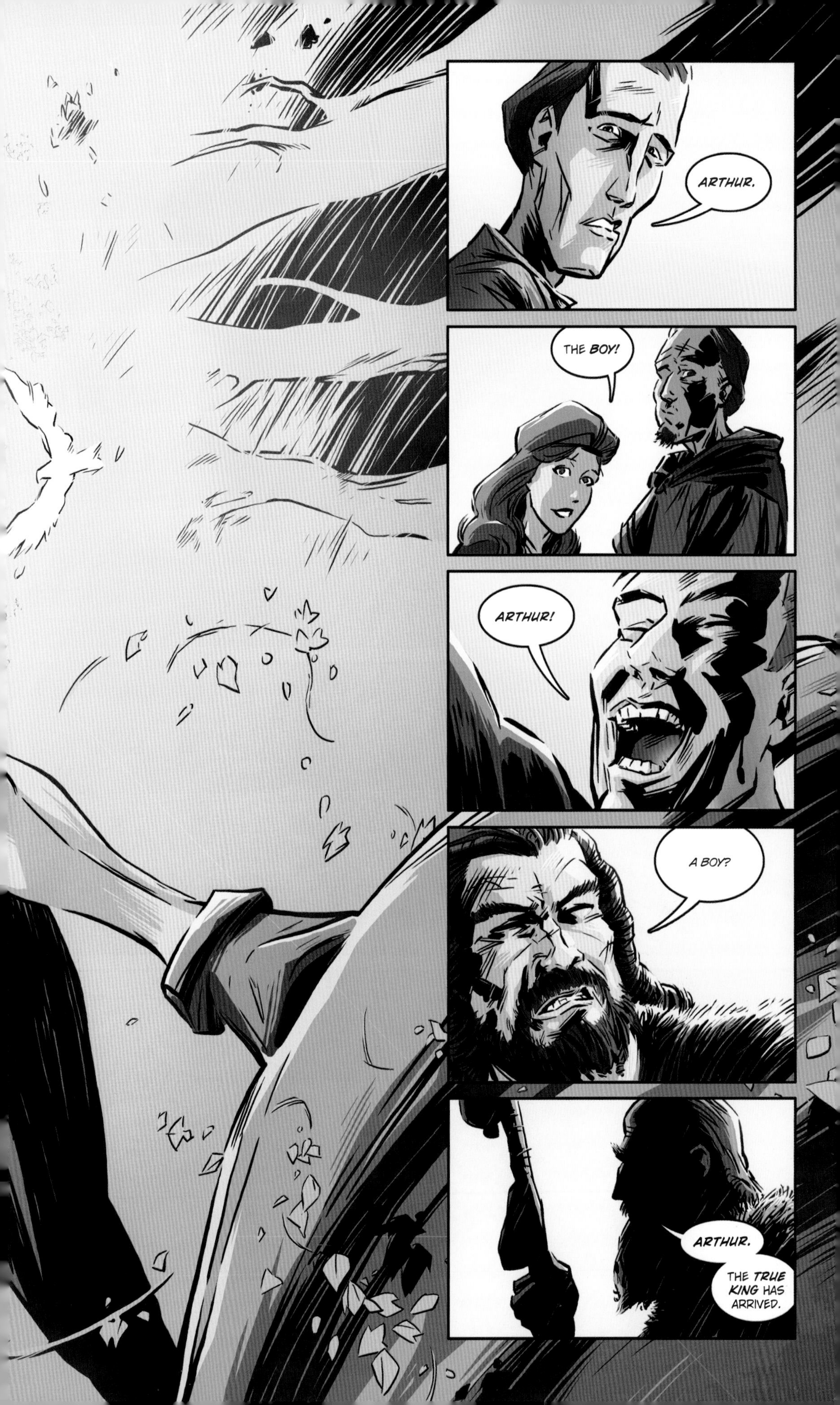
ARTHUR.
THE BOY!
ARTHUR!
A BOY?
ARTHUR.
THE TRUE KING HAS ARRIVED.

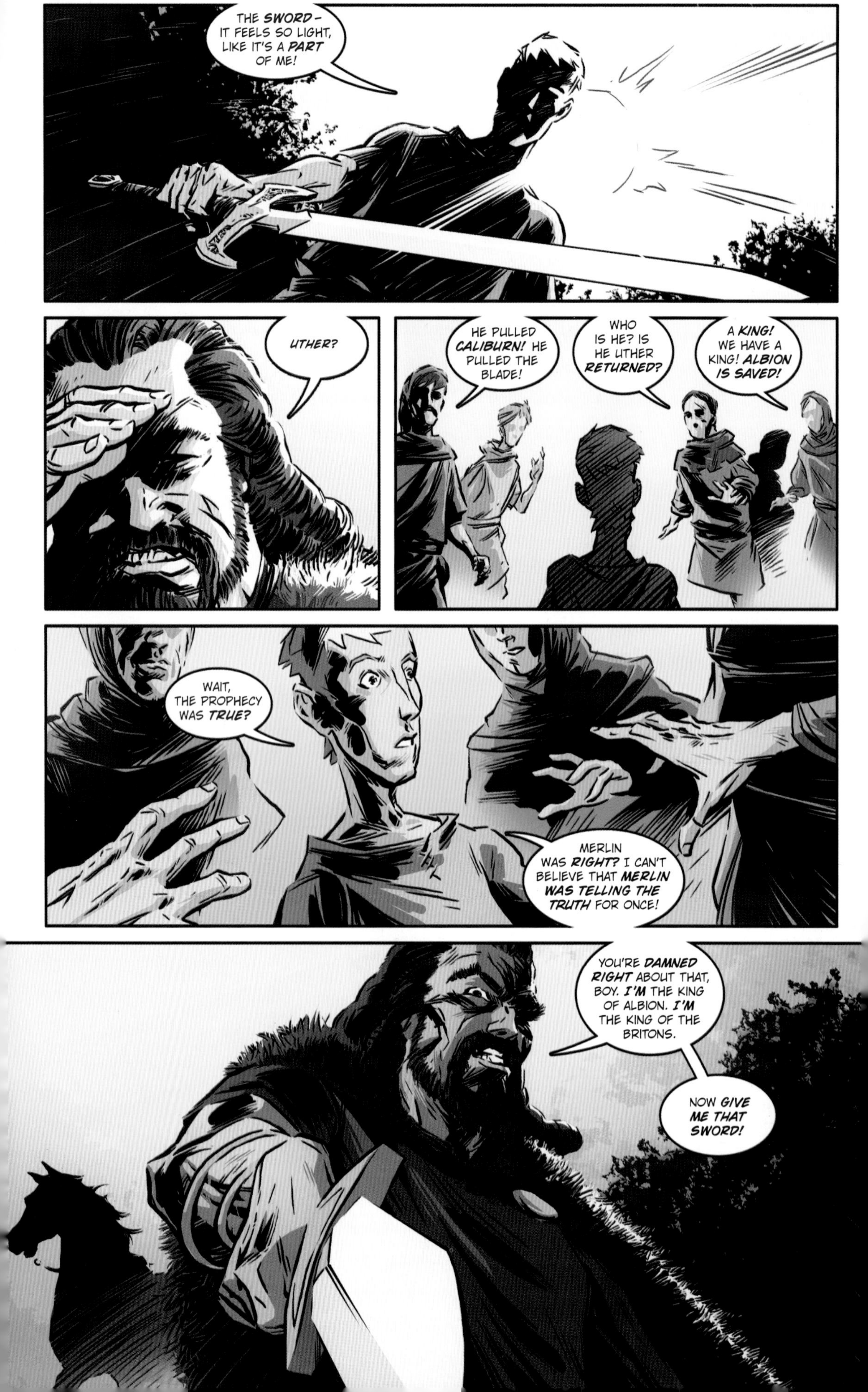
THE SWORD - IT FEELS SO LIGHT, LIKE IT'S A PART OF ME!
UTHER?
HE PULLED CALIBURN! HE PULLED THE BLADE!
WHO IS HE? IS HE UTHER RETURNED?
A KING! WE HAVE A KING! ALBION IS SAVED!
WAIT, THE PROPHECY WAS TRUE?
MERLIN WAS RIGHT? I CAN'T BELIEVE THAT MERLIN WAS TELLING THE TRUTH FOR ONCE!
YOU'RE DAMNED RIGHT ABOUT THAT, BOY. I'M THE KING OF ALBION. I'M THE KING OF THE BRITONS.
NOW GIVE ME THAT SWORD!

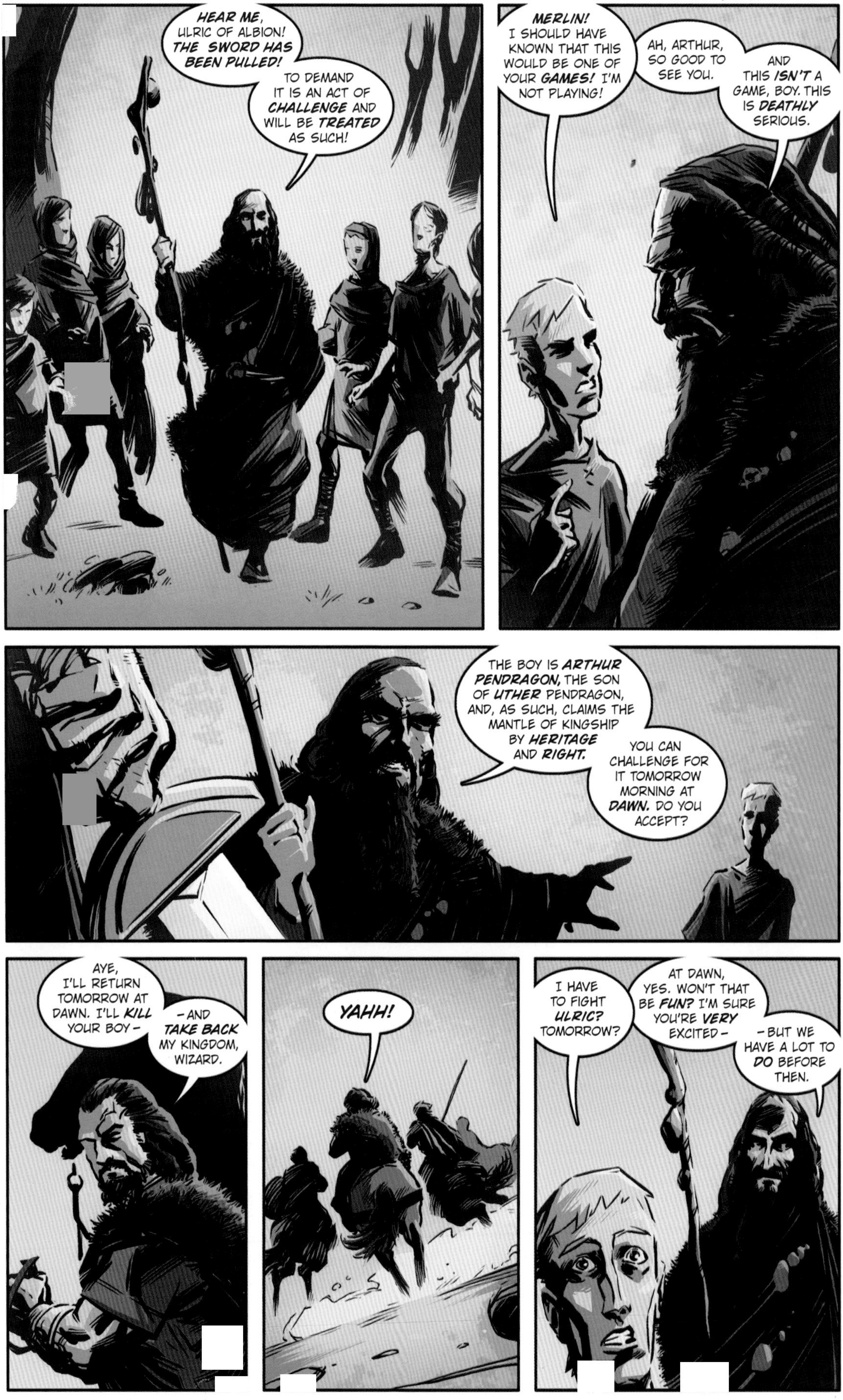
HEAR ME, ULRIC OF ALBION! THE SWORD HAS BEEN PULLED!
TO DEMAND IT IS AN ACT OF CHALLENGE AND WILL BE TREATED AS SUCH!
MERLIN! I SHOULD HAVE KNOWN THAT THIS WOULD BE ONE OF YOUR GAMES! I'M NOT PLAYING!
AH, ARTHUR, SO GOOD TO SEE YOU.
AND THIS ISN'T A GAME, BOY. THIS IS DEATHLY SERIOUS.
THE BOY IS ARTHUR PENDRAGON, THE SON OF UTHER PENDRAGON, AND, AS SUCH, CLAIMS THE MANTLE OF KINGSHIP BY HERITAGE AND RIGHT.
YOU CAN CHALLENGE FOR IT TOMORROW MORNING AT DAWN. DO YOU ACCEPT?
AYE, I'LL RETURN TOMORROW AT DAWN. I'LL KILL YOUR BOY –
– AND TAKE BACK MY KINGDOM, WIZARD.
YAHH!
I HAVE TO FIGHT ULRIC? TOMORROW?
AT DAWN, YES. WON'T THAT BE FUN? I'M SURE YOU'RE VERY EXCITED –
– BUT WE HAVE A LOT TO DO BEFORE THEN.

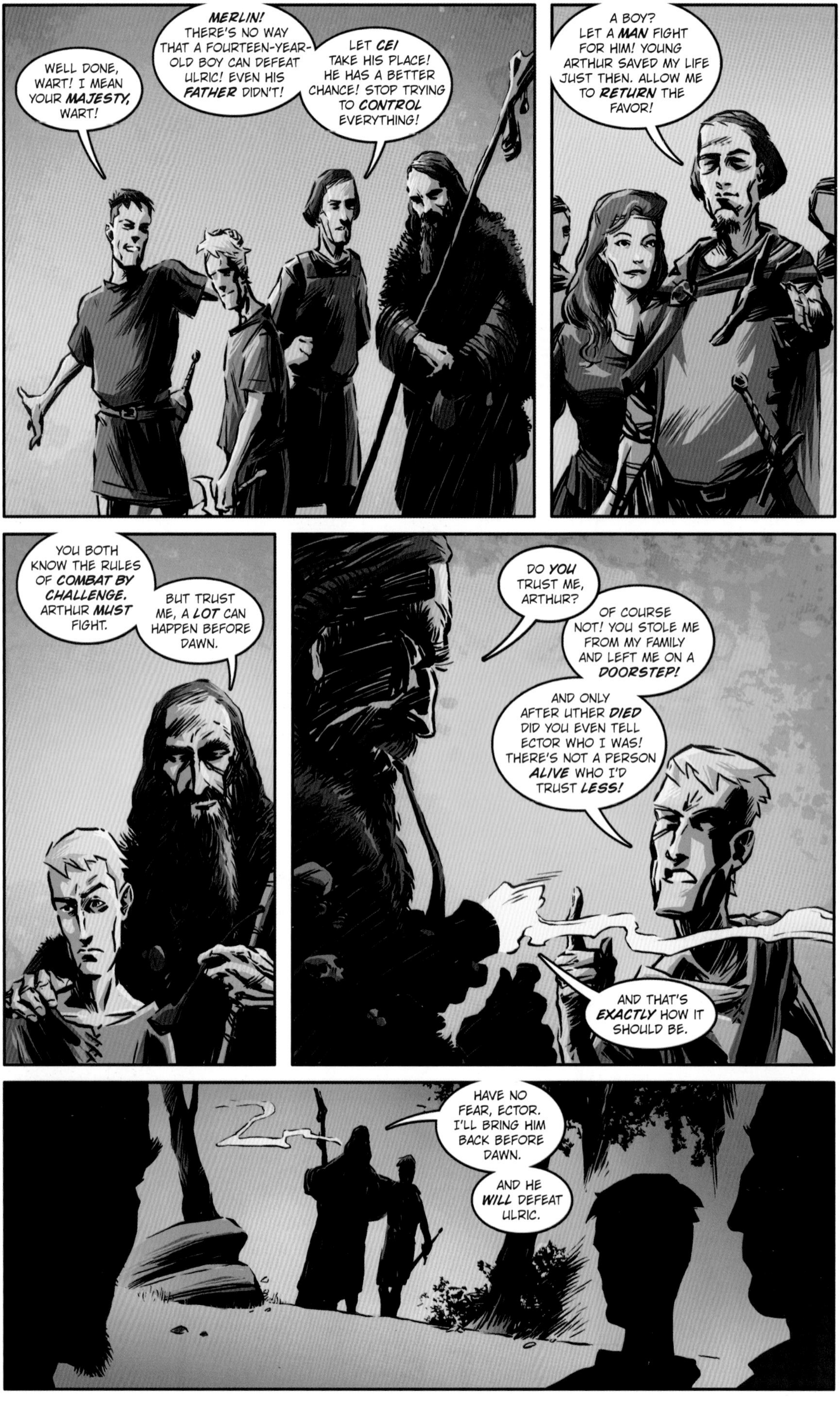

WELL DONE, WART! I MEAN YOUR MAJESTY, WART!
MERLIN! THERE'S NO WAY THAT A FOURTEEN-YEAR-OLD BOY CAN DEFEAT ULRIC! EVEN HIS FATHER DIDN'T!
LET CEI TAKE HIS PLACE! HE HAS A BETTER CHANCE! STOP TRYING TO CONTROL EVERYTHING!
A BOY? LET A MAN FIGHT FOR HIM! YOUNG ARTHUR SAVED MY LIFE JUST THEN. ALLOW ME TO RETURN THE FAVOR!
YOU BOTH KNOW THE RULES OF COMBAT BY CHALLENGE. ARTHUR MUST FIGHT.
BUT TRUST ME, A LOT CAN HAPPEN BEFORE DAWN.
DO YOU TRUST ME, ARTHUR?
OF COURSE NOT! YOU STOLE ME FROM MY FAMILY AND LEFT ME ON A DOORSTEP!
AND ONLY AFTER UTHER DIED DID YOU EVEN TELL ECTOR WHO I WAS! THERE'S NOT A PERSON ALIVE WHO I'D TRUST LESS!
AND THAT'S EXACTLY HOW IT SHOULD BE.
HAVE NO FEAR, ECTOR. I'LL BRING HIM BACK BEFORE DAWN.
AND HE WILL DEFEAT ULRIC.

THE *FAERIE* REALM? ARE YOU *MAD?* I'LL LOSE MY SOUL, OR RETURN A HUNDRED YEARS LATER!

NOT THIS TIME. I'VE BROKERED A DEAL WITH *BRAN THE BLESSED*, THE *KING* OF AVALON. A YEAR WILL PASS THERE IN A MATTER OF *HOURS* HERE.

YOU'LL BE BACK, A YEAR OLDER AND WISER, BEFORE *MIDNIGHT.*

AND HOW WILL YOU MANAGE *THAT?* MAGICALLY AGE ME A FEW YEARS? MAKE ME *STRONGER?*

ACTUALLY, YOU'RE NOT *TOO FAR* OFF THE MARK THERE.

I INTEND TO TAKE YOU SOMEWHERE. A PLACE WHERE TIME FLOWS MUCH *SLOWER* THAN HERE. *AVALON.*

SO I'LL BE GONE FOR A *YEAR* – WHILE CEI AND ECTOR WAIT A *MATTER OF HOURS?*

TO THEM YOU'LL BARELY BE AWAY. BUT A YEAR IN AVALON WILL TEACH YOU MUCH.

THE BEST FIGHTERS WILL TEACH YOU SWORDSMANSHIP STRATEGY – TO *ADD* TO WHAT YOU'VE ALREADY SECRETLY LEARNED.

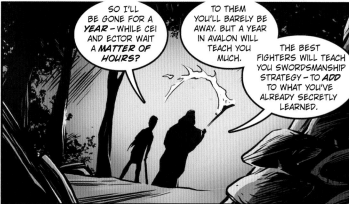

YOU'LL RETURN HERE, AND YOU'LL DEFEAT ULRIC.

YOU'LL SAVE *ALL OF ALBION.* BECAUSE GOD KNOWS, WE *NEED* A SAVIOR RIGHT NOW.

I – I SUPPOSE SO . . .

WELL, THERE YOU GO THEN. JUST ENTER THROUGH THIS *PORTAL* AND WE'LL BE IN *AVALON* BEFORE YOU KNOW IT!

ARTHUR PENDRAGON . . .

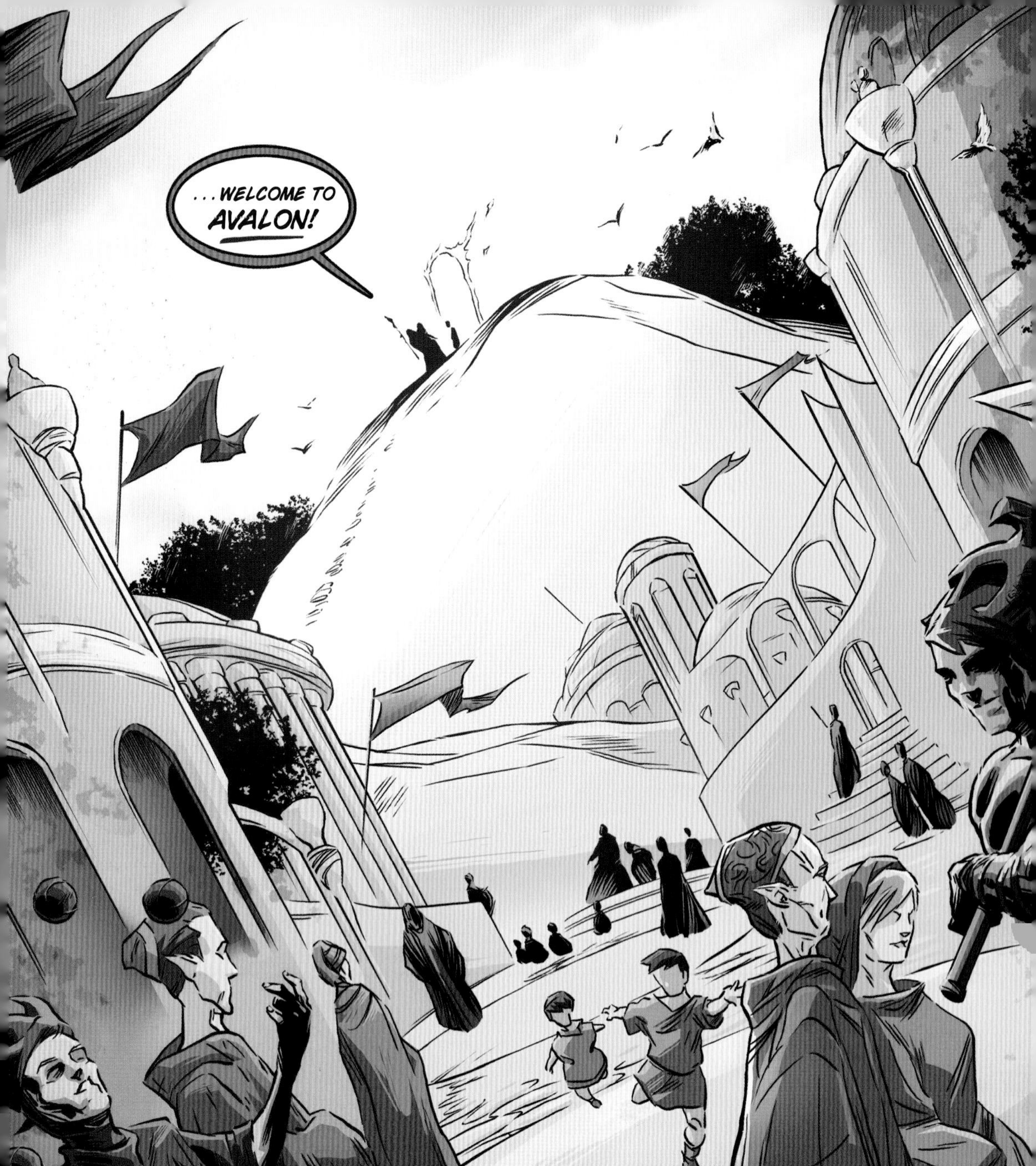
...WELCOME TO AVALON!

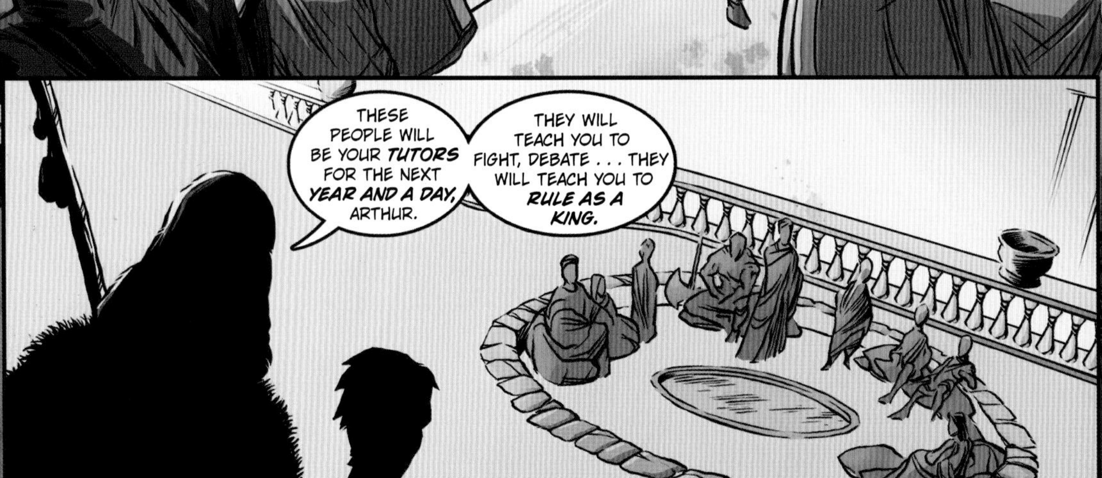
THESE PEOPLE WILL BE YOUR TUTORS FOR THE NEXT YEAR AND A DAY, ARTHUR.
THEY WILL TEACH YOU TO FIGHT, DEBATE . . . THEY WILL TEACH YOU TO RULE AS A KING.

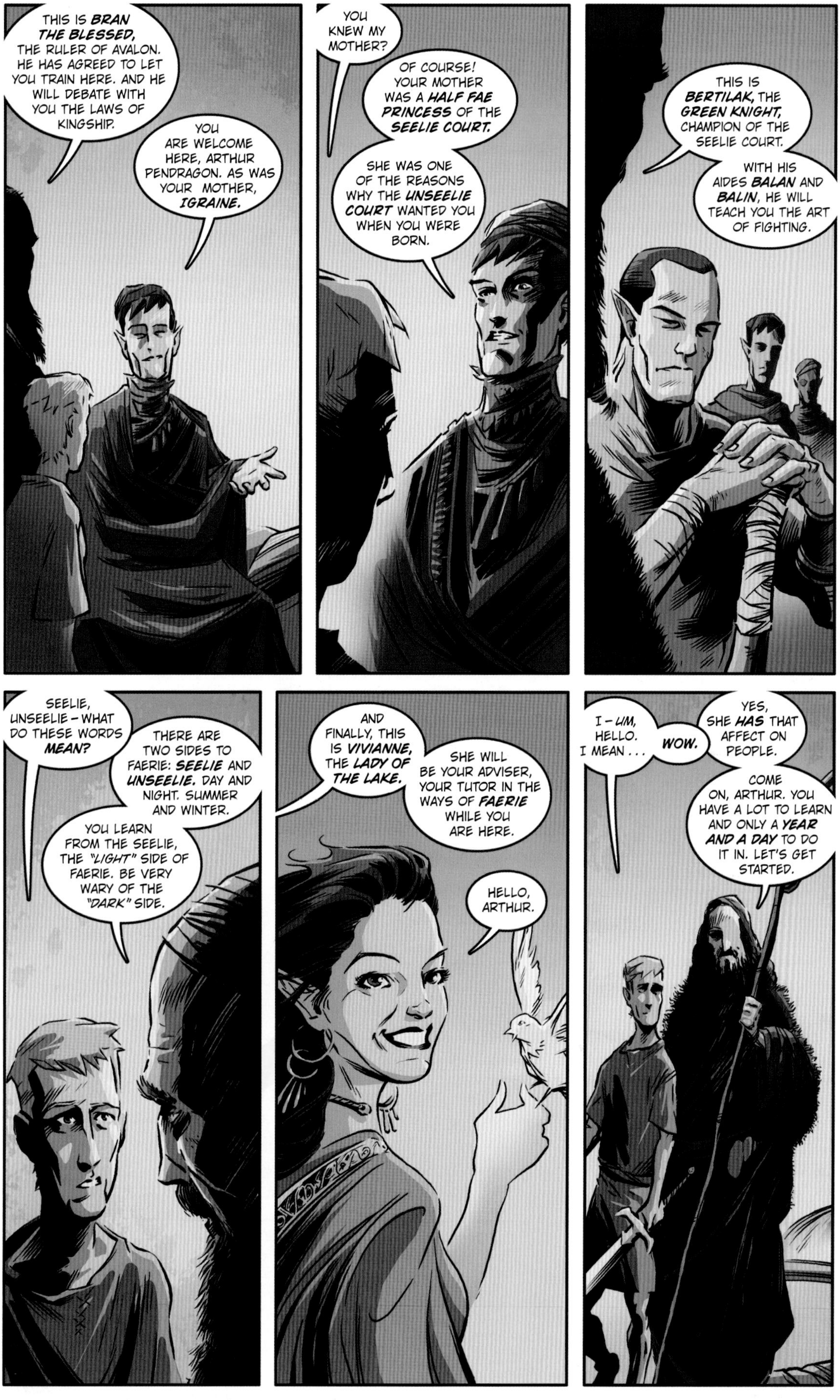
THIS IS BRAN THE BLESSED, THE RULER OF AVALON. HE HAS AGREED TO LET YOU TRAIN HERE. AND HE WILL DEBATE WITH YOU THE LAWS OF KINGSHIP.
YOU ARE WELCOME HERE, ARTHUR PENDRAGON. AS WAS YOUR MOTHER, IGRAINE.
YOU KNEW MY MOTHER?
OF COURSE! YOUR MOTHER WAS A HALF FAE PRINCESS OF THE SEELIE COURT.
SHE WAS ONE OF THE REASONS WHY THE UNSEELIE COURT WANTED YOU WHEN YOU WERE BORN.
THIS IS BERTILAK, THE GREEN KNIGHT, CHAMPION OF THE SEELIE COURT.
WITH HIS AIDES BALAN AND BALIN, HE WILL TEACH YOU THE ART OF FIGHTING.
SEELIE, UNSEELIE – WHAT DO THESE WORDS MEAN?
THERE ARE TWO SIDES TO FAERIE: SEELIE AND UNSEELIE. DAY AND NIGHT. SUMMER AND WINTER.
YOU LEARN FROM THE SEELIE, THE "LIGHT" SIDE OF FAERIE. BE VERY WARY OF THE "DARK" SIDE.
AND FINALLY, THIS IS VIVIANNE, THE LADY OF THE LAKE.
SHE WILL BE YOUR ADVISER, YOUR TUTOR IN THE WAYS OF FAERIE WHILE YOU ARE HERE.
HELLO, ARTHUR.
I – UM, HELLO. I MEAN . . .
WOW.
YES, SHE HAS THAT AFFECT ON PEOPLE.
COME ON, ARTHUR. YOU HAVE A LOT TO LEARN AND ONLY A YEAR AND A DAY TO DO IT IN. LET'S GET STARTED.

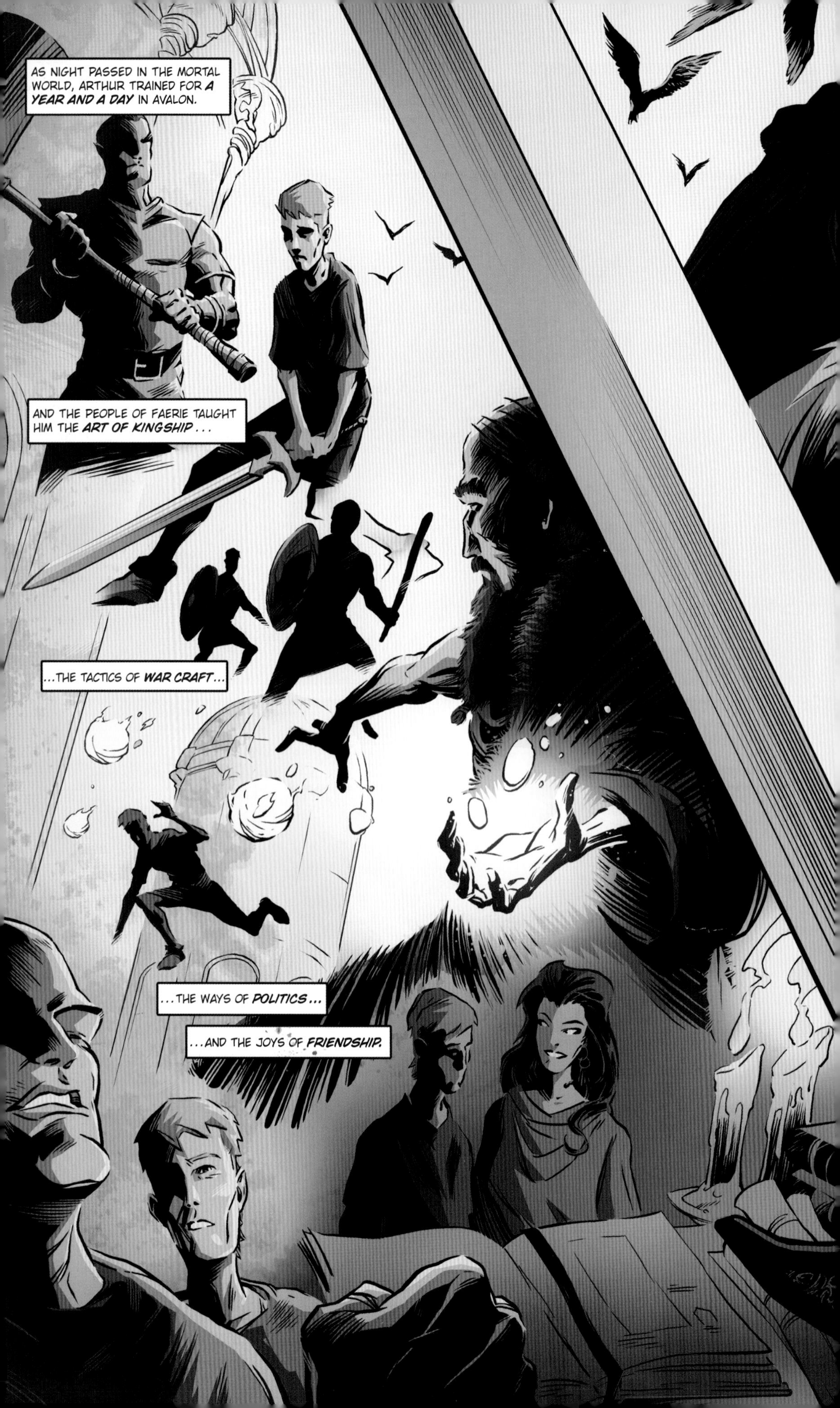
AS NIGHT PASSED IN THE MORTAL WORLD, ARTHUR TRAINED FOR *A YEAR AND A DAY* IN AVALON.
AND THE PEOPLE OF FAERIE TAUGHT HIM THE *ART OF KINGSHIP* . . .
. . .THE TACTICS OF *WAR CRAFT*. . .
. . .THE WAYS OF *POLITICS*. . .
. . .AND THE JOYS OF *FRIENDSHIP.*

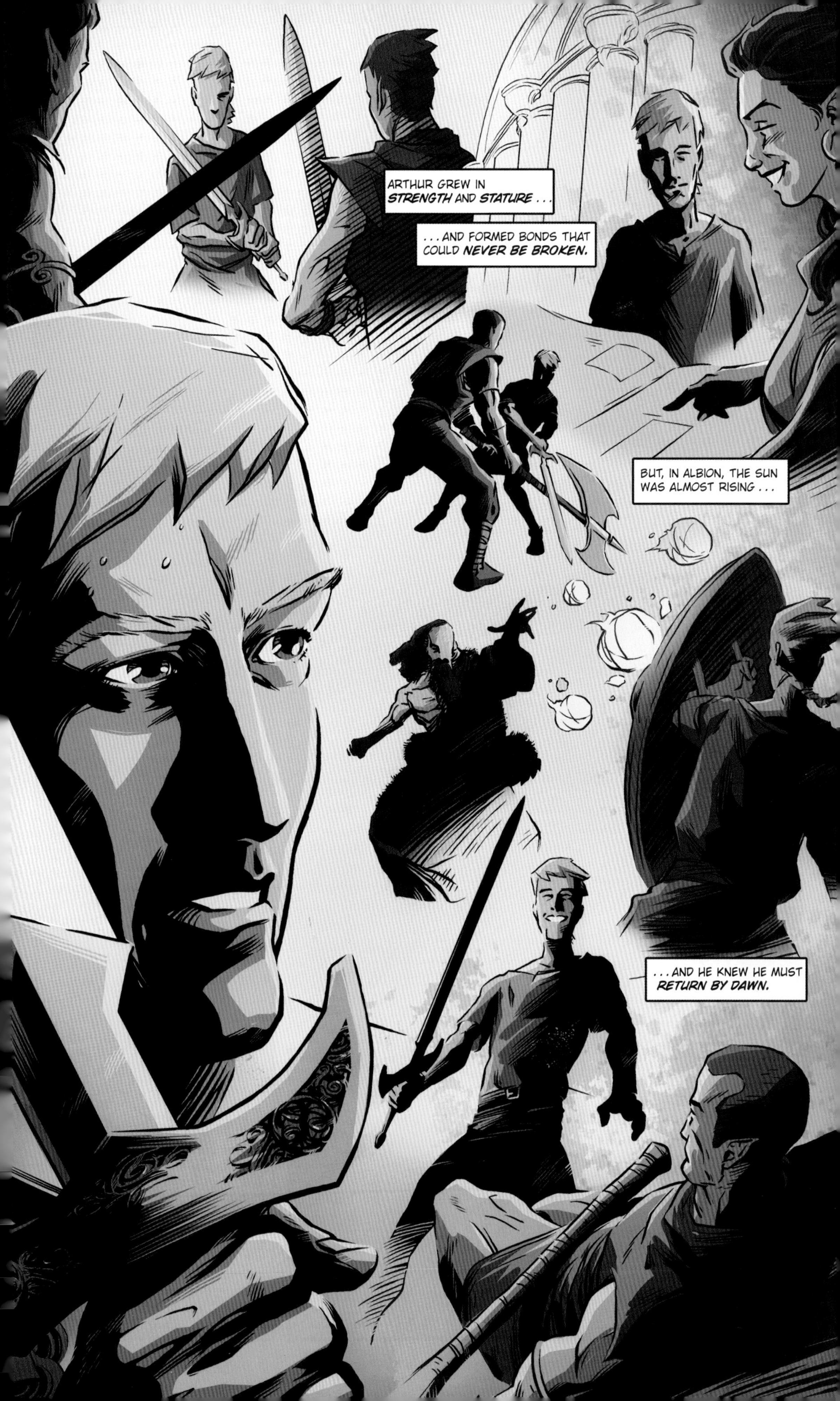
ARTHUR GREW IN
STRENGTH AND STATURE . . .
. . . AND FORMED BONDS THAT
COULD NEVER BE BROKEN.
BUT, IN ALBION, THE SUN
WAS ALMOST RISING . . .
. . . AND HE KNEW HE MUST
RETURN BY DAWN.

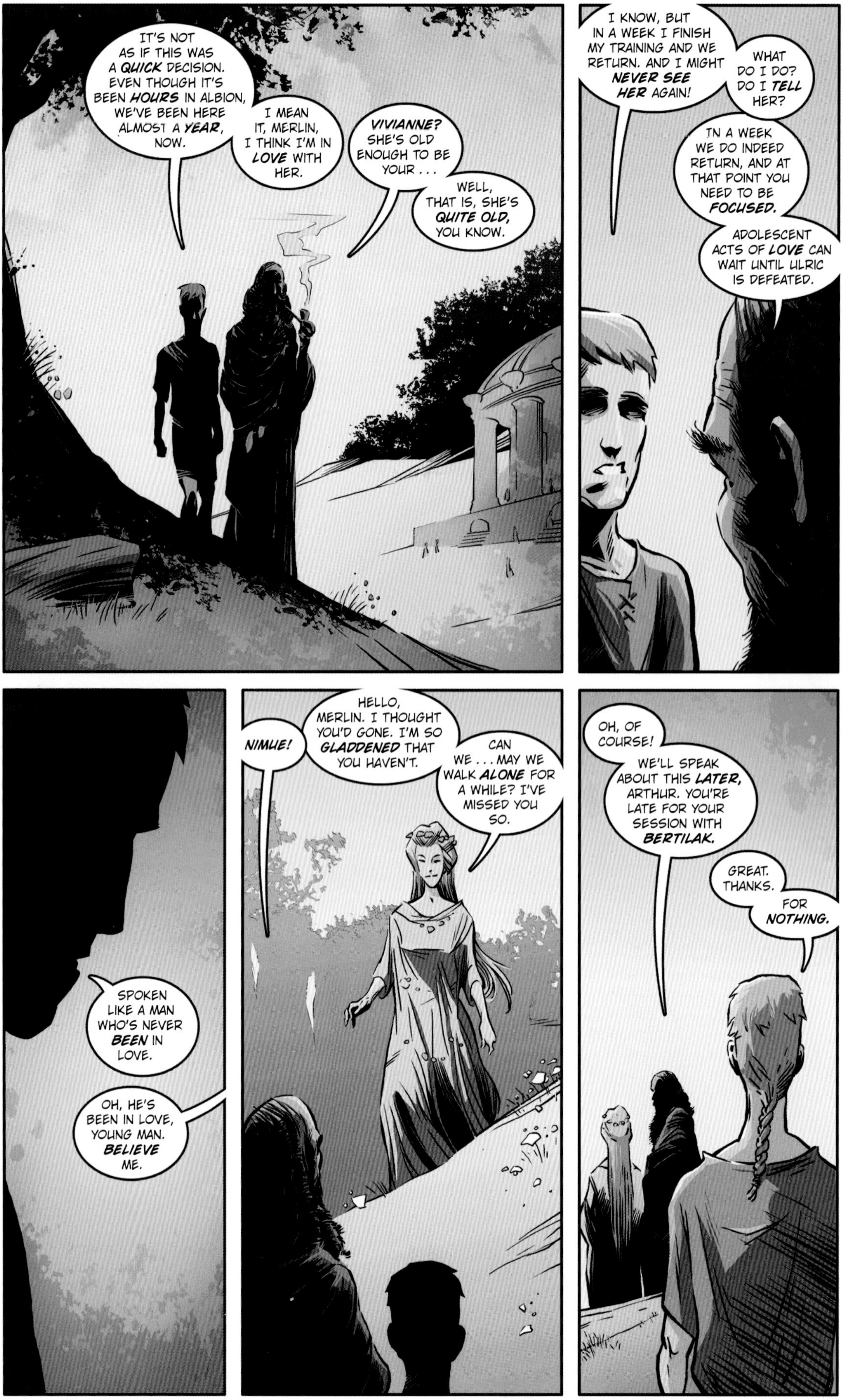
IT'S NOT AS IF THIS WAS A QUICK DECISION. EVEN THOUGH IT'S BEEN HOURS IN ALBION, WE'VE BEEN HERE ALMOST A YEAR, NOW.
I MEAN IT, MERLIN, I THINK I'M IN LOVE WITH HER.
VIVIANNE? SHE'S OLD ENOUGH TO BE YOUR . . .
WELL, THAT IS, SHE'S QUITE OLD, YOU KNOW.
I KNOW, BUT IN A WEEK I FINISH MY TRAINING AND WE RETURN. AND I MIGHT NEVER SEE HER AGAIN!
WHAT DO I DO? DO I TELL HER?
IN A WEEK WE DO INDEED RETURN, AND AT THAT POINT YOU NEED TO BE FOCUSED.
ADOLESCENT ACTS OF LOVE CAN WAIT UNTIL ULRIC IS DEFEATED.
SPOKEN LIKE A MAN WHO'S NEVER BEEN IN LOVE.
OH, HE'S BEEN IN LOVE, YOUNG MAN. BELIEVE ME.
NIMUE!
HELLO, MERLIN. I THOUGHT YOU'D GONE. I'M SO GLADDENED THAT YOU HAVEN'T.
CAN WE . . . MAY WE WALK ALONE FOR A WHILE? I'VE MISSED YOU SO.
OH, OF COURSE!
WE'LL SPEAK ABOUT THIS LATER, ARTHUR. YOU'RE LATE FOR YOUR SESSION WITH BERTILAK.
GREAT. THANKS.
FOR NOTHING.

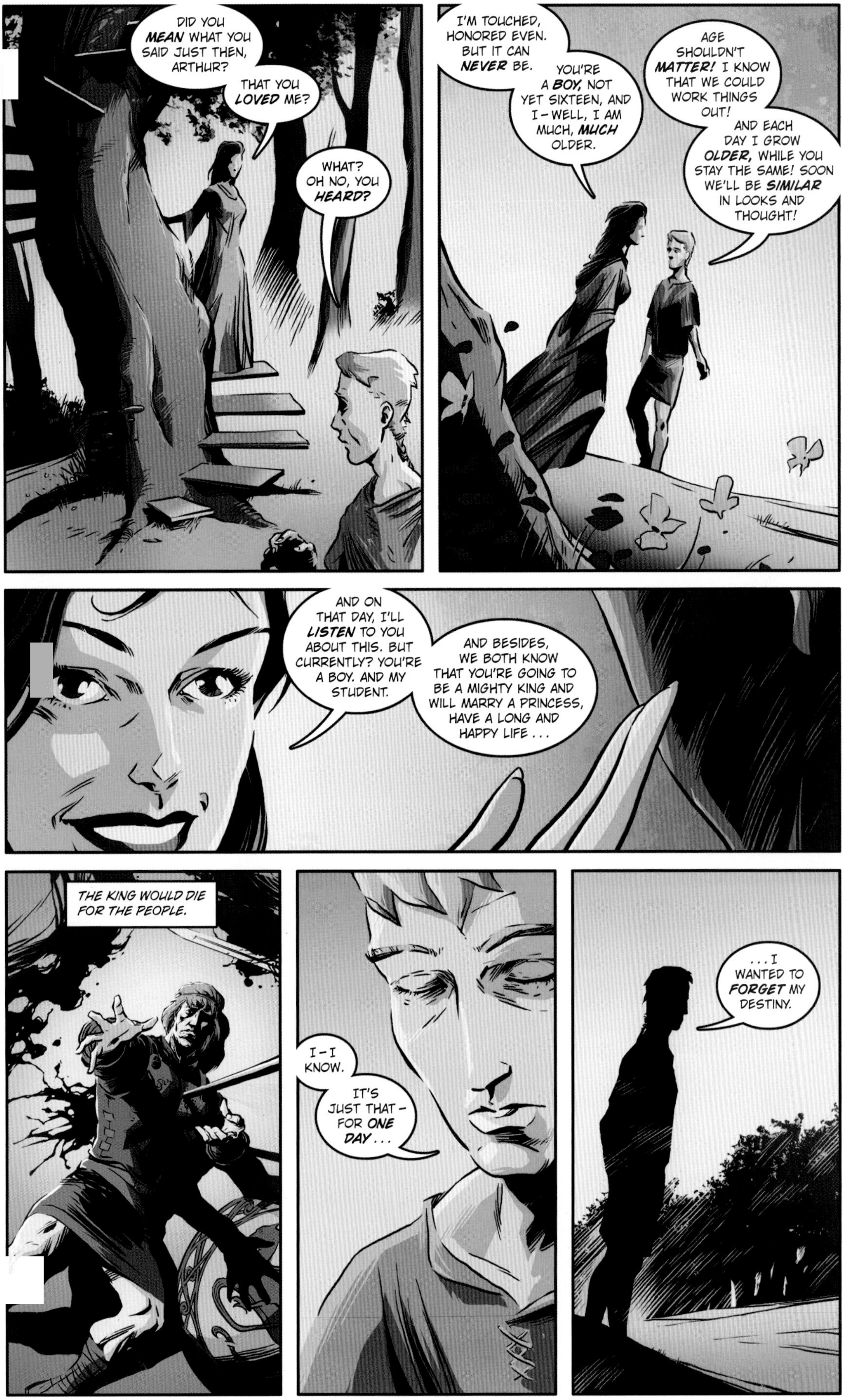
DID YOU MEAN WHAT YOU SAID JUST THEN, ARTHUR?
THAT YOU LOVED ME?
WHAT? OH NO, YOU HEARD?
I'M TOUCHED, HONORED EVEN. BUT IT CAN NEVER BE.
YOU'RE A BOY, NOT YET SIXTEEN, AND I—WELL, I AM MUCH, MUCH OLDER.
AGE SHOULDN'T MATTER! I KNOW THAT WE COULD WORK THINGS OUT!
AND EACH DAY I GROW OLDER, WHILE YOU STAY THE SAME! SOON WE'LL BE SIMILAR IN LOOKS AND THOUGHT!
AND ON THAT DAY, I'LL LISTEN TO YOU ABOUT THIS. BUT CURRENTLY? YOU'RE A BOY. AND MY STUDENT.
AND BESIDES, WE BOTH KNOW THAT YOU'RE GOING TO BE A MIGHTY KING AND WILL MARRY A PRINCESS, HAVE A LONG AND HAPPY LIFE . . .
THE KING WOULD DIE FOR THE PEOPLE.
I—I KNOW.
IT'S JUST THAT—FOR ONE DAY . . .
. . . I WANTED TO FORGET MY DESTINY.

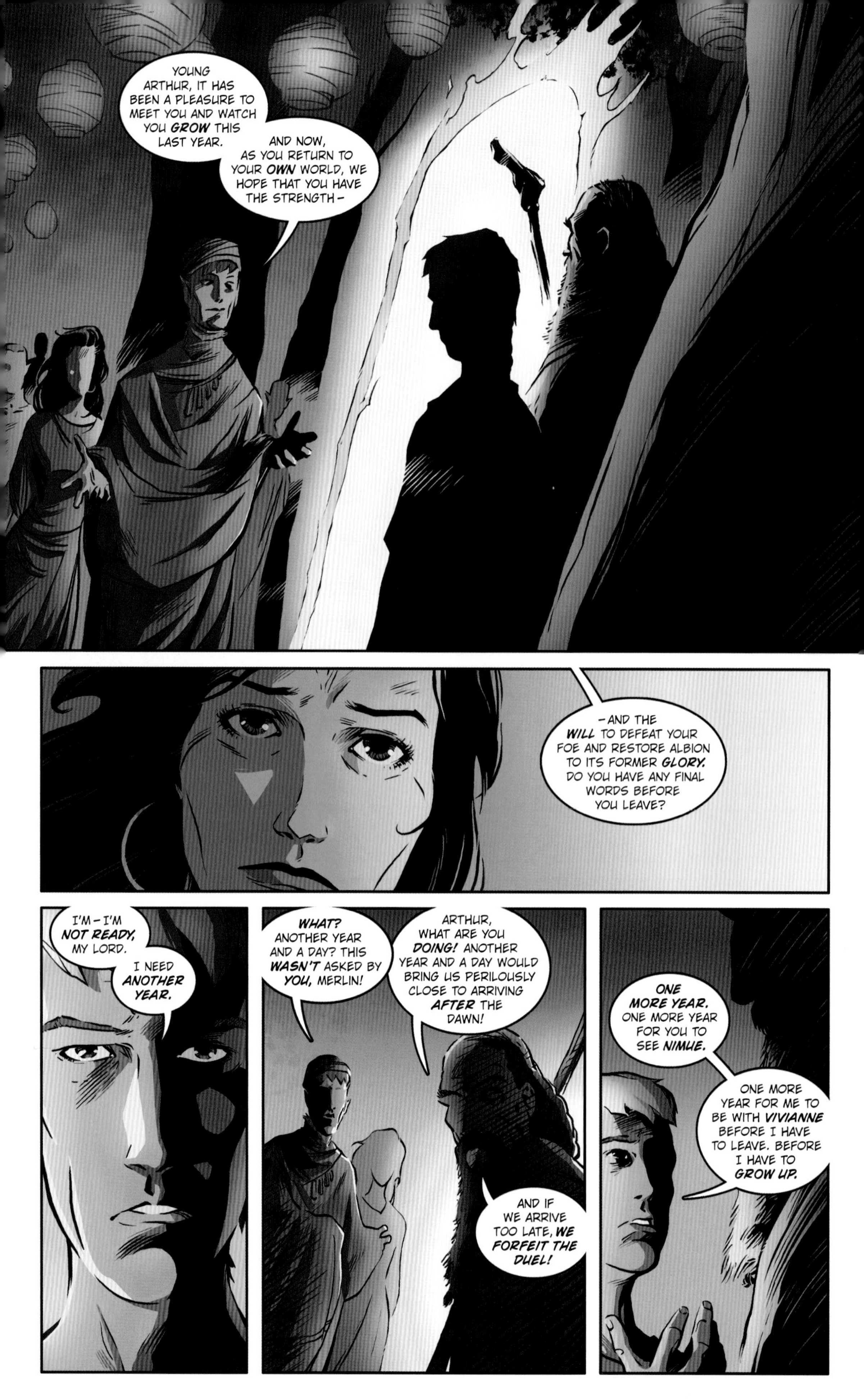
YOUNG ARTHUR, IT HAS BEEN A PLEASURE TO MEET YOU AND WATCH YOU GROW THIS LAST YEAR.
AND NOW, AS YOU RETURN TO YOUR OWN WORLD, WE HOPE THAT YOU HAVE THE STRENGTH–
–AND THE WILL TO DEFEAT YOUR FOE AND RESTORE ALBION TO ITS FORMER GLORY. DO YOU HAVE ANY FINAL WORDS BEFORE YOU LEAVE?
I'M–I'M NOT READY, MY LORD.
I NEED ANOTHER YEAR.
WHAT? ANOTHER YEAR AND A DAY? THIS WASN'T ASKED BY YOU, MERLIN!
ARTHUR, WHAT ARE YOU DOING! ANOTHER YEAR AND A DAY WOULD BRING US PERILOUSLY CLOSE TO ARRIVING AFTER THE DAWN!
AND IF WE ARRIVE TOO LATE, WE FORFEIT THE DUEL!
ONE MORE YEAR. ONE MORE YEAR FOR YOU TO SEE NIMUE.
ONE MORE YEAR FOR ME TO BE WITH VIVIANNE BEFORE I HAVE TO LEAVE. BEFORE I HAVE TO GROW UP.

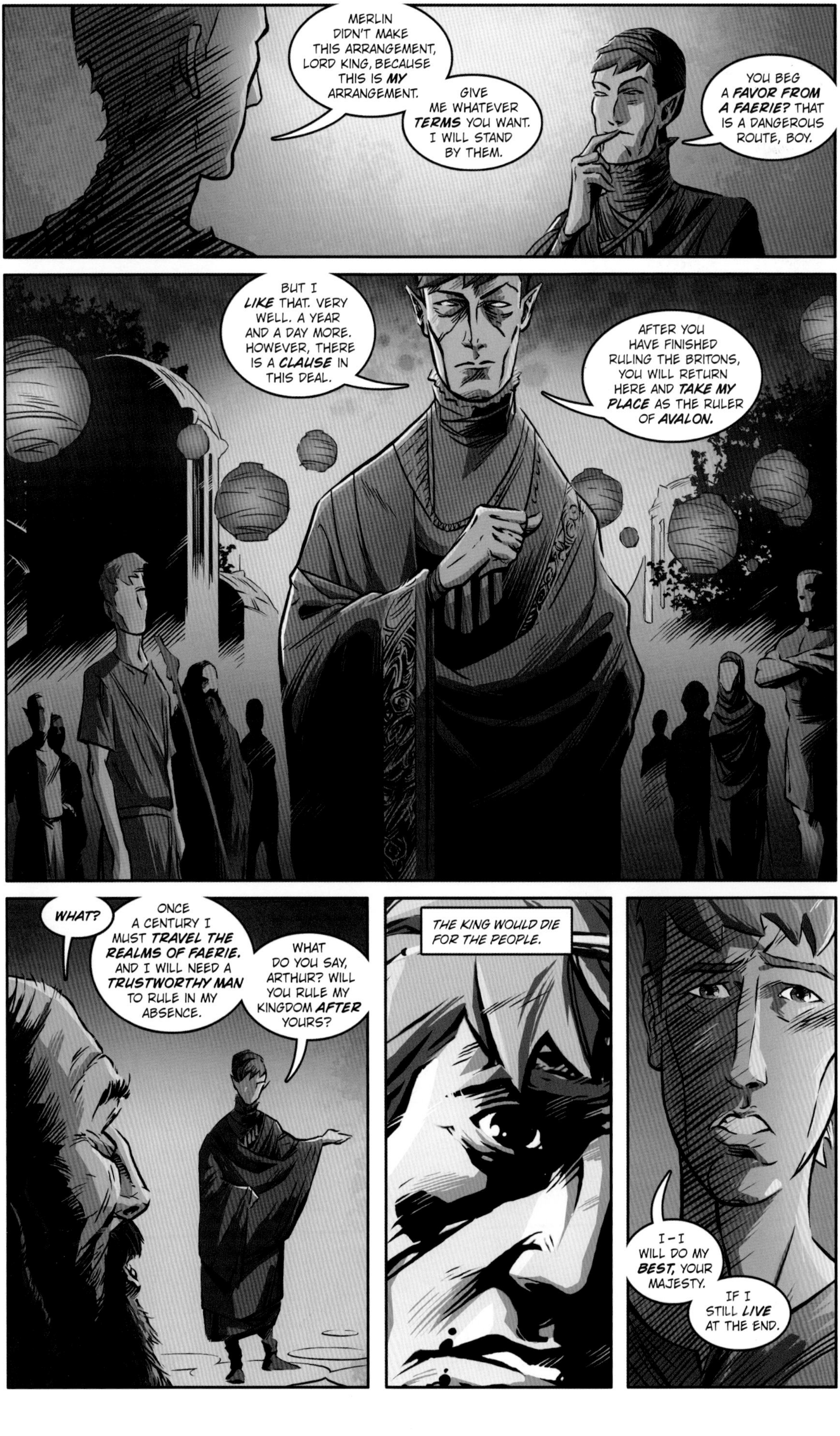
MERLIN DIDN'T MAKE THIS ARRANGEMENT, LORD KING, BECAUSE THIS IS MY ARRANGEMENT.
GIVE ME WHATEVER TERMS YOU WANT. I WILL STAND BY THEM.
YOU BEG A FAVOR FROM A FAERIE? THAT IS A DANGEROUS ROUTE, BOY.
BUT I LIKE THAT. VERY WELL. A YEAR AND A DAY MORE. HOWEVER, THERE IS A CLAUSE IN THIS DEAL.
AFTER YOU HAVE FINISHED RULING THE BRITONS, YOU WILL RETURN HERE AND TAKE MY PLACE AS THE RULER OF AVALON.
WHAT?
ONCE A CENTURY I MUST TRAVEL THE REALMS OF FAERIE. AND I WILL NEED A TRUSTWORTHY MAN TO RULE IN MY ABSENCE.
WHAT DO YOU SAY, ARTHUR? WILL YOU RULE MY KINGDOM AFTER YOURS?
THE KING WOULD DIE FOR THE PEOPLE.
I-I WILL DO MY BEST, YOUR MAJESTY.
IF I STILL LIVE AT THE END.

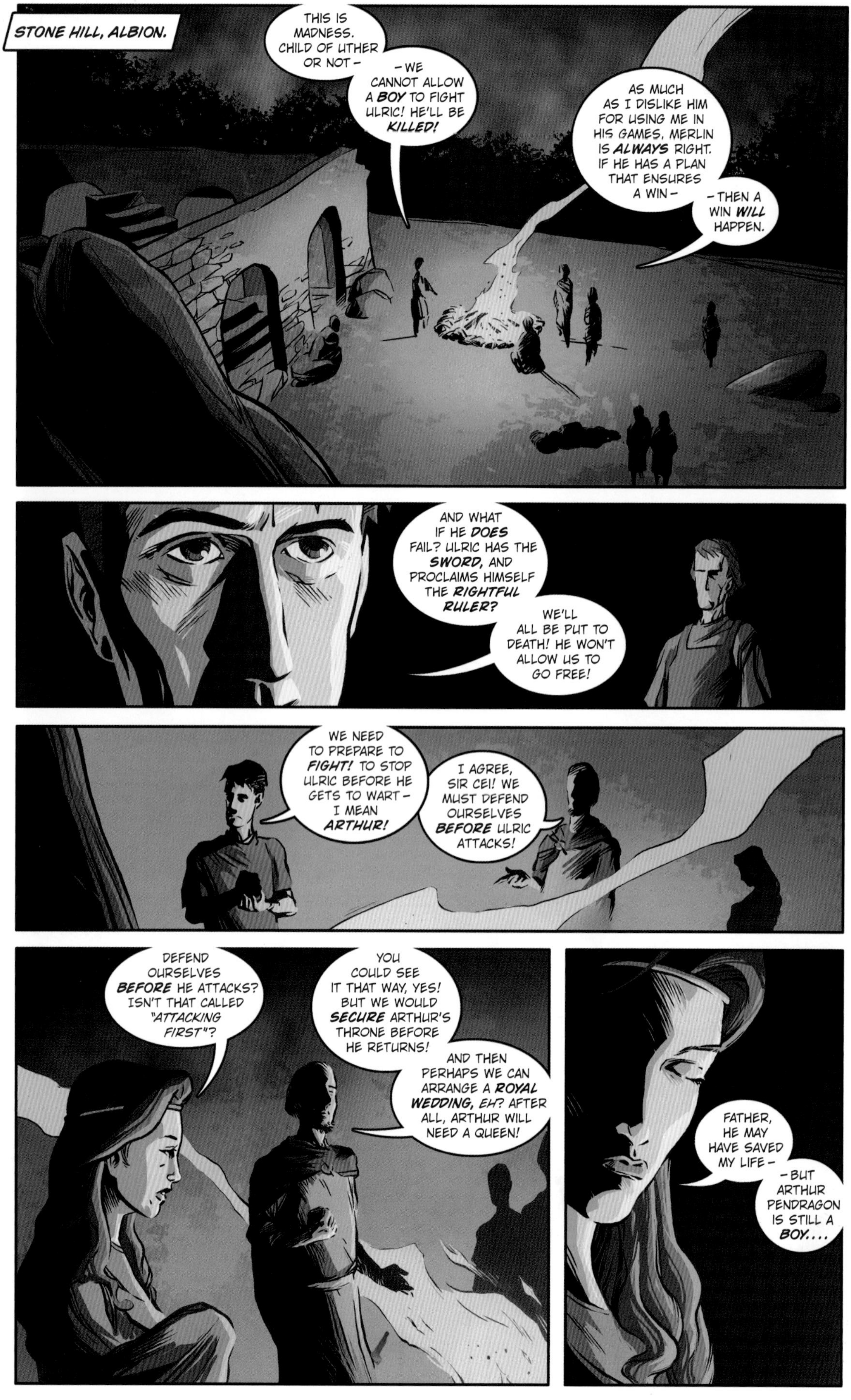
STONE HILL, ALBION.
THIS IS MADNESS. CHILD OF UTHER OR NOT –
– WE CANNOT ALLOW A BOY TO FIGHT ULRIC! HE'LL BE KILLED!
AS MUCH AS I DISLIKE HIM FOR USING ME IN HIS GAMES, MERLIN IS ALWAYS RIGHT. IF HE HAS A PLAN THAT ENSURES A WIN –
– THEN A WIN WILL HAPPEN.
AND WHAT IF HE DOES FAIL? ULRIC HAS THE SWORD, AND PROCLAIMS HIMSELF THE RIGHTFUL RULER?
WE'LL ALL BE PUT TO DEATH! HE WON'T ALLOW US TO GO FREE!
WE NEED TO PREPARE TO FIGHT! TO STOP ULRIC BEFORE HE GETS TO WART – I MEAN ARTHUR!
I AGREE, SIR CEI! WE MUST DEFEND OURSELVES BEFORE ULRIC ATTACKS!
DEFEND OURSELVES BEFORE HE ATTACKS? ISN'T THAT CALLED "ATTACKING FIRST"?
YOU COULD SEE IT THAT WAY, YES! BUT WE WOULD SECURE ARTHUR'S THRONE BEFORE HE RETURNS!
AND THEN PERHAPS WE CAN ARRANGE A ROYAL WEDDING, EH? AFTER ALL, ARTHUR WILL NEED A QUEEN!
FATHER, HE MAY HAVE SAVED MY LIFE –
– BUT ARTHUR PENDRAGON IS STILL A BOY. . . .

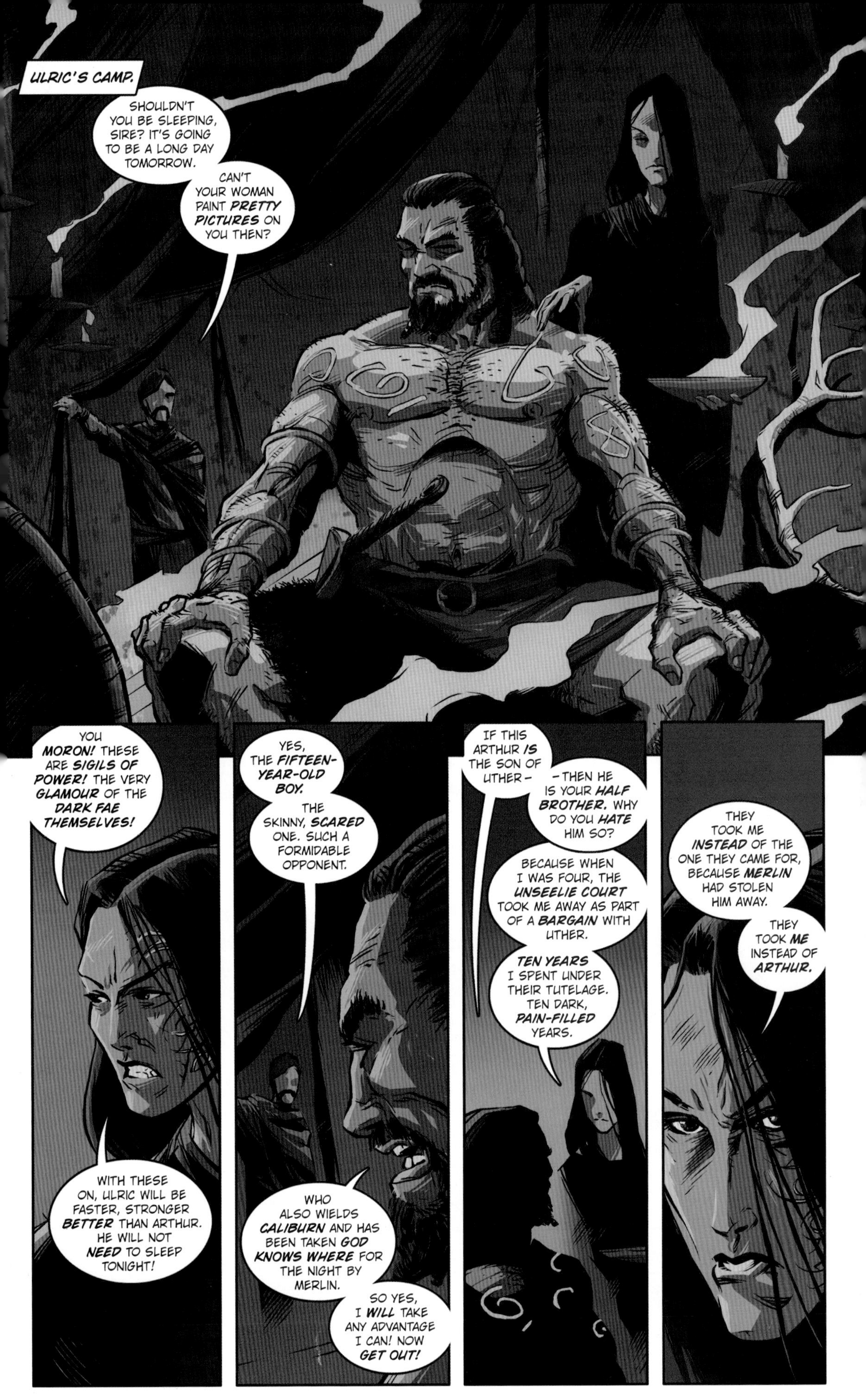
ULRIC'S CAMP.
SHOULDN'T YOU BE SLEEPING, SIRE? IT'S GOING TO BE A LONG DAY TOMORROW.
CAN'T YOUR WOMAN PAINT PRETTY PICTURES ON YOU THEN?
YOU MORON! THESE ARE SIGILS OF POWER! THE VERY GLAMOUR OF THE DARK FAE THEMSELVES!
WITH THESE ON, ULRIC WILL BE FASTER, STRONGER BETTER THAN ARTHUR. HE WILL NOT NEED TO SLEEP TONIGHT!
YES, THE FIFTEEN-YEAR-OLD BOY.
THE SKINNY, SCARED ONE. SUCH A FORMIDABLE OPPONENT.
WHO ALSO WIELDS CALIBURN AND HAS BEEN TAKEN GOD KNOWS WHERE FOR THE NIGHT BY MERLIN.
SO YES, I WILL TAKE ANY ADVANTAGE I CAN! NOW GET OUT!
IF THIS ARTHUR IS THE SON OF UTHER–
–THEN HE IS YOUR HALF BROTHER. WHY DO YOU HATE HIM SO?
BECAUSE WHEN I WAS FOUR, THE UNSEELIE COURT TOOK ME AWAY AS PART OF A BARGAIN WITH UTHER.
TEN YEARS I SPENT UNDER THEIR TUTELAGE. TEN DARK, PAIN-FILLED YEARS.
THEY TOOK ME INSTEAD OF THE ONE THEY CAME FOR, BECAUSE MERLIN HAD STOLEN HIM AWAY.
THEY TOOK ME INSTEAD OF ARTHUR.

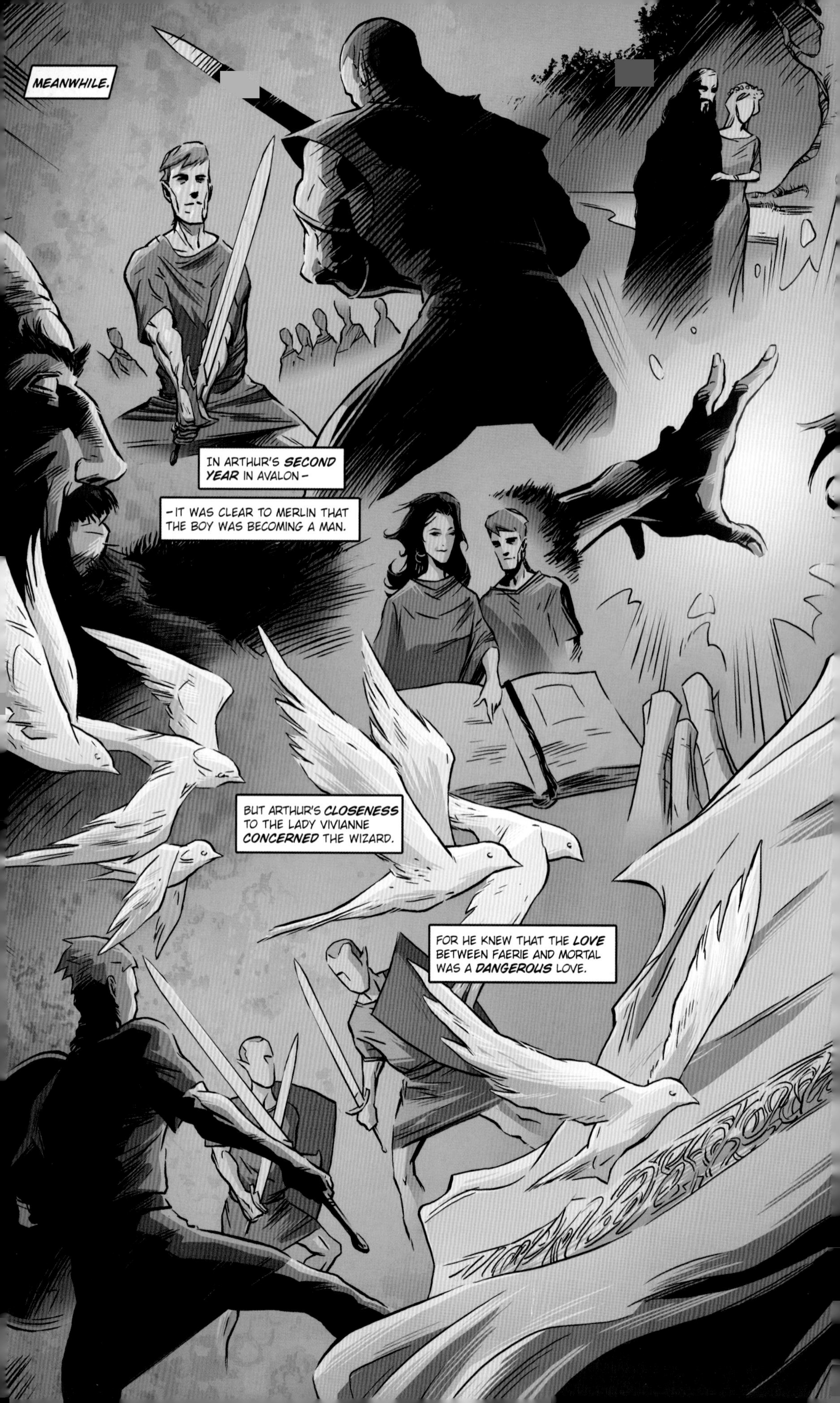
MEANWHILE.
IN ARTHUR'S SECOND YEAR IN AVALON—
—IT WAS CLEAR TO MERLIN THAT THE BOY WAS BECOMING A MAN.
BUT ARTHUR'S CLOSENESS TO THE LADY VIVIANNE CONCERNED THE WIZARD.
FOR HE KNEW THAT THE LOVE BETWEEN FAERIE AND MORTAL WAS A DANGEROUS LOVE.

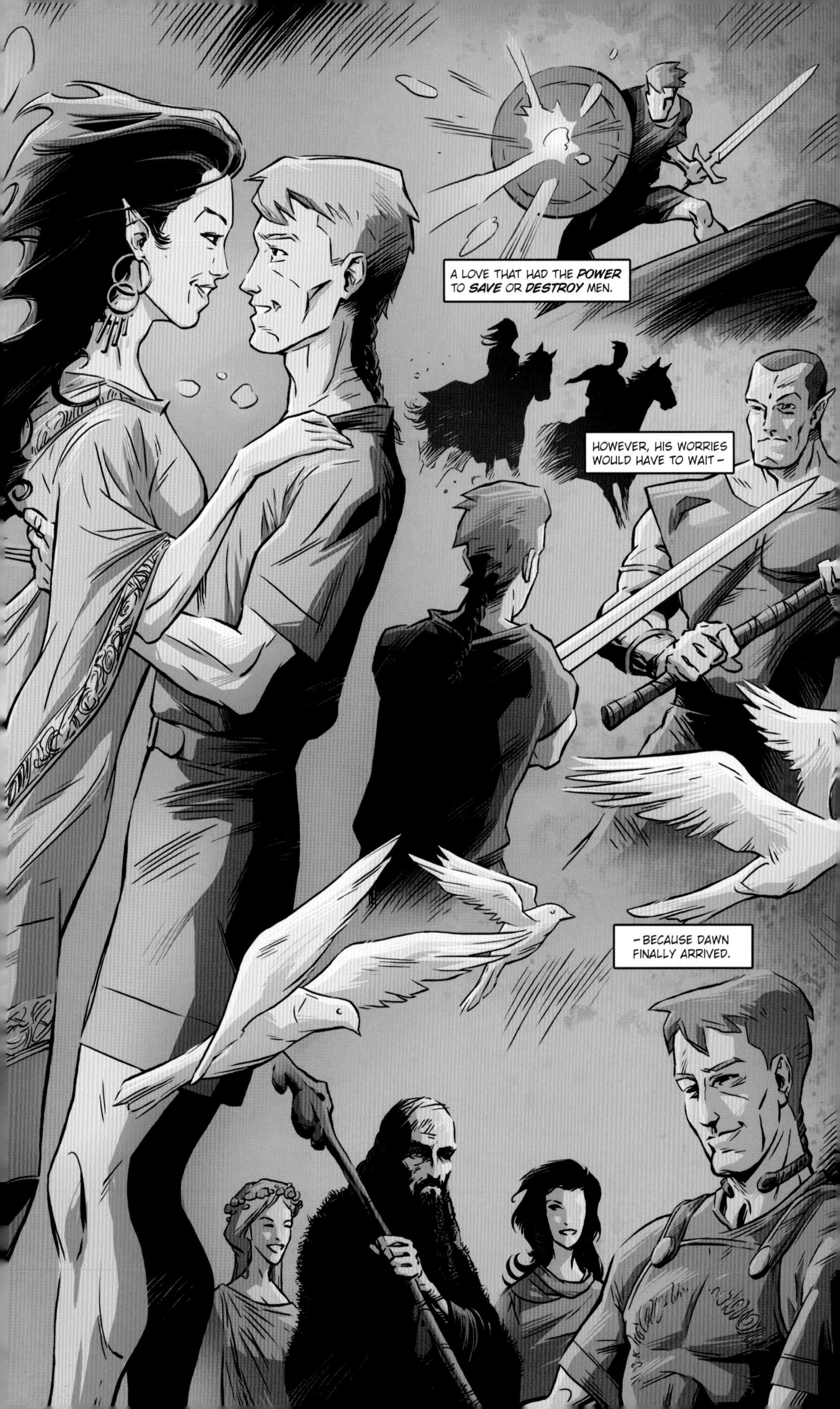
A LOVE THAT HAD THE **POWER** TO **SAVE** OR **DESTROY** MEN.
HOWEVER, HIS WORRIES WOULD HAVE TO WAIT–
–BECAUSE DAWN FINALLY ARRIVED.

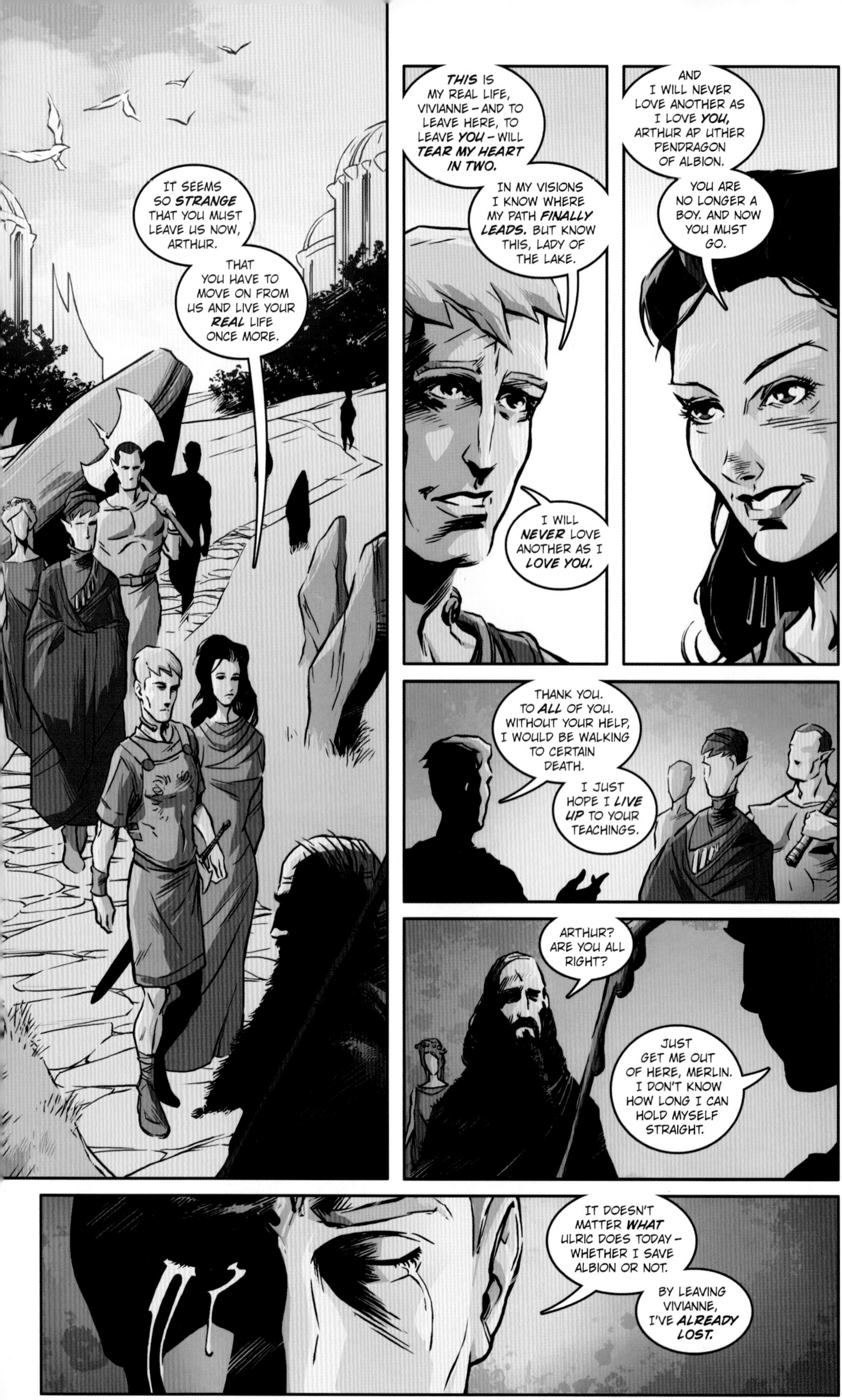
IT SEEMS SO STRANGE THAT YOU MUST LEAVE US NOW, ARTHUR.
THAT YOU HAVE TO MOVE ON FROM US AND LIVE YOUR REAL LIFE ONCE MORE.
THIS IS MY REAL LIFE, VIVIANNE – AND TO LEAVE HERE, TO LEAVE YOU – WILL TEAR MY HEART IN TWO.
IN MY VISIONS I KNOW WHERE MY PATH FINALLY LEADS. BUT KNOW THIS, LADY OF THE LAKE.
I WILL NEVER LOVE ANOTHER AS I LOVE YOU.
AND I WILL NEVER LOVE ANOTHER AS I LOVE YOU, ARTHUR AP UTHER PENDRAGON OF ALBION.
YOU ARE NO LONGER A BOY. AND NOW YOU MUST GO.
THANK YOU. TO ALL OF YOU. WITHOUT YOUR HELP, I WOULD BE WALKING TO CERTAIN DEATH.
I JUST HOPE I LIVE UP TO YOUR TEACHINGS.
ARTHUR? ARE YOU ALL RIGHT?
JUST GET ME OUT OF HERE, MERLIN. I DON'T KNOW HOW LONG I CAN HOLD MYSELF STRAIGHT.
IT DOESN'T MATTER WHAT ULRIC DOES TODAY – WHETHER I SAVE ALBION OR NOT.
BY LEAVING VIVIANNE, I'VE ALREADY LOST.

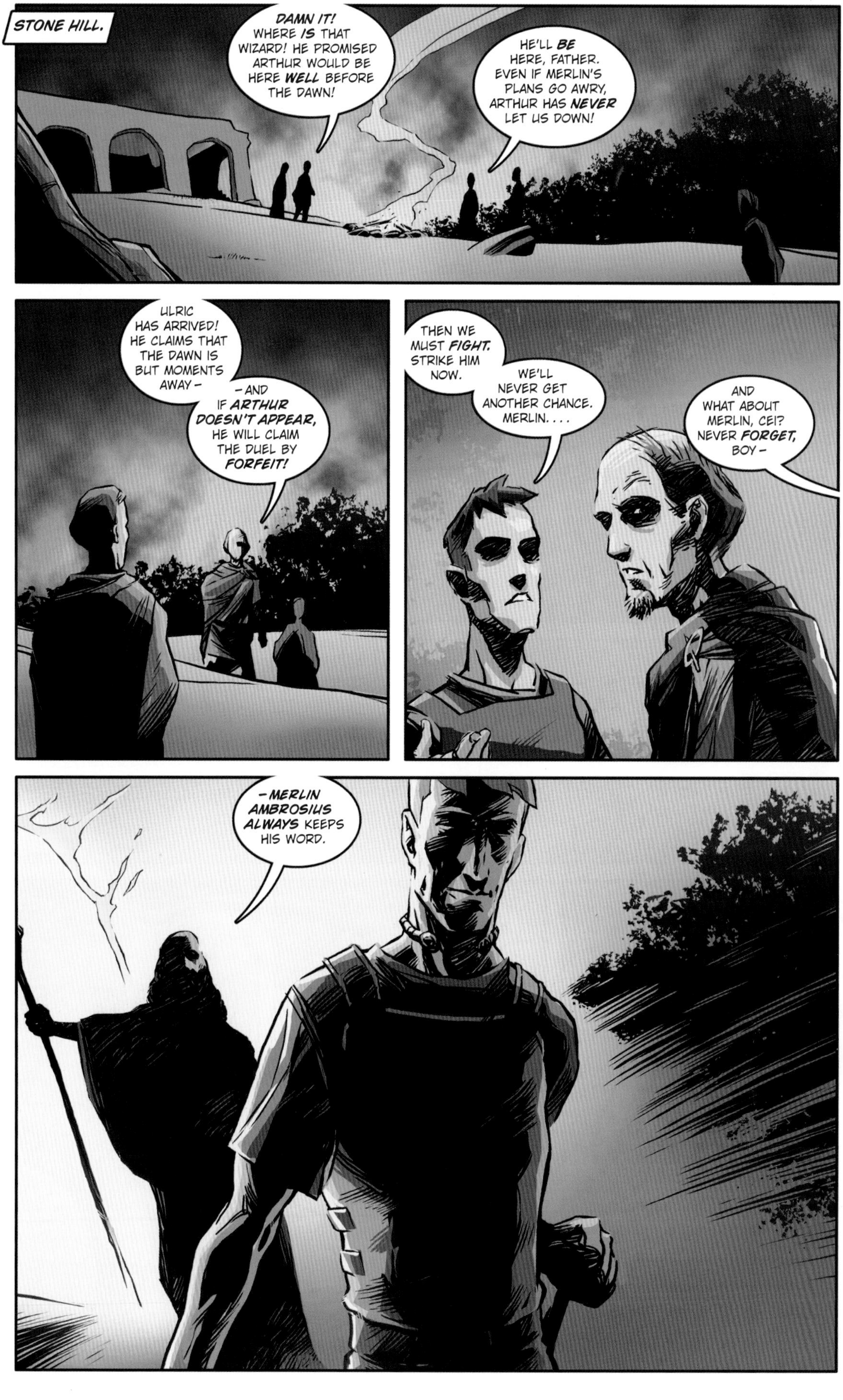
STONE HILL.
DAMN IT! WHERE IS THAT WIZARD! HE PROMISED ARTHUR WOULD BE HERE WELL BEFORE THE DAWN!
HE'LL BE HERE, FATHER. EVEN IF MERLIN'S PLANS GO AWRY, ARTHUR HAS NEVER LET US DOWN!
ULRIC HAS ARRIVED! HE CLAIMS THAT THE DAWN IS BUT MOMENTS AWAY –
– AND IF ARTHUR DOESN'T APPEAR, HE WILL CLAIM THE DUEL BY FORFEIT!
THEN WE MUST FIGHT. STRIKE HIM NOW.
WE'LL NEVER GET ANOTHER CHANCE. MERLIN. . . .
AND WHAT ABOUT MERLIN, CEI? NEVER FORGET, BOY –
– MERLIN AMBROSIUS ALWAYS KEEPS HIS WORD.

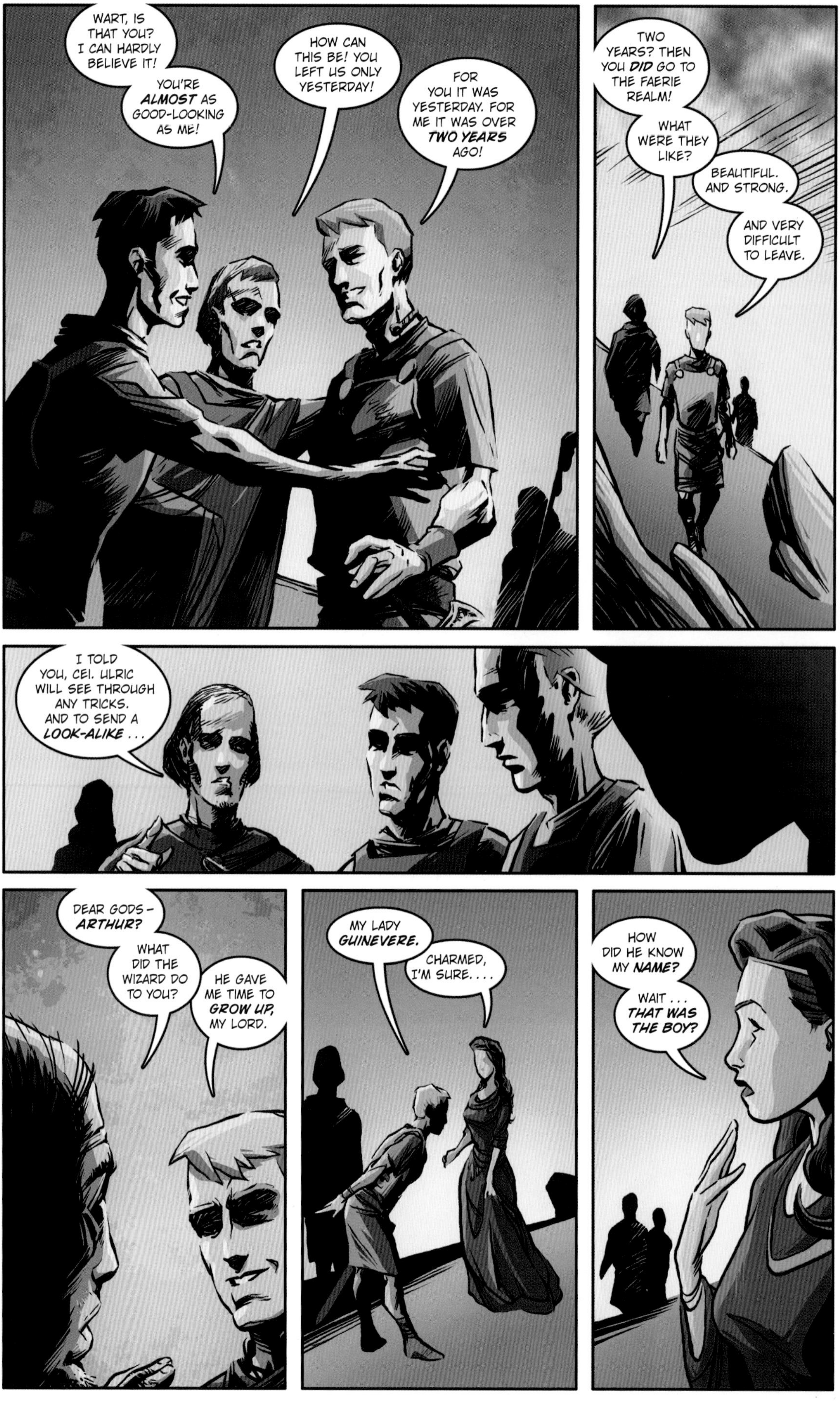
WART, IS THAT YOU? I CAN HARDLY BELIEVE IT!
YOU'RE ALMOST AS GOOD-LOOKING AS ME!
HOW CAN THIS BE! YOU LEFT US ONLY YESTERDAY!
FOR YOU IT WAS YESTERDAY. FOR ME IT WAS OVER TWO YEARS AGO!
TWO YEARS? THEN YOU DID GO TO THE FAERIE REALM!
WHAT WERE THEY LIKE?
BEAUTIFUL. AND STRONG.
AND VERY DIFFICULT TO LEAVE.
I TOLD YOU, CEI. ULRIC WILL SEE THROUGH ANY TRICKS. AND TO SEND A LOOK-ALIKE . . .
DEAR GODS- ARTHUR?
WHAT DID THE WIZARD DO TO YOU?
HE GAVE ME TIME TO GROW UP, MY LORD.
MY LADY GUINEVERE.
CHARMED, I'M SURE. . . .
HOW DID HE KNOW MY NAME?
WAIT . . . THAT WAS THE BOY?

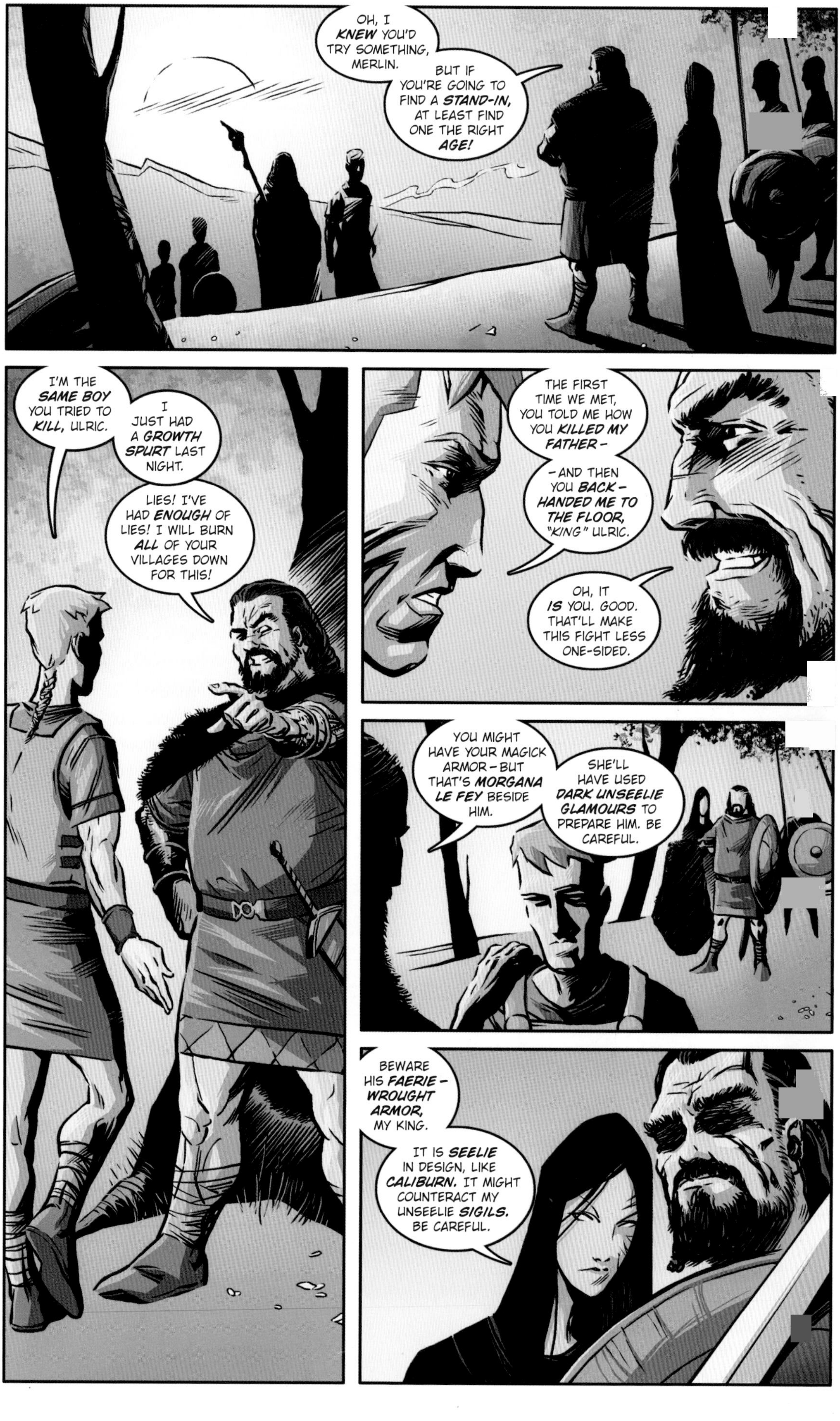
OH, I KNEW YOU'D TRY SOMETHING, MERLIN.
BUT IF YOU'RE GOING TO FIND A STAND-IN, AT LEAST FIND ONE THE RIGHT AGE!
I'M THE SAME BOY YOU TRIED TO KILL, ULRIC.
I JUST HAD A GROWTH SPURT LAST NIGHT.
LIES! I'VE HAD ENOUGH OF LIES! I WILL BURN ALL OF YOUR VILLAGES DOWN FOR THIS!
THE FIRST TIME WE MET, YOU TOLD ME HOW YOU KILLED MY FATHER—
—AND THEN YOU BACK-HANDED ME TO THE FLOOR, "KING" ULRIC.
OH, IT IS YOU. GOOD. THAT'LL MAKE THIS FIGHT LESS ONE-SIDED.
YOU MIGHT HAVE YOUR MAGICK ARMOR—BUT THAT'S MORGANA LE FEY BESIDE HIM.
SHE'LL HAVE USED DARK UNSEELIE GLAMOURS TO PREPARE HIM. BE CAREFUL.
BEWARE HIS FAERIE-WROUGHT ARMOR, MY KING.
IT IS SEELIE IN DESIGN, LIKE CALIBURN. IT MIGHT COUNTERACT MY UNSEELIE SIGILS. BE CAREFUL.

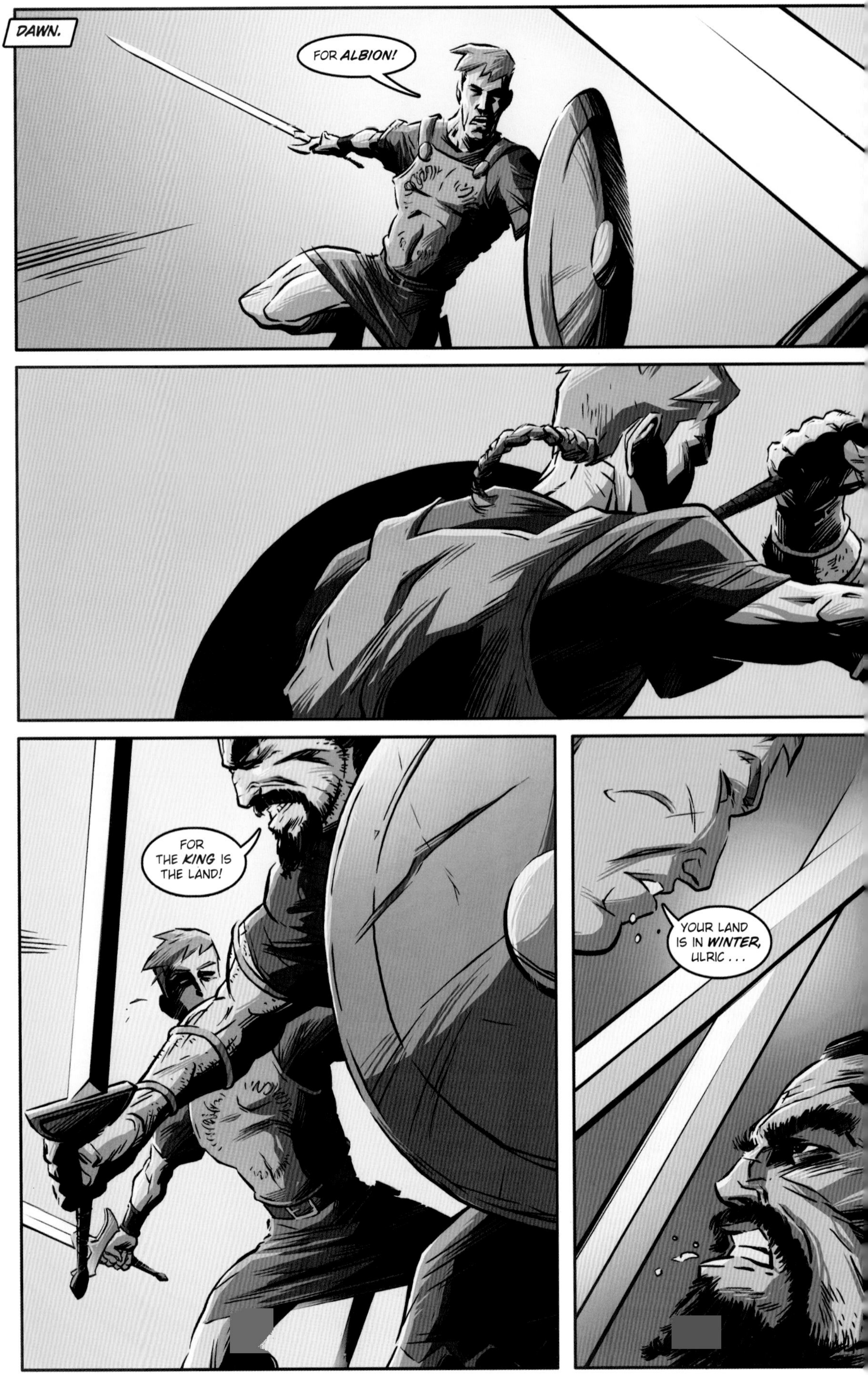
DAWN.
FOR ALBION!
FOR THE KING IS THE LAND!
YOUR LAND IS IN WINTER, ULRIC . . .

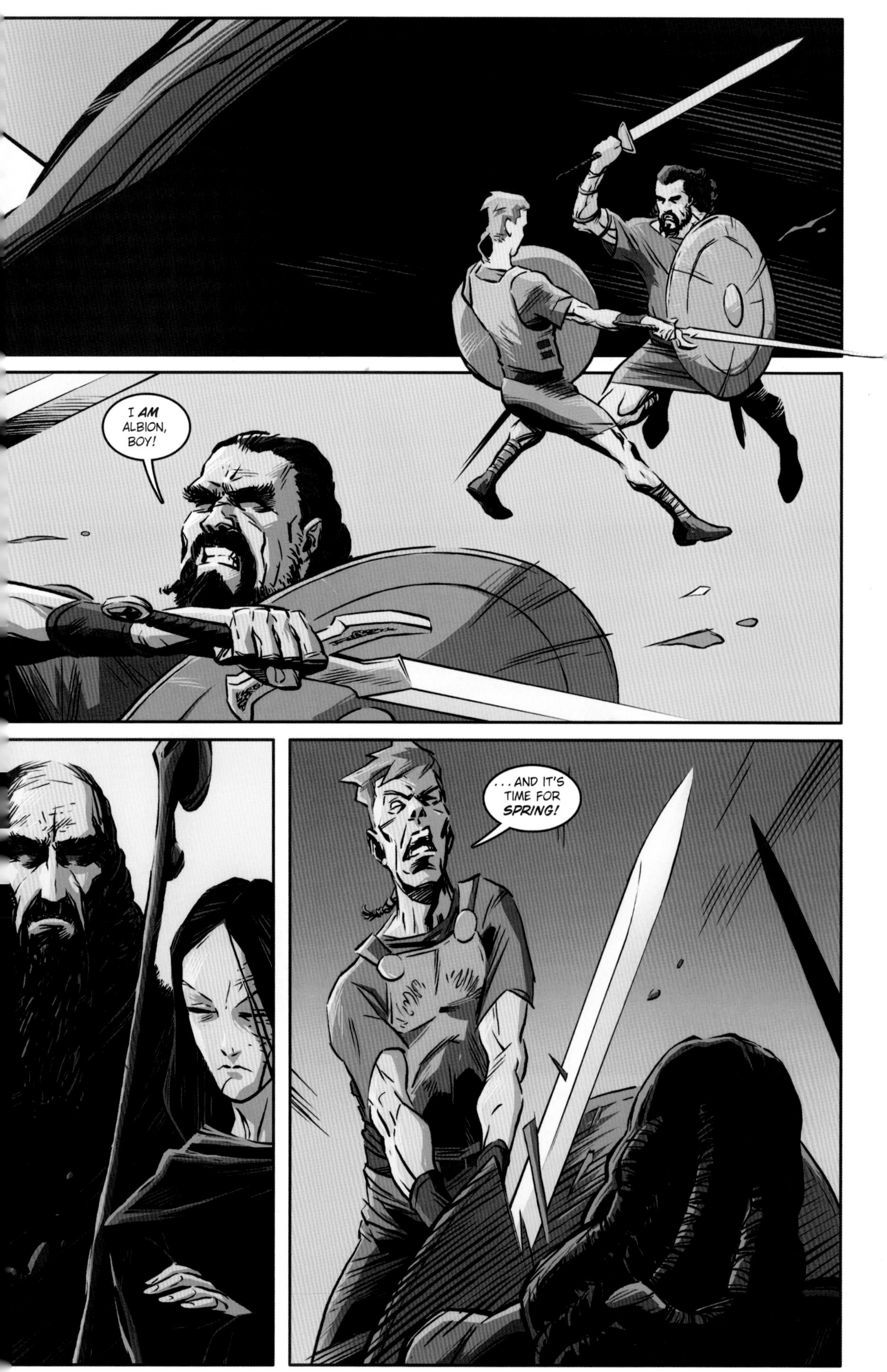
I AM ALBION, BOY!
. . . AND IT'S TIME FOR SPRING!

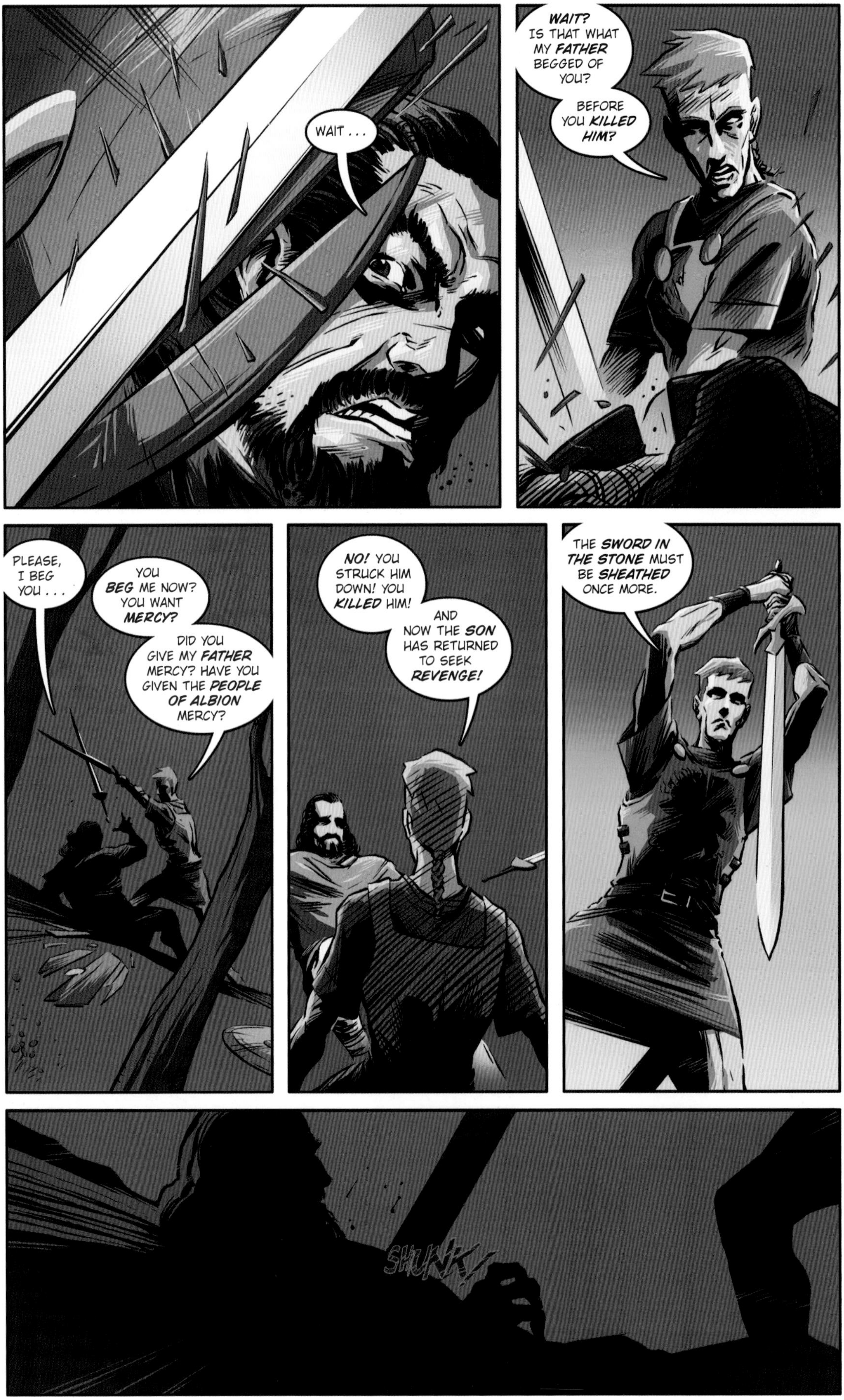

WAIT . . .
WAIT? IS THAT WHAT MY FATHER BEGGED OF YOU?
BEFORE YOU KILLED HIM?
PLEASE, I BEG YOU . . .
YOU BEG ME NOW? YOU WANT MERCY?
DID YOU GIVE MY FATHER MERCY? HAVE YOU GIVEN THE PEOPLE OF ALBION MERCY?
NO! YOU STRUCK HIM DOWN! YOU KILLED HIM!
AND NOW THE SON HAS RETURNED TO SEEK REVENGE!
THE SWORD IN THE STONE MUST BE SHEATHED ONCE MORE.
SHUNK!

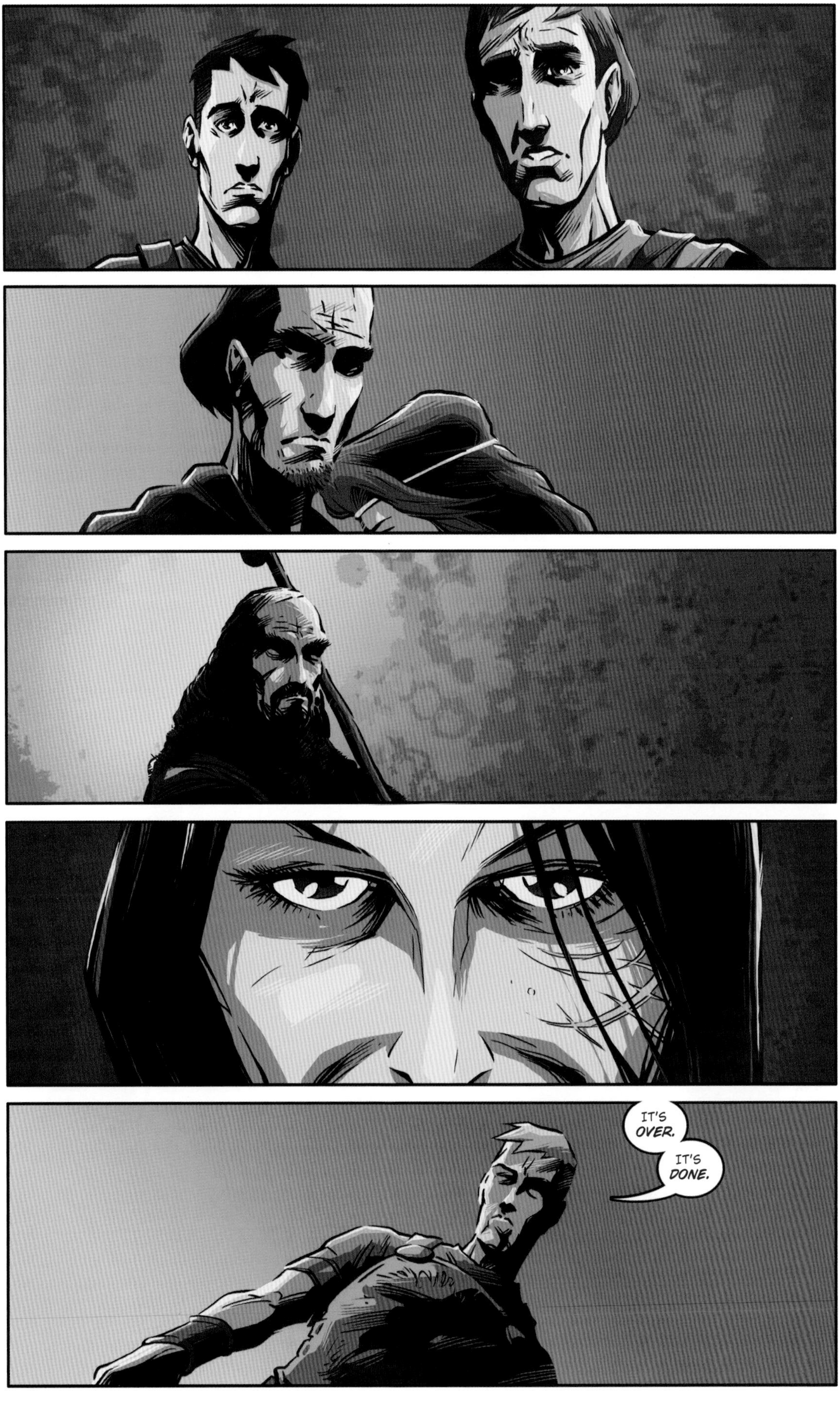
IT'S OVER.
IT'S DONE.

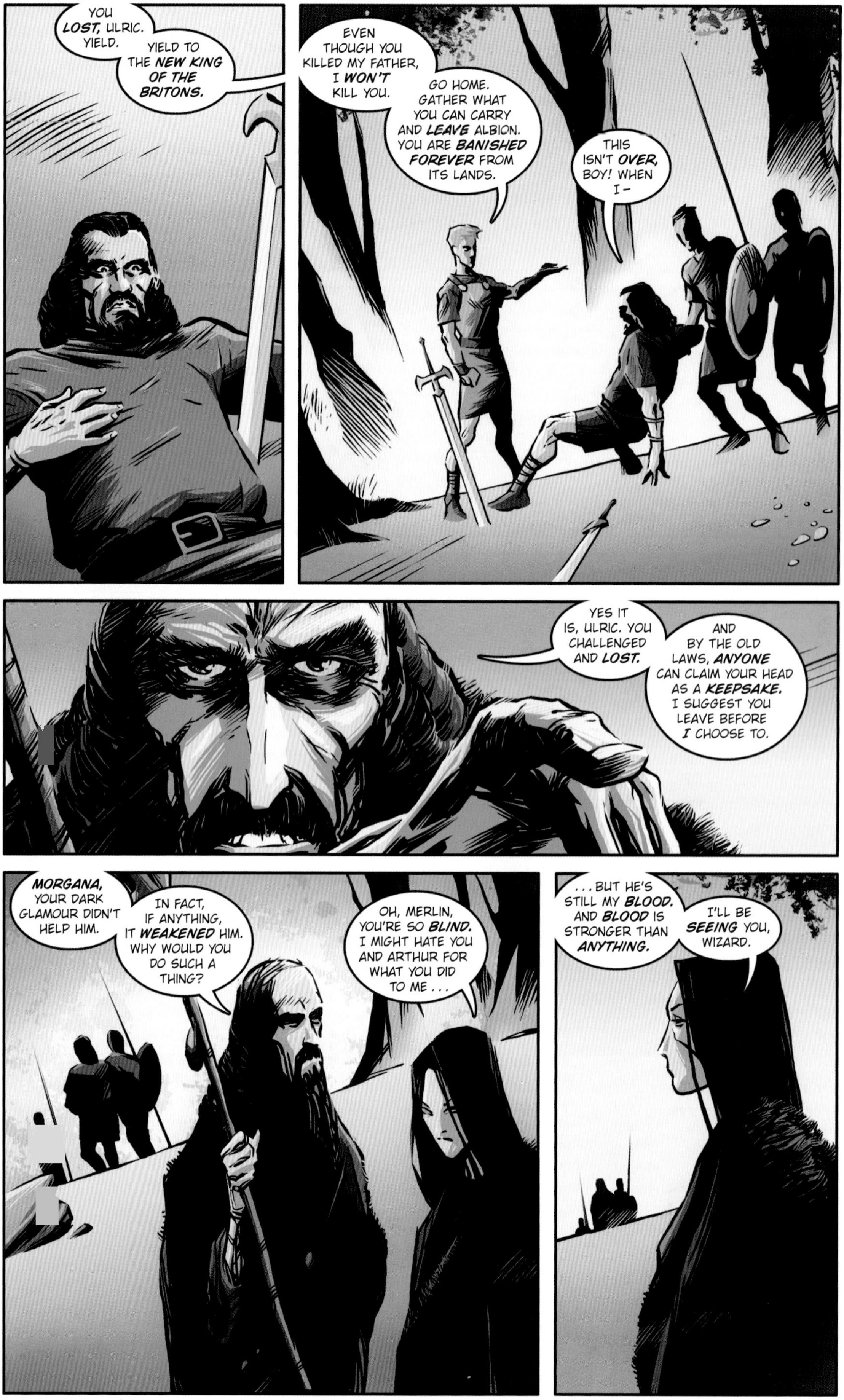
YOU LOST, ULRIC. YIELD.
YIELD TO THE NEW KING OF THE BRITONS.
EVEN THOUGH YOU KILLED MY FATHER, I WON'T KILL YOU.
GO HOME. GATHER WHAT YOU CAN CARRY AND LEAVE ALBION. YOU ARE BANISHED FOREVER FROM ITS LANDS.
THIS ISN'T OVER, BOY! WHEN I–
YES IT IS, ULRIC. YOU CHALLENGED AND LOST.
AND BY THE OLD LAWS, ANYONE CAN CLAIM YOUR HEAD AS A KEEPSAKE. I SUGGEST YOU LEAVE BEFORE I CHOOSE TO.
MORGANA, YOUR DARK GLAMOUR DIDN'T HELP HIM.
IN FACT, IF ANYTHING, IT WEAKENED HIM. WHY WOULD YOU DO SUCH A THING?
OH, MERLIN, YOU'RE SO BLIND. I MIGHT HATE YOU AND ARTHUR FOR WHAT YOU DID TO ME . . .
. . . BUT HE'S STILL MY BLOOD. AND BLOOD IS STRONGER THAN ANYTHING.
I'LL BE SEEING YOU, WIZARD.

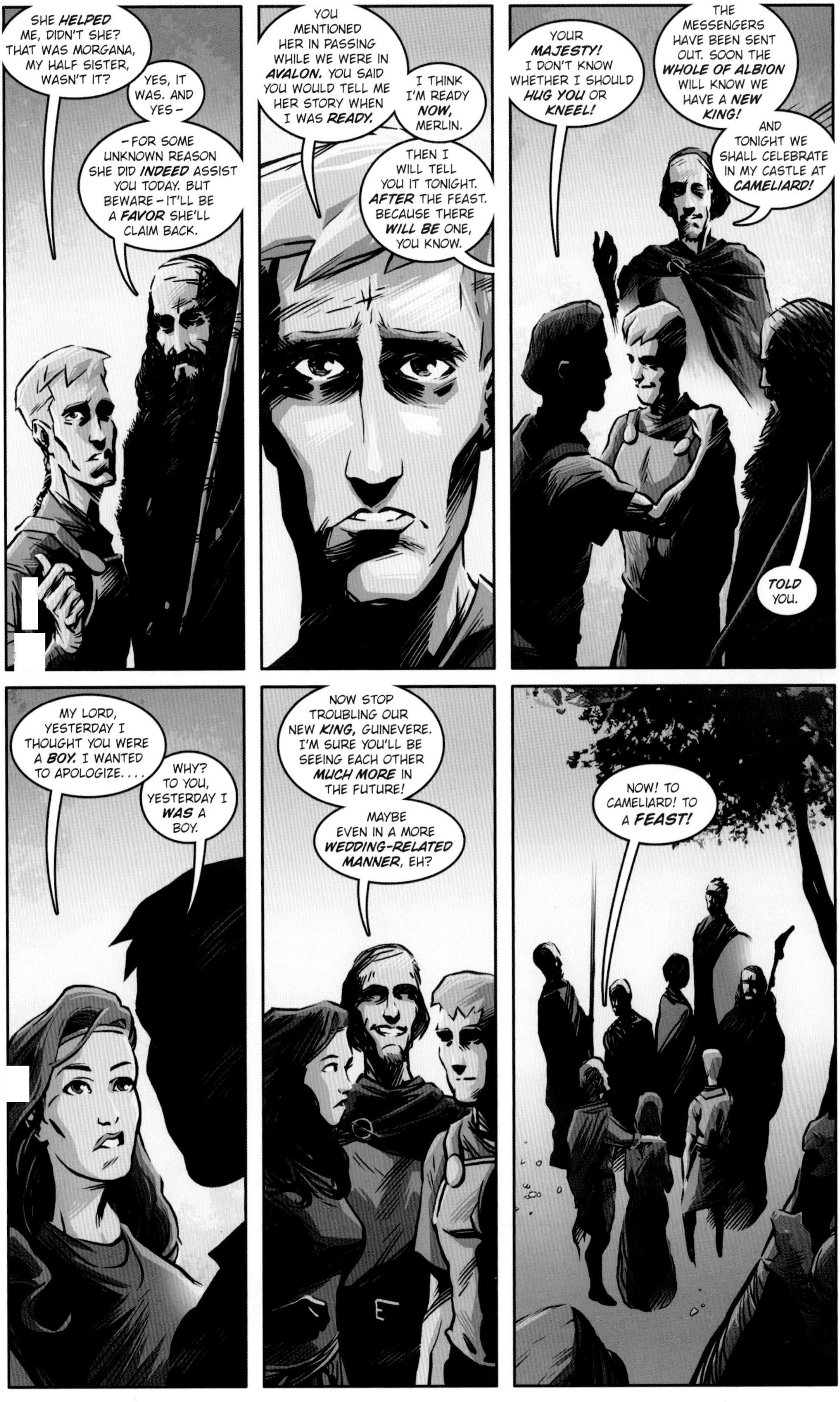
SHE HELPED ME, DIDN'T SHE? THAT WAS MORGANA, MY HALF SISTER, WASN'T IT?
YES, IT WAS. AND YES –
– FOR SOME UNKNOWN REASON SHE DID INDEED ASSIST YOU TODAY. BUT BEWARE – IT'LL BE A FAVOR SHE'LL CLAIM BACK.
YOU MENTIONED HER IN PASSING WHILE WE WERE IN AVALON. YOU SAID YOU WOULD TELL ME HER STORY WHEN I WAS READY.
I THINK I'M READY NOW, MERLIN.
THEN I WILL TELL YOU IT TONIGHT. AFTER THE FEAST. BECAUSE THERE WILL BE ONE, YOU KNOW.
YOUR MAJESTY! I DON'T KNOW WHETHER I SHOULD HUG YOU OR KNEEL!
THE MESSENGERS HAVE BEEN SENT OUT. SOON THE WHOLE OF ALBION WILL KNOW WE HAVE A NEW KING!
AND TONIGHT WE SHALL CELEBRATE IN MY CASTLE AT CAMELIARD!
TOLD YOU.
MY LORD, YESTERDAY I THOUGHT YOU WERE A BOY. I WANTED TO APOLOGIZE. . . .
WHY? TO YOU, YESTERDAY I WAS A BOY.
NOW STOP TROUBLING OUR NEW KING, GUINEVERE. I'M SURE YOU'LL BE SEEING EACH OTHER MUCH MORE IN THE FUTURE!
MAYBE EVEN IN A MORE WEDDING-RELATED MANNER, EH?
NOW! TO CAMELIARD! TO A FEAST!

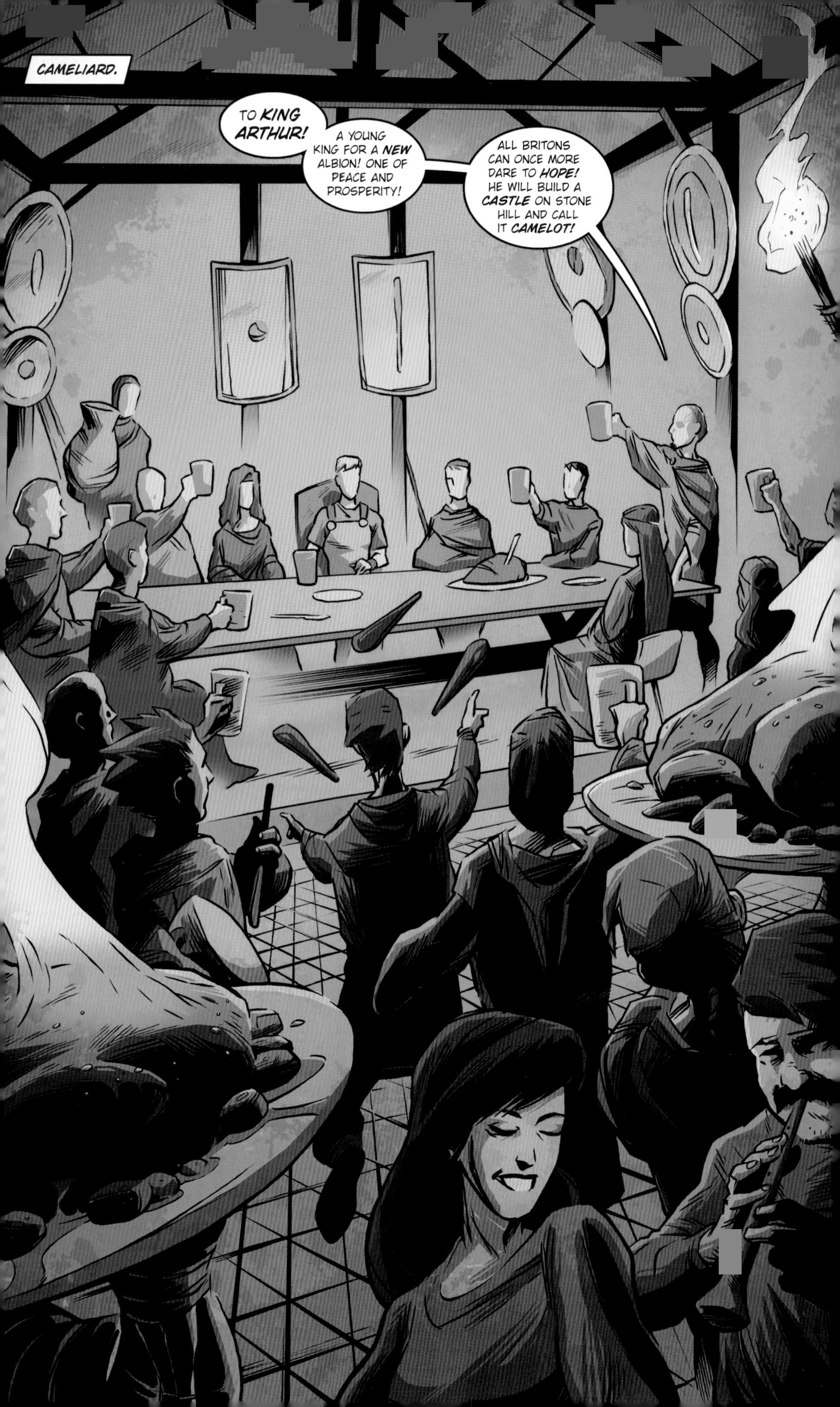
CAMELIARD.
TO KING ARTHUR!
A YOUNG KING FOR A NEW ALBION! ONE OF PEACE AND PROSPERITY!
ALL BRITONS CAN ONCE MORE DARE TO HOPE! HE WILL BUILD A CASTLE ON STONE HILL AND CALL IT CAMELOT!

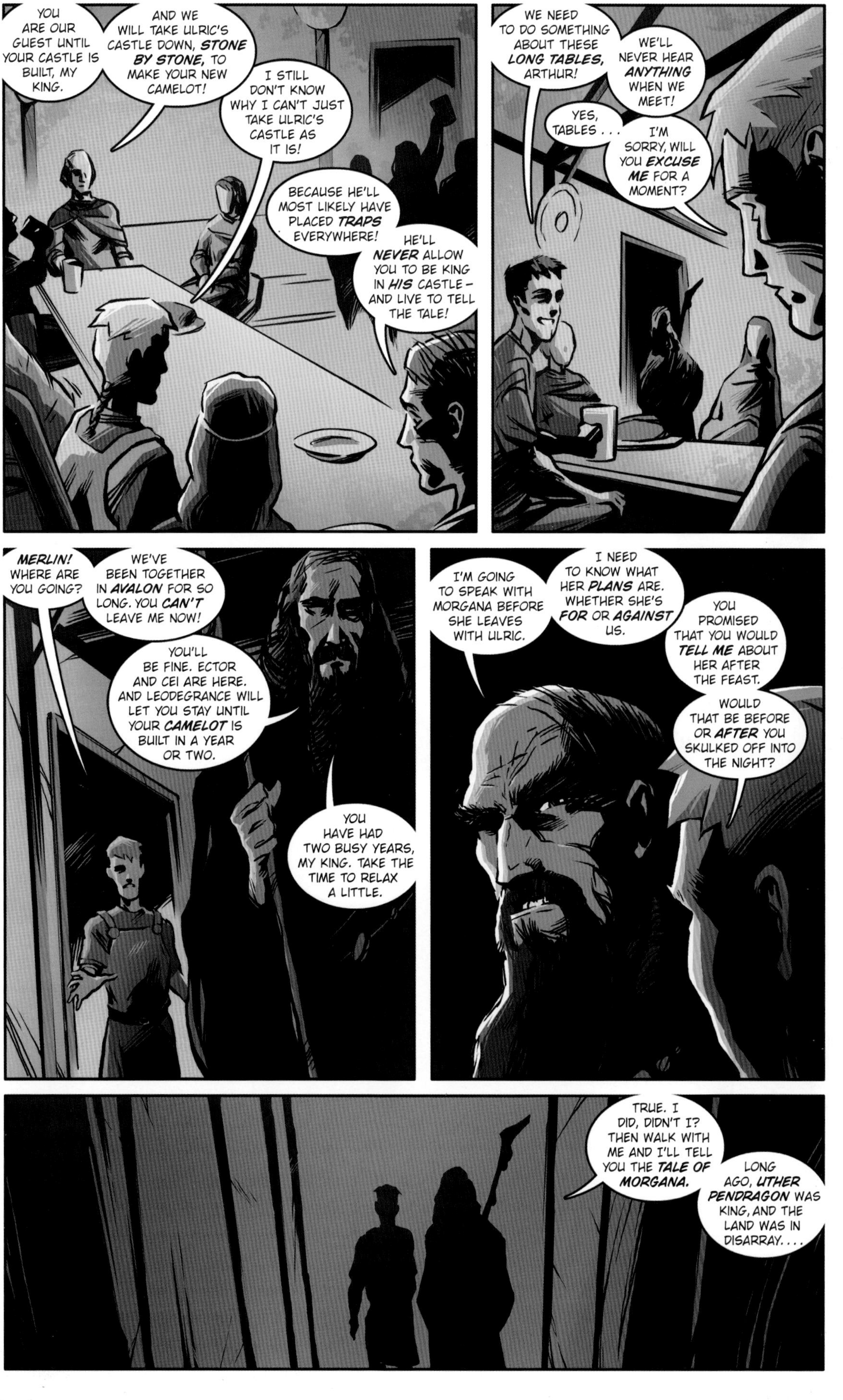
YOU ARE OUR GUEST UNTIL YOUR CASTLE IS BUILT, MY KING.
AND WE WILL TAKE ULRIC'S CASTLE DOWN, STONE BY STONE, TO MAKE YOUR NEW CAMELOT!
I STILL DON'T KNOW WHY I CAN'T JUST TAKE ULRIC'S CASTLE AS IT IS!
BECAUSE HE'LL MOST LIKELY HAVE PLACED TRAPS EVERYWHERE!
HE'LL NEVER ALLOW YOU TO BE KING IN HIS CASTLE – AND LIVE TO TELL THE TALE!
WE NEED TO DO SOMETHING ABOUT THESE LONG TABLES, ARTHUR!
WE'LL NEVER HEAR ANYTHING WHEN WE MEET!
YES, TABLES . . .
I'M SORRY, WILL YOU EXCUSE ME FOR A MOMENT?
MERLIN! WHERE ARE YOU GOING?
WE'VE BEEN TOGETHER IN AVALON FOR SO LONG. YOU CAN'T LEAVE ME NOW!
YOU'LL BE FINE. ECTOR AND CEI ARE HERE. AND LEODEGRANCE WILL LET YOU STAY UNTIL YOUR CAMELOT IS BUILT IN A YEAR OR TWO.
YOU HAVE HAD TWO BUSY YEARS, MY KING. TAKE THE TIME TO RELAX A LITTLE.
I'M GOING TO SPEAK WITH MORGANA BEFORE SHE LEAVES WITH ULRIC.
I NEED TO KNOW WHAT HER PLANS ARE. WHETHER SHE'S FOR OR AGAINST US.
YOU PROMISED THAT YOU WOULD TELL ME ABOUT HER AFTER THE FEAST.
WOULD THAT BE BEFORE OR AFTER YOU SKULKED OFF INTO THE NIGHT?
TRUE. I DID, DIDN'T I? THEN WALK WITH ME AND I'LL TELL YOU THE TALE OF MORGANA.
LONG AGO, UTHER PENDRAGON WAS KING, AND THE LAND WAS IN DISARRAY. . . .

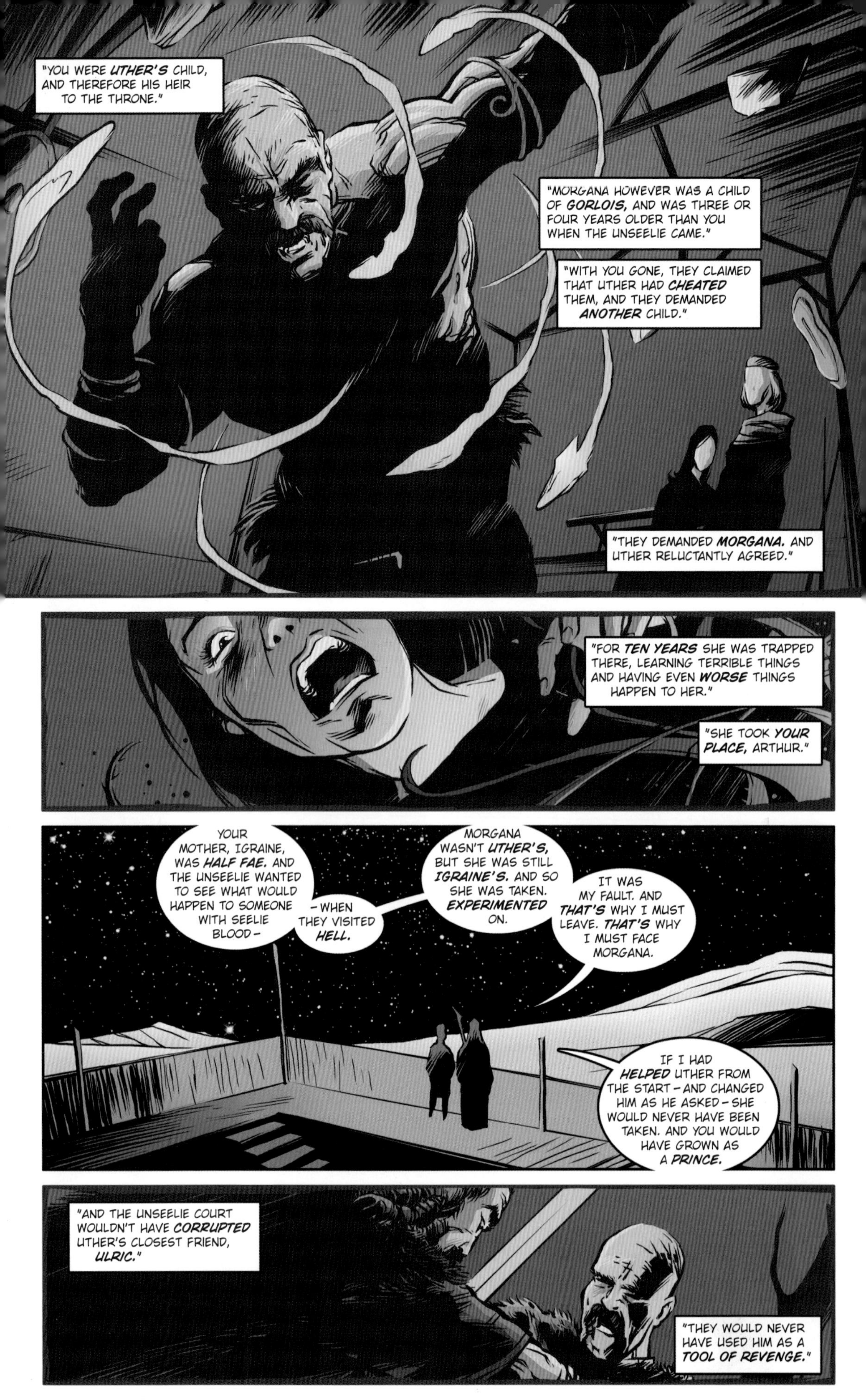

"YOU WERE UTHER'S CHILD, AND THEREFORE HIS HEIR TO THE THRONE."
"MORGANA HOWEVER WAS A CHILD OF GORLOIS, AND WAS THREE OR FOUR YEARS OLDER THAN YOU WHEN THE UNSEELIE CAME."
"WITH YOU GONE, THEY CLAIMED THAT UTHER HAD CHEATED THEM, AND THEY DEMANDED ANOTHER CHILD."
"THEY DEMANDED MORGANA. AND UTHER RELUCTANTLY AGREED."
"FOR TEN YEARS SHE WAS TRAPPED THERE, LEARNING TERRIBLE THINGS AND HAVING EVEN WORSE THINGS HAPPEN TO HER."
"SHE TOOK YOUR PLACE, ARTHUR."
YOUR MOTHER, IGRAINE, WAS HALF FAE. AND THE UNSEELIE WANTED TO SEE WHAT WOULD HAPPEN TO SOMEONE WITH SEELIE BLOOD–
–WHEN THEY VISITED HELL.
MORGANA WASN'T UTHER'S, BUT SHE WAS STILL IGRAINE'S. AND SO SHE WAS TAKEN. EXPERIMENTED ON.
IT WAS MY FAULT. AND THAT'S WHY I MUST LEAVE. THAT'S WHY I MUST FACE MORGANA.
IF I HAD HELPED UTHER FROM THE START – AND CHANGED HIM AS HE ASKED – SHE WOULD NEVER HAVE BEEN TAKEN. AND YOU WOULD HAVE GROWN AS A PRINCE.
"AND THE UNSEELIE COURT WOULDN'T HAVE CORRUPTED UTHER'S CLOSEST FRIEND, ULRIC."
"THEY WOULD NEVER HAVE USED HIM AS A TOOL OF REVENGE."

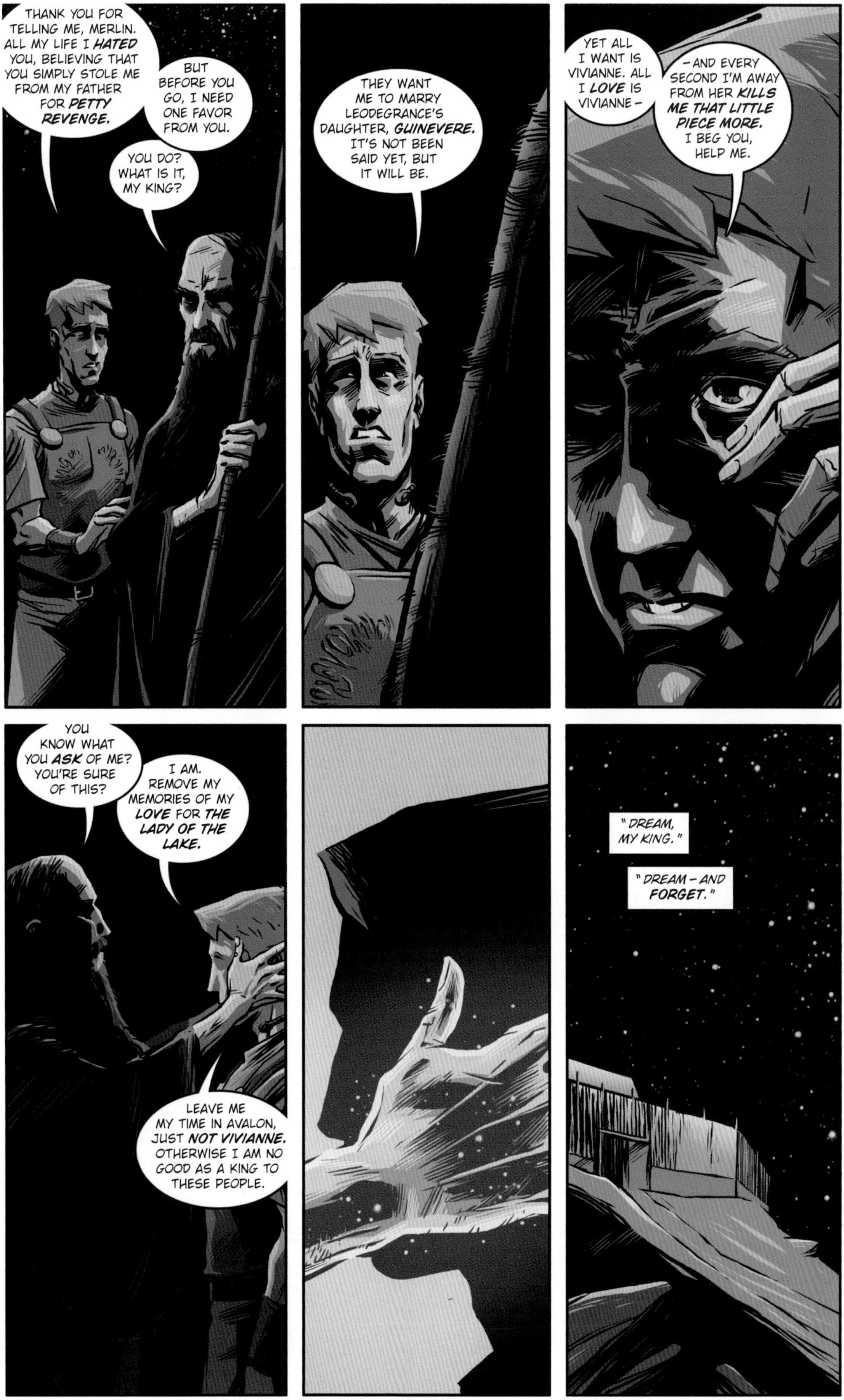
THANK YOU FOR TELLING ME, MERLIN. ALL MY LIFE I *HATED* YOU, BELIEVING THAT YOU SIMPLY STOLE ME FROM MY FATHER FOR *PETTY REVENGE.*
BUT BEFORE YOU GO, I NEED ONE FAVOR FROM YOU.
YOU DO? WHAT IS IT, MY KING?
THEY WANT ME TO MARRY LEODEGRANCE'S DAUGHTER, *GUINEVERE.* IT'S NOT BEEN SAID YET, BUT IT WILL BE.
YET ALL I WANT IS VIVIANNE. ALL I *LOVE* IS VIVIANNE –
– AND EVERY SECOND I'M AWAY FROM HER *KILLS ME THAT LITTLE PIECE MORE.* I BEG YOU, HELP ME.
YOU KNOW WHAT YOU *ASK* OF ME? YOU'RE SURE OF THIS?
I AM. REMOVE MY MEMORIES OF MY *LOVE* FOR *THE LADY OF THE LAKE.*
LEAVE ME MY TIME IN AVALON, JUST *NOT VIVIANNE.* OTHERWISE I AM NO GOOD AS A KING TO THESE PEOPLE.
"*DREAM, MY KING.*"
"*DREAM – AND FORGET.*"

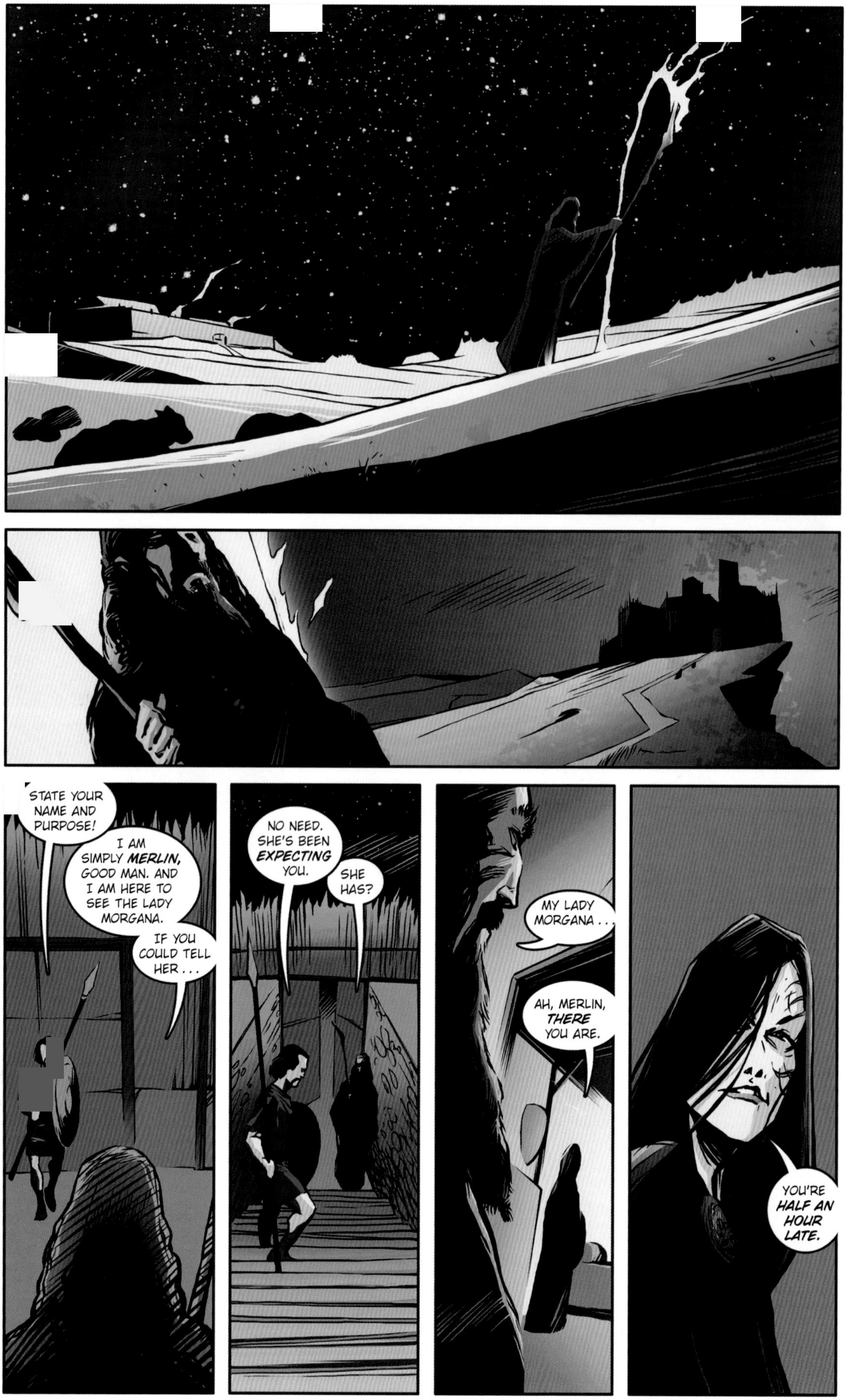
STATE YOUR NAME AND PURPOSE!
I AM SIMPLY MERLIN, GOOD MAN. AND I AM HERE TO SEE THE LADY MORGANA.
IF YOU COULD TELL HER . . .
NO NEED. SHE'S BEEN EXPECTING YOU.
SHE HAS?
MY LADY MORGANA . . .
AH, MERLIN, THERE YOU ARE.
YOU'RE HALF AN HOUR LATE.

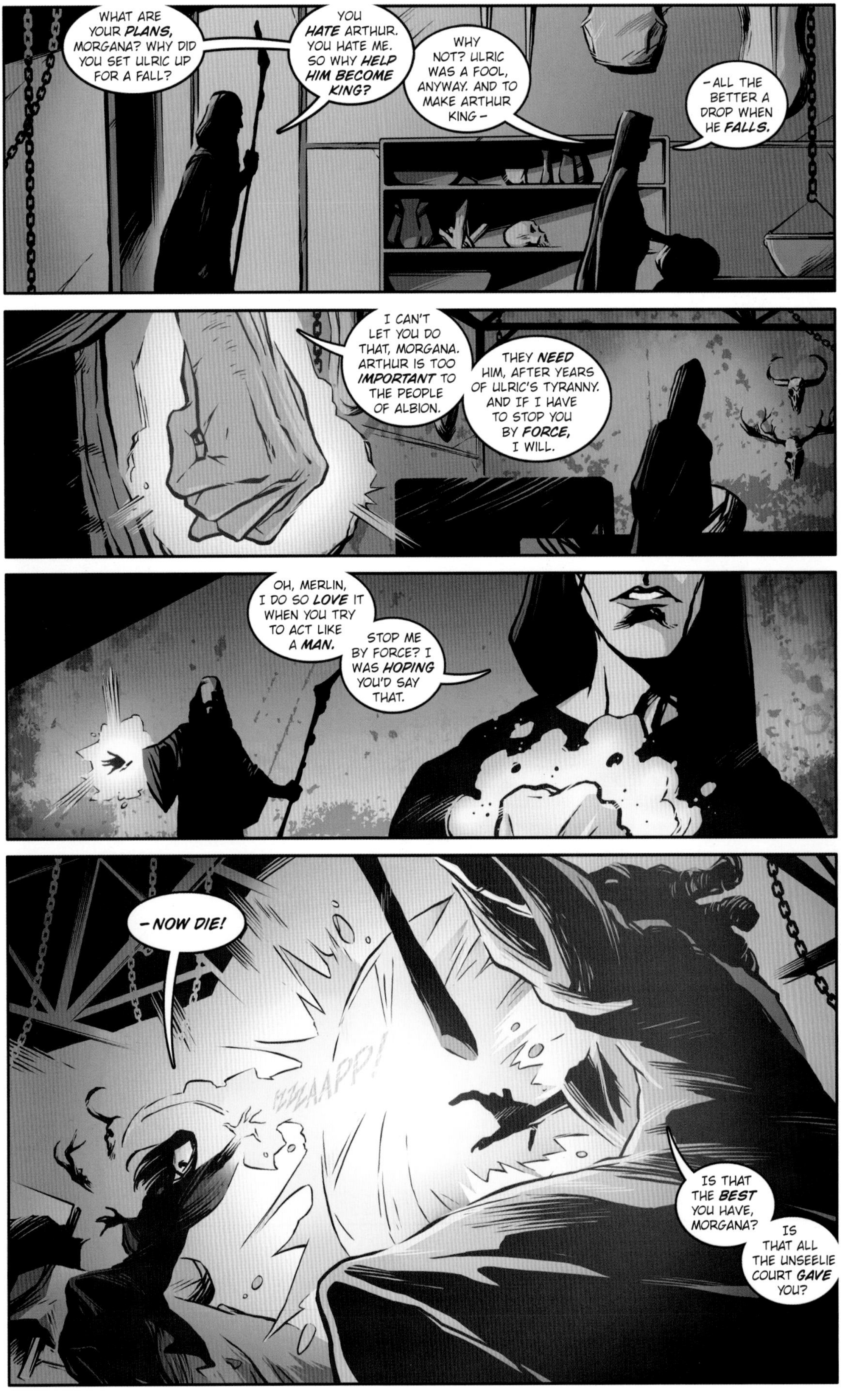

WHAT ARE YOUR PLANS, MORGANA? WHY DID YOU SET ULRIC UP FOR A FALL?
YOU HATE ARTHUR. YOU HATE ME. SO WHY HELP HIM BECOME KING?
WHY NOT? ULRIC WAS A FOOL, ANYWAY. AND TO MAKE ARTHUR KING –
– ALL THE BETTER A DROP WHEN HE FALLS.
I CAN'T LET YOU DO THAT, MORGANA. ARTHUR IS TOO IMPORTANT TO THE PEOPLE OF ALBION.
THEY NEED HIM, AFTER YEARS OF ULRIC'S TYRANNY. AND IF I HAVE TO STOP YOU BY FORCE, I WILL.
OH, MERLIN, I DO SO LOVE IT WHEN YOU TRY TO ACT LIKE A MAN.
STOP ME BY FORCE? I WAS HOPING YOU'D SAY THAT.
– NOW DIE!
ZZZAAPP!
IS THAT THE BEST YOU HAVE, MORGANA?
IS THAT ALL THE UNSEELIE COURT GAVE YOU?

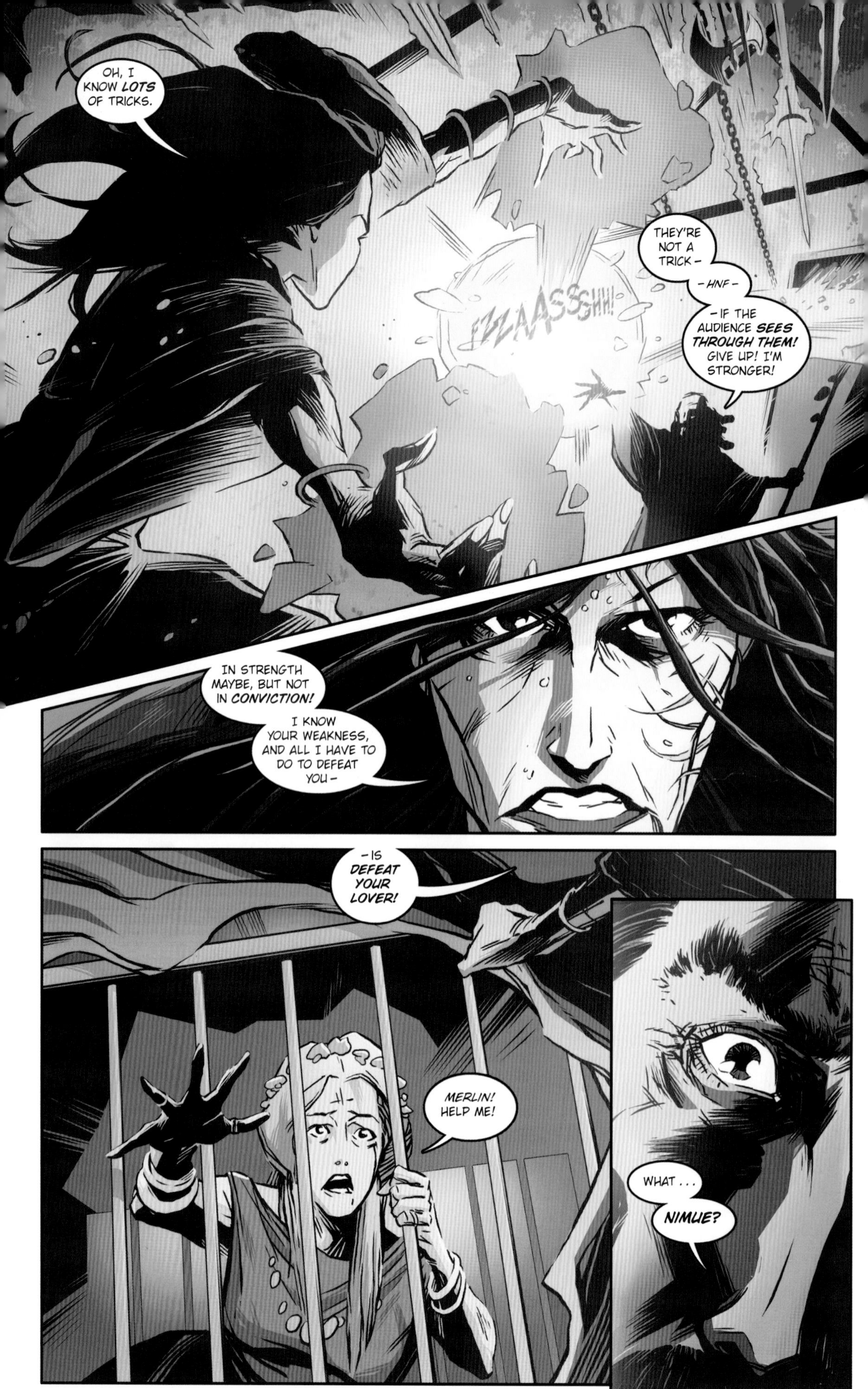

OH, I KNOW LOTS OF TRICKS.
THEY'RE NOT A TRICK –
– HNF –
– IF THE AUDIENCE SEES THROUGH THEM! GIVE UP! I'M STRONGER!
FZZAASSSHH!
IN STRENGTH MAYBE, BUT NOT IN CONVICTION!
I KNOW YOUR WEAKNESS, AND ALL I HAVE TO DO TO DEFEAT YOU –
– IS DEFEAT YOUR LOVER!
MERLIN! HELP ME!
WHAT . . .
NIMUE?

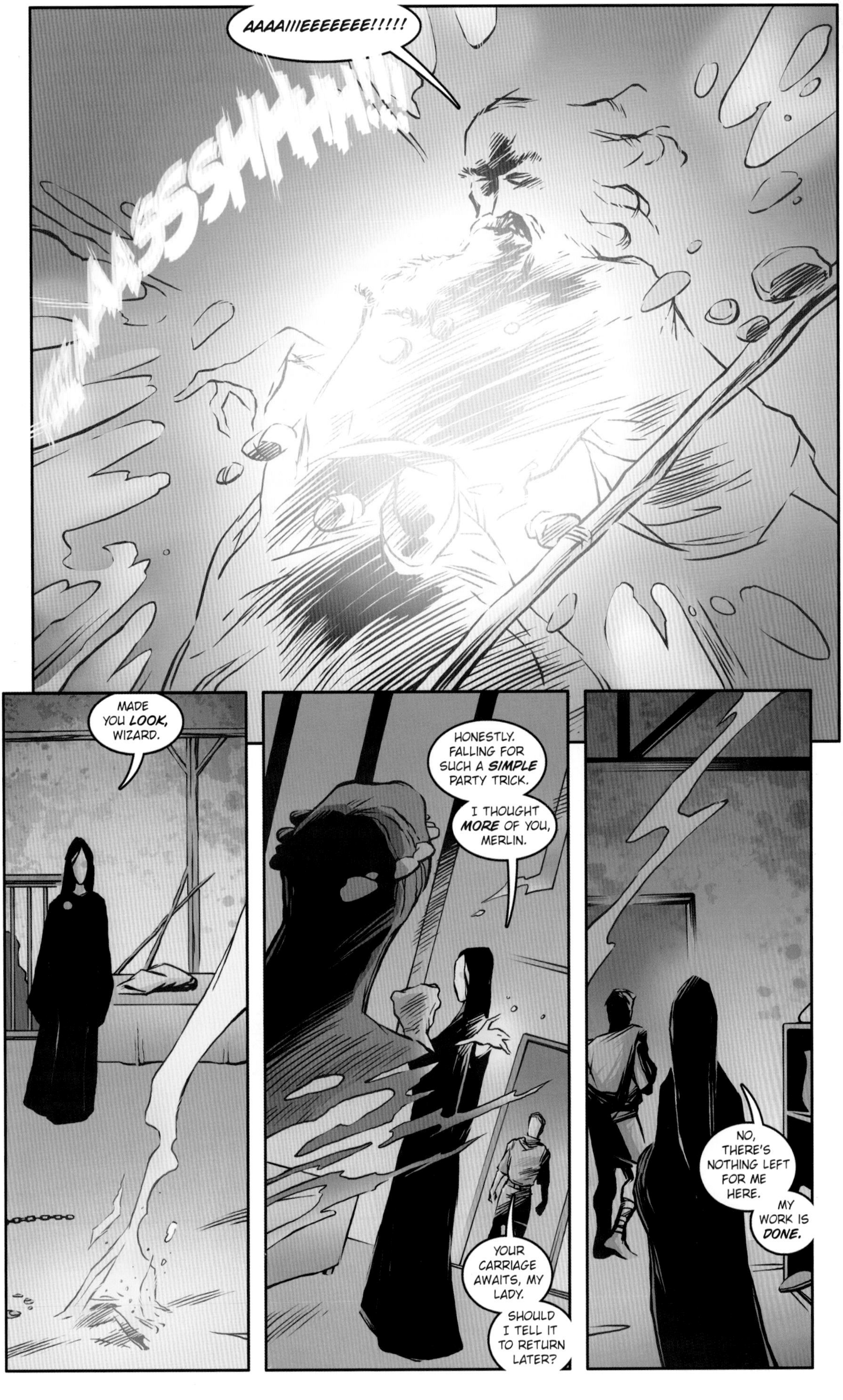
AAAAIIIEEEEEEE!!!!!
CRASSSHHH!!!
MADE YOU *LOOK*, WIZARD.
HONESTLY. FALLING FOR SUCH A *SIMPLE* PARTY TRICK.
I THOUGHT *MORE* OF YOU, MERLIN.
YOUR CARRIAGE AWAITS, MY LADY.
SHOULD I TELL IT TO RETURN LATER?
NO, THERE'S NOTHING LEFT FOR ME HERE.
MY WORK IS *DONE.*

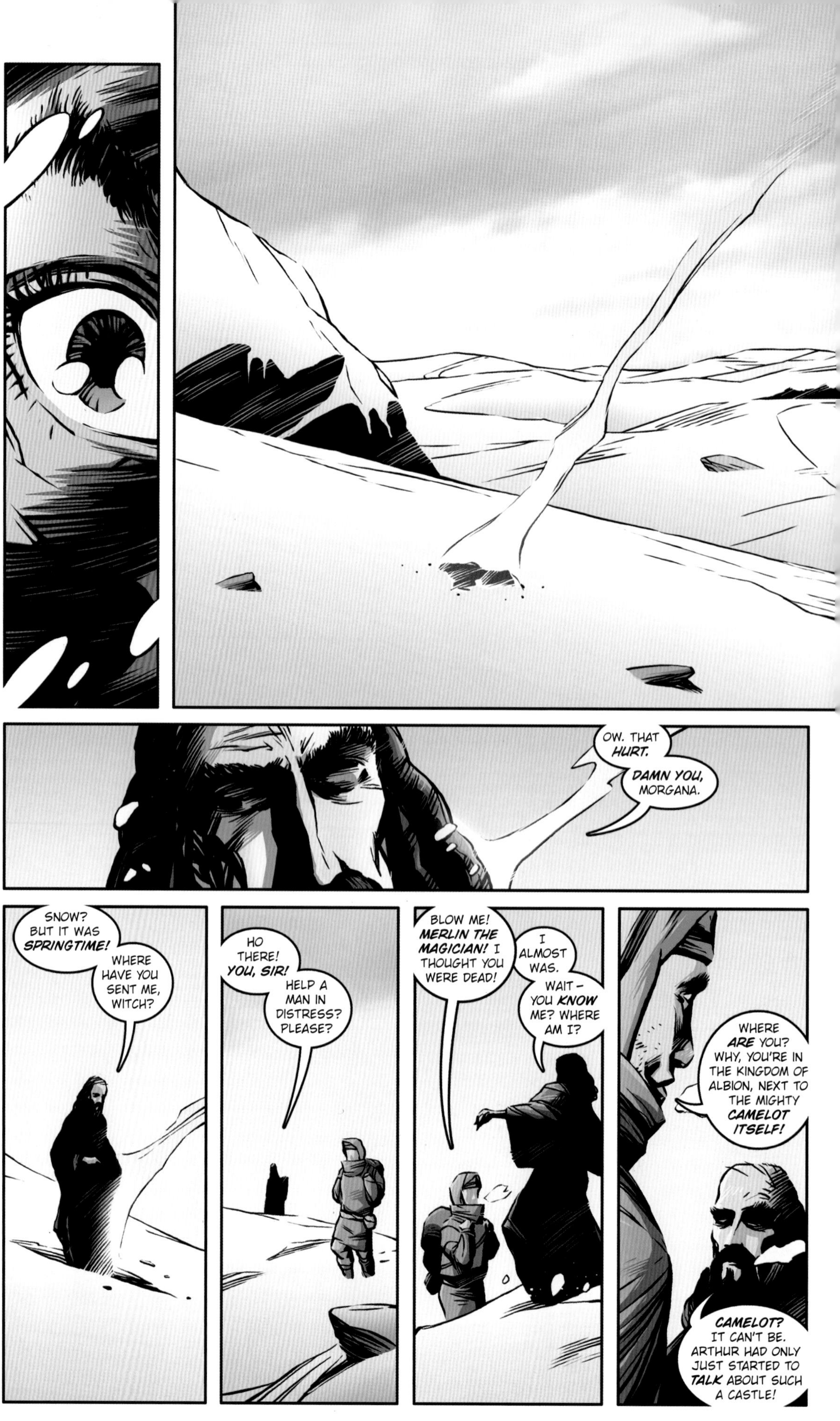
OW. THAT HURT.
DAMN YOU, MORGANA.
SNOW? BUT IT WAS SPRINGTIME!
WHERE HAVE YOU SENT ME, WITCH?
HO THERE! YOU, SIR!
HELP A MAN IN DISTRESS? PLEASE?
BLOW ME! MERLIN THE MAGICIAN! I THOUGHT YOU WERE DEAD!
I ALMOST WAS.
WAIT– YOU KNOW ME? WHERE AM I?
WHERE ARE YOU? WHY, YOU'RE IN THE KINGDOM OF ALBION, NEXT TO THE MIGHTY CAMELOT ITSELF!
CAMELOT? IT CAN'T BE. ARTHUR HAD ONLY JUST STARTED TO TALK ABOUT SUCH A CASTLE!

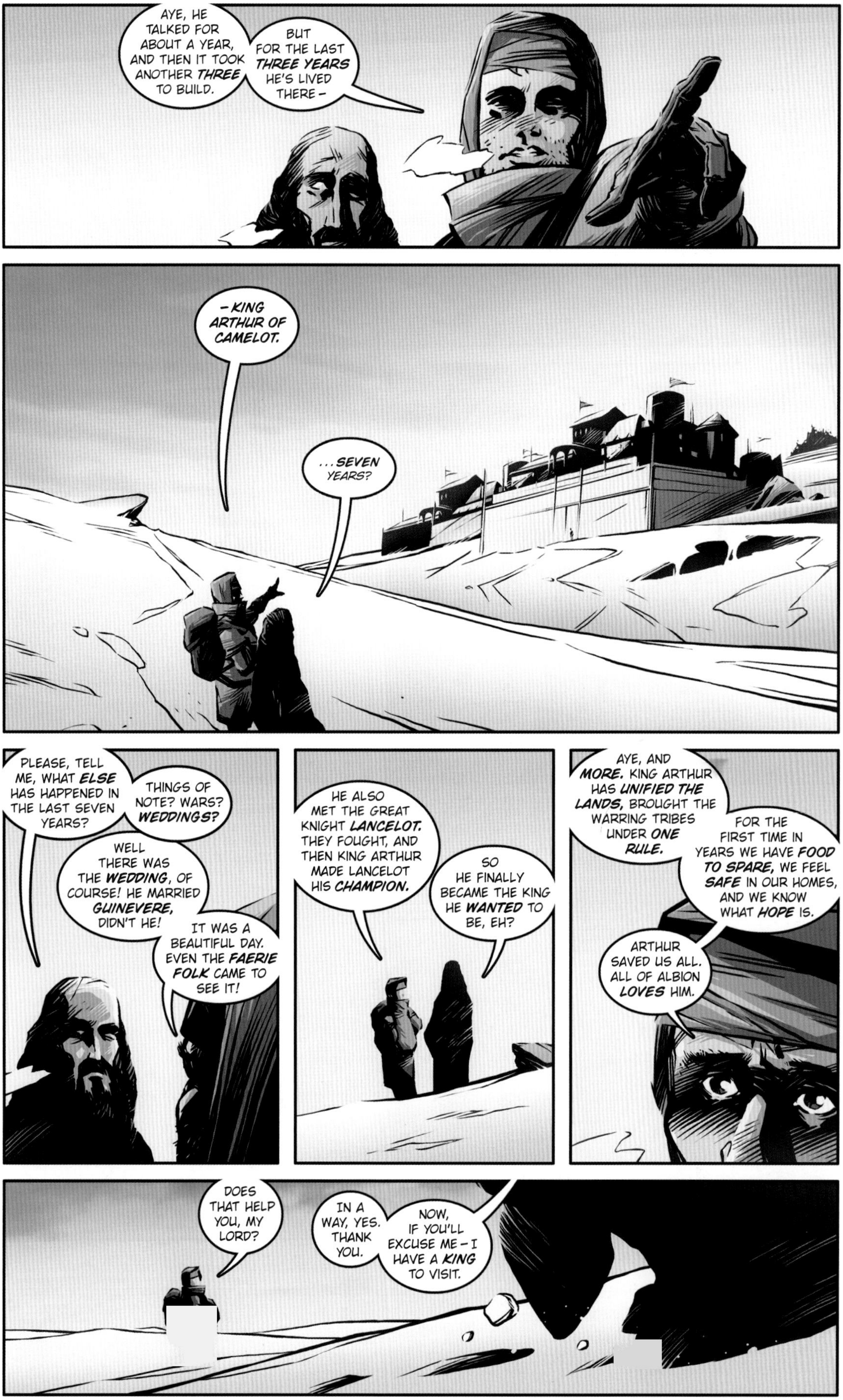
AYE, HE TALKED FOR ABOUT A YEAR, AND THEN IT TOOK ANOTHER THREE TO BUILD.
BUT FOR THE LAST THREE YEARS HE'S LIVED THERE –
– KING ARTHUR OF CAMELOT.
. . . SEVEN YEARS?
PLEASE, TELL ME, WHAT ELSE HAS HAPPENED IN THE LAST SEVEN YEARS?
THINGS OF NOTE? WARS? WEDDINGS?
WELL THERE WAS THE WEDDING, OF COURSE! HE MARRIED GUINEVERE, DIDN'T HE!
IT WAS A BEAUTIFUL DAY. EVEN THE FAERIE FOLK CAME TO SEE IT!
HE ALSO MET THE GREAT KNIGHT LANCELOT. THEY FOUGHT, AND THEN KING ARTHUR MADE LANCELOT HIS CHAMPION.
SO HE FINALLY BECAME THE KING HE WANTED TO BE, EH?
AYE, AND MORE. KING ARTHUR HAS UNIFIED THE LANDS, BROUGHT THE WARRING TRIBES UNDER ONE RULE.
FOR THE FIRST TIME IN YEARS WE HAVE FOOD TO SPARE, WE FEEL SAFE IN OUR HOMES, AND WE KNOW WHAT HOPE IS.
ARTHUR SAVED US ALL. ALL OF ALBION LOVES HIM.
DOES THAT HELP YOU, MY LORD?
IN A WAY, YES. THANK YOU.
NOW, IF YOU'LL EXCUSE ME – I HAVE A KING TO VISIT.

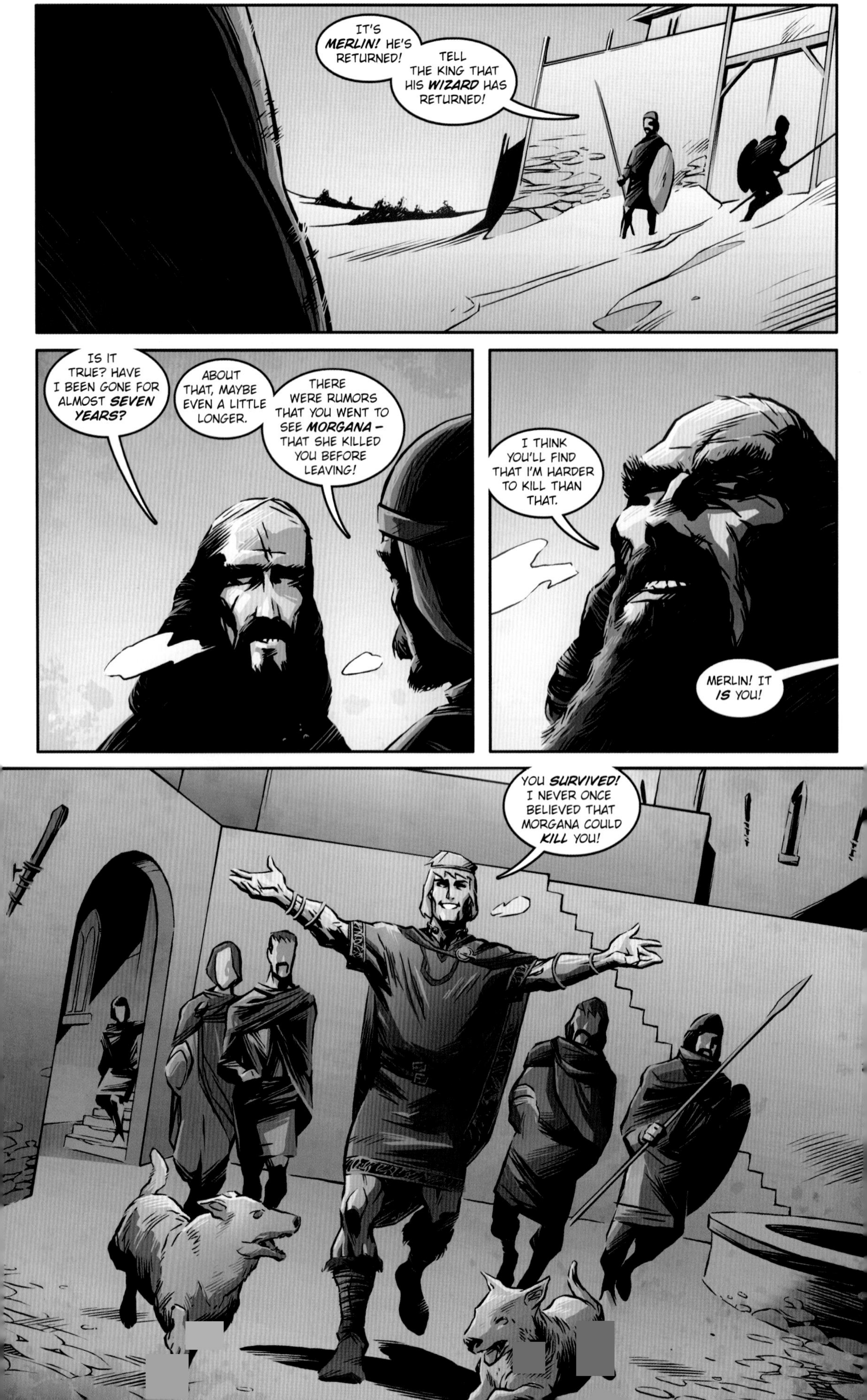
IT'S MERLIN! HE'S RETURNED!
TELL THE KING THAT HIS WIZARD HAS RETURNED!
IS IT TRUE? HAVE I BEEN GONE FOR ALMOST SEVEN YEARS?
ABOUT THAT, MAYBE EVEN A LITTLE LONGER.
THERE WERE RUMORS THAT YOU WENT TO SEE MORGANA — THAT SHE KILLED YOU BEFORE LEAVING!
I THINK YOU'LL FIND THAT I'M HARDER TO KILL THAN THAT.
MERLIN! IT IS YOU!
YOU SURVIVED! I NEVER ONCE BELIEVED THAT MORGANA COULD KILL YOU!

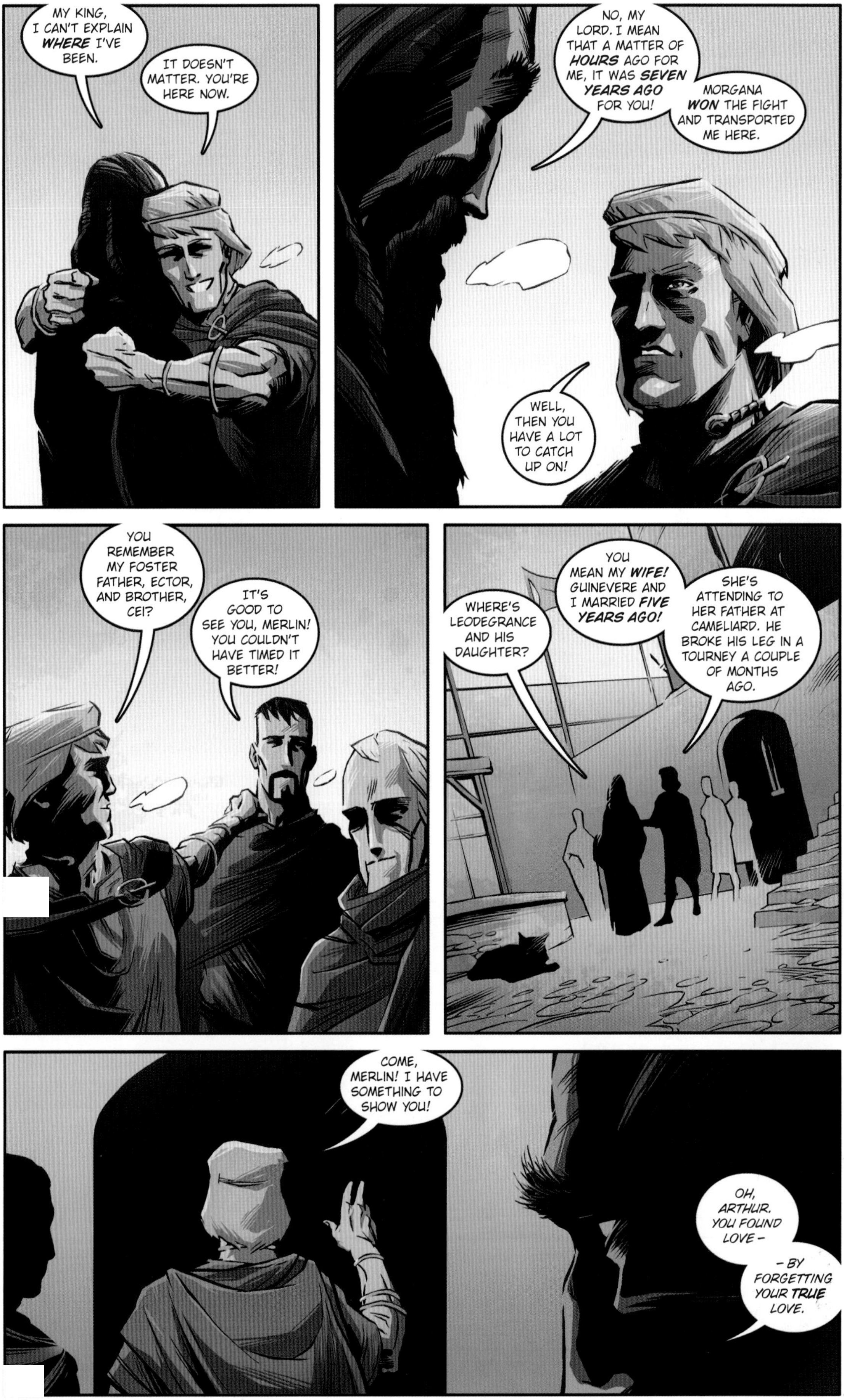
MY KING, I CAN'T EXPLAIN **WHERE** I'VE BEEN.
IT DOESN'T MATTER. YOU'RE HERE NOW.
NO, MY LORD. I MEAN THAT A MATTER OF **HOURS** AGO FOR ME, IT WAS **SEVEN YEARS AGO** FOR YOU!
MORGANA **WON** THE FIGHT AND TRANSPORTED ME HERE.
WELL, THEN YOU HAVE A LOT TO CATCH UP ON!
YOU REMEMBER MY FOSTER FATHER, ECTOR, AND BROTHER, CEI?
IT'S GOOD TO SEE YOU, MERLIN! YOU COULDN'T HAVE TIMED IT BETTER!
WHERE'S LEODEGRANCE AND HIS DAUGHTER?
YOU MEAN MY **WIFE!** GUINEVERE AND I MARRIED **FIVE YEARS AGO!**
SHE'S ATTENDING TO HER FATHER AT CAMELIARD. HE BROKE HIS LEG IN A TOURNEY A COUPLE OF MONTHS AGO.
COME, MERLIN! I HAVE SOMETHING TO SHOW YOU!
*OH, ARTHUR. YOU FOUND LOVE –*
*– BY FORGETTING YOUR **TRUE** LOVE.*

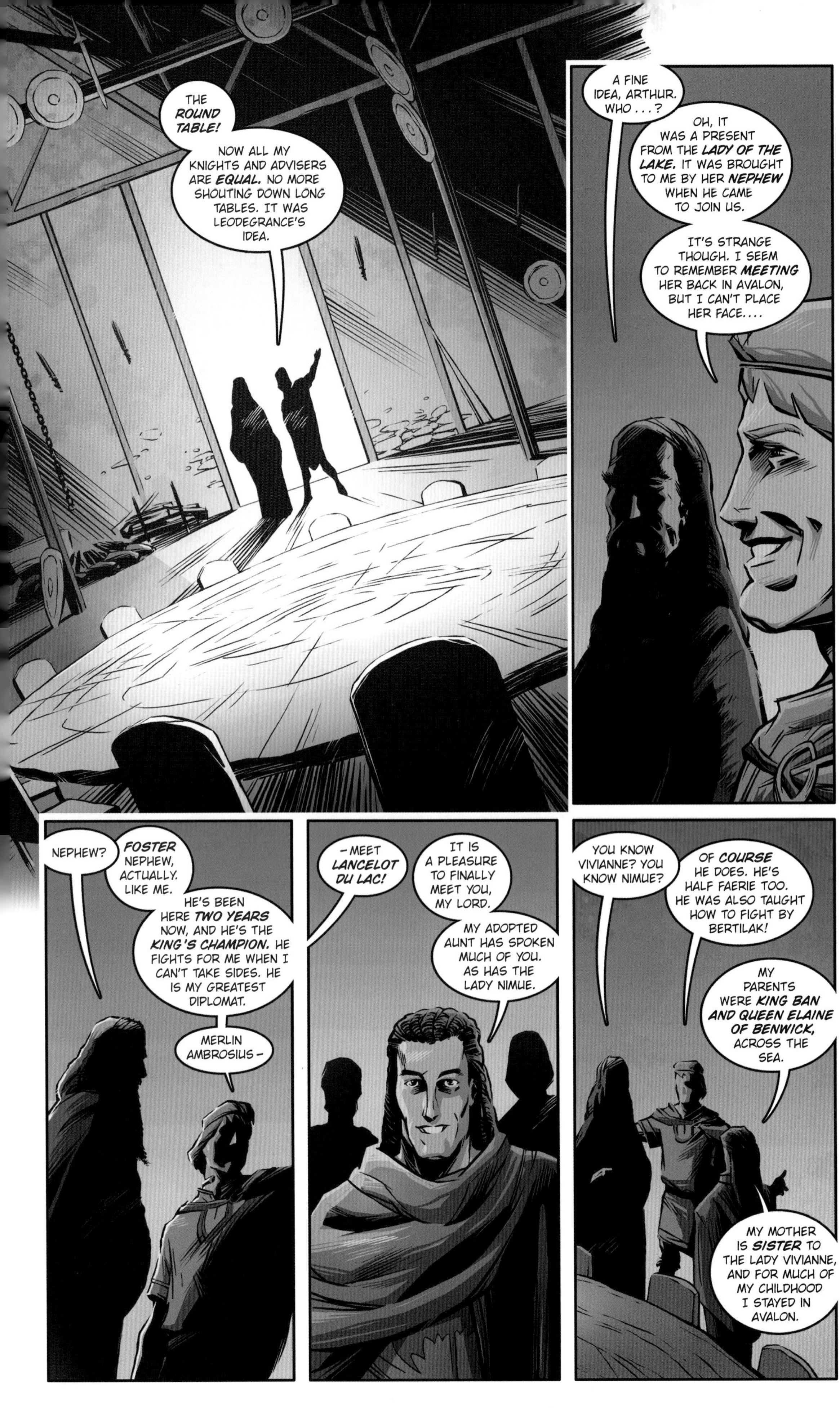

THE ROUND TABLE!
NOW ALL MY KNIGHTS AND ADVISERS ARE EQUAL. NO MORE SHOUTING DOWN LONG TABLES. IT WAS LEODEGRANCE'S IDEA.
A FINE IDEA, ARTHUR. WHO . . . ?
OH, IT WAS A PRESENT FROM THE LADY OF THE LAKE. IT WAS BROUGHT TO ME BY HER NEPHEW WHEN HE CAME TO JOIN US.
IT'S STRANGE THOUGH. I SEEM TO REMEMBER MEETING HER BACK IN AVALON, BUT I CAN'T PLACE HER FACE. . . .
NEPHEW?
FOSTER NEPHEW, ACTUALLY. LIKE ME.
HE'S BEEN HERE TWO YEARS NOW, AND HE'S THE KING'S CHAMPION. HE FIGHTS FOR ME WHEN I CAN'T TAKE SIDES. HE IS MY GREATEST DIPLOMAT.
MERLIN AMBROSIUS–
–MEET LANCELOT DU LAC!
IT IS A PLEASURE TO FINALLY MEET YOU, MY LORD.
MY ADOPTED AUNT HAS SPOKEN MUCH OF YOU. AS HAS THE LADY NIMUE.
YOU KNOW VIVIANNE? YOU KNOW NIMUE?
OF COURSE HE DOES. HE'S HALF FAERIE TOO. HE WAS ALSO TAUGHT HOW TO FIGHT BY BERTILAK!
MY PARENTS WERE KING BAN AND QUEEN ELAINE OF BENWICK, ACROSS THE SEA.
MY MOTHER IS SISTER TO THE LADY VIVIANNE, AND FOR MUCH OF MY CHILDHOOD I STAYED IN AVALON.

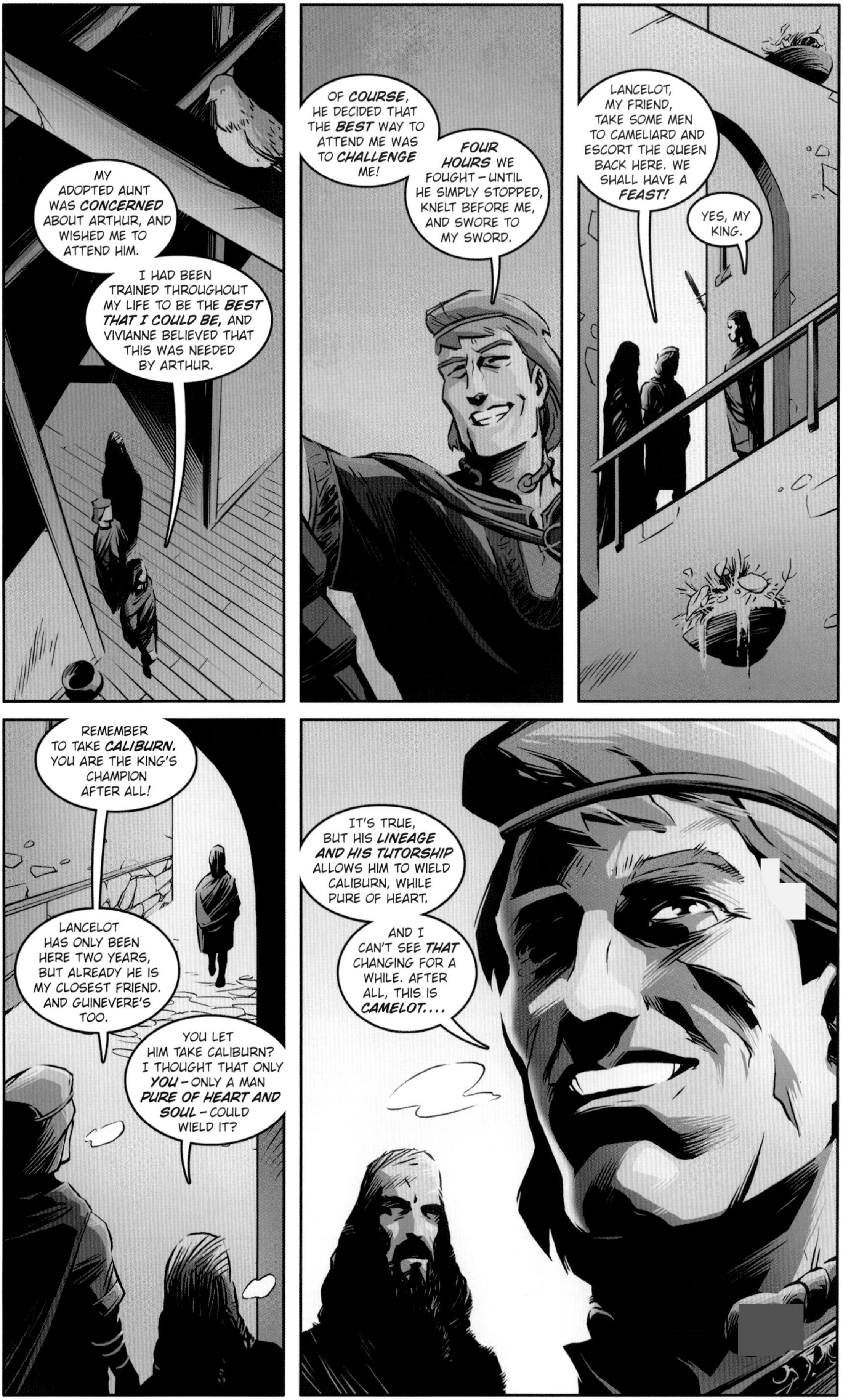
MY ADOPTED AUNT WAS CONCERNED ABOUT ARTHUR, AND WISHED ME TO ATTEND HIM.
I HAD BEEN TRAINED THROUGHOUT MY LIFE TO BE THE BEST THAT I COULD BE, AND VIVIANNE BELIEVED THAT THIS WAS NEEDED BY ARTHUR.
OF COURSE, HE DECIDED THAT THE BEST WAY TO ATTEND ME WAS TO CHALLENGE ME!
FOUR HOURS WE FOUGHT – UNTIL HE SIMPLY STOPPED, KNELT BEFORE ME, AND SWORE TO MY SWORD.
LANCELOT, MY FRIEND, TAKE SOME MEN TO CAMELIARD AND ESCORT THE QUEEN BACK HERE. WE SHALL HAVE A FEAST!
YES, MY KING.
REMEMBER TO TAKE CALIBURN. YOU ARE THE KING'S CHAMPION AFTER ALL!
LANCELOT HAS ONLY BEEN HERE TWO YEARS, BUT ALREADY HE IS MY CLOSEST FRIEND. AND GUINEVERE'S TOO.
YOU LET HIM TAKE CALIBURN? I THOUGHT THAT ONLY YOU – ONLY A MAN PURE OF HEART AND SOUL – COULD WIELD IT?
IT'S TRUE, BUT HIS LINEAGE AND HIS TUTORSHIP ALLOWS HIM TO WIELD CALIBURN, WHILE PURE OF HEART.
AND I CAN'T SEE THAT CHANGING FOR A WHILE. AFTER ALL, THIS IS CAMELOT....

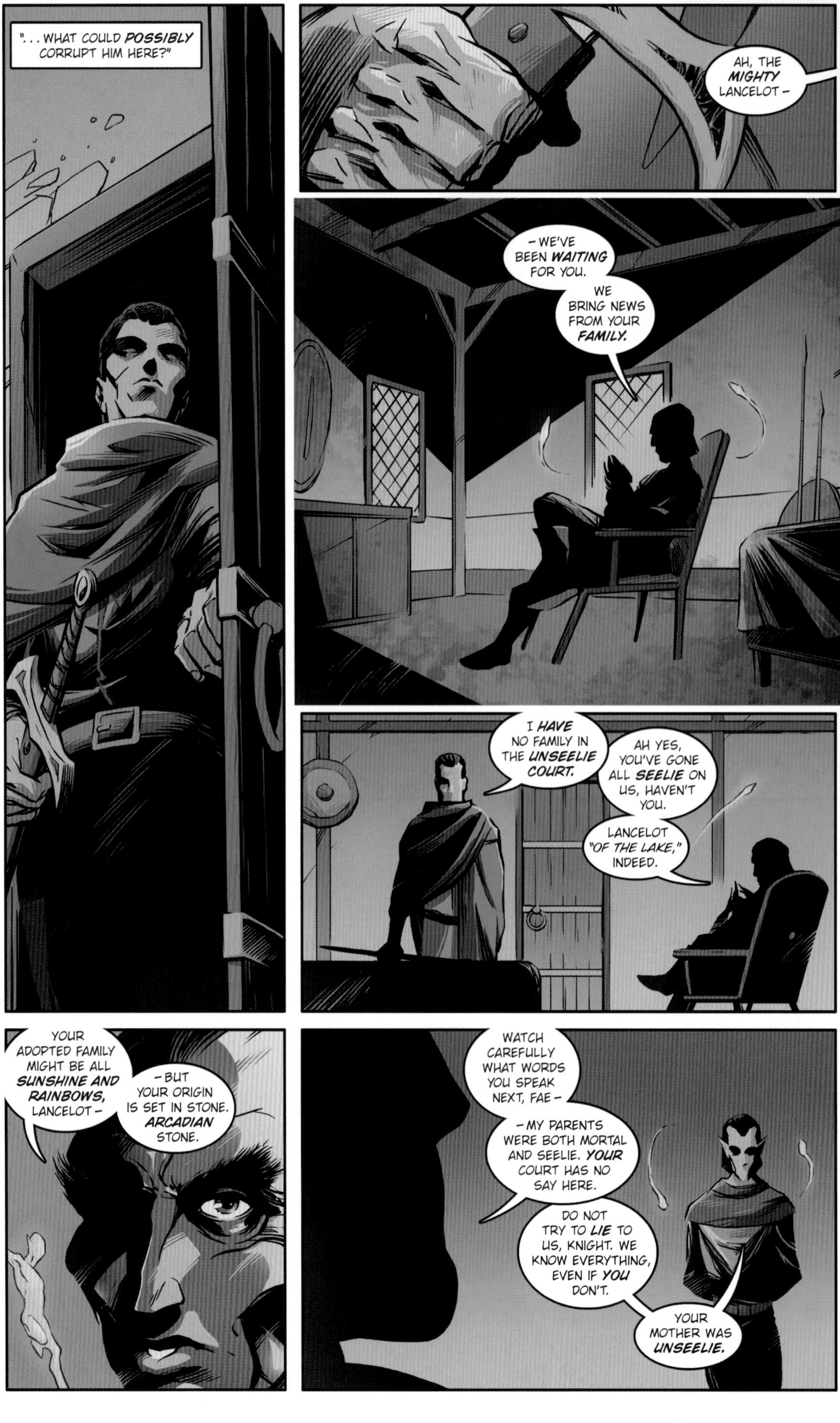
". . . WHAT COULD POSSIBLY CORRUPT HIM HERE?"
AH, THE MIGHTY LANCELOT –
– WE'VE BEEN WAITING FOR YOU.
WE BRING NEWS FROM YOUR FAMILY.
I HAVE NO FAMILY IN THE UNSEELIE COURT.
AH YES, YOU'VE GONE ALL SEELIE ON US, HAVEN'T YOU.
LANCELOT "OF THE LAKE," INDEED.
YOUR ADOPTED FAMILY MIGHT BE ALL SUNSHINE AND RAINBOWS, LANCELOT –
– BUT YOUR ORIGIN IS SET IN STONE. ARCADIAN STONE.
WATCH CAREFULLY WHAT WORDS YOU SPEAK NEXT, FAE –
– MY PARENTS WERE BOTH MORTAL AND SEELIE. YOUR COURT HAS NO SAY HERE.
DO NOT TRY TO LIE TO US, KNIGHT. WE KNOW EVERYTHING, EVEN IF YOU DON'T.
YOUR MOTHER WAS UNSEELIE.

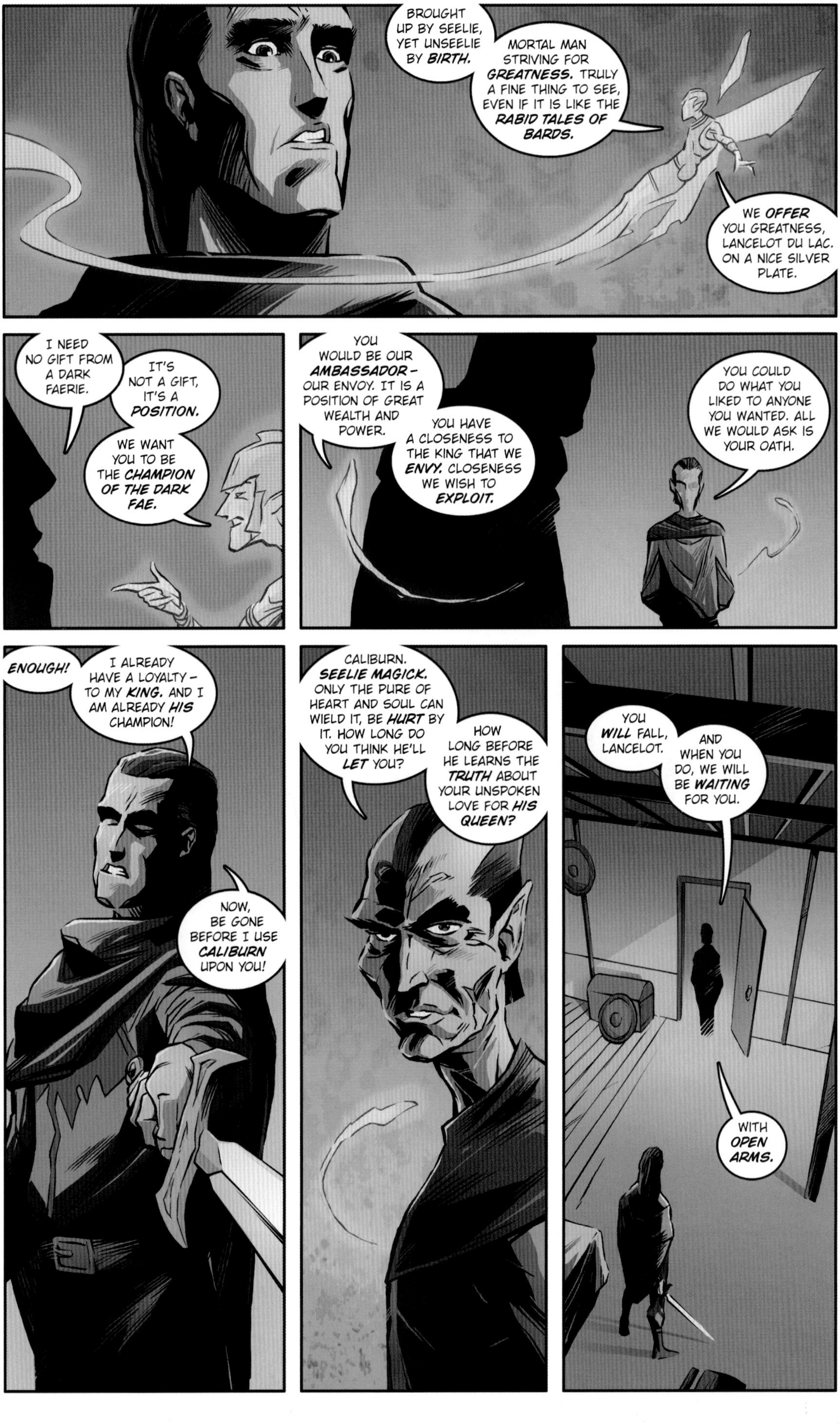
BROUGHT UP BY SEELIE, YET UNSEELIE BY BIRTH.
MORTAL MAN STRIVING FOR GREATNESS. TRULY A FINE THING TO SEE, EVEN IF IT IS LIKE THE RABID TALES OF BARDS.
WE OFFER YOU GREATNESS, LANCELOT DU LAC. ON A NICE SILVER PLATE.
I NEED NO GIFT FROM A DARK FAERIE.
IT'S NOT A GIFT, IT'S A POSITION.
WE WANT YOU TO BE THE CHAMPION OF THE DARK FAE.
YOU WOULD BE OUR AMBASSADOR - OUR ENVOY. IT IS A POSITION OF GREAT WEALTH AND POWER.
YOU HAVE A CLOSENESS TO THE KING THAT WE ENVY. CLOSENESS WE WISH TO EXPLOIT.
YOU COULD DO WHAT YOU LIKED TO ANYONE YOU WANTED. ALL WE WOULD ASK IS YOUR OATH.
ENOUGH!
I ALREADY HAVE A LOYALTY - TO MY KING. AND I AM ALREADY HIS CHAMPION!
NOW, BE GONE BEFORE I USE CALIBURN UPON YOU!
CALIBURN. SEELIE MAGICK. ONLY THE PURE OF HEART AND SOUL CAN WIELD IT, BE HURT BY IT. HOW LONG DO YOU THINK HE'LL LET YOU?
HOW LONG BEFORE HE LEARNS THE TRUTH ABOUT YOUR UNSPOKEN LOVE FOR HIS QUEEN?
YOU WILL FALL, LANCELOT.
AND WHEN YOU DO, WE WILL BE WAITING FOR YOU.
WITH OPEN ARMS.

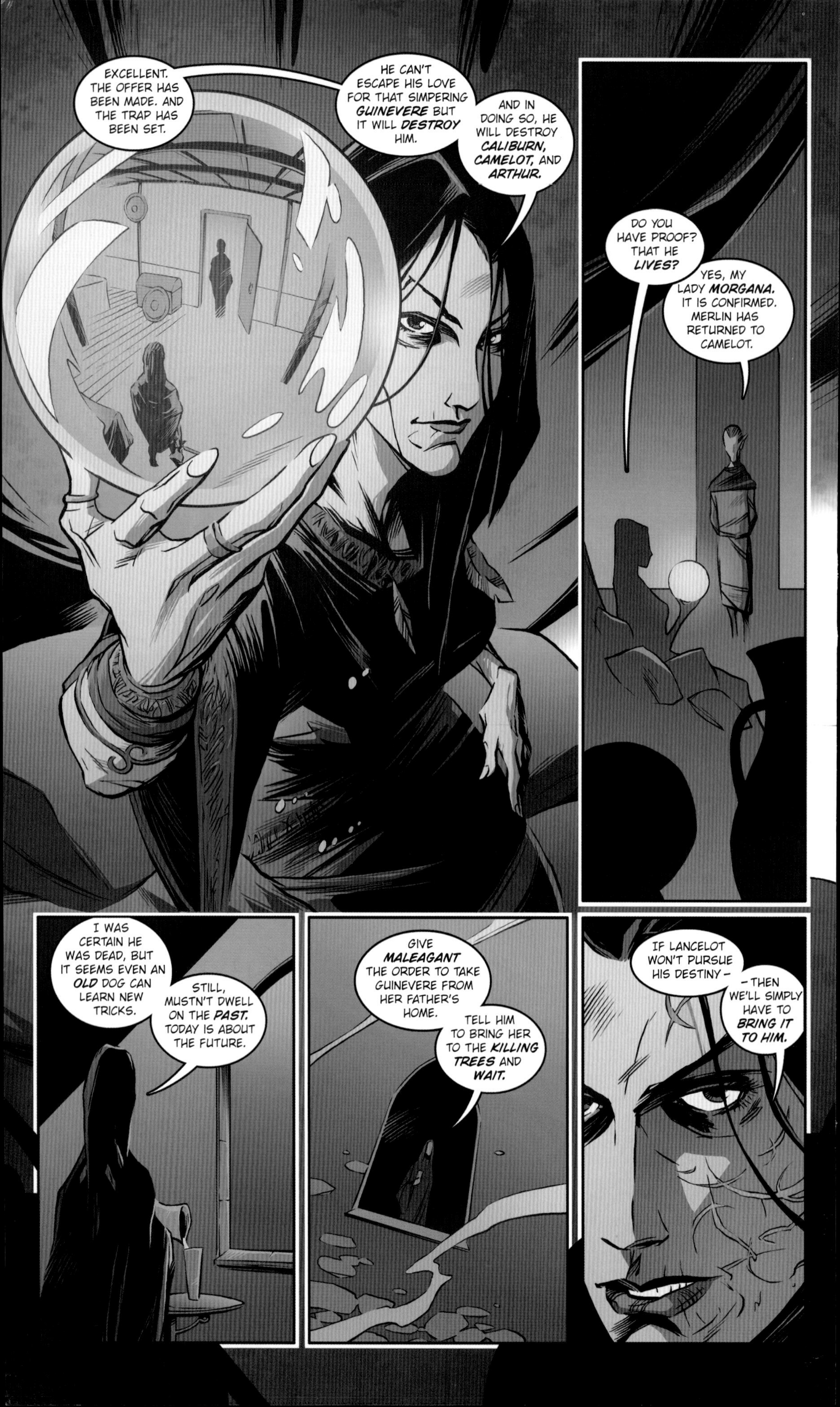

EXCELLENT. THE OFFER HAS BEEN MADE. AND THE TRAP HAS BEEN SET.
HE CAN'T ESCAPE HIS LOVE FOR THAT SIMPERING GUINEVERE BUT IT WILL DESTROY HIM.
AND IN DOING SO, HE WILL DESTROY CALIBURN, CAMELOT, AND ARTHUR.
DO YOU HAVE PROOF? THAT HE LIVES?
YES, MY LADY MORGANA. IT IS CONFIRMED. MERLIN HAS RETURNED TO CAMELOT.
I WAS CERTAIN HE WAS DEAD, BUT IT SEEMS EVEN AN OLD DOG CAN LEARN NEW TRICKS.
STILL, MUSTN'T DWELL ON THE PAST. TODAY IS ABOUT THE FUTURE.
GIVE MALEAGANT THE ORDER TO TAKE GUINEVERE FROM HER FATHER'S HOME.
TELL HIM TO BRING HER TO THE KILLING TREES AND WAIT.
IF LANCELOT WON'T PURSUE HIS DESTINY —
— THEN WE'LL SIMPLY HAVE TO BRING IT TO HIM.

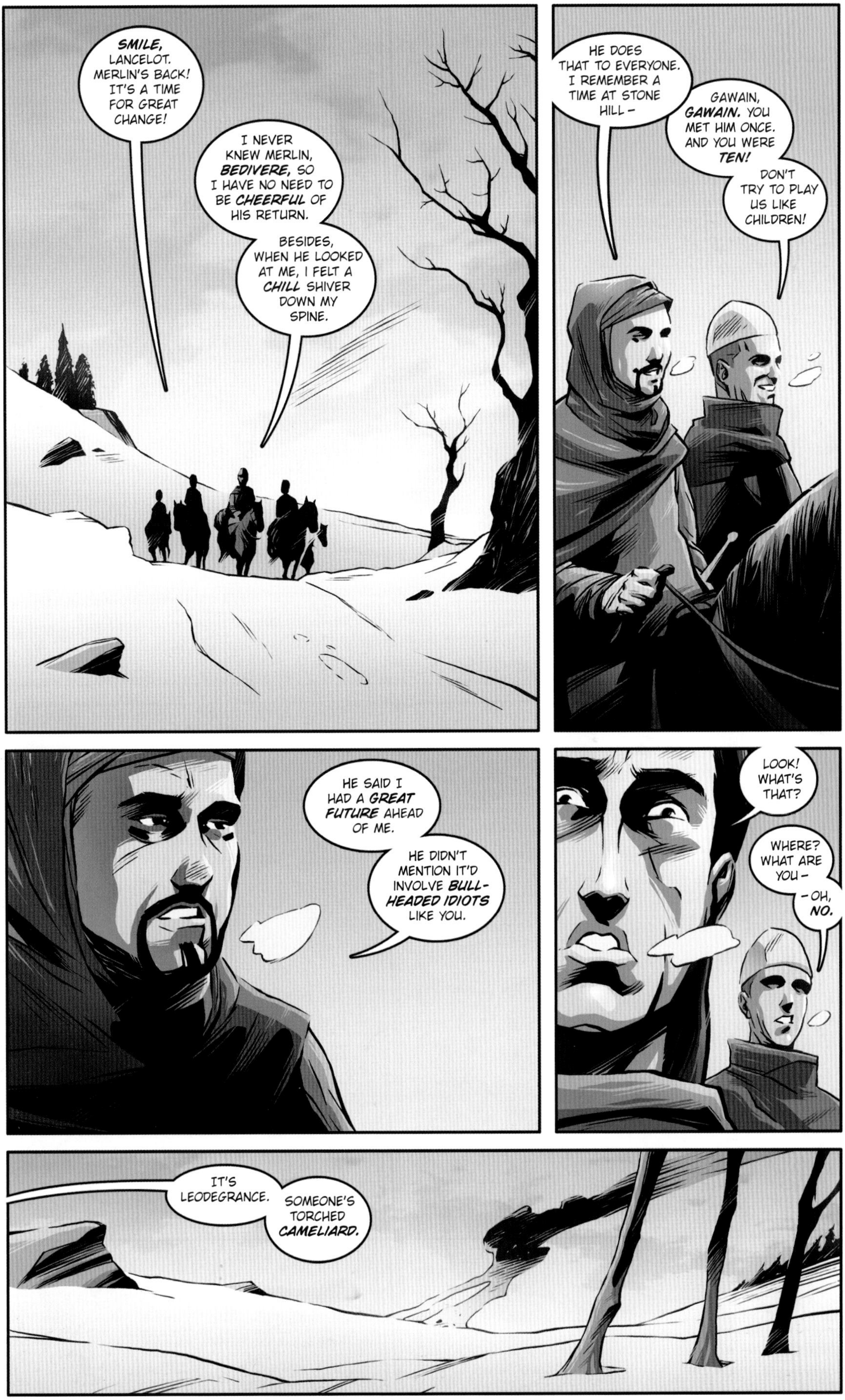
SMILE, LANCELOT. MERLIN'S BACK! IT'S A TIME FOR GREAT CHANGE!
I NEVER KNEW MERLIN, BEDIVERE, SO I HAVE NO NEED TO BE CHEERFUL OF HIS RETURN.
BESIDES, WHEN HE LOOKED AT ME, I FELT A CHILL SHIVER DOWN MY SPINE.
HE DOES THAT TO EVERYONE. I REMEMBER A TIME AT STONE HILL –
GAWAIN, GAWAIN. YOU MET HIM ONCE. AND YOU WERE TEN!
DON'T TRY TO PLAY US LIKE CHILDREN!
HE SAID I HAD A GREAT FUTURE AHEAD OF ME.
HE DIDN'T MENTION IT'D INVOLVE BULL-HEADED IDIOTS LIKE YOU.
LOOK! WHAT'S THAT?
WHERE? WHAT ARE YOU –
– OH, NO.
IT'S LEODEGRANCE.
SOMEONE'S TORCHED CAMELIARD.

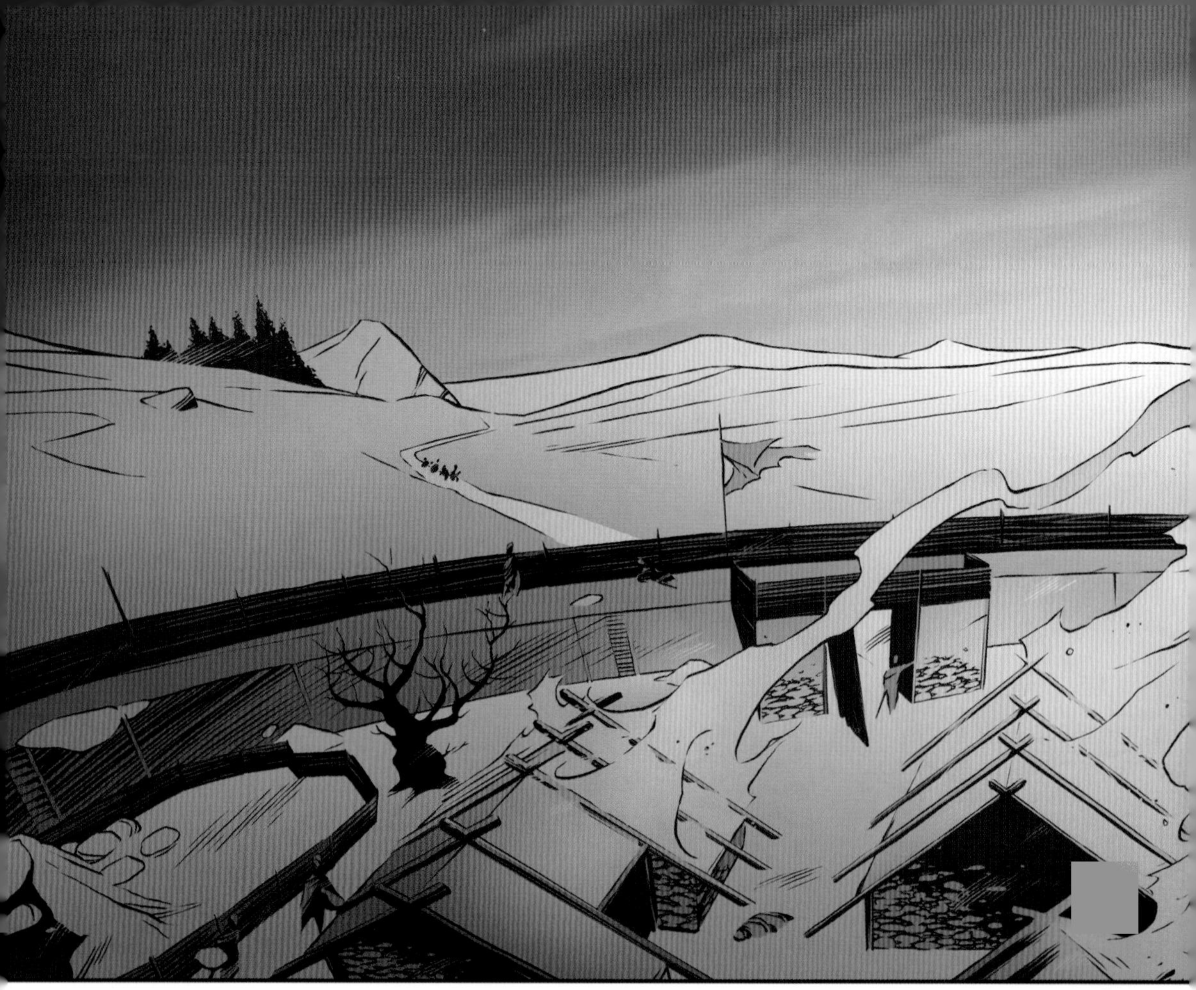

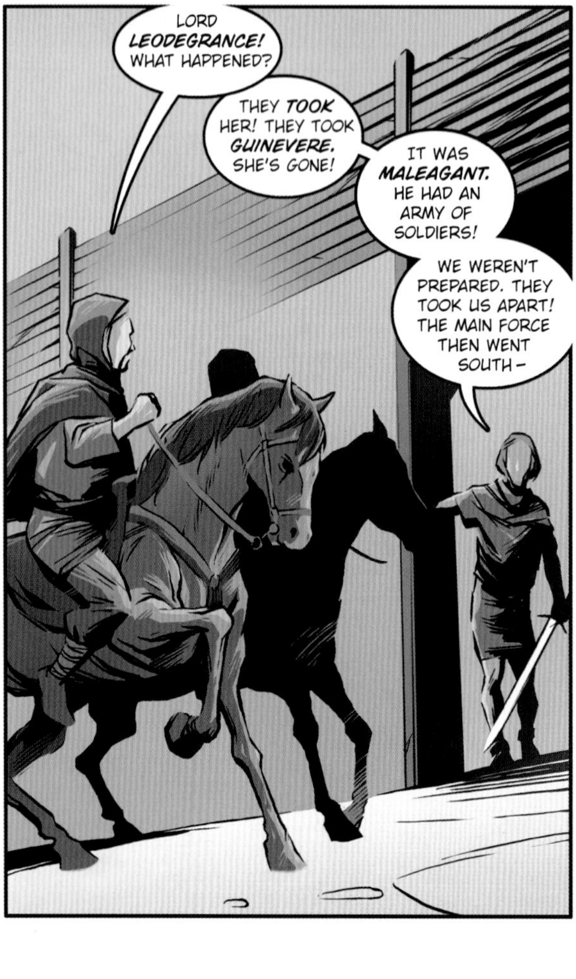
LORD LEODEGRANCE! WHAT HAPPENED?
THEY TOOK HER! THEY TOOK GUINEVERE. SHE'S GONE!
IT WAS MALEAGANT. HE HAD AN ARMY OF SOLDIERS!
WE WEREN'T PREPARED. THEY TOOK US APART! THE MAIN FORCE THEN WENT SOUTH–

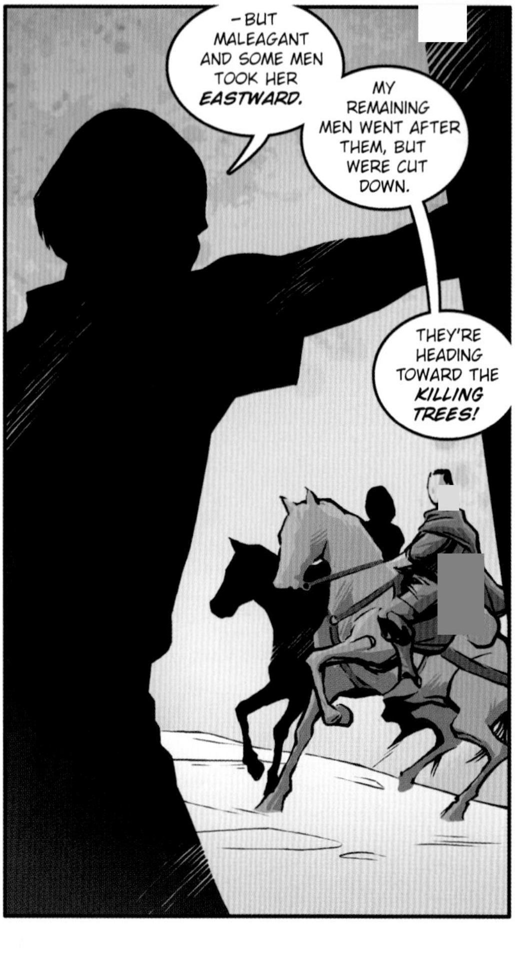
–BUT MALEAGANT AND SOME MEN TOOK HER EASTWARD.
MY REMAINING MEN WENT AFTER THEM, BUT WERE CUT DOWN.
THEY'RE HEADING TOWARD THE KILLING TREES!

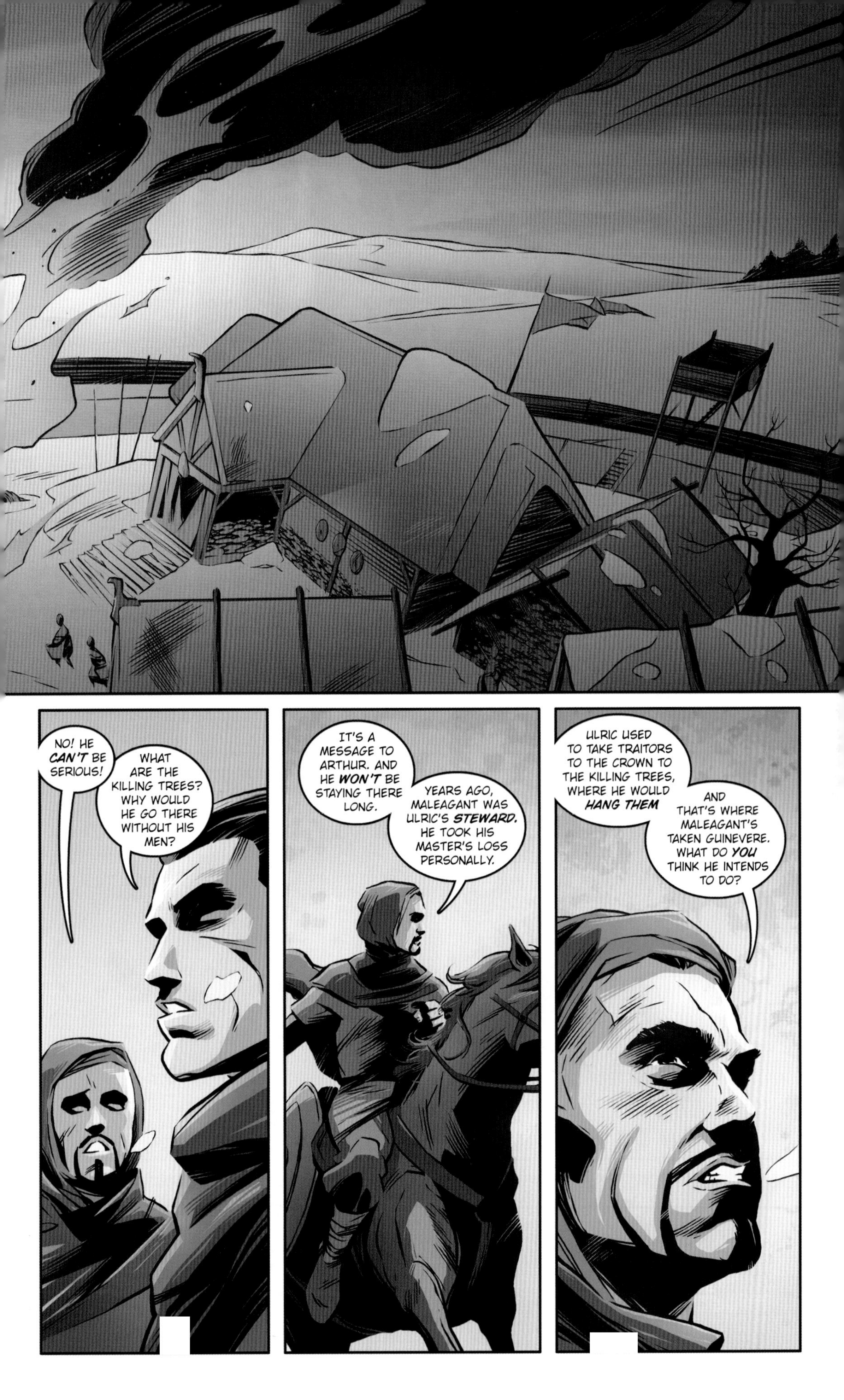

NO! HE CAN'T BE SERIOUS!
WHAT ARE THE KILLING TREES? WHY WOULD HE GO THERE WITHOUT HIS MEN?
IT'S A MESSAGE TO ARTHUR. AND HE WON'T BE STAYING THERE LONG.
YEARS AGO, MALEAGANT WAS ULRIC'S STEWARD. HE TOOK HIS MASTER'S LOSS PERSONALLY.
ULRIC USED TO TAKE TRAITORS TO THE CROWN TO THE KILLING TREES, WHERE HE WOULD HANG THEM
AND THAT'S WHERE MALEAGANT'S TAKEN GUINEVERE. WHAT DO YOU THINK HE INTENDS TO DO?

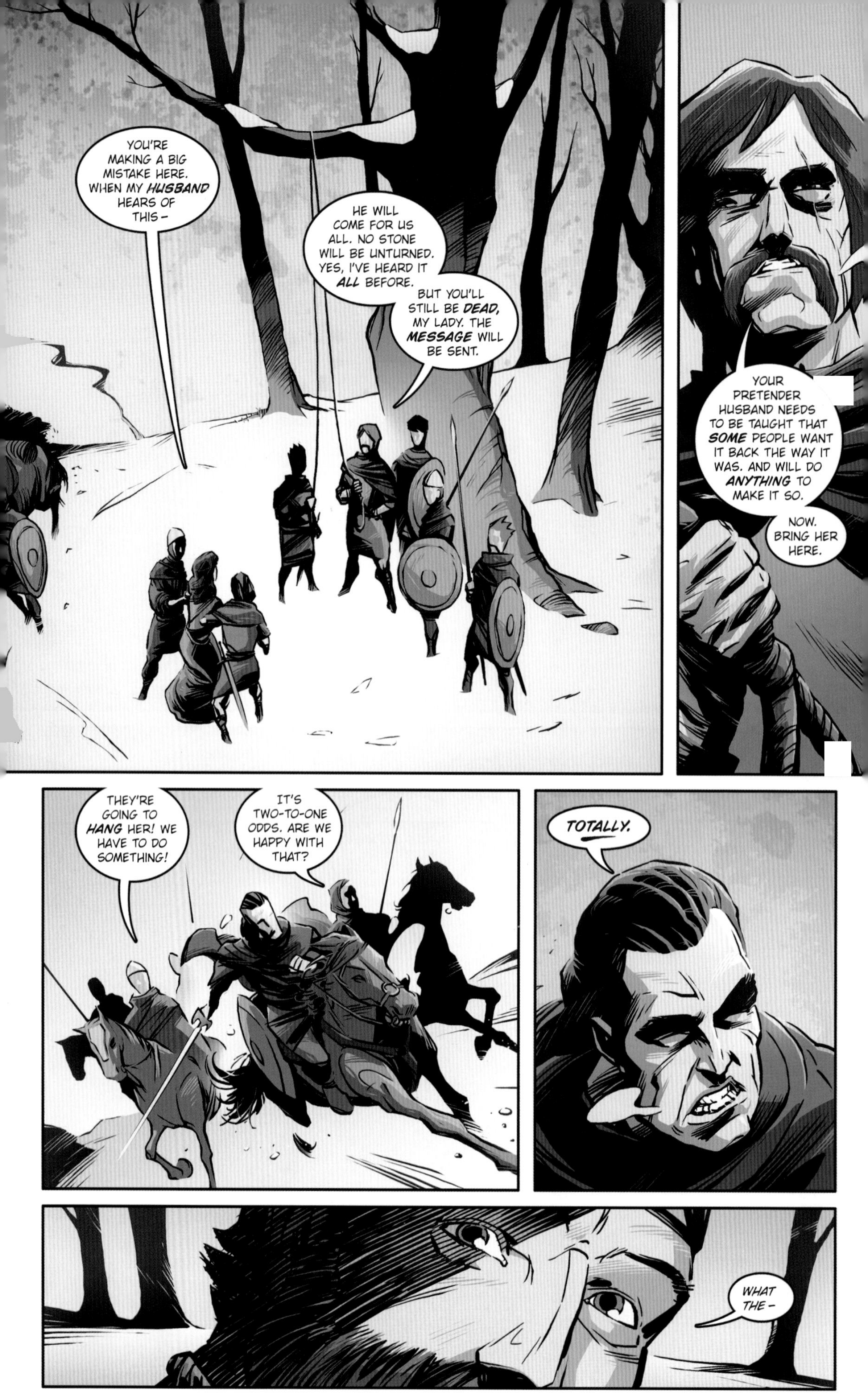

YOU'RE MAKING A BIG MISTAKE HERE. WHEN MY *HUSBAND* HEARS OF THIS –
HE WILL COME FOR US ALL. NO STONE WILL BE UNTURNED. YES, I'VE HEARD IT *ALL* BEFORE.
BUT YOU'LL STILL BE *DEAD,* MY LADY. THE *MESSAGE* WILL BE SENT.
YOUR PRETENDER HUSBAND NEEDS TO BE TAUGHT THAT *SOME* PEOPLE WANT IT BACK THE WAY IT WAS. AND WILL DO *ANYTHING* TO MAKE IT SO.
NOW. BRING HER HERE.
THEY'RE GOING TO *HANG* HER! WE HAVE TO DO SOMETHING!
IT'S TWO-TO-ONE ODDS. ARE WE HAPPY WITH THAT?
*TOTALLY.*
WHAT THE –

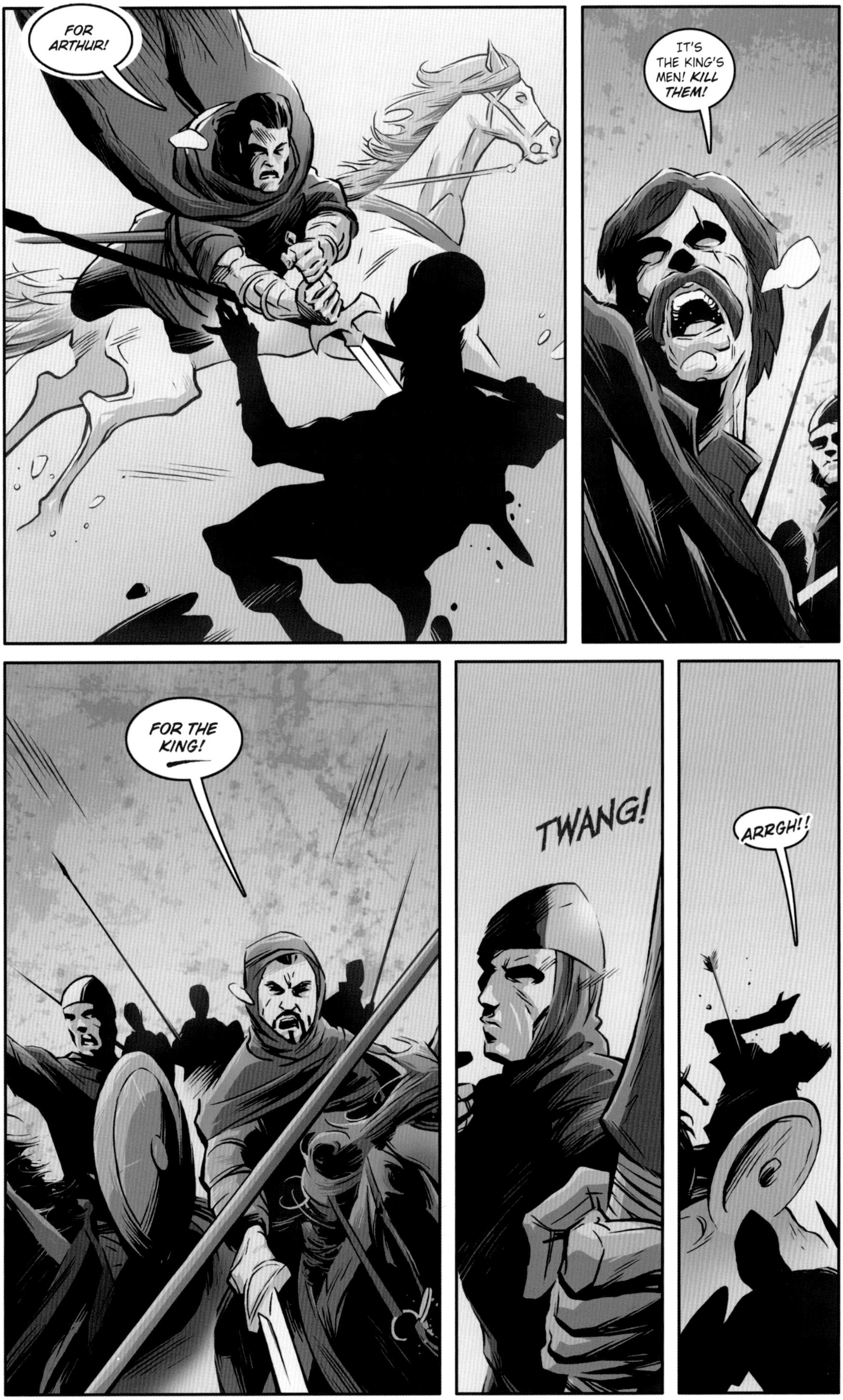
FOR ARTHUR!
IT'S THE KING'S MEN! KILL THEM!
FOR THE KING!
TWANG!
ARRGH!!

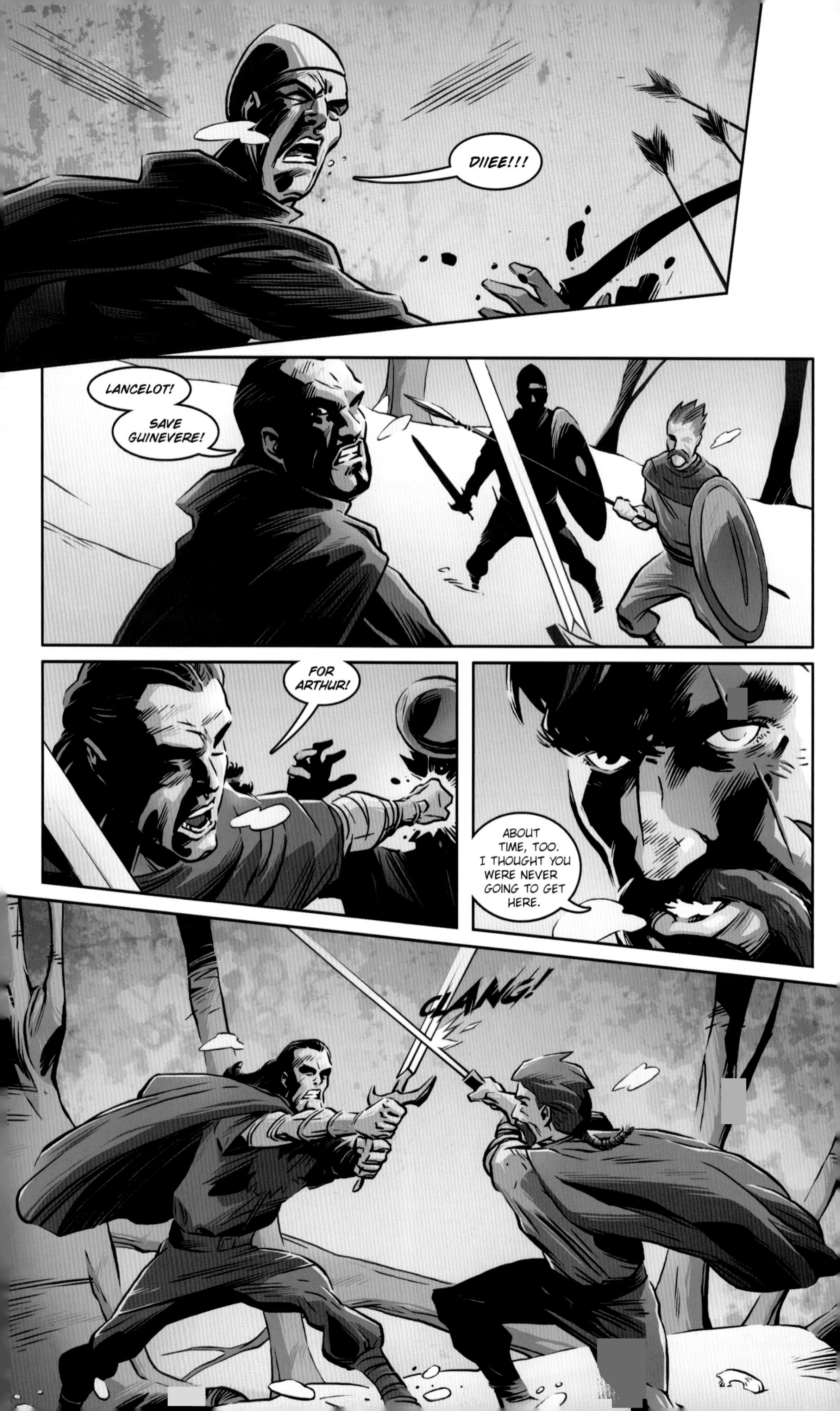
DIIEE!!!
LANCELOT!
SAVE GUINEVERE!
FOR ARTHUR!
ABOUT TIME, TOO. I THOUGHT YOU WERE NEVER GOING TO GET HERE.
CLANG!

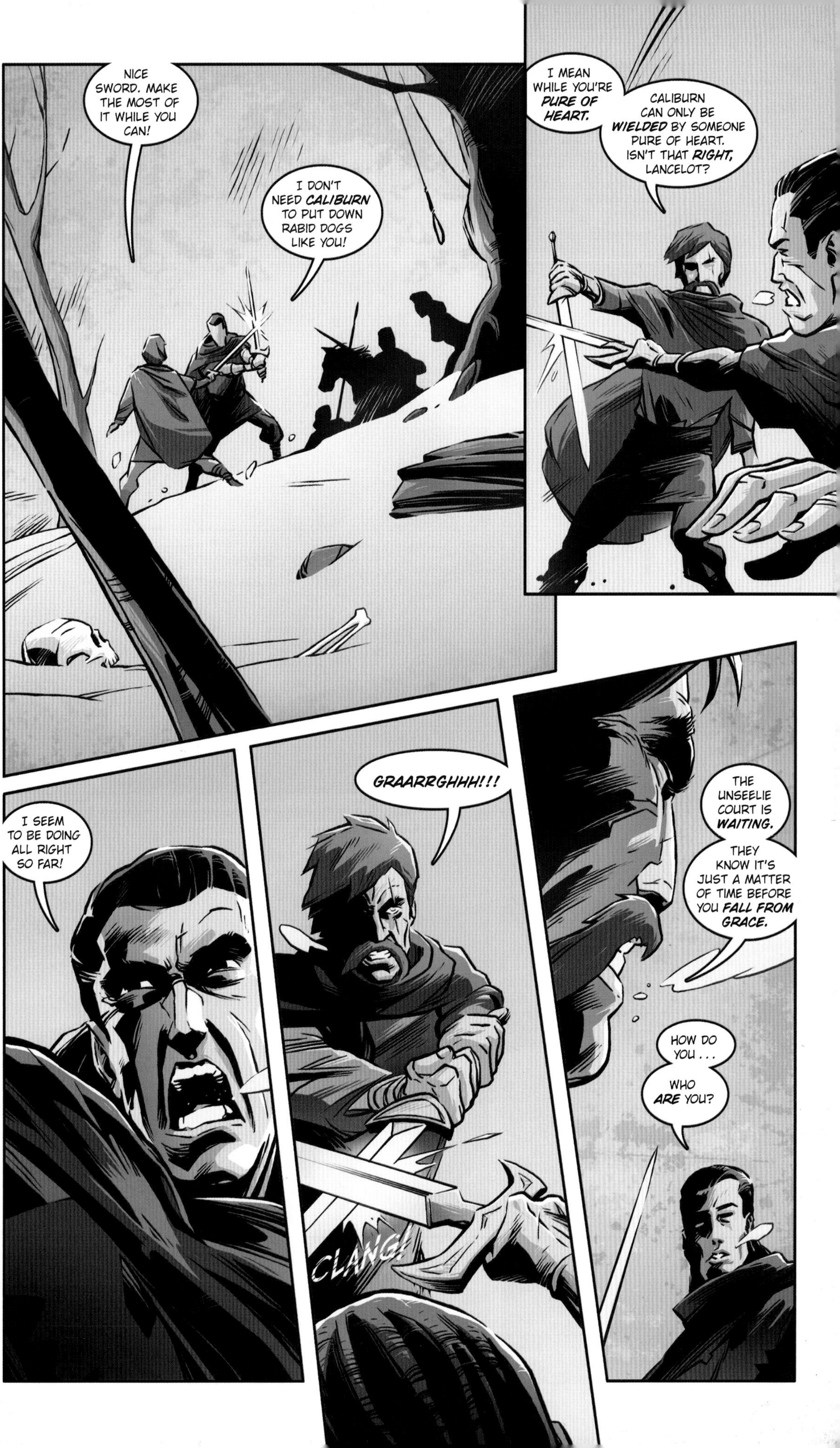
NICE SWORD. MAKE THE MOST OF IT WHILE YOU CAN!
I DON'T NEED CALIBURN TO PUT DOWN RABID DOGS LIKE YOU!
I MEAN WHILE YOU'RE PURE OF HEART.
CALIBURN CAN ONLY BE WIELDED BY SOMEONE PURE OF HEART. ISN'T THAT RIGHT, LANCELOT?
I SEEM TO BE DOING ALL RIGHT SO FAR!
GRAARRGHHH!!!
CLANG!
THE UNSEELIE COURT IS WAITING.
THEY KNOW IT'S JUST A MATTER OF TIME BEFORE YOU FALL FROM GRACE.
HOW DO YOU . . .
WHO ARE YOU?

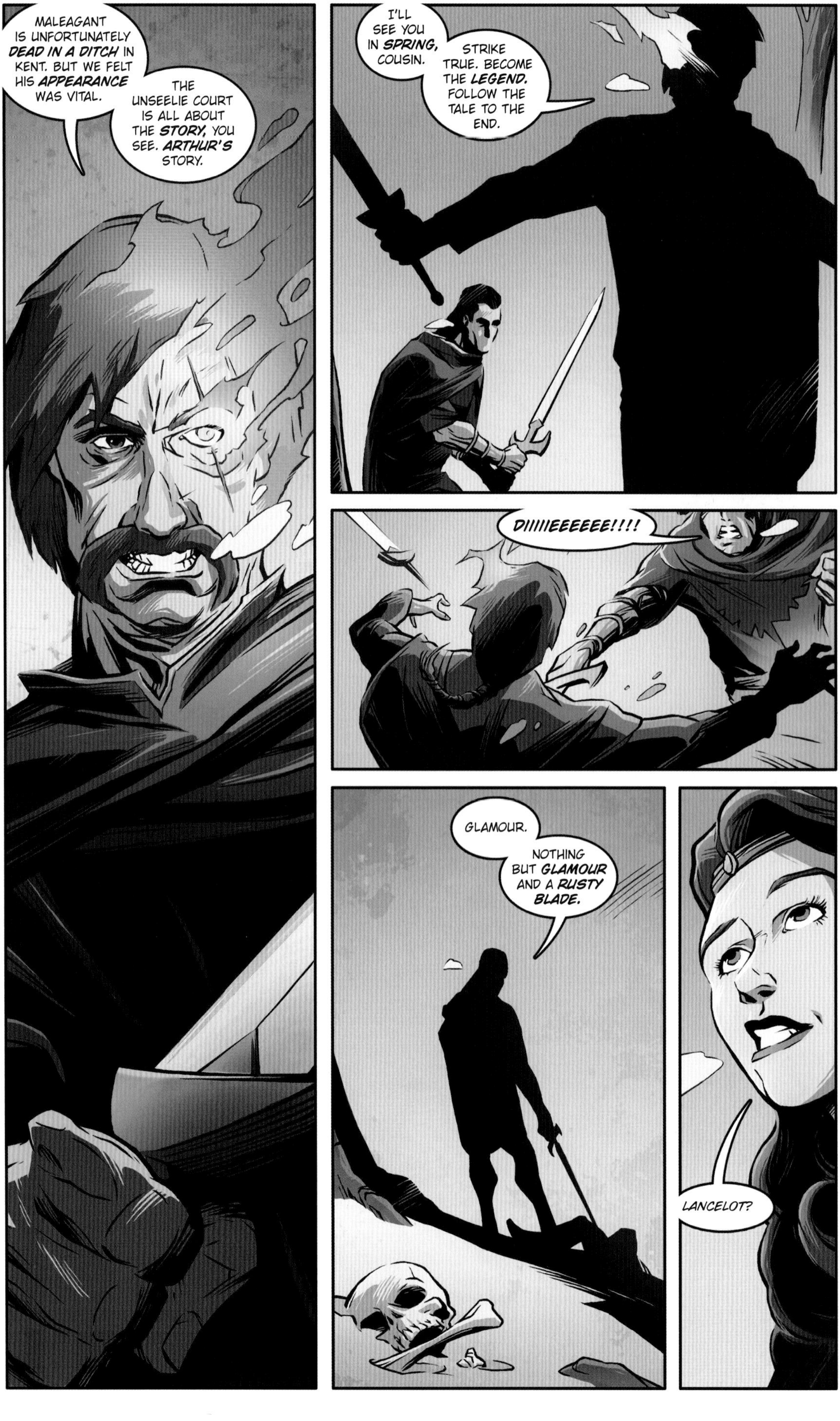
MALEAGANT IS UNFORTUNATELY *DEAD IN A DITCH* IN KENT. BUT WE FELT HIS *APPEARANCE* WAS VITAL.
THE UNSEELIE COURT IS ALL ABOUT THE *STORY,* YOU SEE. *ARTHUR'S* STORY.
I'LL SEE YOU IN *SPRING,* COUSIN.
STRIKE TRUE. BECOME THE *LEGEND.* FOLLOW THE TALE TO THE END.
DIIIIIEEEEEE!!!!
GLAMOUR.
NOTHING BUT *GLAMOUR* AND A *RUSTY BLADE.*
LANCELOT?

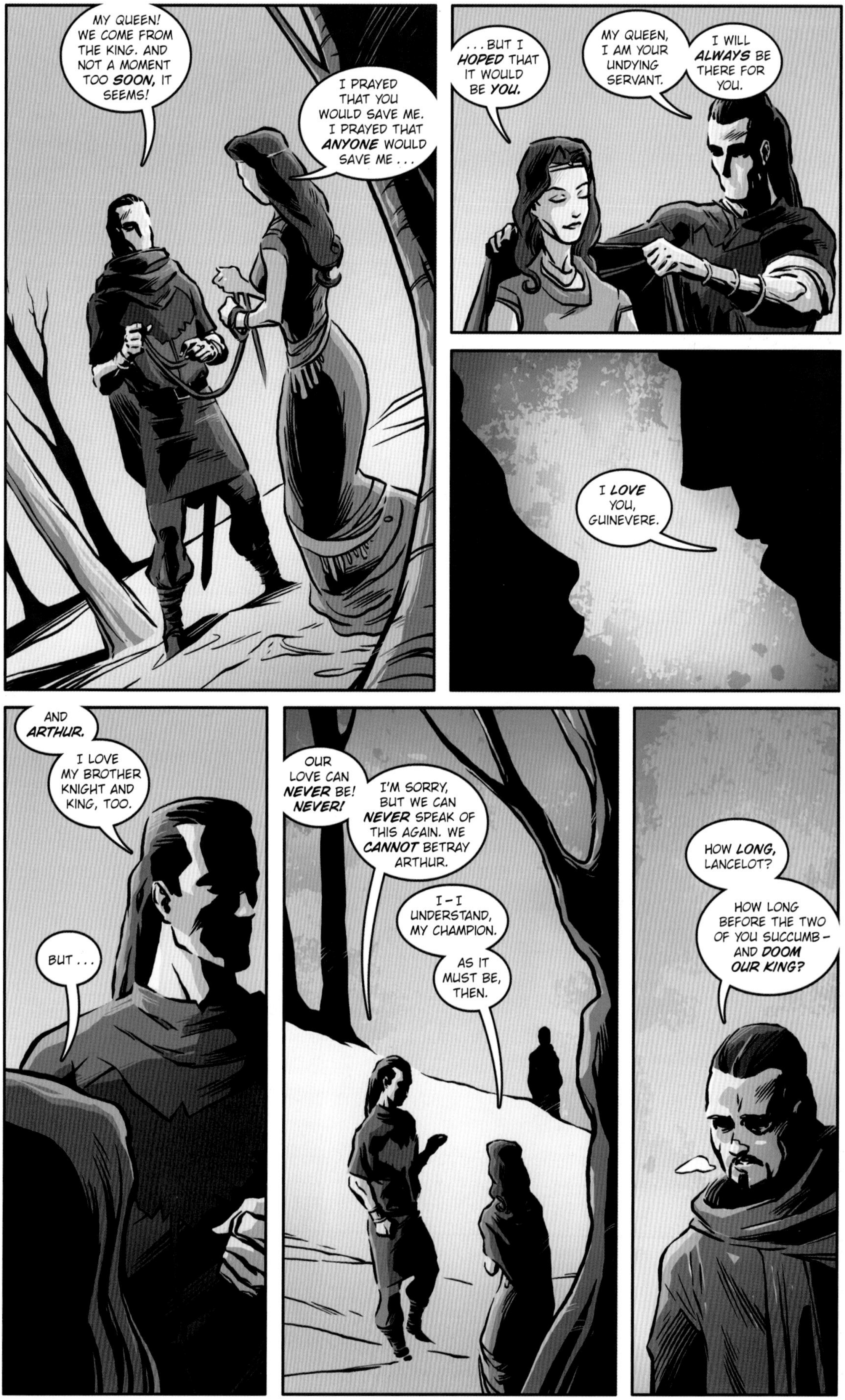
MY QUEEN! WE COME FROM THE KING. AND NOT A MOMENT TOO SOON, IT SEEMS!
I PRAYED THAT YOU WOULD SAVE ME. I PRAYED THAT ANYONE WOULD SAVE ME . . .
. . . BUT I HOPED THAT IT WOULD BE YOU.
MY QUEEN, I AM YOUR UNDYING SERVANT.
I WILL ALWAYS BE THERE FOR YOU.
I LOVE YOU, GUINEVERE.
AND ARTHUR.
I LOVE MY BROTHER KNIGHT AND KING, TOO.
BUT . . .
OUR LOVE CAN NEVER BE! NEVER!
I'M SORRY, BUT WE CAN NEVER SPEAK OF THIS AGAIN. WE CANNOT BETRAY ARTHUR.
I-I UNDERSTAND, MY CHAMPION.
AS IT MUST BE, THEN.
HOW LONG, LANCELOT?
HOW LONG BEFORE THE TWO OF YOU SUCCUMB-AND DOOM OUR KING?

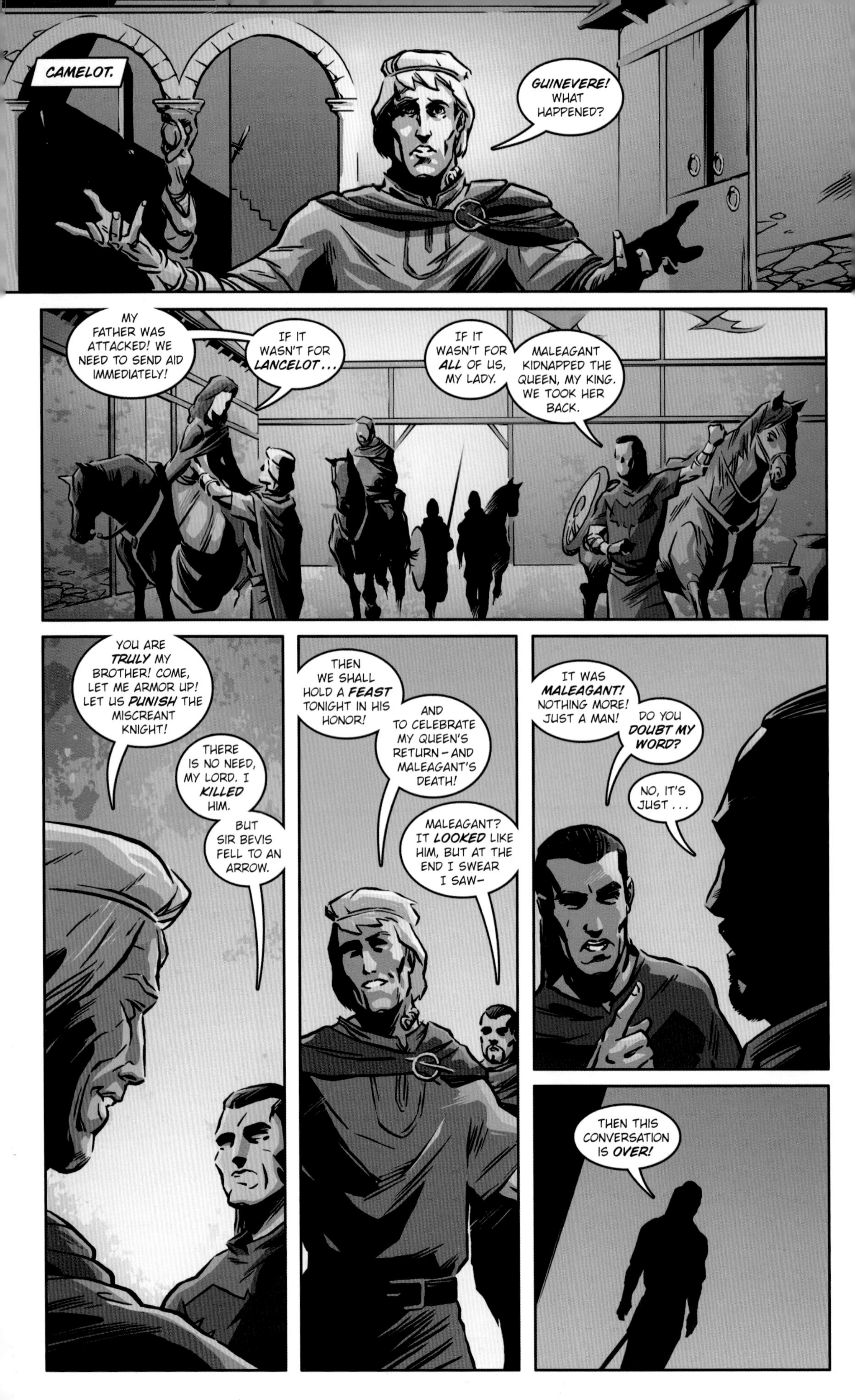
CAMELOT.
GUINEVERE! WHAT HAPPENED?
MY FATHER WAS ATTACKED! WE NEED TO SEND AID IMMEDIATELY!
IF IT WASN'T FOR LANCELOT...
IF IT WASN'T FOR ALL OF US, MY LADY.
MALEAGANT KIDNAPPED THE QUEEN, MY KING. WE TOOK HER BACK.
YOU ARE TRULY MY BROTHER! COME, LET ME ARMOR UP! LET US PUNISH THE MISCREANT KNIGHT!
THERE IS NO NEED, MY LORD. I KILLED HIM.
BUT SIR BEVIS FELL TO AN ARROW.
THEN WE SHALL HOLD A FEAST TONIGHT IN HIS HONOR!
AND TO CELEBRATE MY QUEEN'S RETURN – AND MALEAGANT'S DEATH!
MALEAGANT? IT LOOKED LIKE HIM, BUT AT THE END I SWEAR I SAW–
IT WAS MALEAGANT! NOTHING MORE! JUST A MAN!
DO YOU DOUBT MY WORD?
NO, IT'S JUST . . .
THEN THIS CONVERSATION IS OVER!

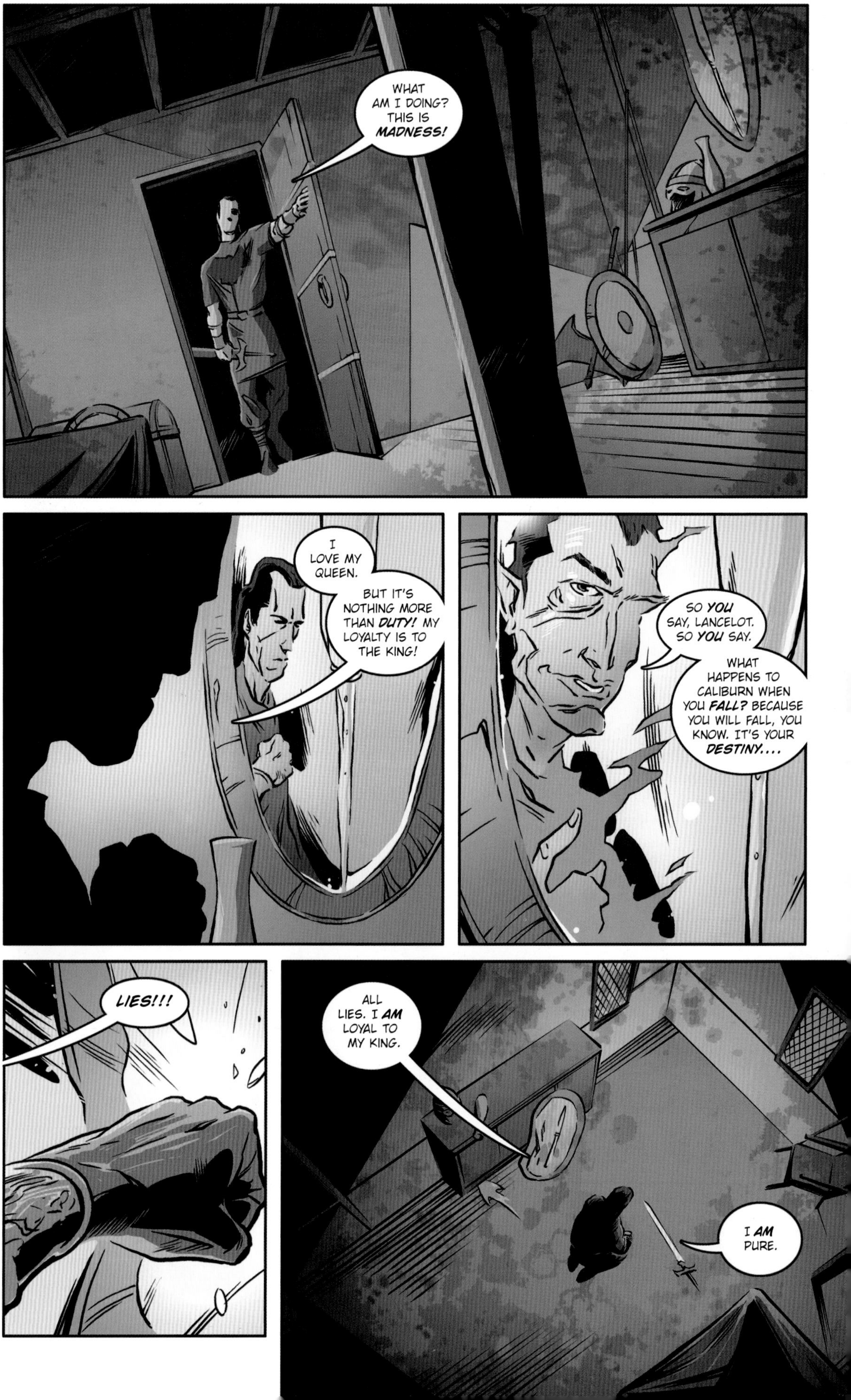
WHAT AM I DOING? THIS IS MADNESS!
I LOVE MY QUEEN.
BUT IT'S NOTHING MORE THAN DUTY! MY LOYALTY IS TO THE KING!
SO YOU SAY, LANCELOT. SO YOU SAY.
WHAT HAPPENS TO CALIBURN WHEN YOU FALL? BECAUSE YOU WILL FALL, YOU KNOW. IT'S YOUR DESTINY....
LIES!!!
ALL LIES. I AM LOYAL TO MY KING.
I AM PURE.

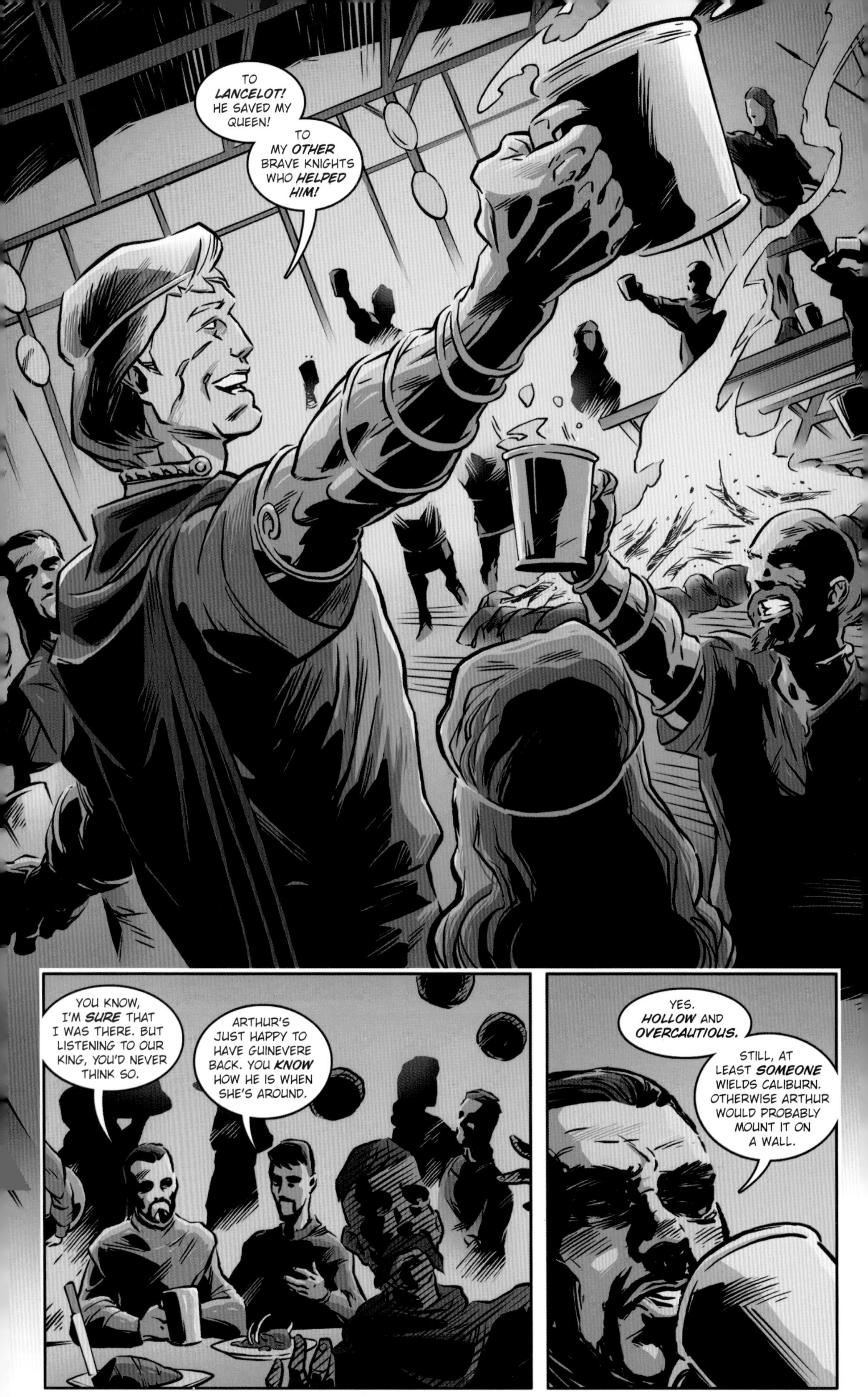
TO LANCELOT! HE SAVED MY QUEEN!
TO MY OTHER BRAVE KNIGHTS WHO HELPED HIM!
YOU KNOW, I'M SURE THAT I WAS THERE. BUT LISTENING TO OUR KING, YOU'D NEVER THINK SO.
ARTHUR'S JUST HAPPY TO HAVE GUINEVERE BACK. YOU KNOW HOW HE IS WHEN SHE'S AROUND.
YES. HOLLOW AND OVERCAUTIOUS.
STILL, AT LEAST SOMEONE WIELDS CALIBURN. OTHERWISE ARTHUR WOULD PROBABLY MOUNT IT ON A WALL.

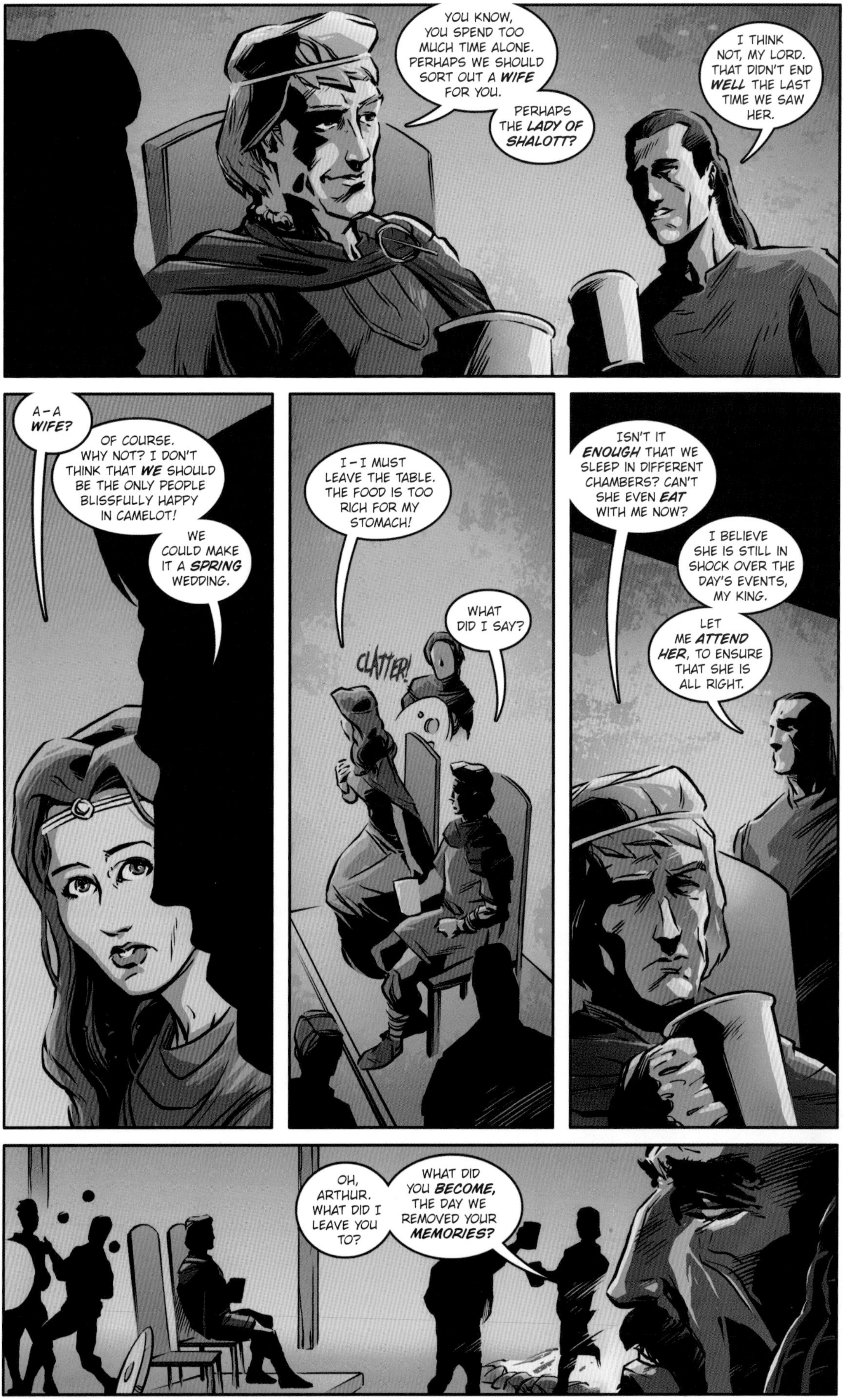

YOU KNOW, YOU SPEND TOO MUCH TIME ALONE. PERHAPS WE SHOULD SORT OUT A WIFE FOR YOU.
PERHAPS THE LADY OF SHALOTT?
I THINK NOT, MY LORD. THAT DIDN'T END WELL THE LAST TIME WE SAW HER.
A-A WIFE?
OF COURSE. WHY NOT? I DON'T THINK THAT WE SHOULD BE THE ONLY PEOPLE BLISSFULLY HAPPY IN CAMELOT!
WE COULD MAKE IT A SPRING WEDDING.
I-I MUST LEAVE THE TABLE. THE FOOD IS TOO RICH FOR MY STOMACH!
CLATTER!
WHAT DID I SAY?
ISN'T IT ENOUGH THAT WE SLEEP IN DIFFERENT CHAMBERS? CAN'T SHE EVEN EAT WITH ME NOW?
I BELIEVE SHE IS STILL IN SHOCK OVER THE DAY'S EVENTS, MY KING.
LET ME ATTEND HER, TO ENSURE THAT SHE IS ALL RIGHT.
OH, ARTHUR. WHAT DID I LEAVE YOU TO?
WHAT DID YOU BECOME, THE DAY WE REMOVED YOUR MEMORIES?

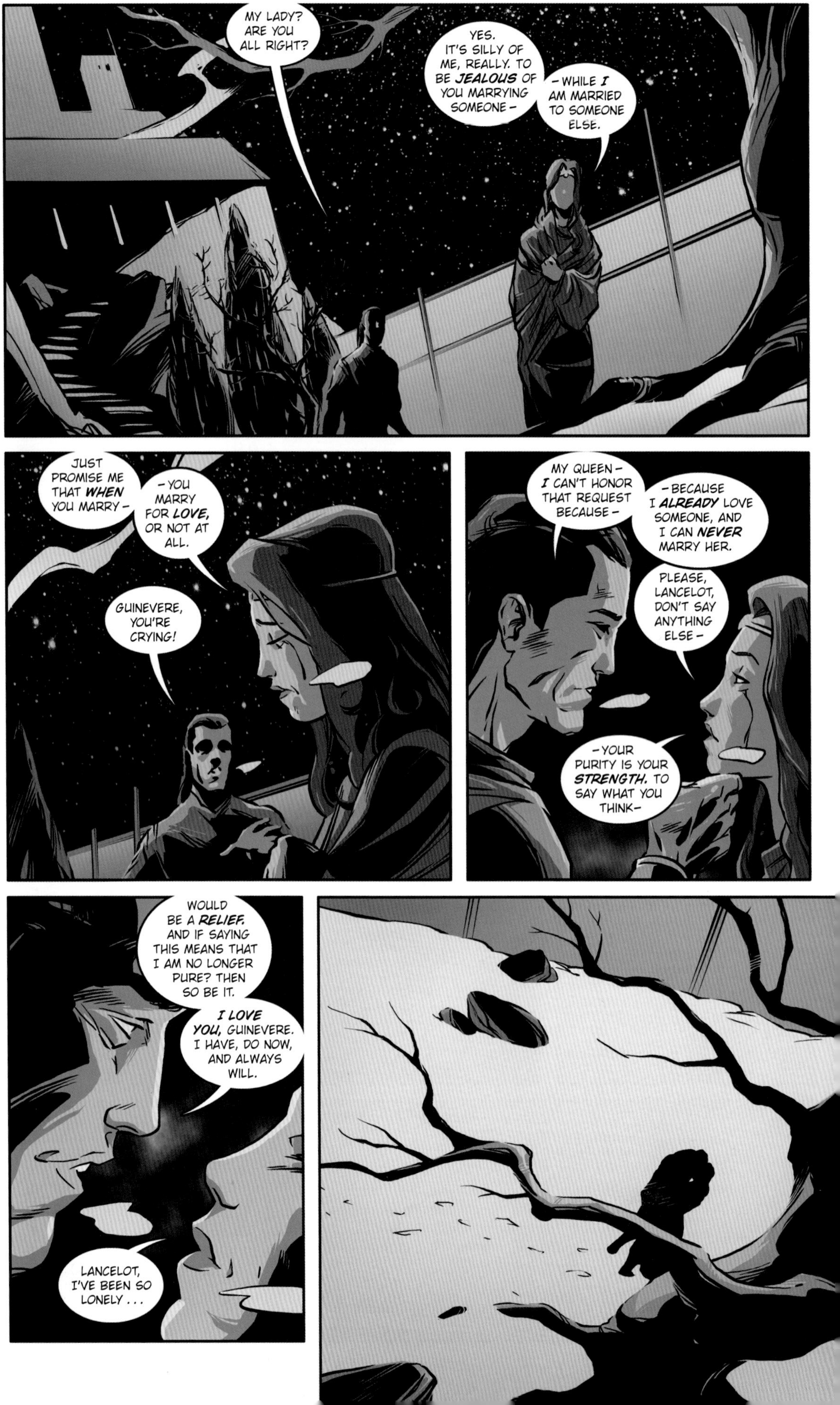
MY LADY? ARE YOU ALL RIGHT?
YES. IT'S SILLY OF ME, REALLY. TO BE JEALOUS OF YOU MARRYING SOMEONE –
– WHILE I AM MARRIED TO SOMEONE ELSE.
JUST PROMISE ME THAT WHEN YOU MARRY –
– YOU MARRY FOR LOVE, OR NOT AT ALL.
GUINEVERE, YOU'RE CRYING!
MY QUEEN – I CAN'T HONOR THAT REQUEST BECAUSE –
– BECAUSE I ALREADY LOVE SOMEONE, AND I CAN NEVER MARRY HER.
PLEASE, LANCELOT, DON'T SAY ANYTHING ELSE –
– YOUR PURITY IS YOUR STRENGTH. TO SAY WHAT YOU THINK–
WOULD BE A RELIEF. AND IF SAYING THIS MEANS THAT I AM NO LONGER PURE? THEN SO BE IT.
I LOVE YOU, GUINEVERE. I HAVE, DO NOW, AND ALWAYS WILL.
LANCELOT, I'VE BEEN SO LONELY . . .

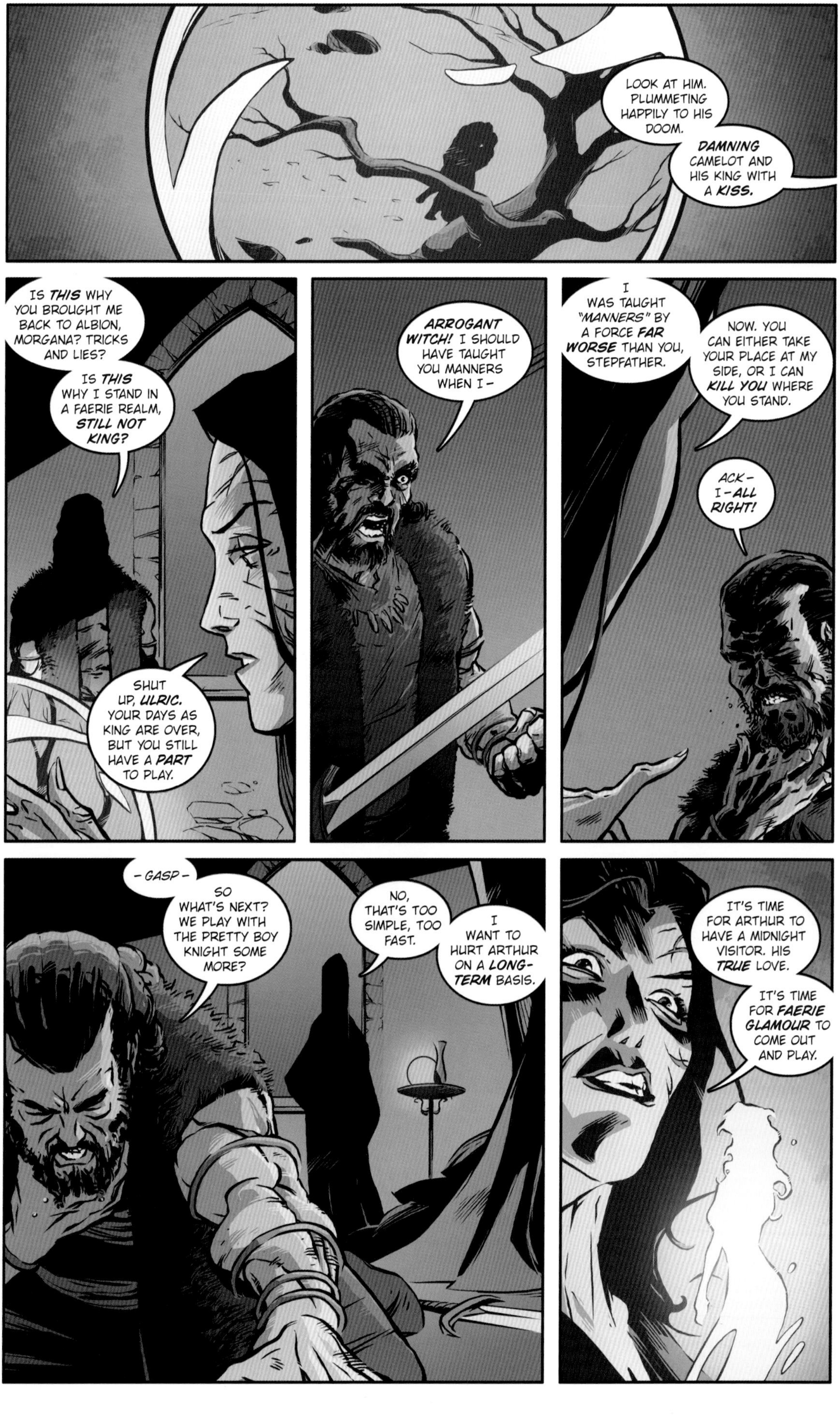

LOOK AT HIM. PLUMMETING HAPPILY TO HIS DOOM.
DAMNING CAMELOT AND HIS KING WITH A KISS.
IS THIS WHY YOU BROUGHT ME BACK TO ALBION, MORGANA? TRICKS AND LIES?
IS THIS WHY I STAND IN A FAERIE REALM, STILL NOT KING?
SHUT UP, ULRIC. YOUR DAYS AS KING ARE OVER, BUT YOU STILL HAVE A PART TO PLAY.
ARROGANT WITCH! I SHOULD HAVE TAUGHT YOU MANNERS WHEN I –
I WAS TAUGHT "MANNERS" BY A FORCE FAR WORSE THAN YOU, STEPFATHER.
NOW. YOU CAN EITHER TAKE YOUR PLACE AT MY SIDE, OR I CAN KILL YOU WHERE YOU STAND.
ACK – I – ALL RIGHT!
– GASP –
SO WHAT'S NEXT? WE PLAY WITH THE PRETTY BOY KNIGHT SOME MORE?
NO, THAT'S TOO SIMPLE, TOO FAST.
I WANT TO HURT ARTHUR ON A LONG-TERM BASIS.
IT'S TIME FOR ARTHUR TO HAVE A MIDNIGHT VISITOR. HIS TRUE LOVE.
IT'S TIME FOR FAERIE GLAMOUR TO COME OUT AND PLAY.

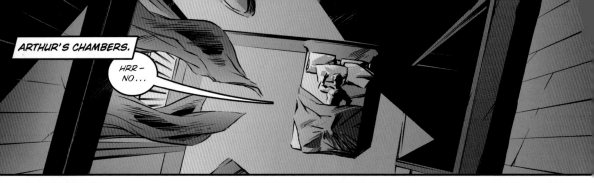

ARTHUR'S CHAMBERS.

HRR— NO...

WHA— WHO'S THAT?

GUINEVERE? IS THAT YOU?

IT IS I, ARTHUR.

YOUR *TRUE* LOVE.

VIVIANNE? WHAT ARE YOU— NO, *STOP*— GET OFF—

WHY DO YOU STOP ME? YOU *LOVE* ME. YOU *WANT* ME. YOU CREATED THIS *GLAMOUR* OF ME.

*ACCEPT* ME. TAKE ME IN YOUR ARMS.

LOVE ME.

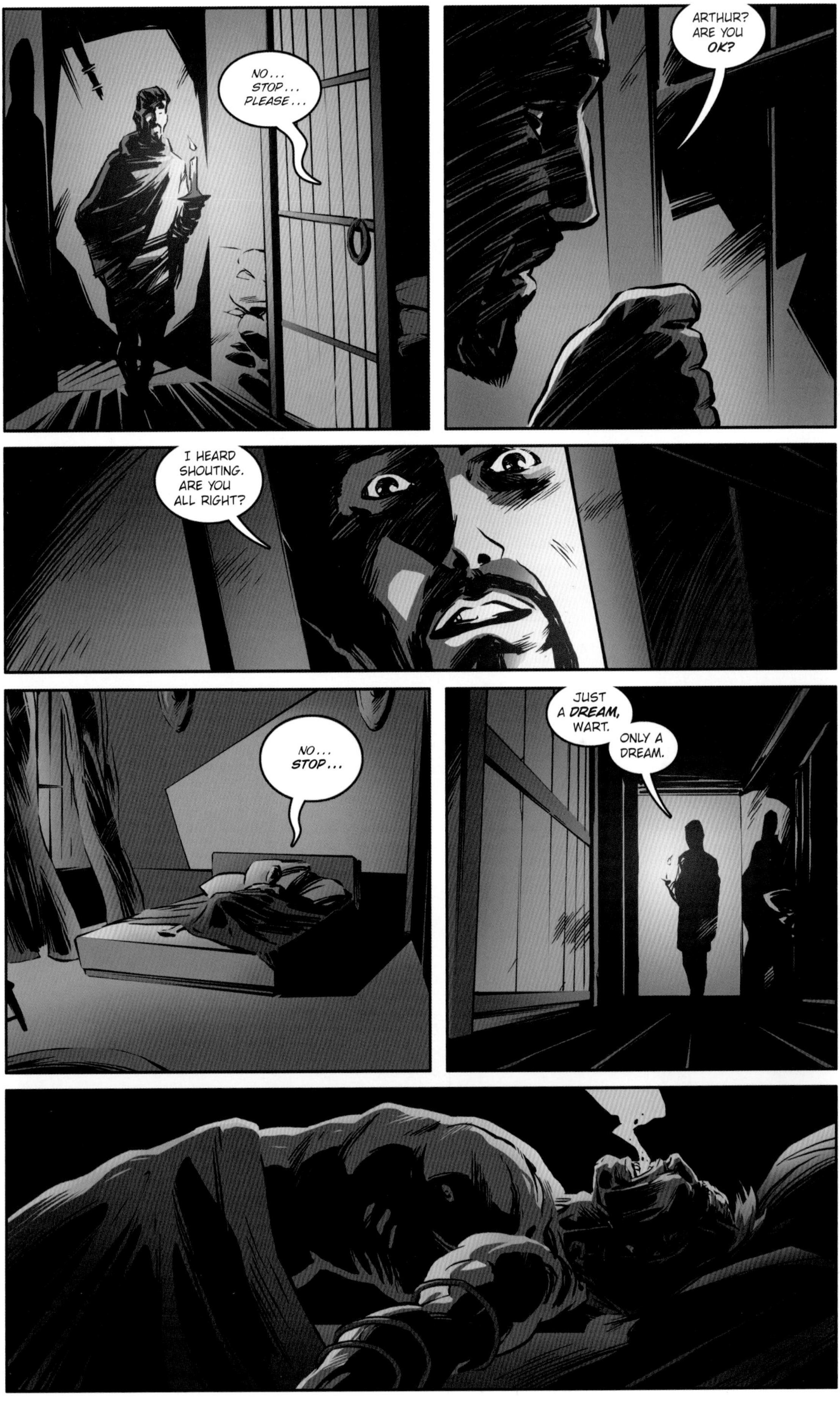
NO... STOP... PLEASE...
ARTHUR? ARE YOU OK?
I HEARD SHOUTING. ARE YOU ALL RIGHT?
NO... STOP...
JUST A DREAM, WART.
ONLY A DREAM.

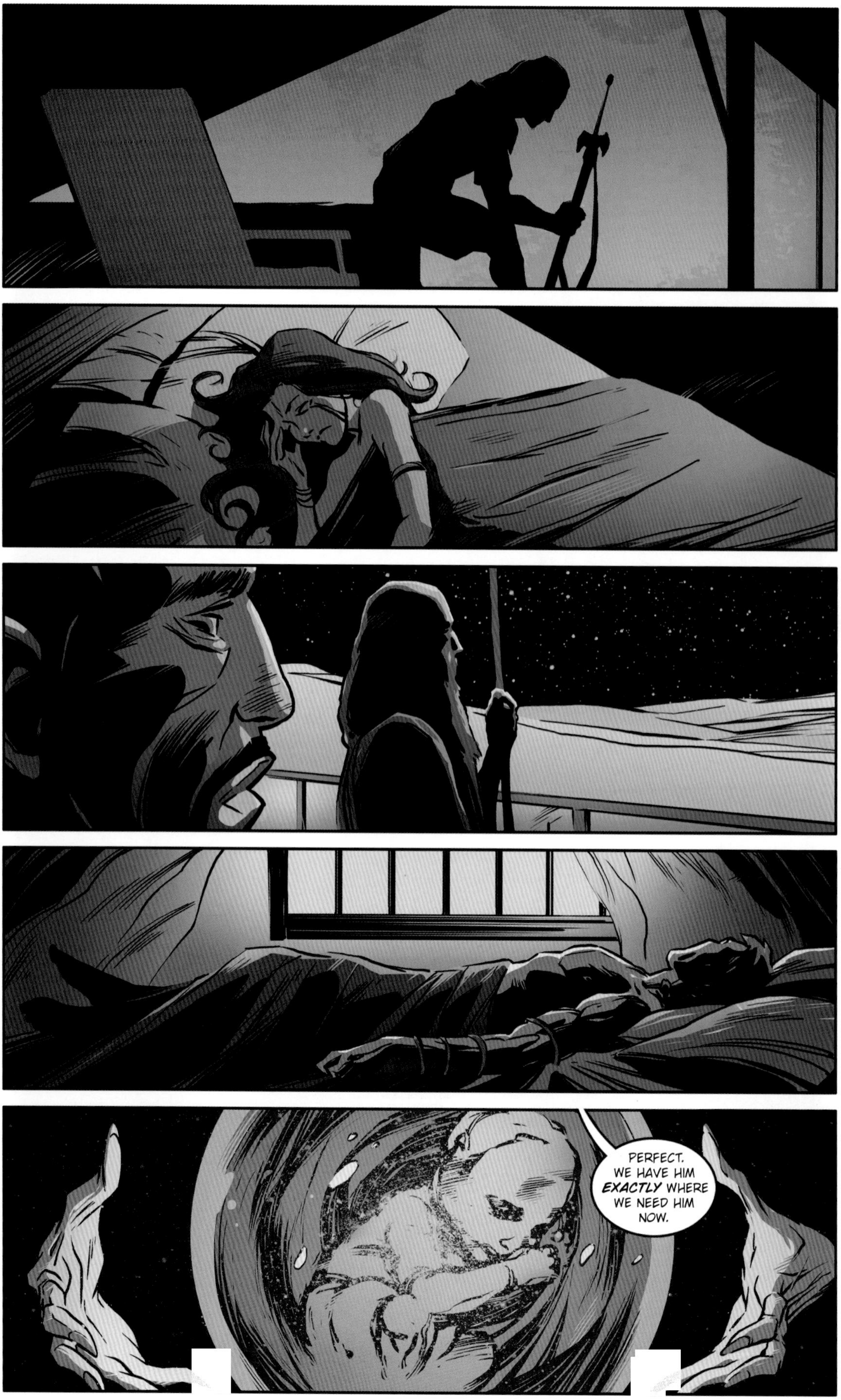
PERFECT. WE HAVE HIM EXACTLY WHERE WE NEED HIM NOW.

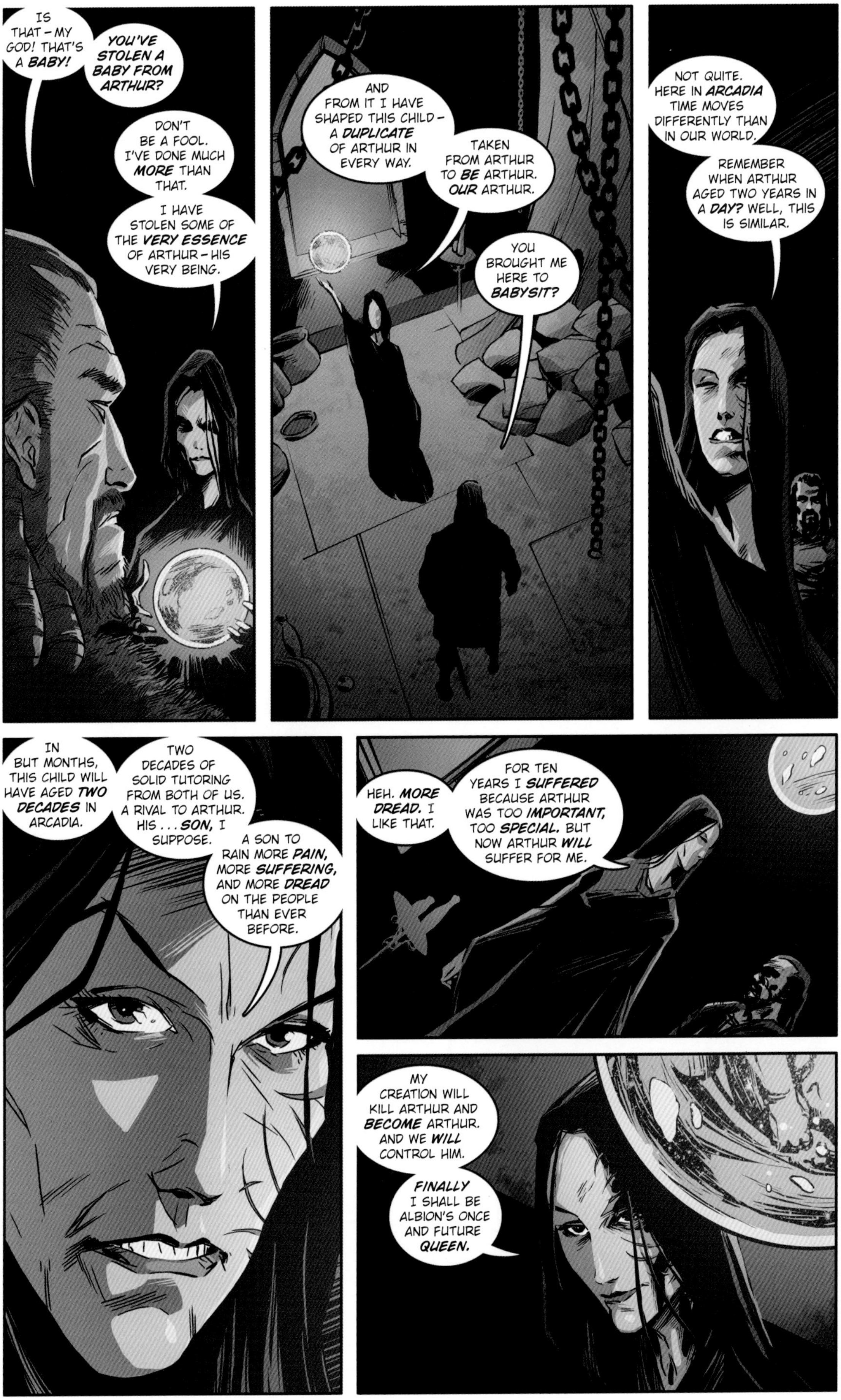
IS THAT – MY GOD! THAT'S A BABY!
YOU'VE STOLEN A BABY FROM ARTHUR?
DON'T BE A FOOL. I'VE DONE MUCH MORE THAN THAT.
I HAVE STOLEN SOME OF THE VERY ESSENCE OF ARTHUR – HIS VERY BEING.
AND FROM IT I HAVE SHAPED THIS CHILD – A DUPLICATE OF ARTHUR IN EVERY WAY.
TAKEN FROM ARTHUR TO BE ARTHUR. OUR ARTHUR.
YOU BROUGHT ME HERE TO BABYSIT?
NOT QUITE. HERE IN ARCADIA TIME MOVES DIFFERENTLY THAN IN OUR WORLD.
REMEMBER WHEN ARTHUR AGED TWO YEARS IN A DAY? WELL, THIS IS SIMILAR.
IN BUT MONTHS, THIS CHILD WILL HAVE AGED TWO DECADES IN ARCADIA.
TWO DECADES OF SOLID TUTORING FROM BOTH OF US. A RIVAL TO ARTHUR. HIS . . . SON, I SUPPOSE.
A SON TO RAIN MORE PAIN, MORE SUFFERING, AND MORE DREAD ON THE PEOPLE THAN EVER BEFORE.
HEH. MORE DREAD. I LIKE THAT.
FOR TEN YEARS I SUFFERED BECAUSE ARTHUR WAS TOO IMPORTANT, TOO SPECIAL. BUT NOW ARTHUR WILL SUFFER FOR ME.
MY CREATION WILL KILL ARTHUR AND BECOME ARTHUR. AND WE WILL CONTROL HIM.
FINALLY I SHALL BE ALBION'S ONCE AND FUTURE QUEEN.

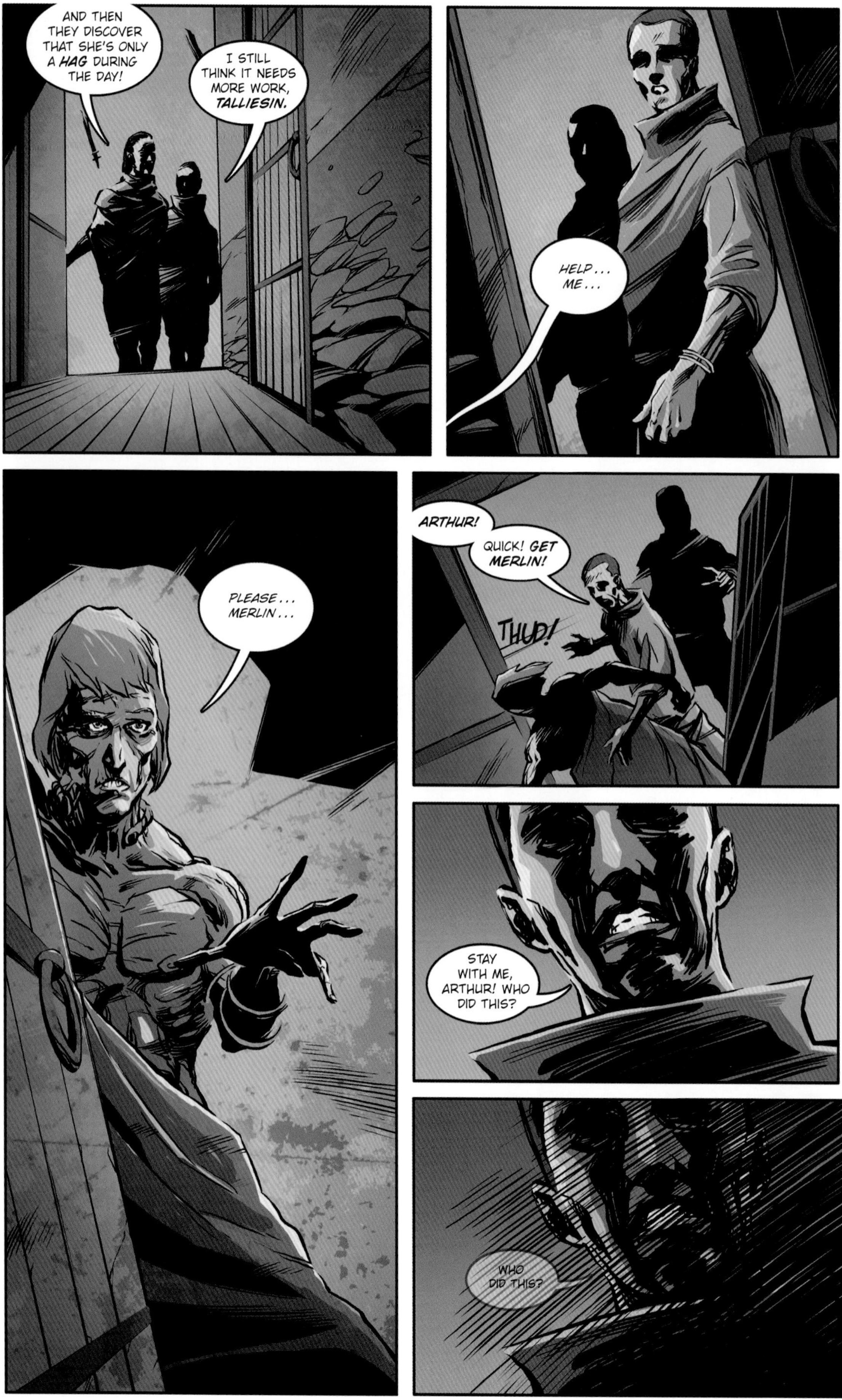
AND THEN THEY DISCOVER THAT SHE'S ONLY A HAG DURING THE DAY!
I STILL THINK IT NEEDS MORE WORK, TALLIESIN.
HELP... ME...
PLEASE... MERLIN...
ARTHUR!
QUICK! GET MERLIN!
THUD!
STAY WITH ME, ARTHUR! WHO DID THIS?
WHO DID THIS?

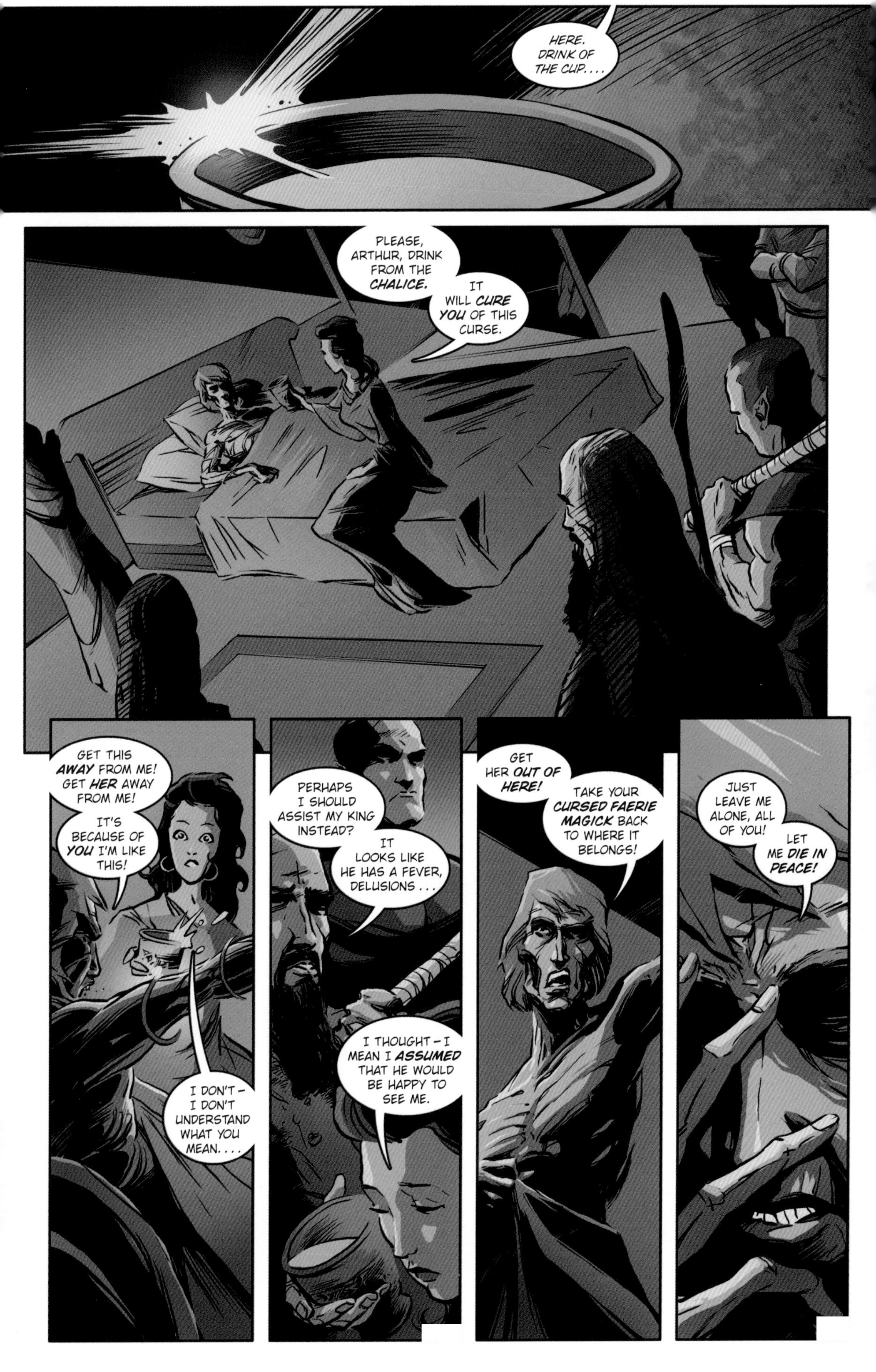
HERE. DRINK OF THE CUP. . . .
PLEASE, ARTHUR, DRINK FROM THE **CHALICE.**
IT WILL **CURE YOU** OF THIS CURSE.
GET THIS **AWAY** FROM ME! GET **HER** AWAY FROM ME!
IT'S BECAUSE OF **YOU** I'M LIKE THIS!
I DON'T - I DON'T UNDERSTAND WHAT YOU MEAN. . . .
PERHAPS I SHOULD ASSIST MY KING INSTEAD?
IT LOOKS LIKE HE HAS A FEVER, DELUSIONS . . .
I THOUGHT - I MEAN I **ASSUMED** THAT HE WOULD BE HAPPY TO SEE ME.
GET HER **OUT OF HERE!**
TAKE YOUR **CURSED FAERIE MAGICK** BACK TO WHERE IT BELONGS!
JUST LEAVE ME ALONE, ALL OF YOU!
LET ME **DIE IN PEACE!**

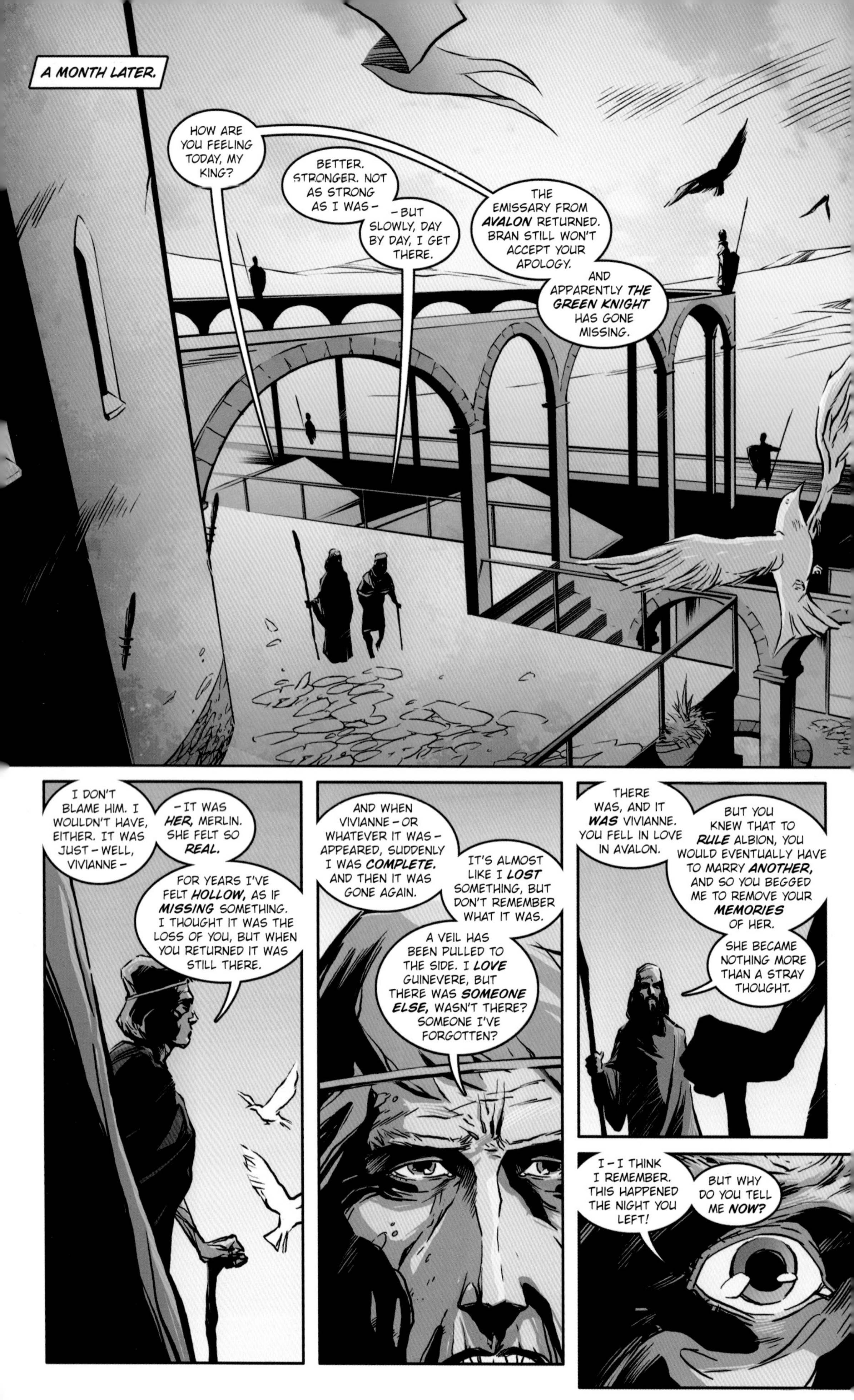
A MONTH LATER.
HOW ARE YOU FEELING TODAY, MY KING?
BETTER. STRONGER. NOT AS STRONG AS I WAS–
–BUT SLOWLY, DAY BY DAY, I GET THERE.
THE EMISSARY FROM AVALON RETURNED. BRAN STILL WON'T ACCEPT YOUR APOLOGY.
AND APPARENTLY THE GREEN KNIGHT HAS GONE MISSING.
I DON'T BLAME HIM. I WOULDN'T HAVE, EITHER. IT WAS JUST–WELL, VIVIANNE–
–IT WAS HER, MERLIN. SHE FELT SO REAL.
FOR YEARS I'VE FELT HOLLOW, AS IF MISSING SOMETHING. I THOUGHT IT WAS THE LOSS OF YOU, BUT WHEN YOU RETURNED IT WAS STILL THERE.
AND WHEN VIVIANNE–OR WHATEVER IT WAS–APPEARED, SUDDENLY I WAS COMPLETE. AND THEN IT WAS GONE AGAIN.
IT'S ALMOST LIKE I LOST SOMETHING, BUT DON'T REMEMBER WHAT IT WAS.
A VEIL HAS BEEN PULLED TO THE SIDE. I LOVE GUINEVERE, BUT THERE WAS SOMEONE ELSE, WASN'T THERE? SOMEONE I'VE FORGOTTEN?
THERE WAS, AND IT WAS VIVIANNE. YOU FELL IN LOVE IN AVALON.
BUT YOU KNEW THAT TO RULE ALBION, YOU WOULD EVENTUALLY HAVE TO MARRY ANOTHER, AND SO YOU BEGGED ME TO REMOVE YOUR MEMORIES OF HER.
SHE BECAME NOTHING MORE THAN A STRAY THOUGHT.
I–I THINK I REMEMBER. THIS HAPPENED THE NIGHT YOU LEFT!
BUT WHY DO YOU TELL ME NOW?

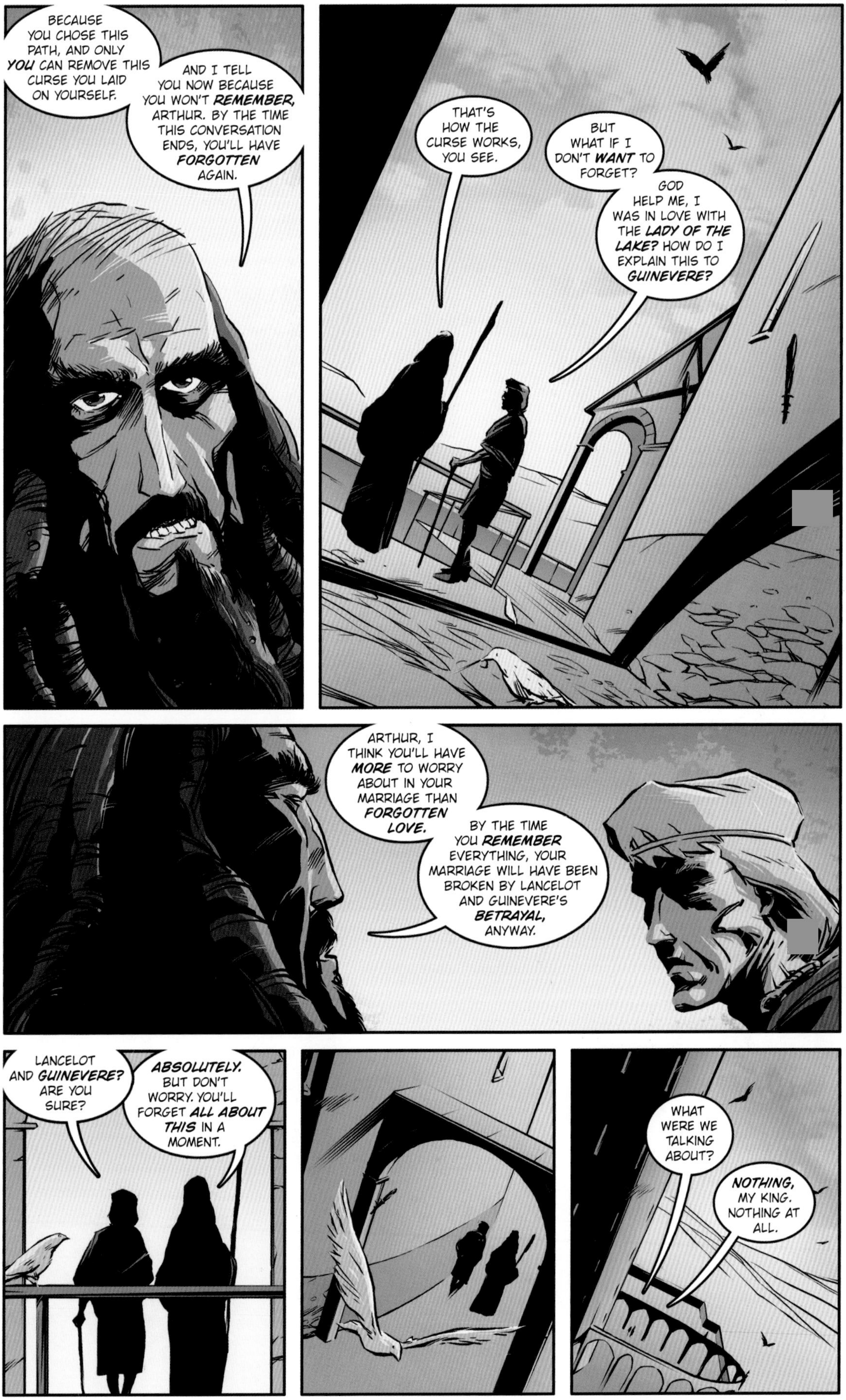
BECAUSE YOU CHOSE THIS PATH, AND ONLY YOU CAN REMOVE THIS CURSE YOU LAID ON YOURSELF.
AND I TELL YOU NOW BECAUSE YOU WON'T REMEMBER, ARTHUR. BY THE TIME THIS CONVERSATION ENDS, YOU'LL HAVE FORGOTTEN AGAIN.
THAT'S HOW THE CURSE WORKS, YOU SEE.
BUT WHAT IF I DON'T WANT TO FORGET?
GOD HELP ME, I WAS IN LOVE WITH THE LADY OF THE LAKE? HOW DO I EXPLAIN THIS TO GUINEVERE?
ARTHUR, I THINK YOU'LL HAVE MORE TO WORRY ABOUT IN YOUR MARRIAGE THAN FORGOTTEN LOVE.
BY THE TIME YOU REMEMBER EVERYTHING, YOUR MARRIAGE WILL HAVE BEEN BROKEN BY LANCELOT AND GUINEVERE'S BETRAYAL, ANYWAY.
LANCELOT AND GUINEVERE? ARE YOU SURE?
ABSOLUTELY. BUT DON'T WORRY. YOU'LL FORGET ALL ABOUT THIS IN A MOMENT.
WHAT WERE WE TALKING ABOUT?
NOTHING, MY KING. NOTHING AT ALL.

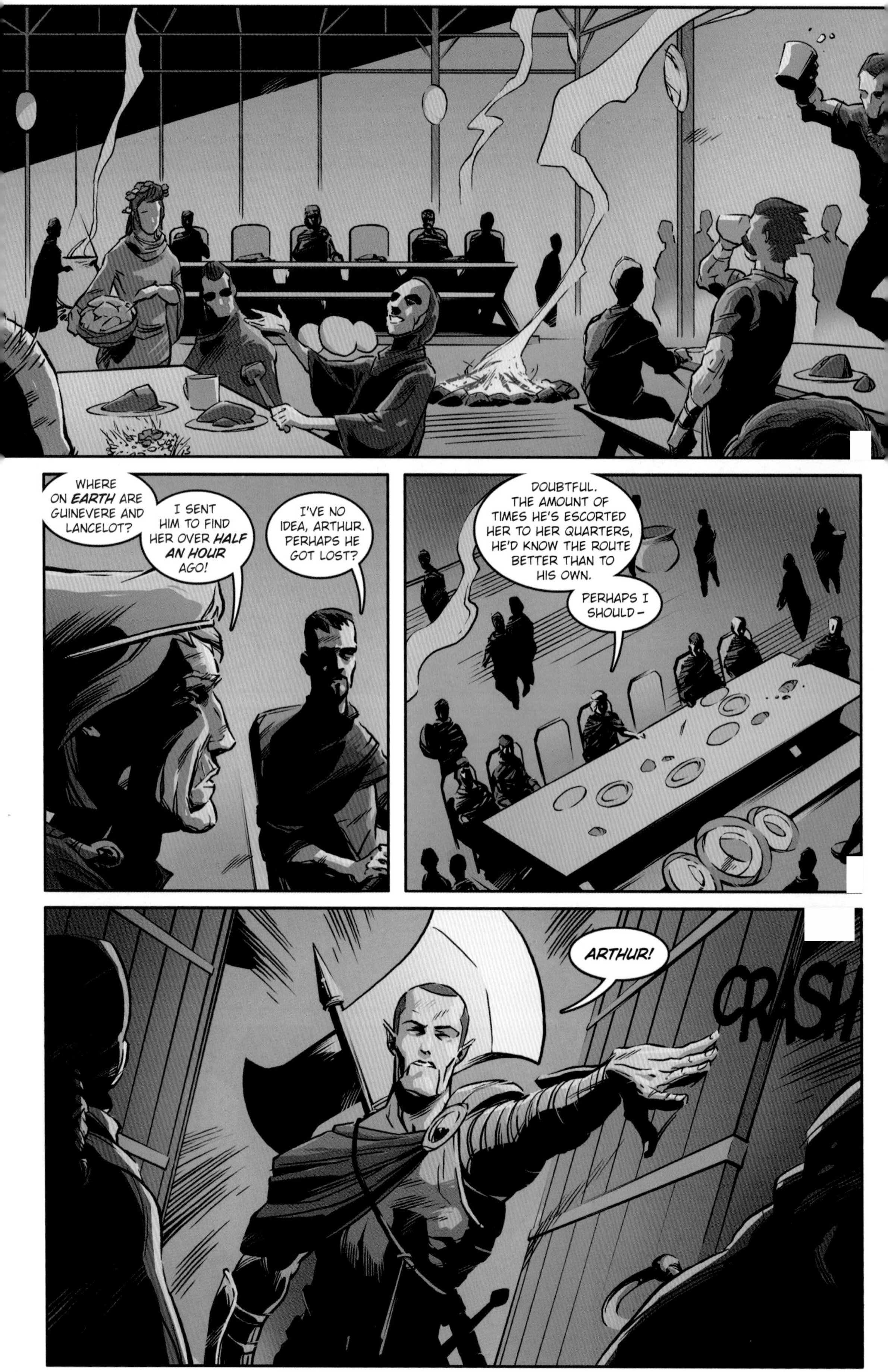
WHERE ON EARTH ARE GUINEVERE AND LANCELOT?
I SENT HIM TO FIND HER OVER HALF AN HOUR AGO!
I'VE NO IDEA, ARTHUR. PERHAPS HE GOT LOST?
DOUBTFUL. THE AMOUNT OF TIMES HE'S ESCORTED HER TO HER QUARTERS, HE'D KNOW THE ROUTE BETTER THAN TO HIS OWN.
PERHAPS I SHOULD–
ARTHUR!
CRASH

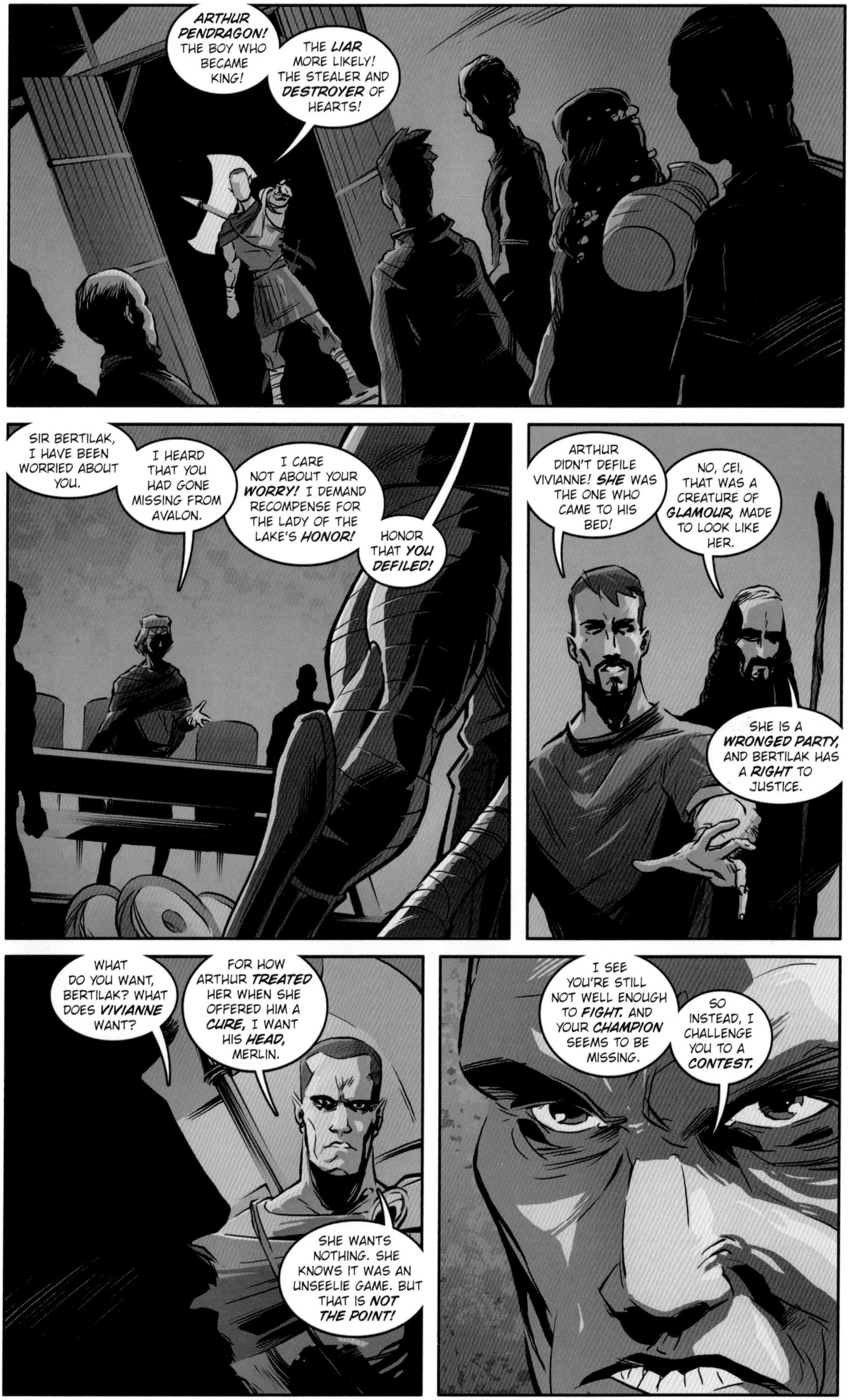
ARTHUR PENDRAGON! THE BOY WHO BECAME KING!
THE LIAR MORE LIKELY! THE STEALER AND DESTROYER OF HEARTS!
SIR BERTILAK, I HAVE BEEN WORRIED ABOUT YOU.
I HEARD THAT YOU HAD GONE MISSING FROM AVALON.
I CARE NOT ABOUT YOUR WORRY! I DEMAND RECOMPENSE FOR THE LADY OF THE LAKE'S HONOR!
HONOR THAT YOU DEFILED!
ARTHUR DIDN'T DEFILE VIVIANNE! SHE WAS THE ONE WHO CAME TO HIS BED!
NO, CEI, THAT WAS A CREATURE OF GLAMOUR, MADE TO LOOK LIKE HER.
SHE IS A WRONGED PARTY, AND BERTILAK HAS A RIGHT TO JUSTICE.
WHAT DO YOU WANT, BERTILAK? WHAT DOES VIVIANNE WANT?
FOR HOW ARTHUR TREATED HER WHEN SHE OFFERED HIM A CURE, I WANT HIS HEAD, MERLIN.
SHE WANTS NOTHING. SHE KNOWS IT WAS AN UNSEELIE GAME. BUT THAT IS NOT THE POINT!
I SEE YOU'RE STILL NOT WELL ENOUGH TO FIGHT. AND YOUR CHAMPION SEEMS TO BE MISSING.
SO INSTEAD, I CHALLENGE YOU TO A CONTEST.

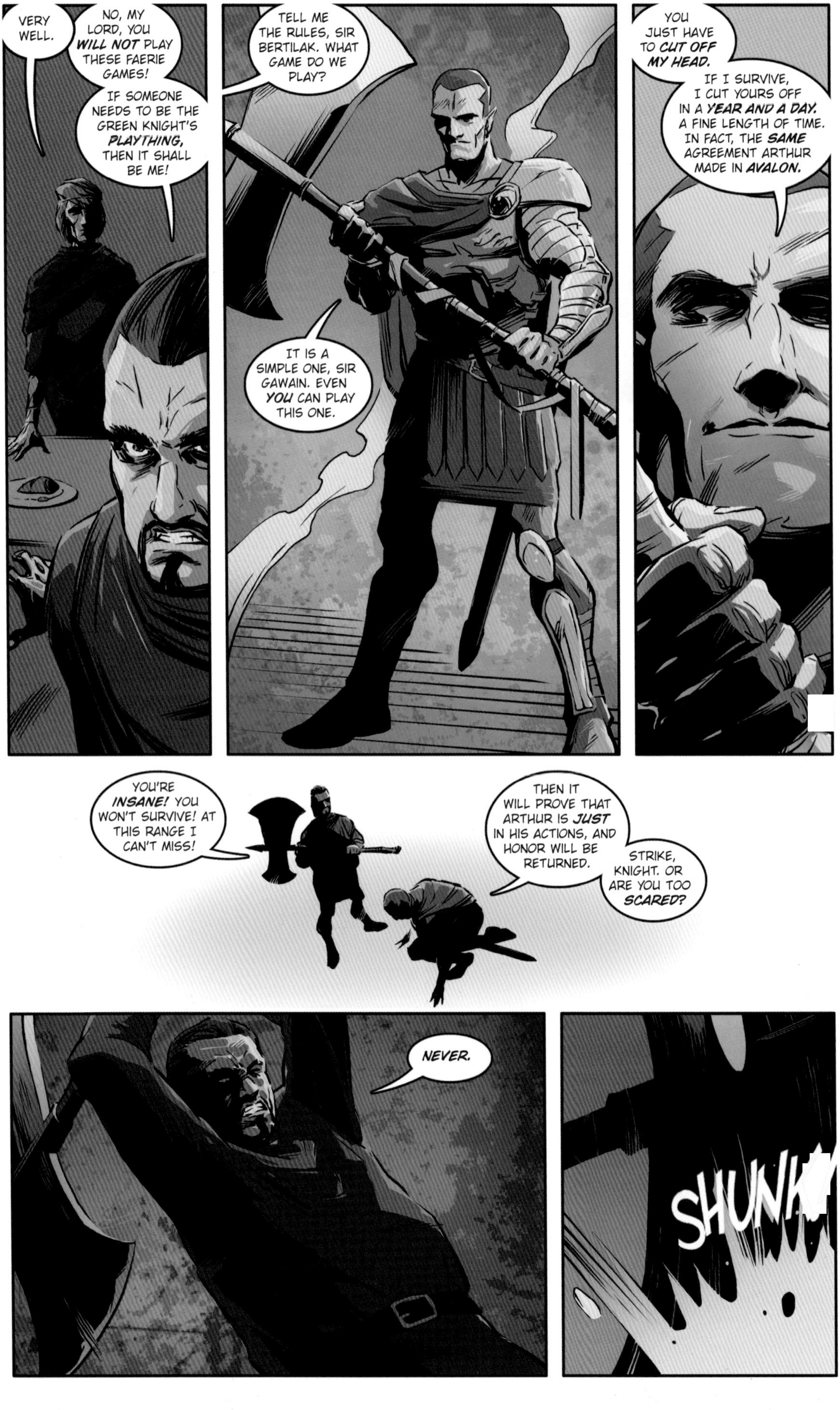

VERY WELL.
NO, MY LORD, YOU WILL NOT PLAY THESE FAERIE GAMES!
IF SOMEONE NEEDS TO BE THE GREEN KNIGHT'S PLAYTHING, THEN IT SHALL BE ME!
TELL ME THE RULES, SIR BERTILAK. WHAT GAME DO WE PLAY?
IT IS A SIMPLE ONE, SIR GAWAIN. EVEN YOU CAN PLAY THIS ONE.
YOU JUST HAVE TO CUT OFF MY HEAD.
IF I SURVIVE, I CUT YOURS OFF IN A YEAR AND A DAY. A FINE LENGTH OF TIME. IN FACT, THE SAME AGREEMENT ARTHUR MADE IN AVALON.
YOU'RE INSANE! YOU WON'T SURVIVE! AT THIS RANGE I CAN'T MISS!
THEN IT WILL PROVE THAT ARTHUR IS JUST IN HIS ACTIONS, AND HONOR WILL BE RETURNED.
STRIKE, KNIGHT. OR ARE YOU TOO SCARED?
NEVER.
SHUNK

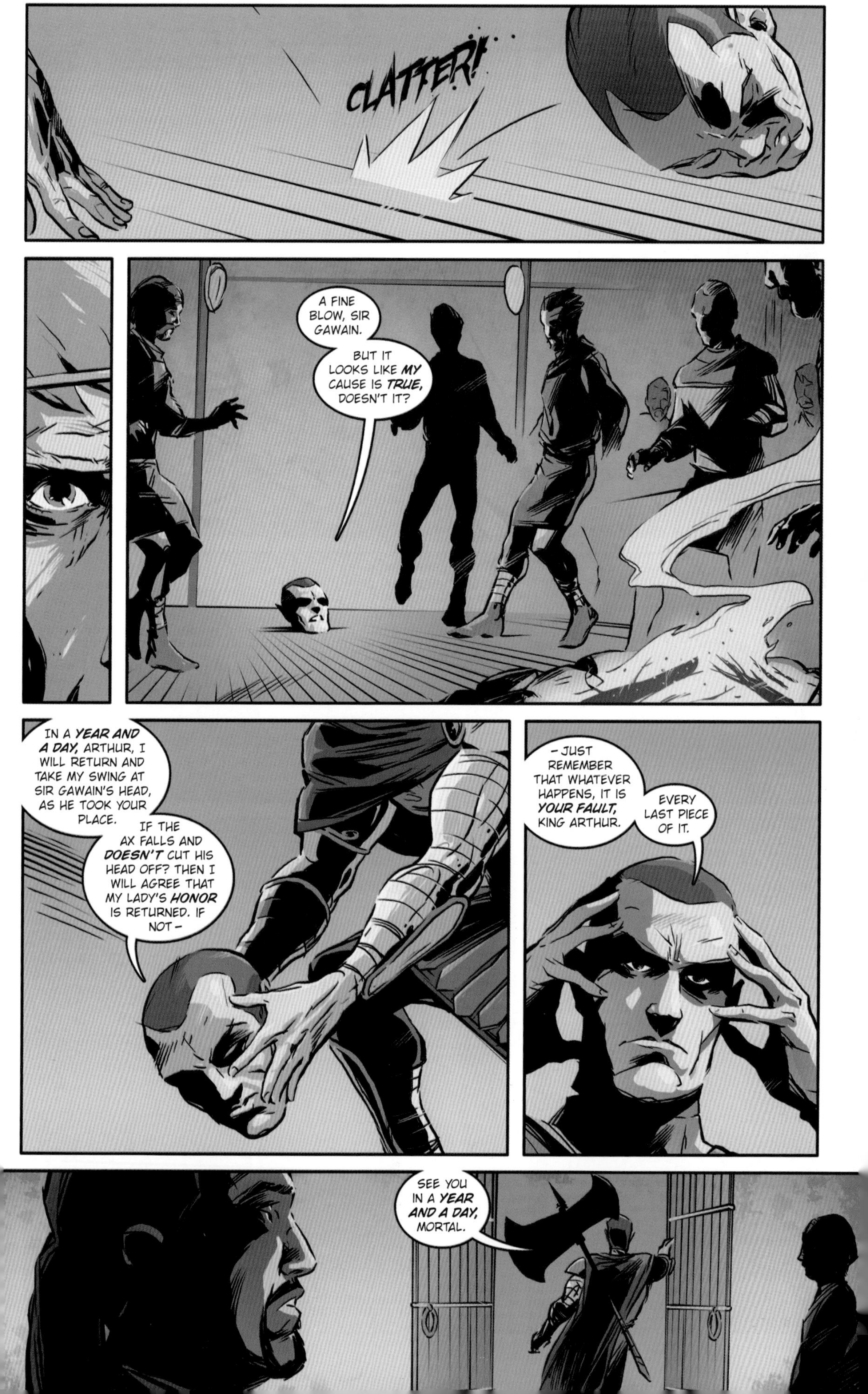
CLATTER!
A FINE BLOW, SIR GAWAIN.
BUT IT LOOKS LIKE MY CAUSE IS TRUE, DOESN'T IT?
IN A YEAR AND A DAY, ARTHUR, I WILL RETURN AND TAKE MY SWING AT SIR GAWAIN'S HEAD, AS HE TOOK YOUR PLACE.
IF THE AX FALLS AND DOESN'T CUT HIS HEAD OFF? THEN I WILL AGREE THAT MY LADY'S HONOR IS RETURNED. IF NOT –
– JUST REMEMBER THAT WHATEVER HAPPENS, IT IS YOUR FAULT, KING ARTHUR.
EVERY LAST PIECE OF IT.
SEE YOU IN A YEAR AND A DAY, MORTAL.

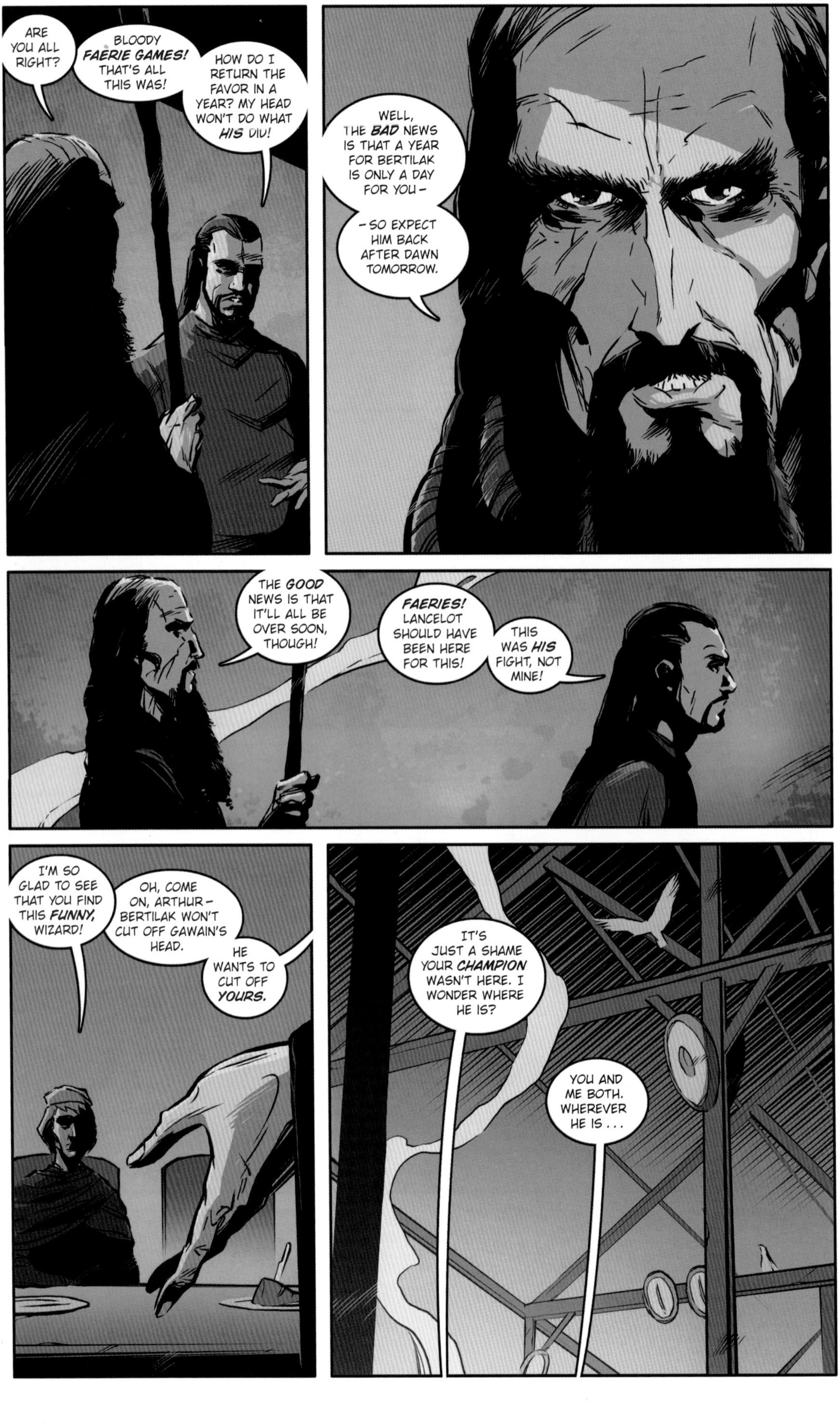

ARE YOU ALL RIGHT?
BLOODY FAERIE GAMES! THAT'S ALL THIS WAS!
HOW DO I RETURN THE FAVOR IN A YEAR? MY HEAD WON'T DO WHAT HIS DID!
WELL, THE BAD NEWS IS THAT A YEAR FOR BERTILAK IS ONLY A DAY FOR YOU –
– SO EXPECT HIM BACK AFTER DAWN TOMORROW.
THE GOOD NEWS IS THAT IT'LL ALL BE OVER SOON, THOUGH!
FAERIES! LANCELOT SHOULD HAVE BEEN HERE FOR THIS!
THIS WAS HIS FIGHT, NOT MINE!
I'M SO GLAD TO SEE THAT YOU FIND THIS FUNNY, WIZARD!
OH, COME ON, ARTHUR – BERTILAK WON'T CUT OFF GAWAIN'S HEAD.
HE WANTS TO CUT OFF YOURS.
IT'S JUST A SHAME YOUR CHAMPION WASN'T HERE. I WONDER WHERE HE IS?
YOU AND ME BOTH. WHEREVER HE IS . . .

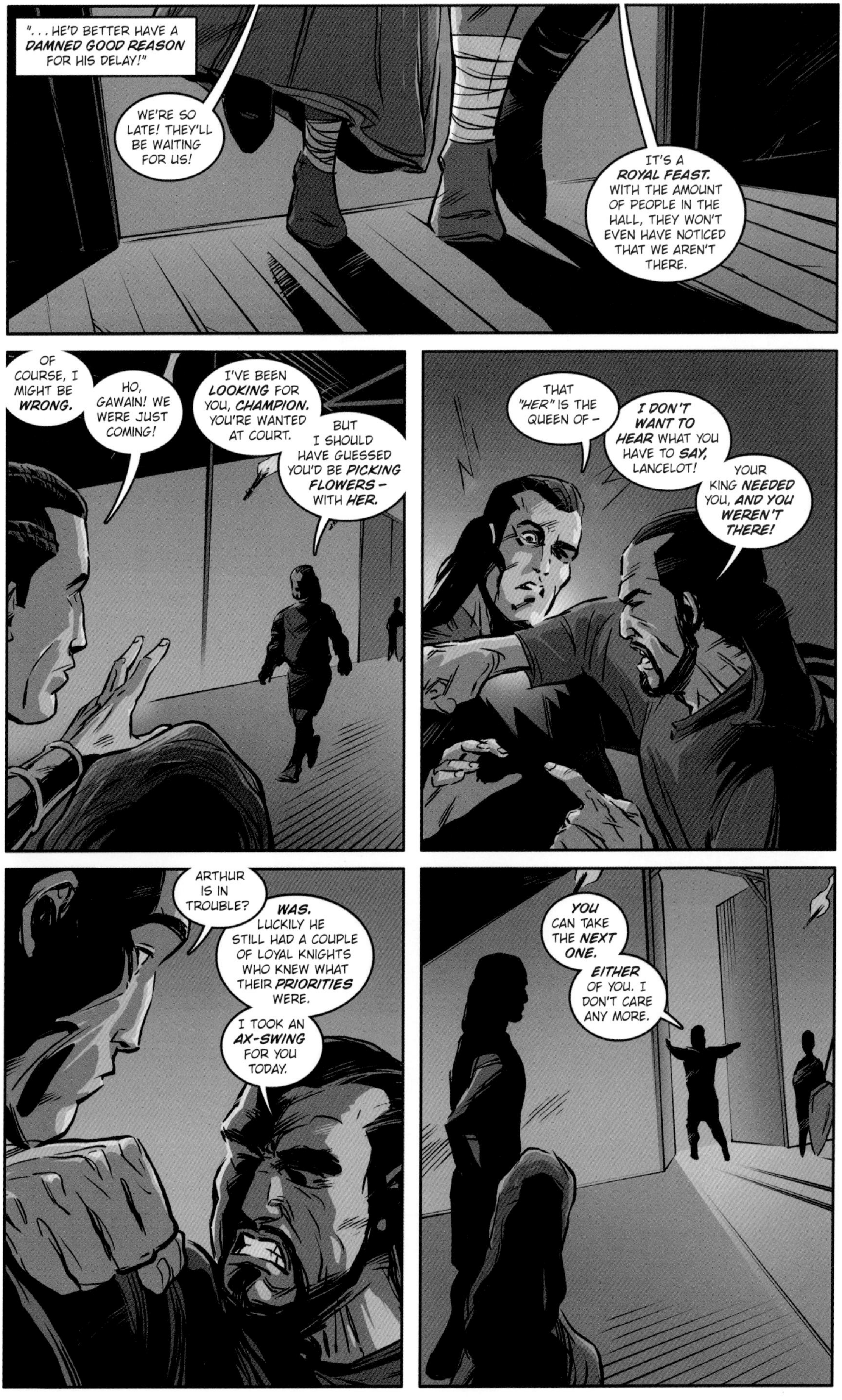
". . . HE'D BETTER HAVE A DAMNED GOOD REASON FOR HIS DELAY!"
WE'RE SO LATE! THEY'LL BE WAITING FOR US!
IT'S A ROYAL FEAST. WITH THE AMOUNT OF PEOPLE IN THE HALL, THEY WON'T EVEN HAVE NOTICED THAT WE AREN'T THERE.
OF COURSE, I MIGHT BE WRONG.
HO, GAWAIN! WE WERE JUST COMING!
I'VE BEEN LOOKING FOR YOU, CHAMPION. YOU'RE WANTED AT COURT.
BUT I SHOULD HAVE GUESSED YOU'D BE PICKING FLOWERS – WITH HER.
THAT "HER" IS THE QUEEN OF –
I DON'T WANT TO HEAR WHAT YOU HAVE TO SAY, LANCELOT!
YOUR KING NEEDED YOU, AND YOU WEREN'T THERE!
ARTHUR IS IN TROUBLE?
WAS. LUCKILY HE STILL HAD A COUPLE OF LOYAL KNIGHTS WHO KNEW WHAT THEIR PRIORITIES WERE.
I TOOK AN AX-SWING FOR YOU TODAY.
YOU CAN TAKE THE NEXT ONE.
EITHER OF YOU. I DON'T CARE ANY MORE.

I FOUND YOUR MISSING CHAMPION, MY LORD.

MY KING, I AM *SORRY* FOR OUR DELAY.

THE QUEEN WAS FEELING UNWELL AND I HAD TO WAIT FOR HER. BUT GAWAIN'S WORDS—

THE FEAST HAS *ENDED*, MY QUEEN. WHICH MEANS THAT YOU'RE NOT LATE—YOU WERE *ABSENT ENTIRELY*.

AND IF *EITHER* OF YOU HAVE AN ISSUE WITH GAWAIN, WHO TOOK LANCELOT'S PLACE TONIGHT IN MY *DEFENSE*—

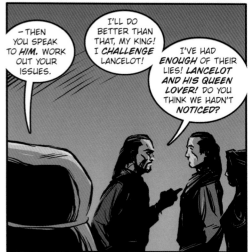

—THEN YOU SPEAK TO *HIM*. WORK OUT YOUR ISSUES.

I'LL DO BETTER THAN THAT, MY KING! I *CHALLENGE* LANCELOT!

I'VE HAD *ENOUGH* OF THEIR LIES! *LANCELOT AND HIS QUEEN LOVER!* DO YOU THINK WE HADN'T *NOTICED?*

I SAW YOU AT THE *CARAVAN!* WE'VE SEEN YOU IN THE *GARDEN!*

THERE'S NOT A *KNIGHT IN CAMELOT* WHO DOESN'T KNOW OF YOUR SECRET! YOU MAKE A *MOCKERY* OF THE MARRIAGE—

OH, TRUST ME, GAWAIN, *THAT* ISN'T A MOCKERY OF THEIR MARRIAGE—

—BUT I'M ABOUT TO SHOW YOU SOMETHING THAT *IS*.

HELLO, *BROTHER.*

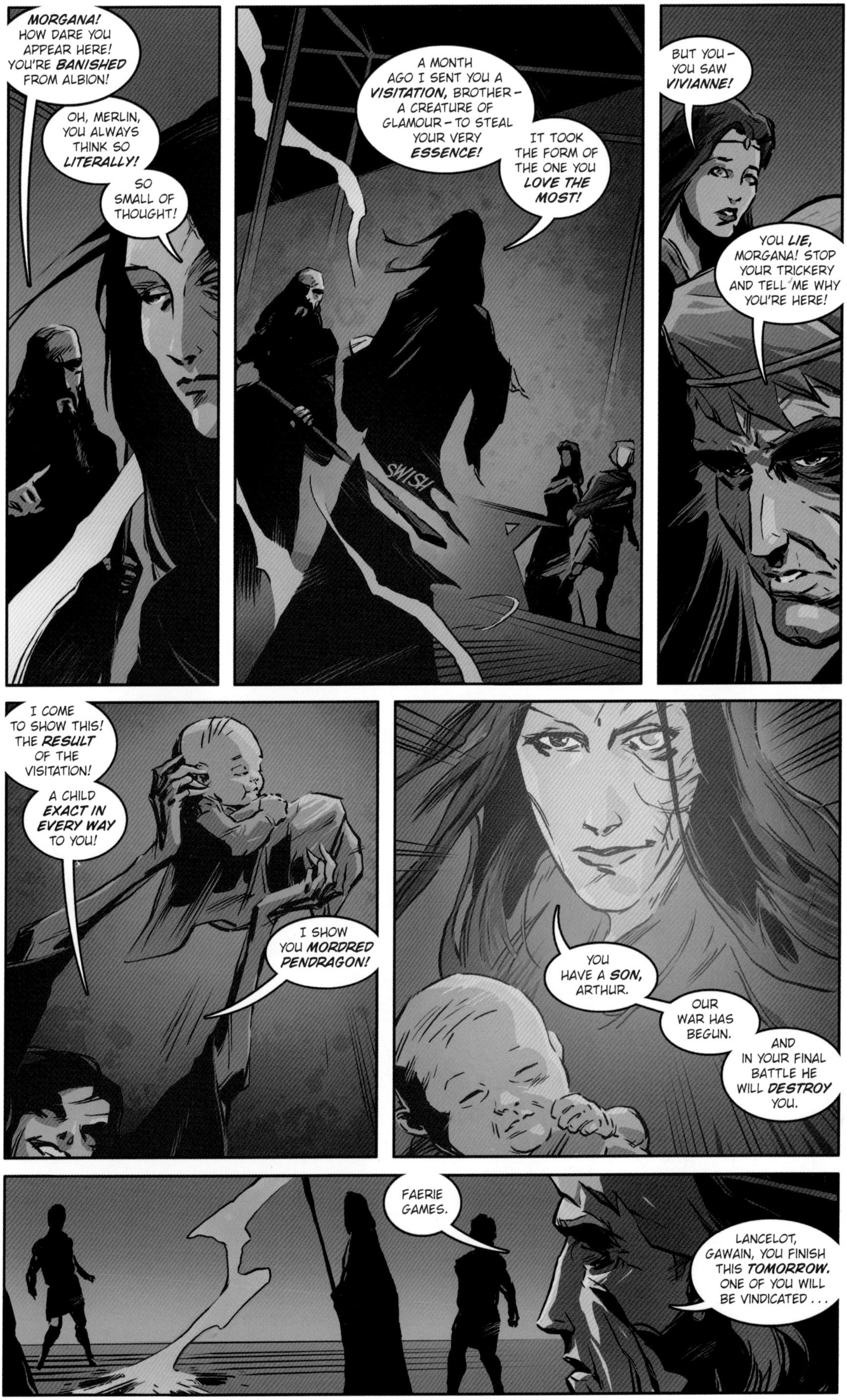

MORGANA! HOW DARE YOU APPEAR HERE! YOU'RE BANISHED FROM ALBION!
OH, MERLIN, YOU ALWAYS THINK SO LITERALLY!
SO SMALL OF THOUGHT!
A MONTH AGO I SENT YOU A VISITATION, BROTHER – A CREATURE OF GLAMOUR – TO STEAL YOUR VERY ESSENCE!
IT TOOK THE FORM OF THE ONE YOU LOVE THE MOST!
SWISH
BUT YOU – YOU SAW VIVIANNE!
YOU LIE, MORGANA! STOP YOUR TRICKERY AND TELL ME WHY YOU'RE HERE!
I COME TO SHOW THIS! THE RESULT OF THE VISITATION!
A CHILD EXACT IN EVERY WAY TO YOU!
I SHOW YOU MORDRED PENDRAGON!
YOU HAVE A SON, ARTHUR.
OUR WAR HAS BEGUN.
AND IN YOUR FINAL BATTLE HE WILL DESTROY YOU.
FAERIE GAMES.
LANCELOT, GAWAIN, YOU FINISH THIS TOMORROW. ONE OF YOU WILL BE VINDICATED . . .

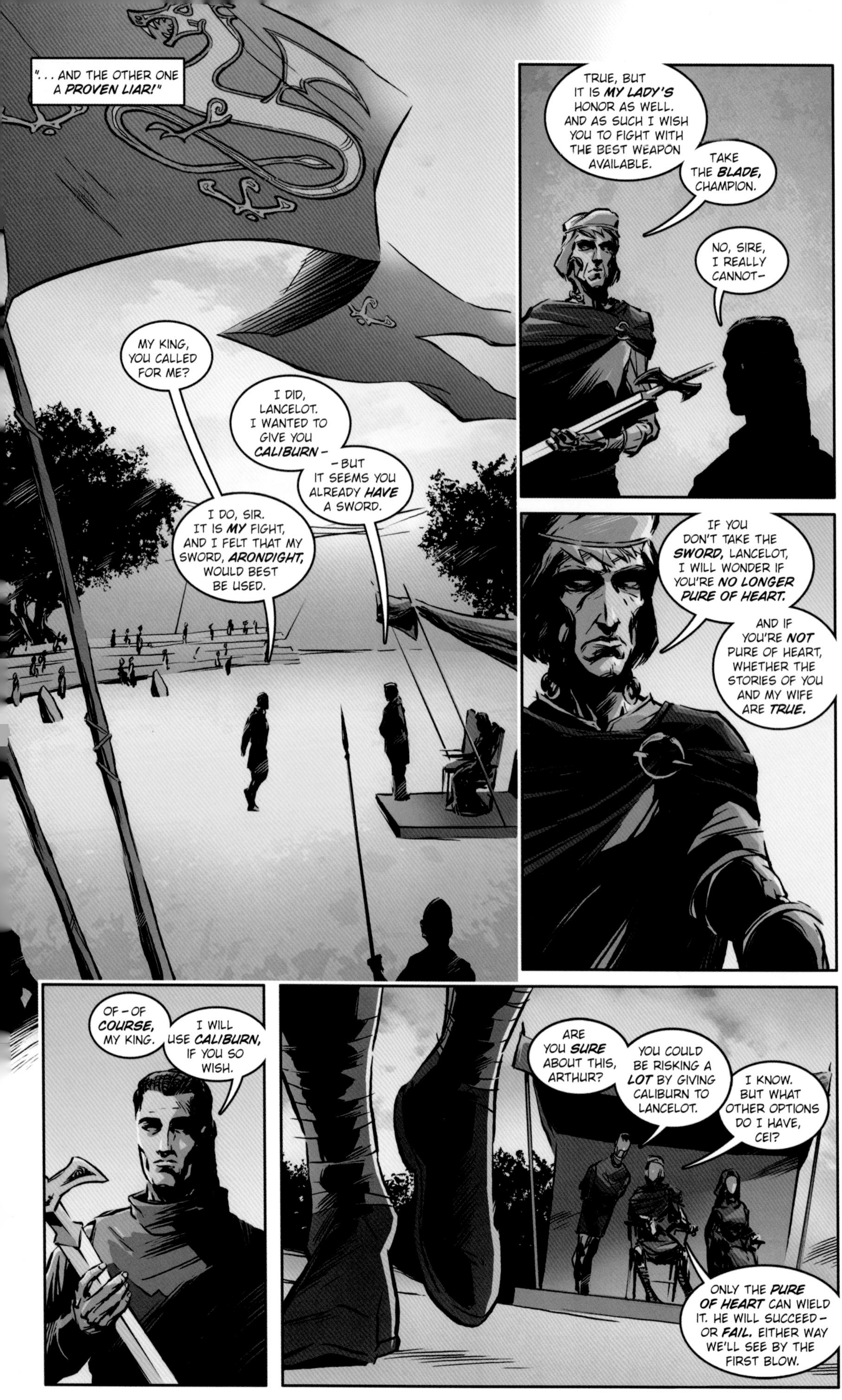
". . . AND THE OTHER ONE A *PROVEN LIAR!*"
MY KING, YOU CALLED FOR ME?
I DID, LANCELOT. I WANTED TO GIVE YOU *CALIBURN* –
– BUT IT SEEMS YOU ALREADY *HAVE* A SWORD.
I DO, SIR. IT IS *MY* FIGHT, AND I FELT THAT MY SWORD, *ARONDIGHT,* WOULD BEST BE USED.
TRUE, BUT IT IS *MY LADY'S* HONOR AS WELL. AND AS SUCH I WISH YOU TO FIGHT WITH THE BEST WEAPON AVAILABLE.
TAKE THE *BLADE,* CHAMPION.
NO, SIRE, I REALLY CANNOT–
IF YOU DON'T TAKE THE *SWORD,* LANCELOT, I WILL WONDER IF YOU'RE *NO LONGER PURE OF HEART.*
AND IF YOU'RE *NOT* PURE OF HEART, WHETHER THE STORIES OF YOU AND MY WIFE ARE *TRUE.*
OF – OF *COURSE,* MY KING.
I WILL USE *CALIBURN,* IF YOU SO WISH.
ARE YOU *SURE* ABOUT THIS, ARTHUR?
YOU COULD BE RISKING A *LOT* BY GIVING CALIBURN TO LANCELOT.
I KNOW. BUT WHAT OTHER OPTIONS DO I HAVE, CEI?
ONLY THE *PURE OF HEART* CAN WIELD IT. HE WILL SUCCEED – OR *FAIL.* EITHER WAY WE'LL SEE BY THE FIRST BLOW.

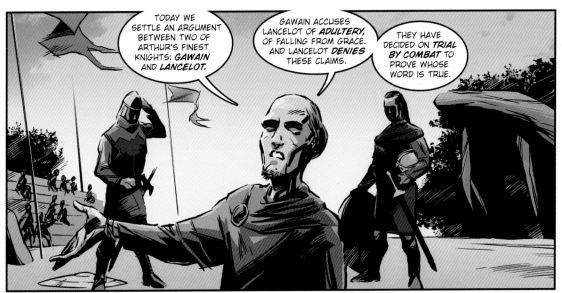

TODAY WE SETTLE AN ARGUMENT BETWEEN TWO OF ARTHUR'S FINEST KNIGHTS: *GAWAIN* AND *LANCELOT.*

GAWAIN ACCUSES LANCELOT OF *ADULTERY,* OF FALLING FROM GRACE. AND LANCELOT *DENIES* THESE CLAIMS.

THEY HAVE DECIDED ON *TRIAL BY COMBAT* TO PROVE WHOSE WORD IS TRUE.

IF THIS FIGHT ENDS AND YOU ARE PROVEN A *LIAR?* FOR WHAT YOU HAVE SAID ABOUT MY DAUGHTER –

– I WILL *CUT OUT YOUR SPLEEN* WITH A CUTLERY KNIFE.

AND YOU – IF YOU PROVE TO BE A *FALSE* KNIGHT –

– I'LL LEAVE YOU TO *ARTHUR.* AND IT'LL BE *WORSE.*

*FIGHT!*

I DON'T WANT TO *FIGHT* YOU, GAWAIN. YOU'RE MY BROTHER KNIGHT–

I'M NO BROTHER TO *ADULTEROUS SCUM* LIKE YOU! YOU'VE BROKEN THE CIRCLE! *DOOMED US ALL!*

AND THAT HARLOT IS NO *QUEEN OF MINE!*

NEVER CALL GUINEVERE THAT!

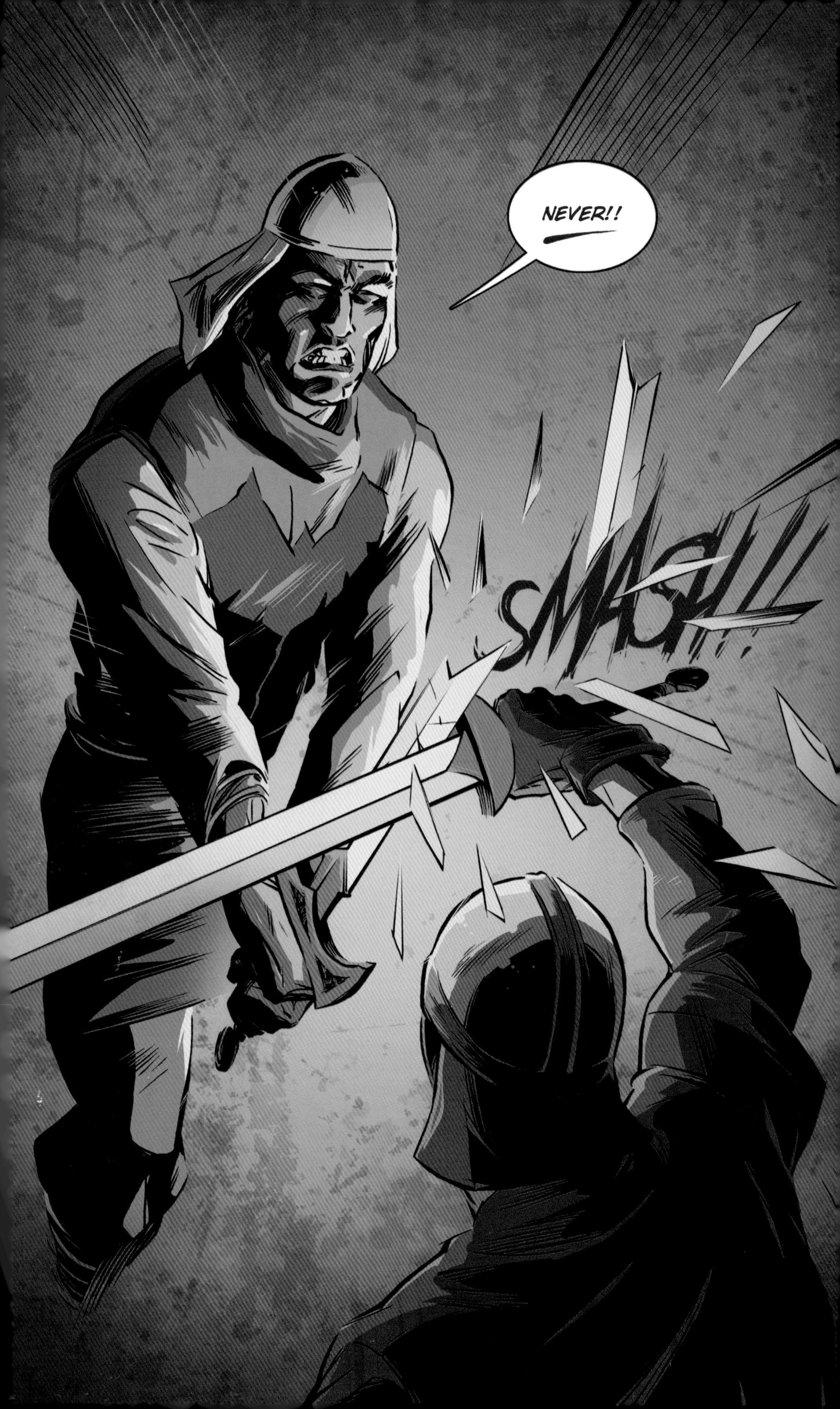
NEVER!!
SMASH!!

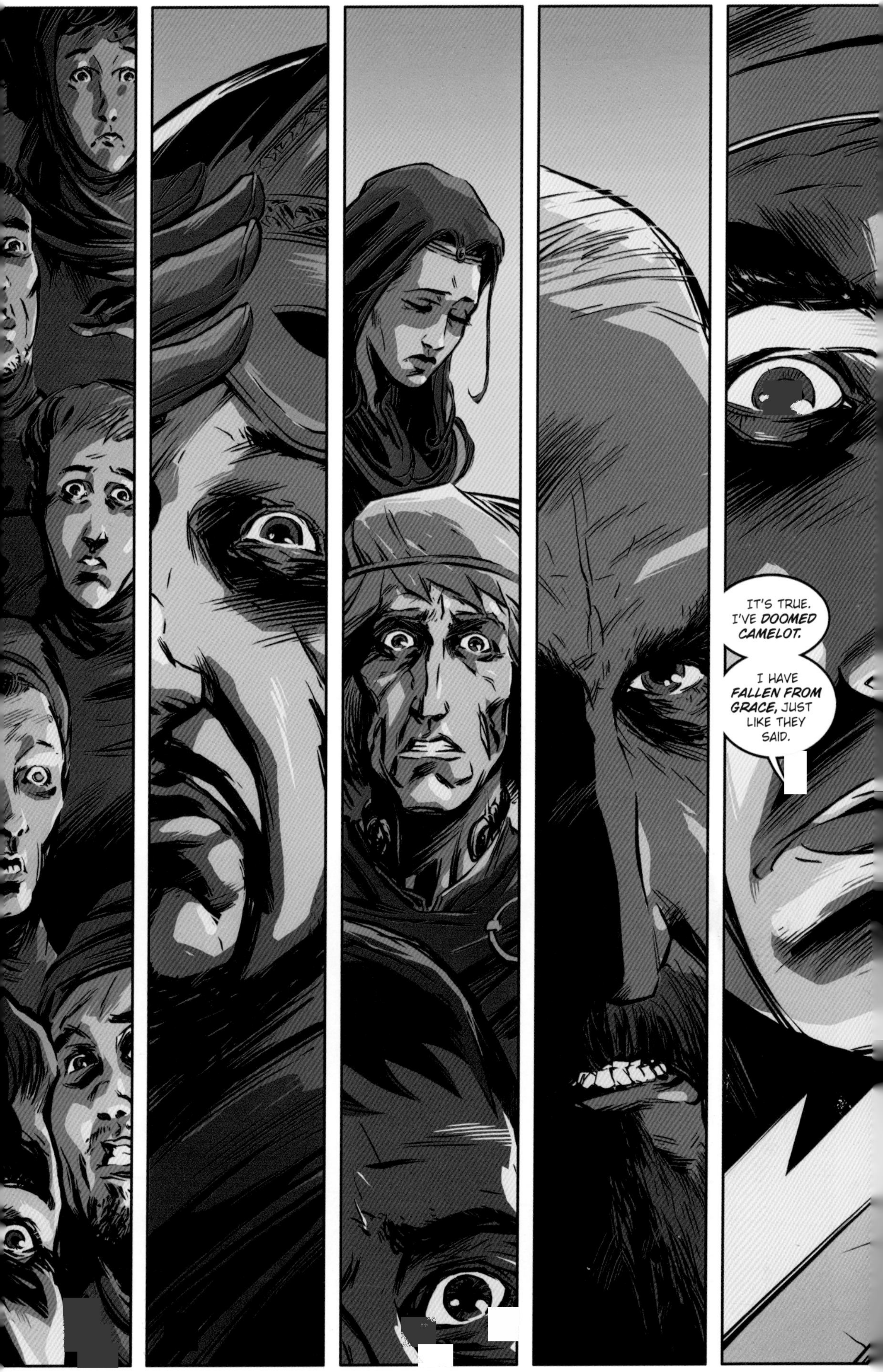
IT'S TRUE. I'VE *DOOMED CAMELOT.*
I HAVE *FALLEN FROM GRACE,* JUST LIKE THEY SAID.

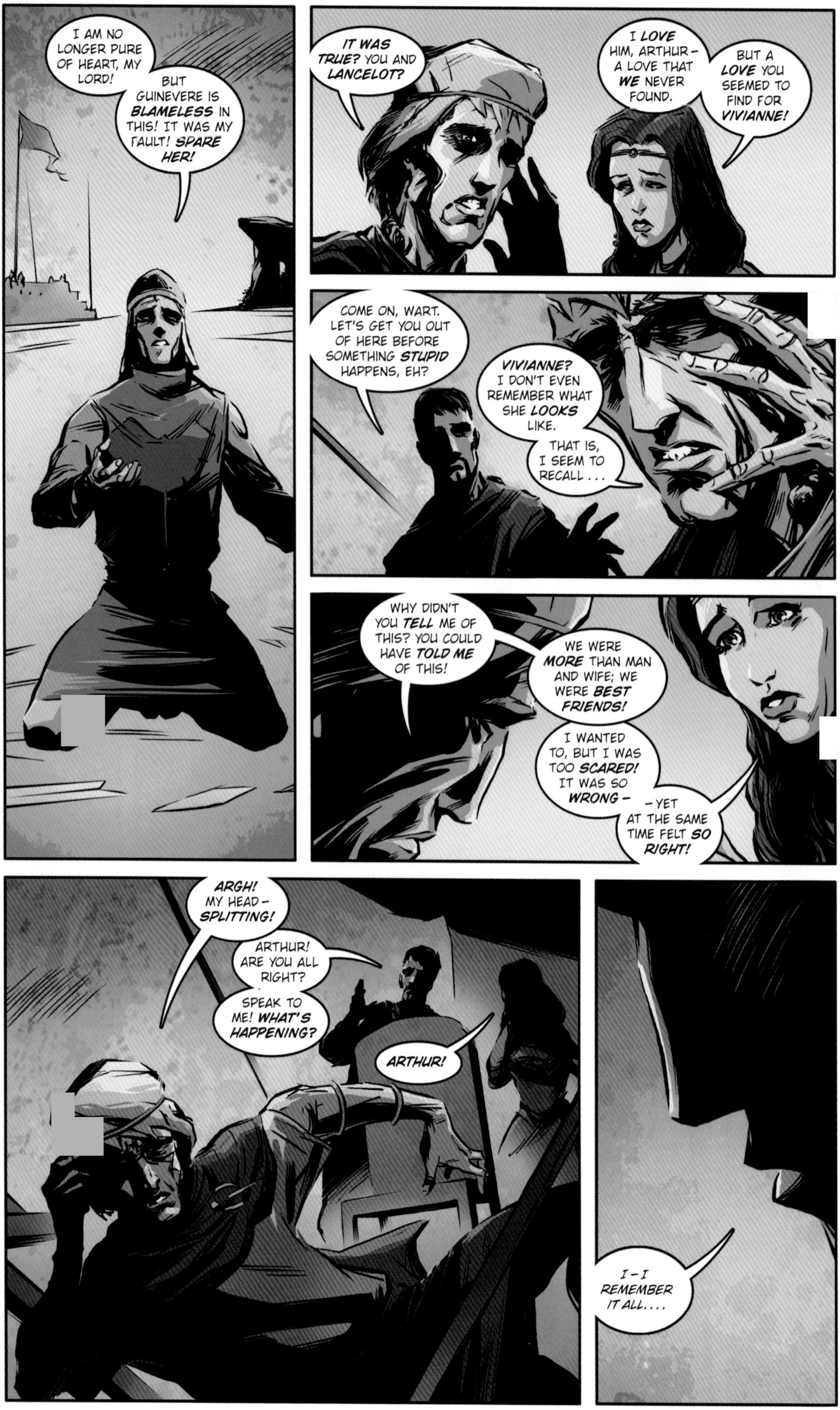
I AM NO LONGER PURE OF HEART, MY LORD!
BUT GUINEVERE IS BLAMELESS IN THIS! IT WAS MY FAULT! SPARE HER!
IT WAS TRUE? YOU AND LANCELOT?
I LOVE HIM, ARTHUR – A LOVE THAT WE NEVER FOUND.
BUT A LOVE YOU SEEMED TO FIND FOR VIVIANNE!
COME ON, WART. LET'S GET YOU OUT OF HERE BEFORE SOMETHING STUPID HAPPENS, EH?
VIVIANNE? I DON'T EVEN REMEMBER WHAT SHE LOOKS LIKE.
THAT IS, I SEEM TO RECALL . . .
WHY DIDN'T YOU TELL ME OF THIS? YOU COULD HAVE TOLD ME OF THIS!
WE WERE MORE THAN MAN AND WIFE; WE WERE BEST FRIENDS!
I WANTED TO, BUT I WAS TOO SCARED! IT WAS SO WRONG –
– YET AT THE SAME TIME FELT SO RIGHT!
ARGH! MY HEAD – SPLITTING!
ARTHUR! ARE YOU ALL RIGHT?
SPEAK TO ME! WHAT'S HAPPENING?
ARTHUR!
I – I REMEMBER IT ALL. . . .

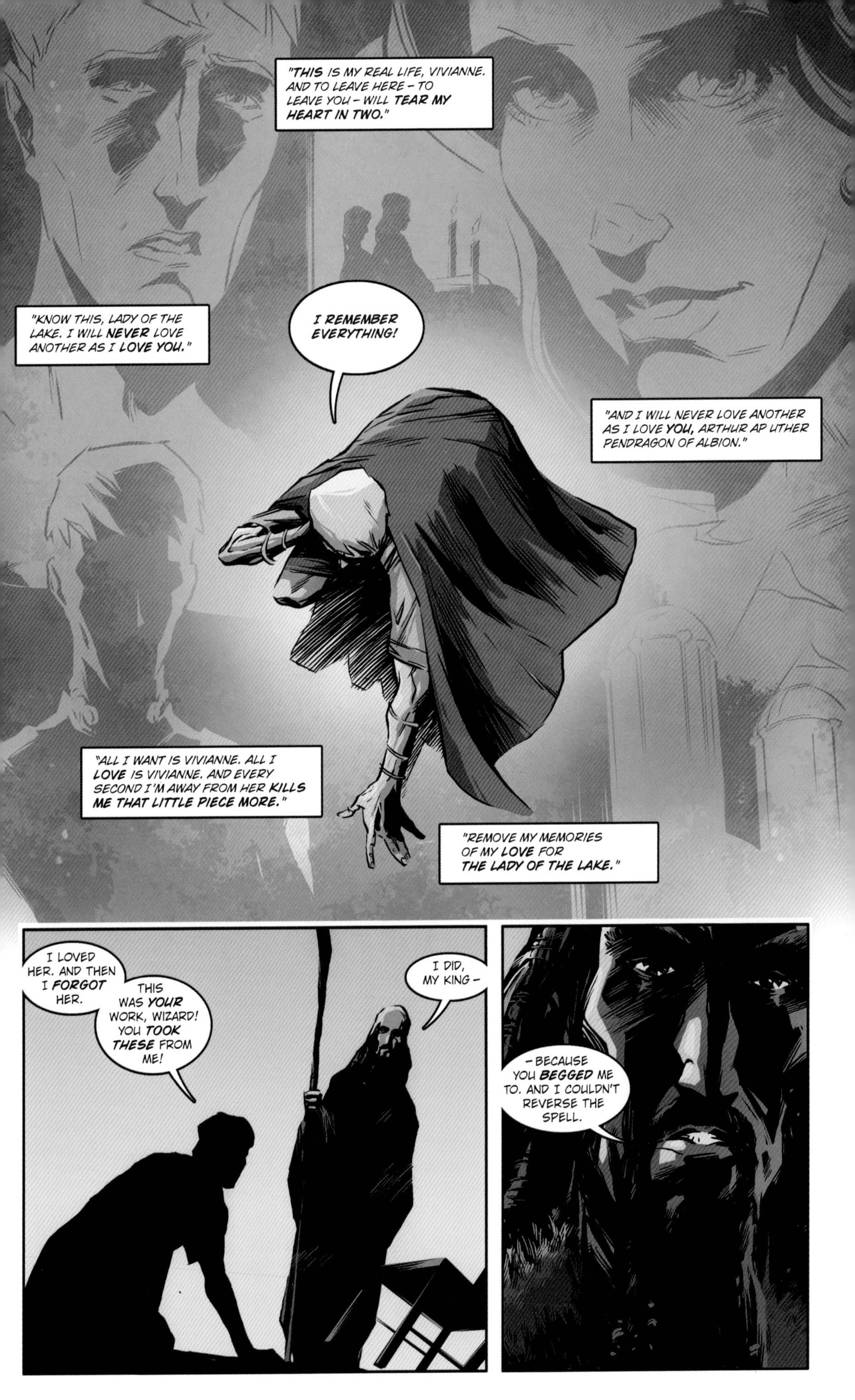

"THIS IS MY REAL LIFE, VIVIANNE. AND TO LEAVE HERE – TO LEAVE YOU – WILL TEAR MY HEART IN TWO."
"KNOW THIS, LADY OF THE LAKE. I WILL NEVER LOVE ANOTHER AS I LOVE YOU."
I REMEMBER EVERYTHING!
"AND I WILL NEVER LOVE ANOTHER AS I LOVE YOU, ARTHUR AP UTHER PENDRAGON OF ALBION."
"ALL I WANT IS VIVIANNE. ALL I LOVE IS VIVIANNE. AND EVERY SECOND I'M AWAY FROM HER KILLS ME THAT LITTLE PIECE MORE."
"REMOVE MY MEMORIES OF MY LOVE FOR THE LADY OF THE LAKE."
I LOVED HER. AND THEN I FORGOT HER.
THIS WAS YOUR WORK, WIZARD! YOU TOOK THESE FROM ME!
I DID, MY KING –
– BECAUSE YOU BEGGED ME TO. AND I COULDN'T REVERSE THE SPELL.

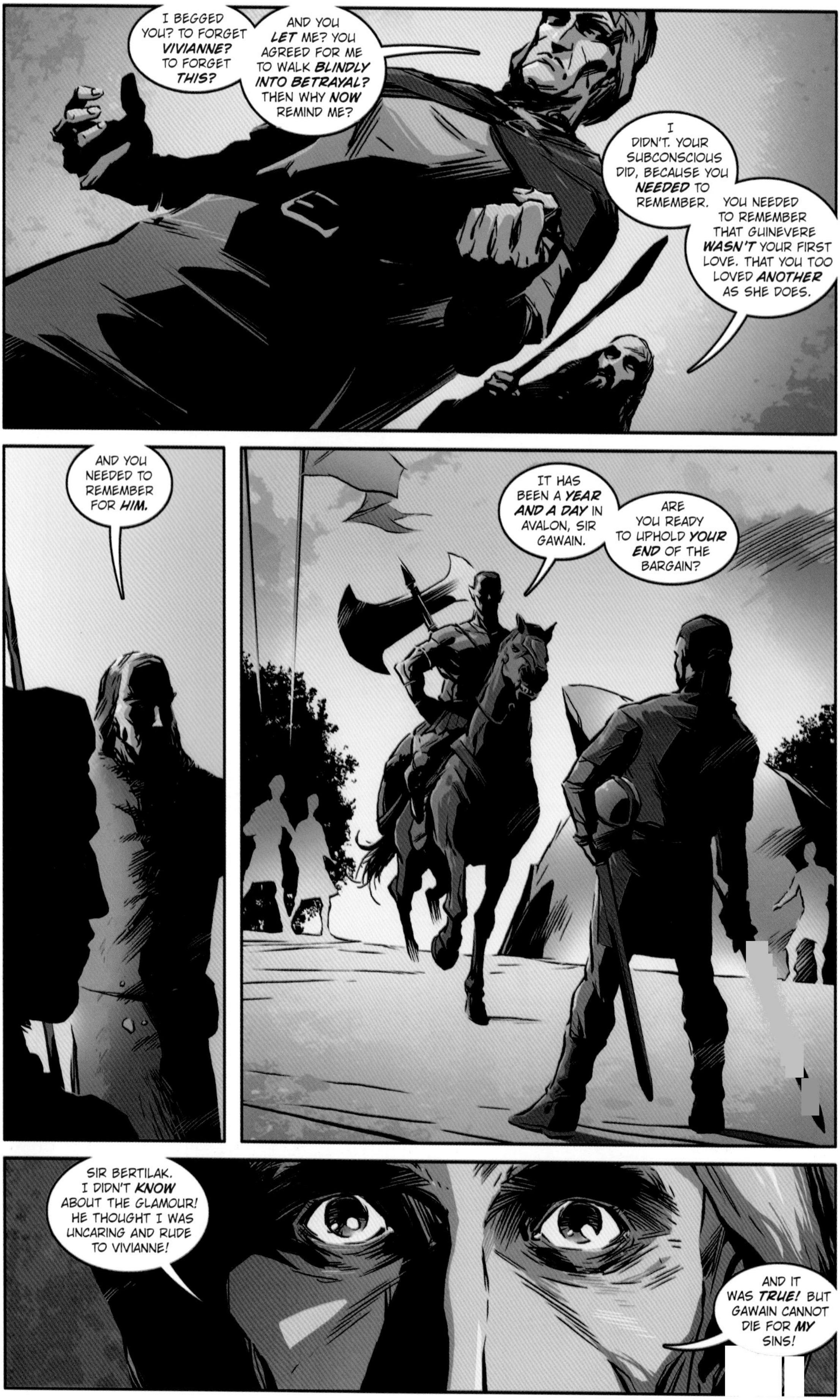
I BEGGED YOU? TO FORGET VIVIANNE? TO FORGET THIS?
AND YOU LET ME? YOU AGREED FOR ME TO WALK BLINDLY INTO BETRAYAL? THEN WHY NOW REMIND ME?
I DIDN'T. YOUR SUBCONSCIOUS DID, BECAUSE YOU NEEDED TO REMEMBER.
YOU NEEDED TO REMEMBER THAT GUINEVERE WASN'T YOUR FIRST LOVE. THAT YOU TOO LOVED ANOTHER AS SHE DOES.
AND YOU NEEDED TO REMEMBER FOR HIM.
IT HAS BEEN A YEAR AND A DAY IN AVALON, SIR GAWAIN.
ARE YOU READY TO UPHOLD YOUR END OF THE BARGAIN?
SIR BERTILAK. I DIDN'T KNOW ABOUT THE GLAMOUR! HE THOUGHT I WAS UNCARING AND RUDE TO VIVIANNE!
AND IT WAS TRUE! BUT GAWAIN CANNOT DIE FOR MY SINS!

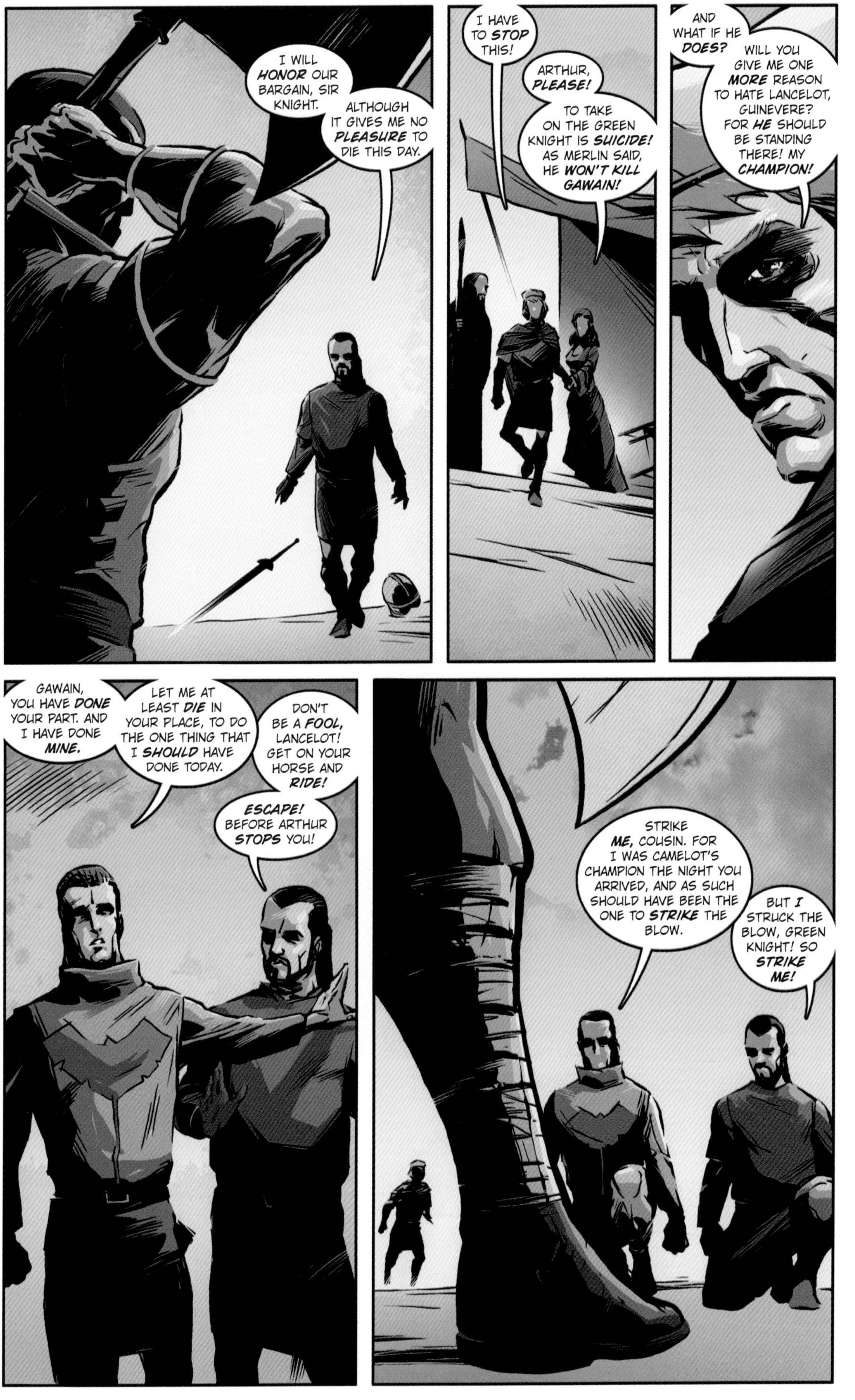

I WILL HONOR OUR BARGAIN, SIR KNIGHT.
ALTHOUGH IT GIVES ME NO PLEASURE TO DIE THIS DAY.
I HAVE TO STOP THIS!
ARTHUR, PLEASE!
TO TAKE ON THE GREEN KNIGHT IS SUICIDE! AS MERLIN SAID, HE WON'T KILL GAWAIN!
AND WHAT IF HE DOES?
WILL YOU GIVE ME ONE MORE REASON TO HATE LANCELOT, GUINEVERE? FOR HE SHOULD BE STANDING THERE! MY CHAMPION!
GAWAIN, YOU HAVE DONE YOUR PART. AND I HAVE DONE MINE.
LET ME AT LEAST DIE IN YOUR PLACE, TO DO THE ONE THING THAT I SHOULD HAVE DONE TODAY.
DON'T BE A FOOL, LANCELOT! GET ON YOUR HORSE AND RIDE!
ESCAPE! BEFORE ARTHUR STOPS YOU!
STRIKE ME, COUSIN. FOR I WAS CAMELOT'S CHAMPION THE NIGHT YOU ARRIVED, AND AS SUCH SHOULD HAVE BEEN THE ONE TO STRIKE THE BLOW.
BUT I STRUCK THE BLOW, GREEN KNIGHT! SO STRIKE ME!

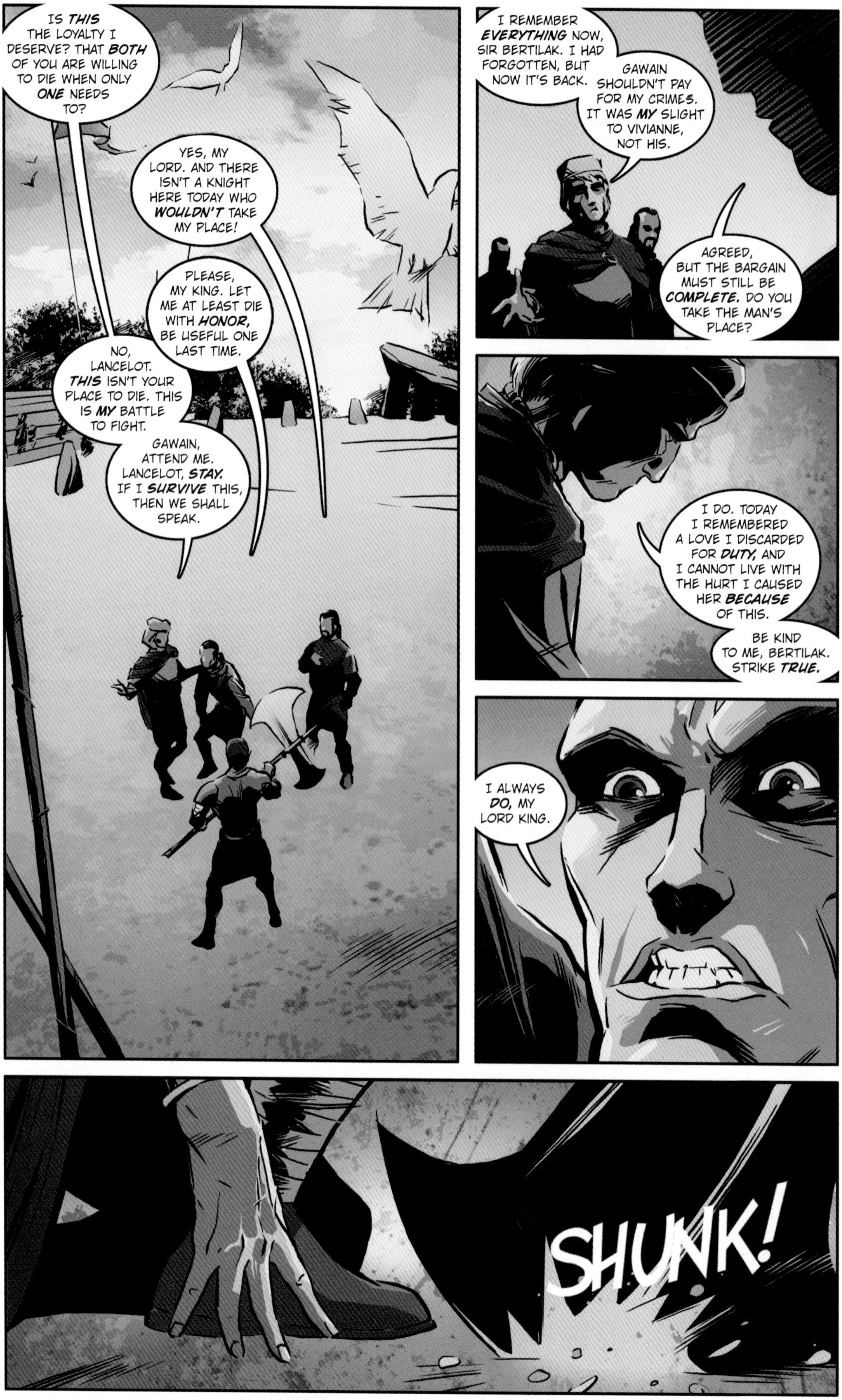
IS THIS THE LOYALTY I DESERVE? THAT BOTH OF YOU ARE WILLING TO DIE WHEN ONLY ONE NEEDS TO?
YES, MY LORD. AND THERE ISN'T A KNIGHT HERE TODAY WHO WOULDN'T TAKE MY PLACE!
PLEASE, MY KING. LET ME AT LEAST DIE WITH HONOR, BE USEFUL ONE LAST TIME.
NO, LANCELOT. THIS ISN'T YOUR PLACE TO DIE. THIS IS MY BATTLE TO FIGHT.
GAWAIN, ATTEND ME. LANCELOT, STAY. IF I SURVIVE THIS, THEN WE SHALL SPEAK.
I REMEMBER EVERYTHING NOW, SIR BERTILAK. I HAD FORGOTTEN, BUT NOW IT'S BACK.
GAWAIN SHOULDN'T PAY FOR MY CRIMES. IT WAS MY SLIGHT TO VIVIANNE, NOT HIS.
AGREED, BUT THE BARGAIN MUST STILL BE COMPLETE. DO YOU TAKE THE MAN'S PLACE?
I DO. TODAY I REMEMBERED A LOVE I DISCARDED FOR DUTY, AND I CANNOT LIVE WITH THE HURT I CAUSED HER BECAUSE OF THIS.
BE KIND TO ME, BERTILAK. STRIKE TRUE.
I ALWAYS DO, MY LORD KING.
SHUNK!

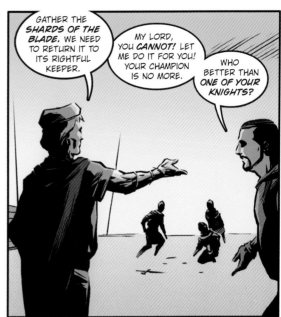

WHERE ONCE I SAW A *BOY,* NOW I SEE A MAN.

YOU HAVE REGAINED YOUR LOST MEMORIES, AND YOUR DEBT IS FULFILLED.

YOU ARE THE *TRUE* KING ONCE MORE.

GATHER THE *SHARDS OF THE BLADE.* WE NEED TO RETURN IT TO ITS RIGHTFUL KEEPER.

MY LORD, YOU *CANNOT!* LET ME DO IT FOR YOU! YOUR CHAMPION IS NO MORE.

WHO BETTER THAN *ONE OF YOUR KNIGHTS?*

TOO LONG HAVE I LET *OTHERS* FIGHT MY BATTLES, GAWAIN. IT IS TIME TO FACE MY FOES IN PERSON.

AND YOU HAVE TAKEN MY PLACE *TOO MANY* TIMES ALREADY, MY FRIEND. IT IS TIME FOR YOU TO REST.

GUINEVERE, WE BOTH LOVE *OTHERS.* BUT WHILE I MADE MYSELF FORGET, YOU WERE FORCED TO *LIVE* WITH YOUR SECRET.

LANCELOT, I CANNOT HATE YOU FOR FOLLOWING WHERE *FATE* LED YOU, AS I MUST FOLLOW MYSELF. SO GO IN PEACE.

*HEAR THIS!* NOBODY SHALL TOUCH GUINEVERE OR LANCELOT! THEY ARE *BANISHED FROM CAMELOT—*

—BUT STILL *WELCOME IN ALBION!*

A GOOD CHOICE, ARTHUR.

FOR WE HAVE *PLANS* FOR LANCELOT.

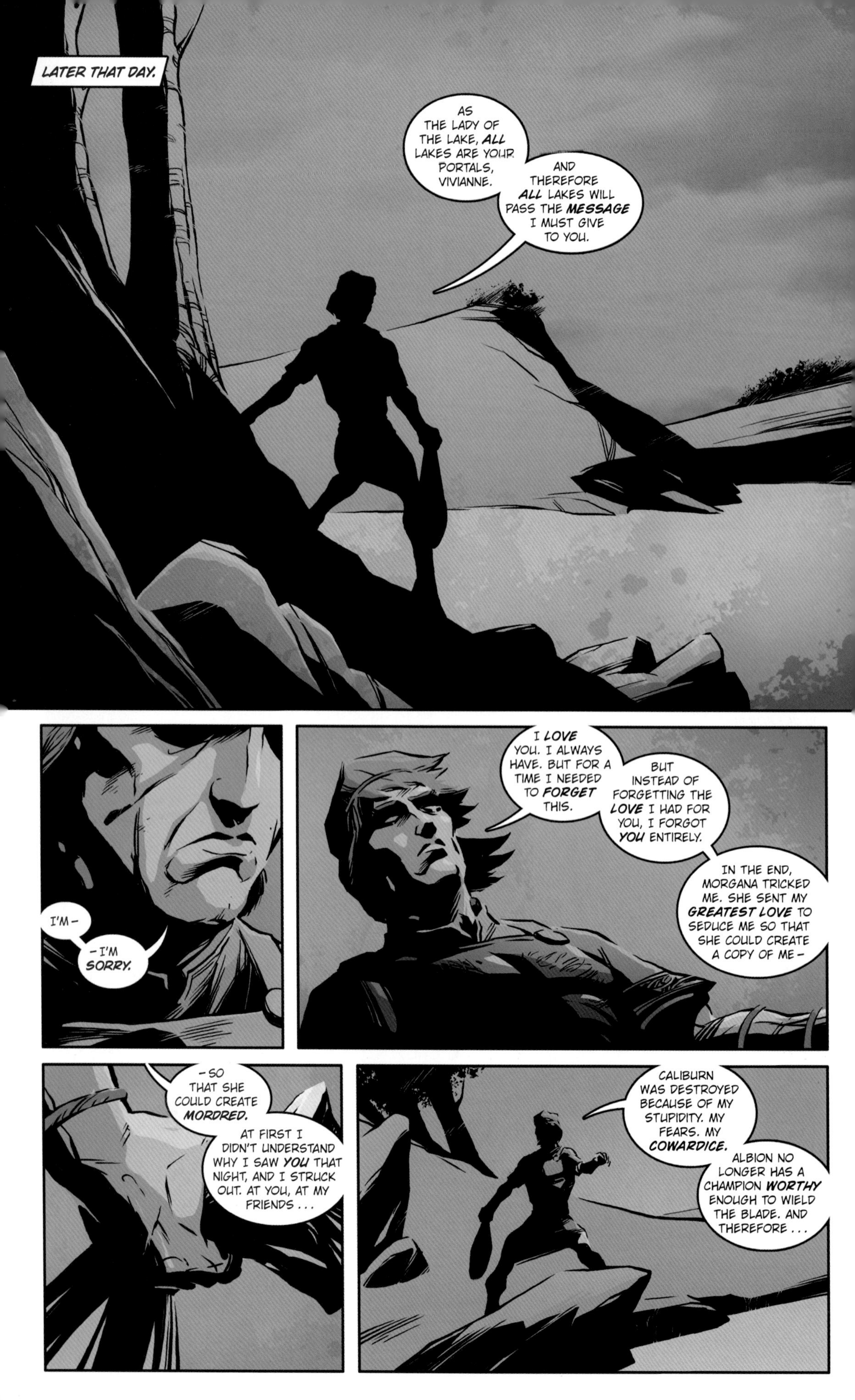
LATER THAT DAY.
AS THE LADY OF THE LAKE, ALL LAKES ARE YOUR PORTALS, VIVIANNE.
AND THEREFORE ALL LAKES WILL PASS THE MESSAGE I MUST GIVE TO YOU.
I'M–
–I'M SORRY.
I LOVE YOU. I ALWAYS HAVE. BUT FOR A TIME I NEEDED TO FORGET THIS.
BUT INSTEAD OF FORGETTING THE LOVE I HAD FOR YOU, I FORGOT YOU ENTIRELY.
IN THE END, MORGANA TRICKED ME. SHE SENT MY GREATEST LOVE TO SEDUCE ME SO THAT SHE COULD CREATE A COPY OF ME–
–SO THAT SHE COULD CREATE MORDRED.
AT FIRST I DIDN'T UNDERSTAND WHY I SAW YOU THAT NIGHT, AND I STRUCK OUT. AT YOU, AT MY FRIENDS . . .
CALIBURN WAS DESTROYED BECAUSE OF MY STUPIDITY. MY FEARS. MY COWARDICE.
ALBION NO LONGER HAS A CHAMPION WORTHY ENOUGH TO WIELD THE BLADE. AND THEREFORE . . .

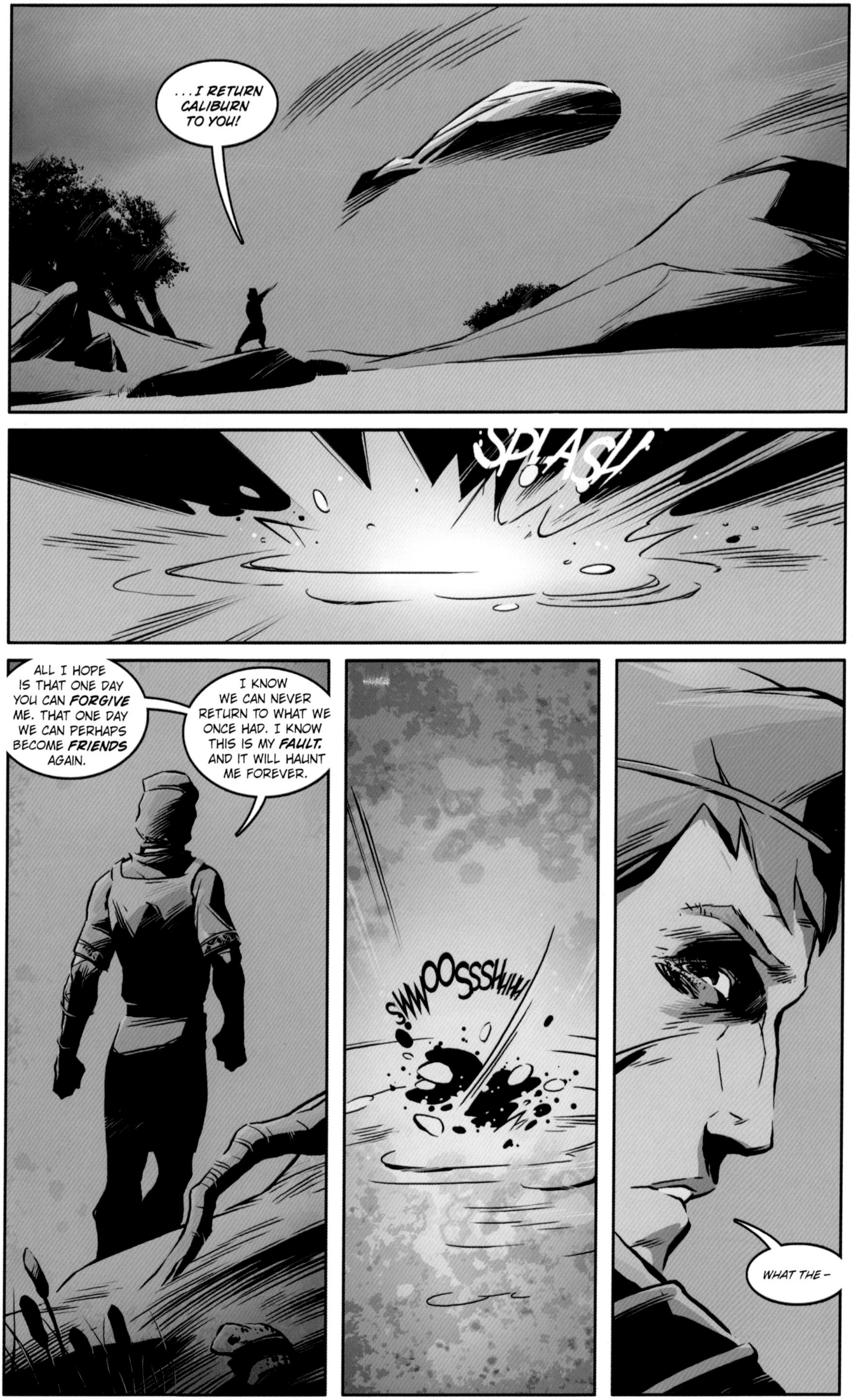
...I RETURN CALIBURN TO YOU!
SPLASH
ALL I HOPE IS THAT ONE DAY YOU CAN FORGIVE ME. THAT ONE DAY WE CAN PERHAPS BECOME FRIENDS AGAIN.
I KNOW WE CAN NEVER RETURN TO WHAT WE ONCE HAD. I KNOW THIS IS MY FAULT. AND IT WILL HAUNT ME FOREVER.
SWWOOSSSHHH
WHAT THE –

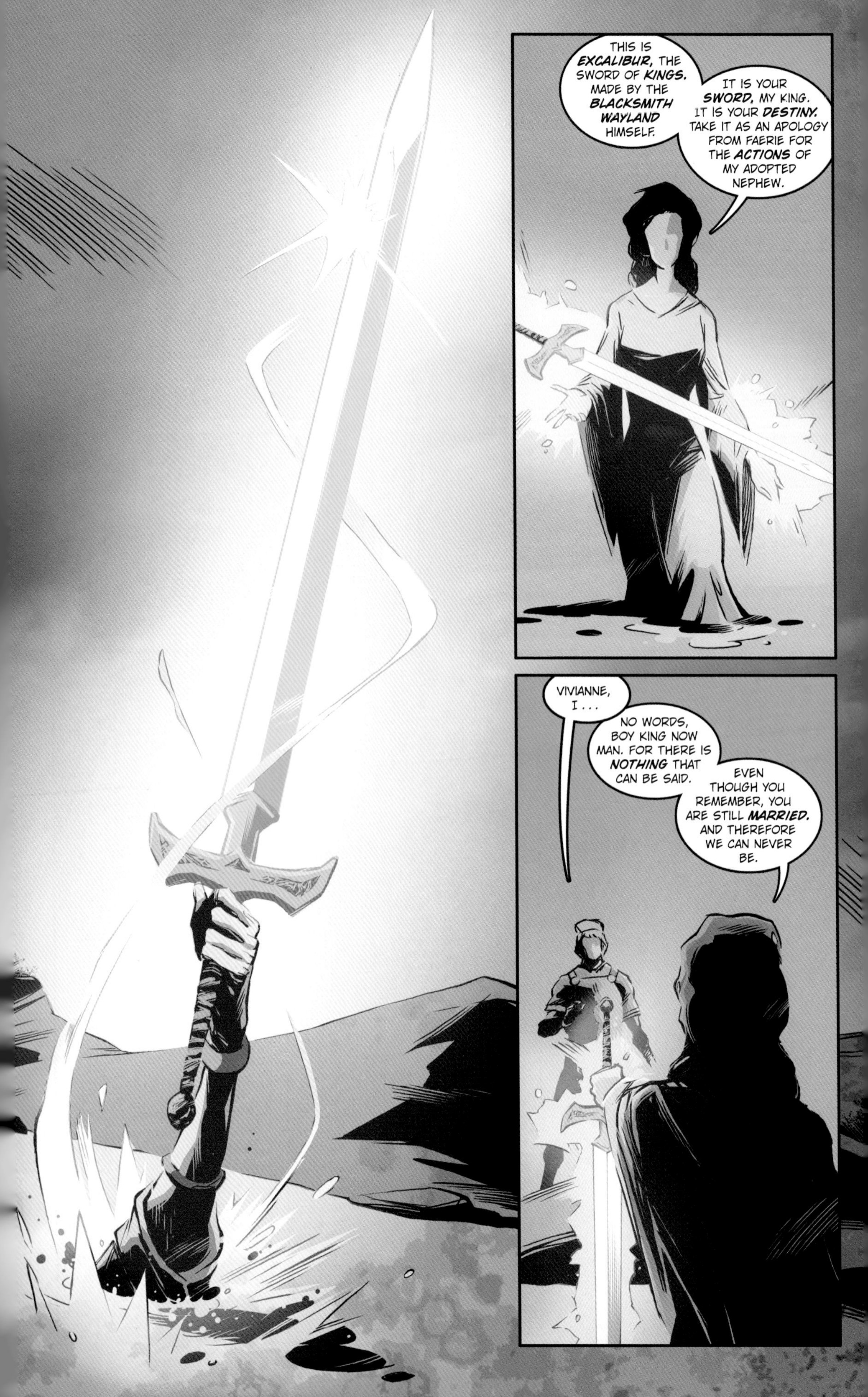
THIS IS **EXCALIBUR,** THE SWORD OF **KINGS.** MADE BY THE **BLACKSMITH WAYLAND** HIMSELF.
IT IS YOUR **SWORD,** MY KING. IT IS YOUR **DESTINY.** TAKE IT AS AN APOLOGY FROM FAERIE FOR THE **ACTIONS** OF MY ADOPTED NEPHEW.
VIVIANNE, I . . .
NO WORDS, BOY KING NOW MAN. FOR THERE IS **NOTHING** THAT CAN BE SAID.
EVEN THOUGH YOU REMEMBER, YOU ARE STILL **MARRIED.** AND THEREFORE WE CAN NEVER BE.

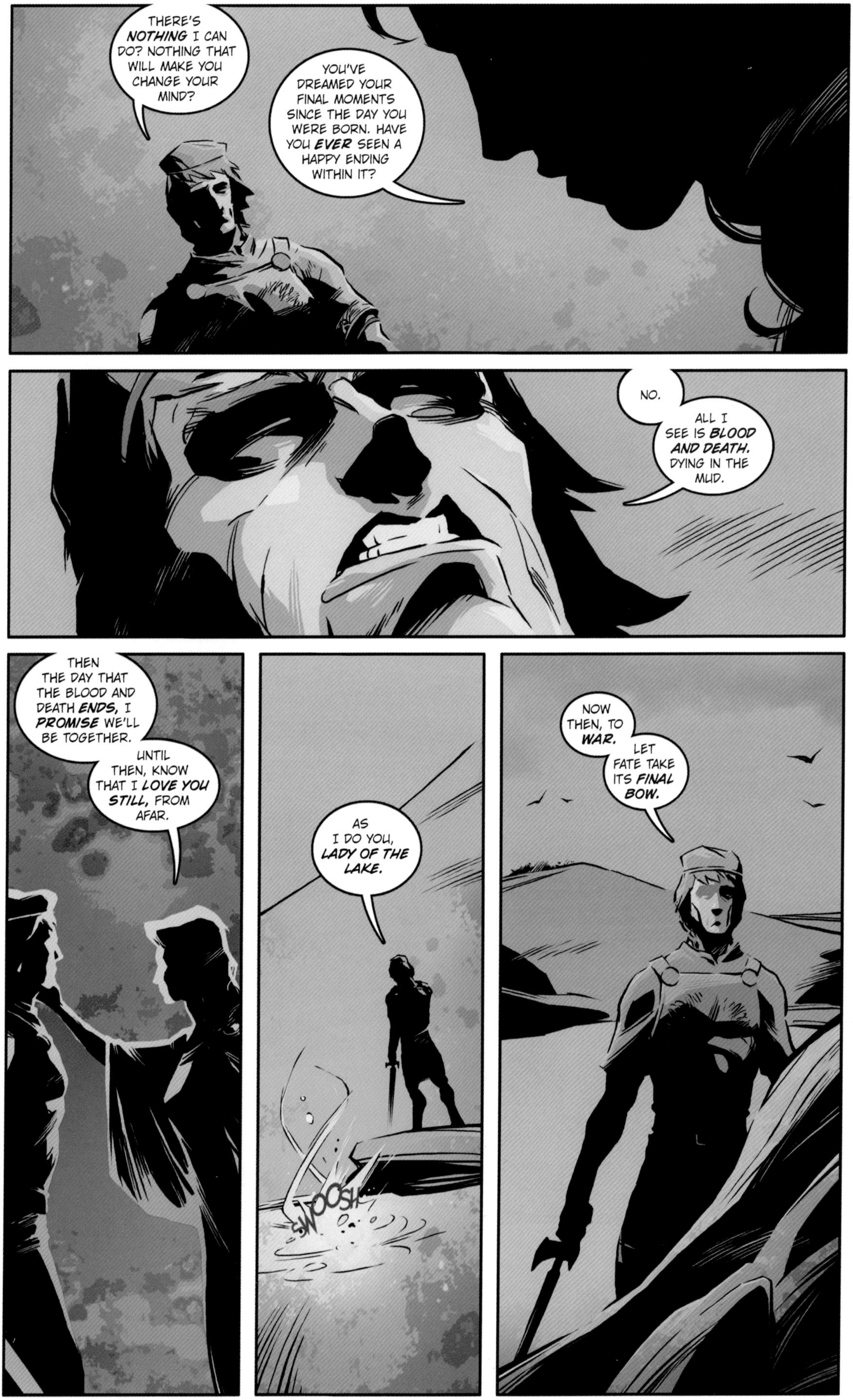

THERE'S NOTHING I CAN DO? NOTHING THAT WILL MAKE YOU CHANGE YOUR MIND?
YOU'VE DREAMED YOUR FINAL MOMENTS SINCE THE DAY YOU WERE BORN. HAVE YOU EVER SEEN A HAPPY ENDING WITHIN IT?
NO.
ALL I SEE IS BLOOD AND DEATH. DYING IN THE MUD.
THEN THE DAY THAT THE BLOOD AND DEATH ENDS, I PROMISE WE'LL BE TOGETHER.
UNTIL THEN, KNOW THAT I LOVE YOU STILL, FROM AFAR.
AS I DO YOU, LADY OF THE LAKE.
SWOOSH
NOW THEN, TO WAR.
LET FATE TAKE ITS FINAL BOW.

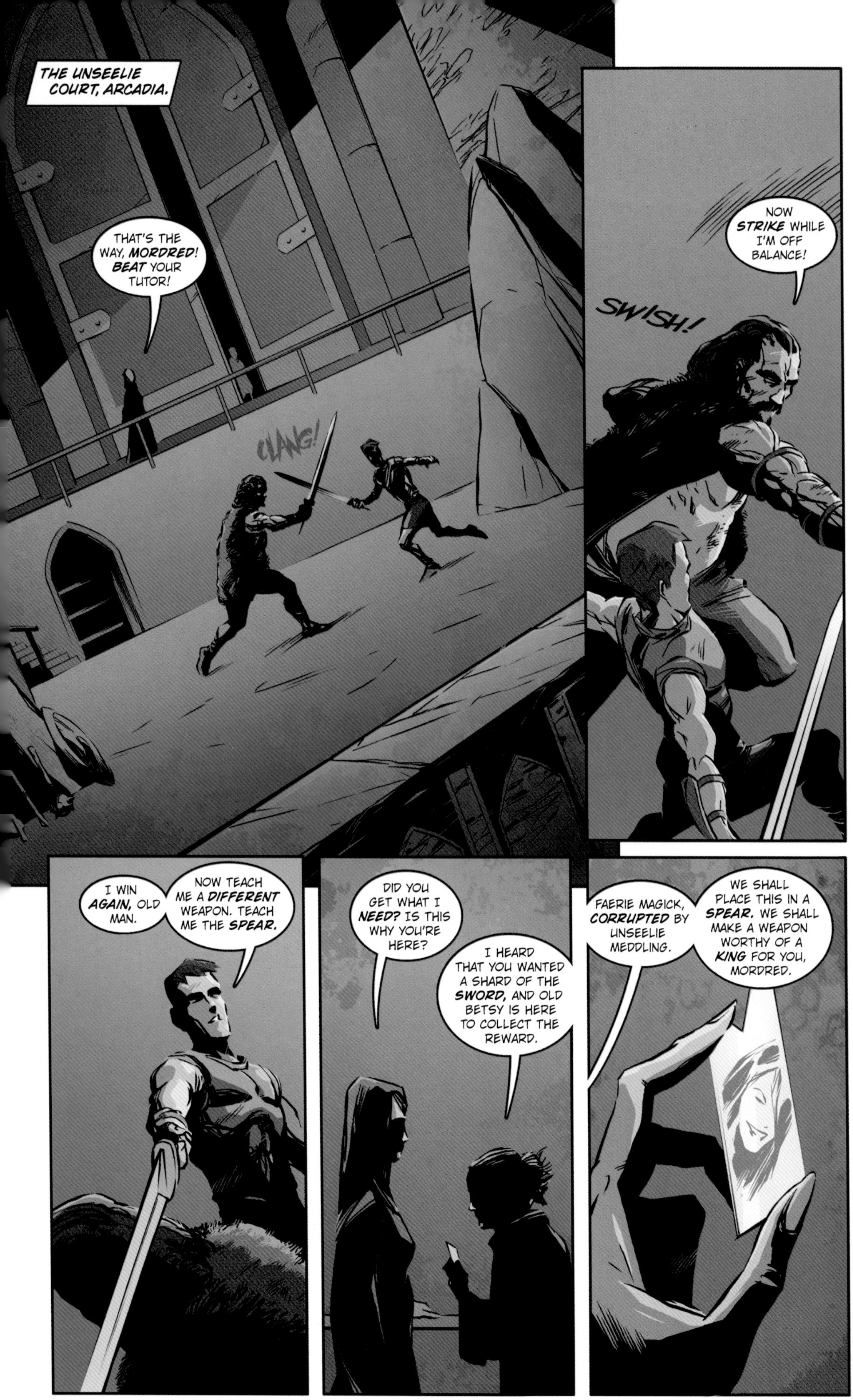
THE UNSEELIE COURT, ARCADIA.
THAT'S THE WAY, MORDRED! BEAT YOUR TUTOR!
CLANG!
NOW STRIKE WHILE I'M OFF BALANCE!
SWISH!
I WIN AGAIN, OLD MAN.
NOW TEACH ME A DIFFERENT WEAPON. TEACH ME THE SPEAR.
DID YOU GET WHAT I NEED? IS THIS WHY YOU'RE HERE?
I HEARD THAT YOU WANTED A SHARD OF THE SWORD, AND OLD BETSY IS HERE TO COLLECT THE REWARD.
FAERIE MAGICK, CORRUPTED BY UNSEELIE MEDDLING.
WE SHALL PLACE THIS IN A SPEAR. WE SHALL MAKE A WEAPON WORTHY OF A KING FOR YOU, MORDRED.

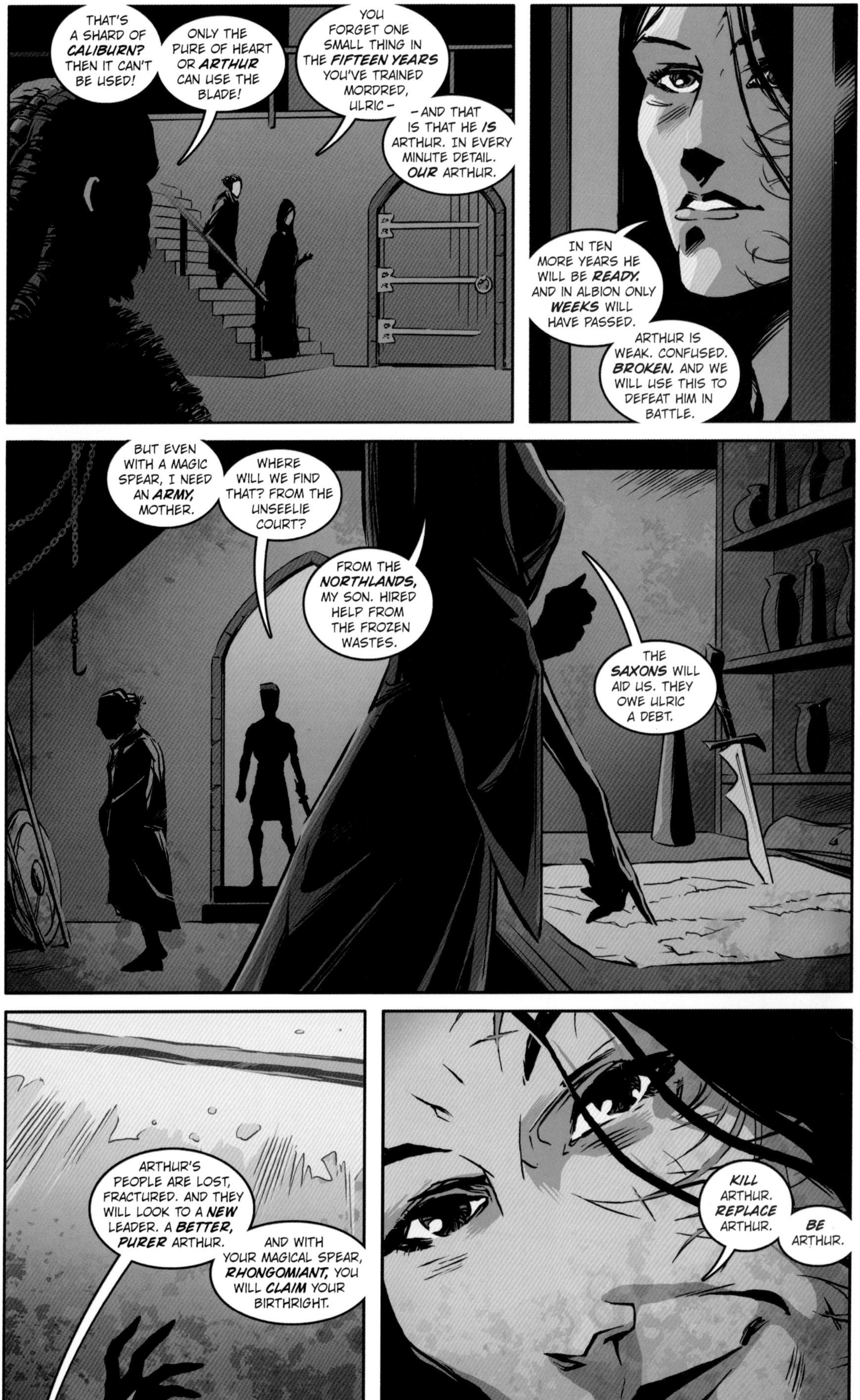
THAT'S A SHARD OF CALIBURN? THEN IT CAN'T BE USED!
ONLY THE PURE OF HEART OR ARTHUR CAN USE THE BLADE!
YOU FORGET ONE SMALL THING IN THE FIFTEEN YEARS YOU'VE TRAINED MORDRED, ULRIC –
– AND THAT IS THAT HE IS ARTHUR. IN EVERY MINUTE DETAIL. OUR ARTHUR.
IN TEN MORE YEARS HE WILL BE READY. AND IN ALBION ONLY WEEKS WILL HAVE PASSED.
ARTHUR IS WEAK. CONFUSED. BROKEN. AND WE WILL USE THIS TO DEFEAT HIM IN BATTLE.
BUT EVEN WITH A MAGIC SPEAR, I NEED AN ARMY, MOTHER.
WHERE WILL WE FIND THAT? FROM THE UNSEELIE COURT?
FROM THE NORTHLANDS, MY SON. HIRED HELP FROM THE FROZEN WASTES.
THE SAXONS WILL AID US. THEY OWE ULRIC A DEBT.
ARTHUR'S PEOPLE ARE LOST, FRACTURED. AND THEY WILL LOOK TO A NEW LEADER. A BETTER, PURER ARTHUR.
AND WITH YOUR MAGICAL SPEAR, RHONGOMIANT, YOU WILL CLAIM YOUR BIRTHRIGHT.
KILL ARTHUR. REPLACE ARTHUR.
BE ARTHUR.

CAMELOT.

WHAT DO I *DO*, MERLIN? HOW DO I *DEFEAT* MORGANA?

I THINK WE BOTH KNOW THAT THIS IS A BATTLE WE WON'T WALK AWAY FROM *ALIVE*, MY KING.

BUT NO MATTER WHAT, WE *MUST* STOP MORGANA AND THE UNSEELIE COURT.

THE REPORTS SAY THAT *SAXONS* ARE INVADING — THAT THEY HEAD FOR CAMELOT. IS THIS THE *START*?

IS THIS HOW IT ALL *ENDS*?

DEAR ECTOR, I DID INDEED.

I RELEASE YOU ALL FROM YOUR *OATHS* TO ME.

*WHAT?*

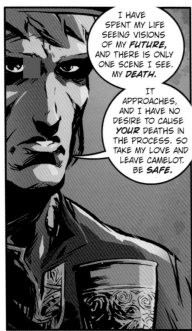

I HAVE SPENT MY LIFE SEEING VISIONS OF MY *FUTURE*, AND THERE IS ONLY ONE SCENE I SEE. MY *DEATH.*

IT APPROACHES, AND I HAVE NO DESIRE TO CAUSE *YOUR* DEATHS IN THE PROCESS. SO TAKE MY LOVE AND LEAVE CAMELOT. BE *SAFE.*

IF YOU DECIDE TO STAY — TO STAND *WITH* ME — THEN DRINK WITH ME FROM THIS MOST *HOLY OF GRAILS*, THE *CHALICE* GIVEN TO ME BY THE SEELIE COURT IN MY DARKEST HOUR.

BECOME MY BROTHERS *ONCE MORE* IN THIS MOST SOLEMN PACT.

I'VE LOOKED AFTER YOU ALL MY LIFE, WART. NO REASON TO STOP NOW.

UNTIL THE *VERY END.*

YOU'RE MY *SON*, ARTHUR — MORE SO THAN UTHER'S. I RAISED YOU.

AND I'LL BE DAMNED IF I *DESERT* YOU NOW. UNTIL THE END IT IS.

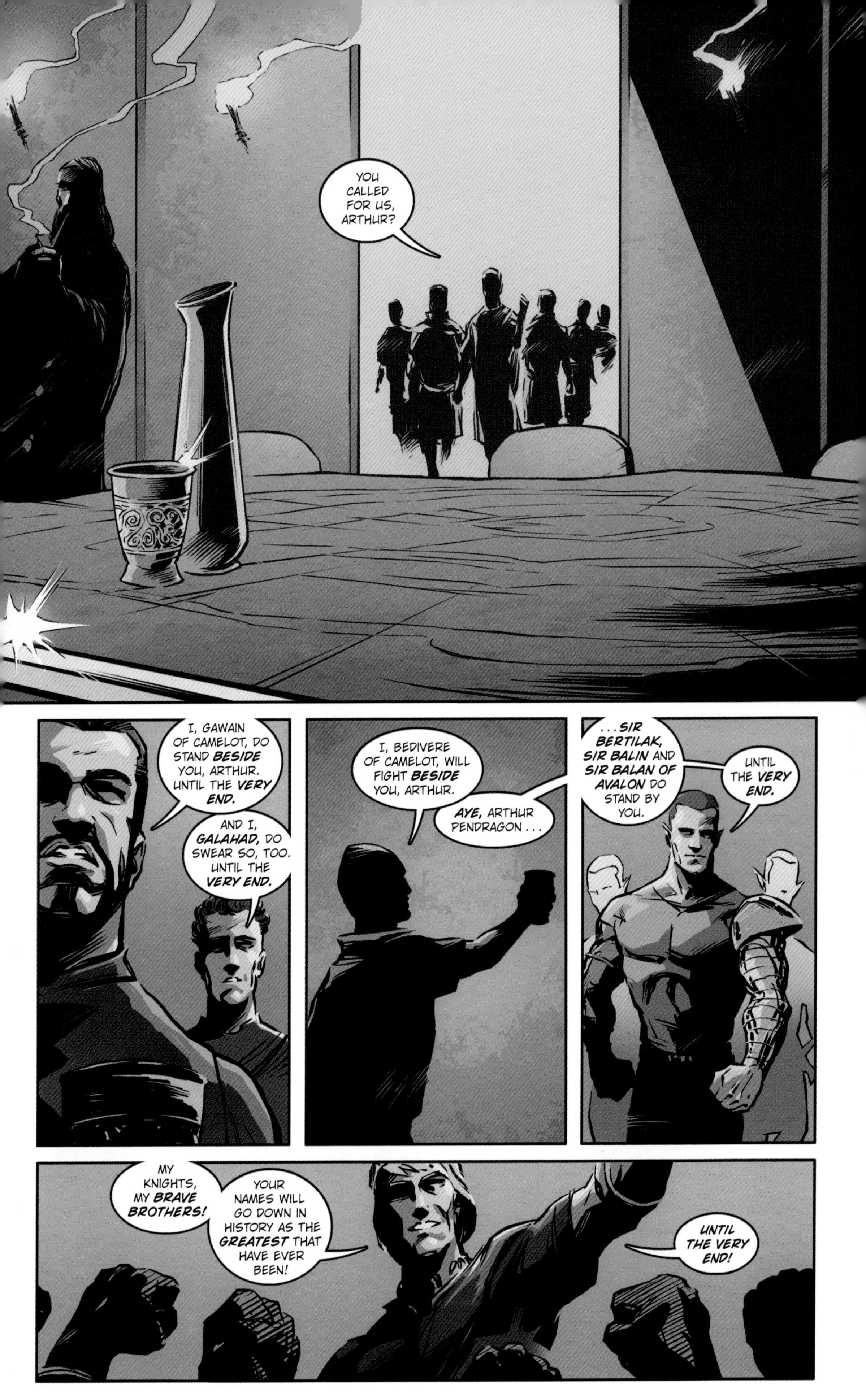

YOU CALLED FOR US, ARTHUR?
I, GAWAIN OF CAMELOT, DO STAND BESIDE YOU, ARTHUR. UNTIL THE VERY END.
AND I, GALAHAD, DO SWEAR SO, TOO. UNTIL THE VERY END.
I, BEDIVERE OF CAMELOT, WILL FIGHT BESIDE YOU, ARTHUR.
AYE, ARTHUR PENDRAGON . . .
. . . SIR BERTILAK, SIR BALIN AND SIR BALAN OF AVALON DO STAND BY YOU.
UNTIL THE VERY END.
MY KNIGHTS, MY BRAVE BROTHERS!
YOUR NAMES WILL GO DOWN IN HISTORY AS THE GREATEST THAT HAVE EVER BEEN!
UNTIL THE VERY END!

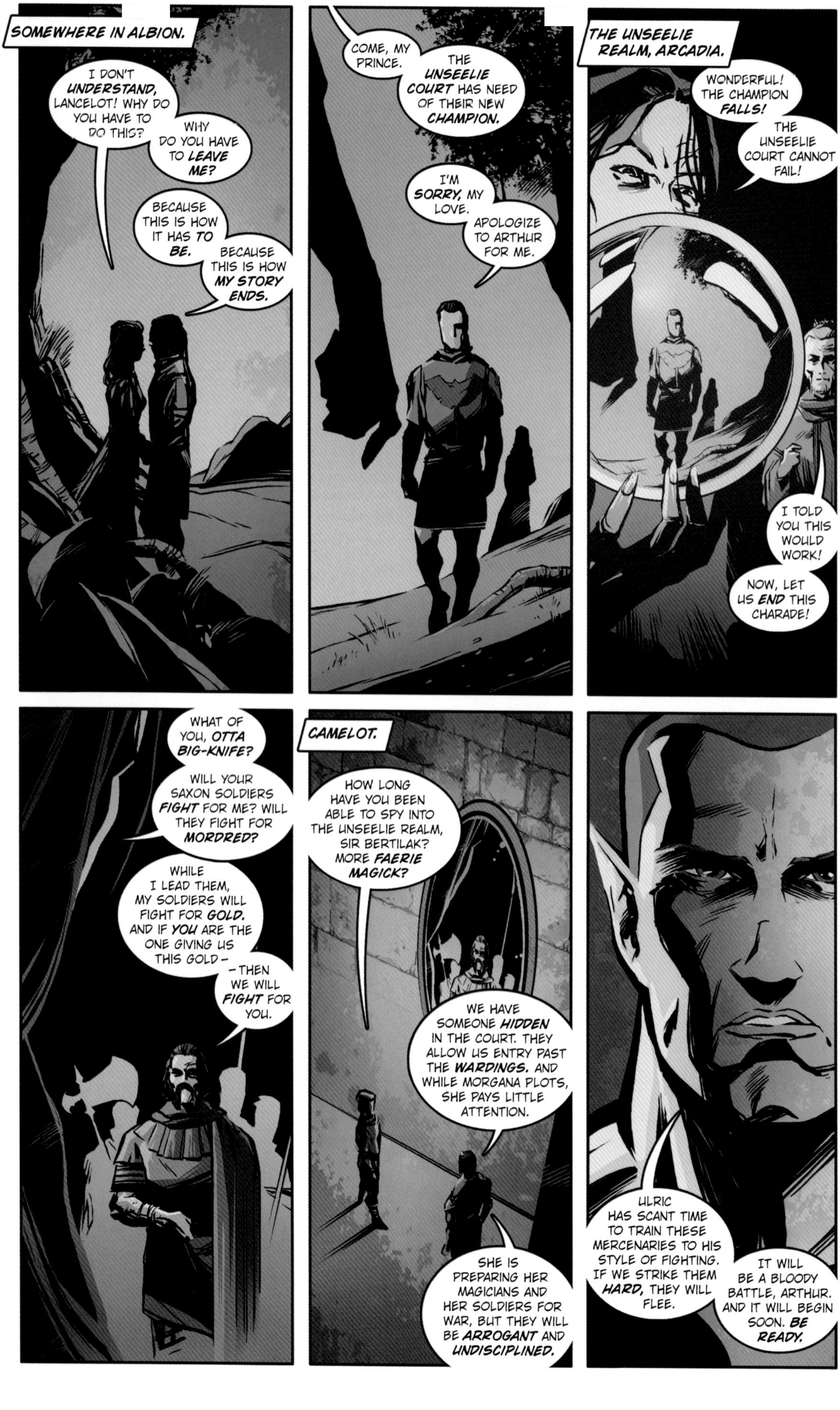

SOMEWHERE IN ALBION.
I DON'T UNDERSTAND, LANCELOT! WHY DO YOU HAVE TO DO THIS?
WHY DO YOU HAVE TO LEAVE ME?
BECAUSE THIS IS HOW IT HAS TO BE.
BECAUSE THIS IS HOW MY STORY ENDS.
COME, MY PRINCE.
THE UNSEELIE COURT HAS NEED OF THEIR NEW CHAMPION.
I'M SORRY, MY LOVE.
APOLOGIZE TO ARTHUR FOR ME.
THE UNSEELIE REALM, ARCADIA.
WONDERFUL! THE CHAMPION FALLS!
THE UNSEELIE COURT CANNOT FAIL!
I TOLD YOU THIS WOULD WORK!
NOW, LET US END THIS CHARADE!
WHAT OF YOU, OTTA BIG-KNIFE?
WILL YOUR SAXON SOLDIERS FIGHT FOR ME? WILL THEY FIGHT FOR MORDRED?
WHILE I LEAD THEM, MY SOLDIERS WILL FIGHT FOR GOLD. AND IF YOU ARE THE ONE GIVING US THIS GOLD—
—THEN WE WILL FIGHT FOR YOU.
CAMELOT.
HOW LONG HAVE YOU BEEN ABLE TO SPY INTO THE UNSEELIE REALM, SIR BERTILAK? MORE FAERIE MAGICK?
WE HAVE SOMEONE HIDDEN IN THE COURT. THEY ALLOW US ENTRY PAST THE WARDINGS. AND WHILE MORGANA PLOTS, SHE PAYS LITTLE ATTENTION.
SHE IS PREPARING HER MAGICIANS AND HER SOLDIERS FOR WAR, BUT THEY WILL BE ARROGANT AND UNDISCIPLINED.
ULRIC HAS SCANT TIME TO TRAIN THESE MERCENARIES TO HIS STYLE OF FIGHTING. IF WE STRIKE THEM HARD, THEY WILL FLEE.
IT WILL BE A BLOODY BATTLE, ARTHUR. AND IT WILL BEGIN SOON. BE READY.

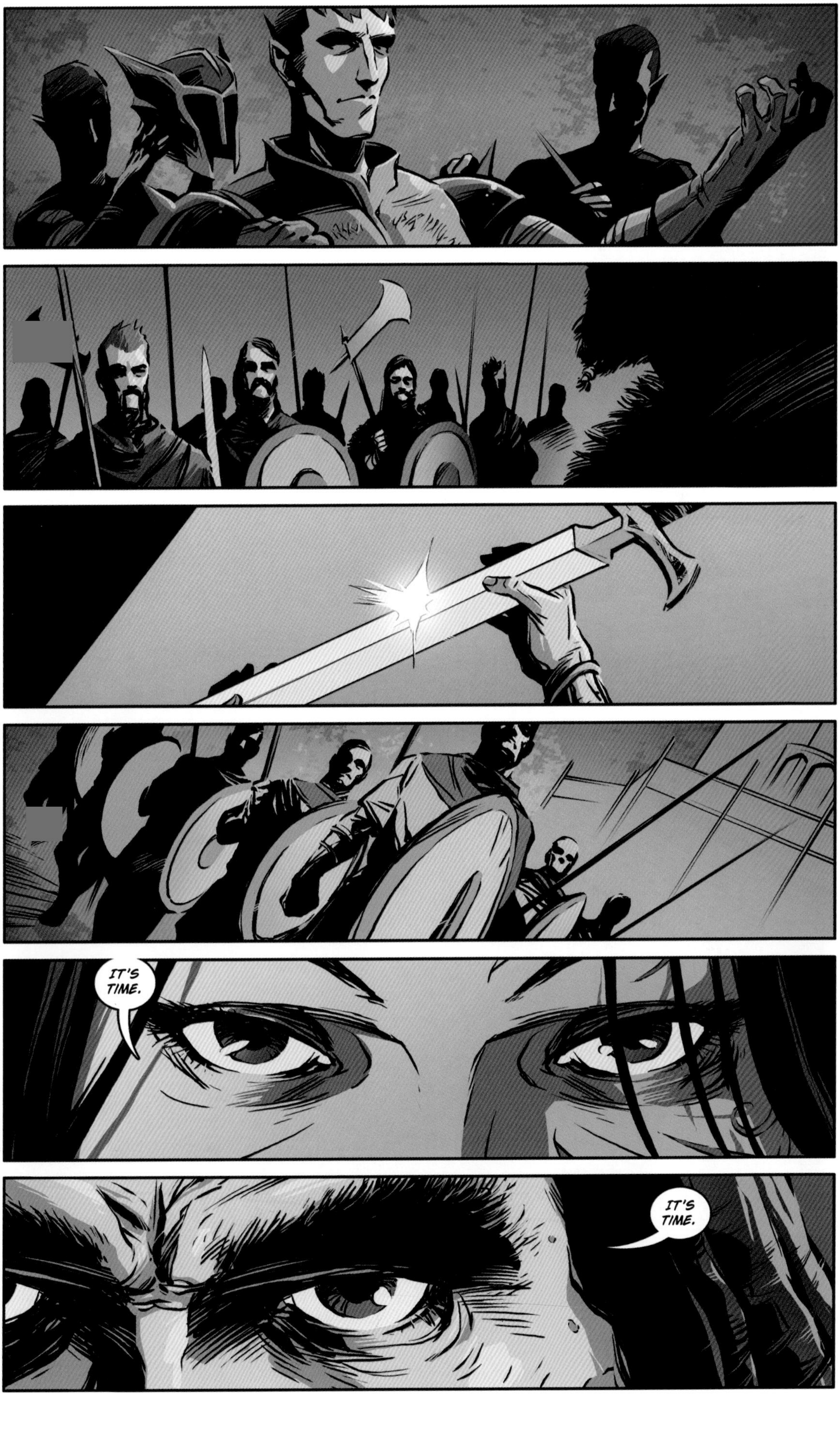
IT'S TIME.
IT'S TIME.

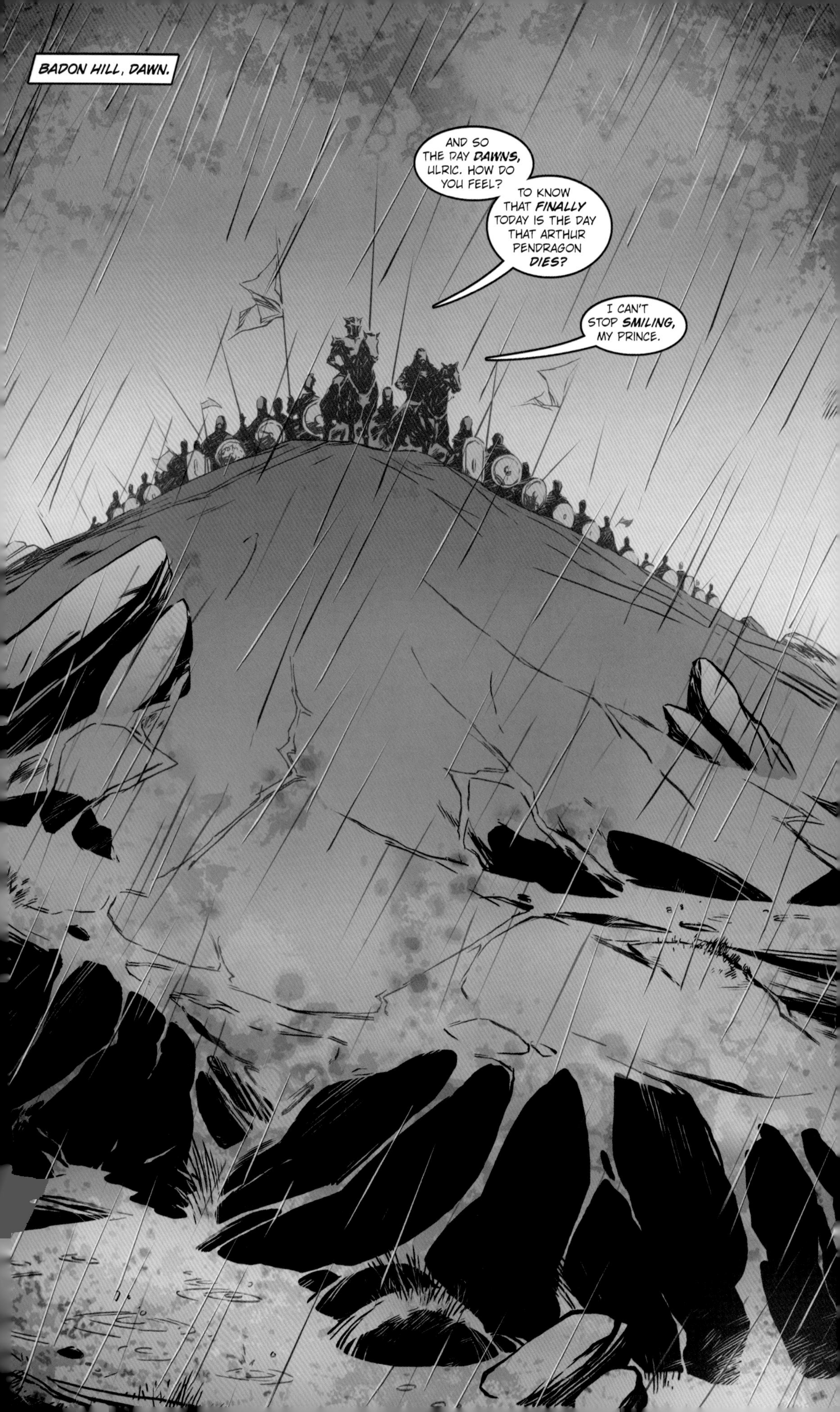
BADON HILL, DAWN.
AND SO THE DAY DAWNS, ULRIC. HOW DO YOU FEEL?
TO KNOW THAT FINALLY TODAY IS THE DAY THAT ARTHUR PENDRAGON DIES?
I CAN'T STOP SMILING, MY PRINCE.

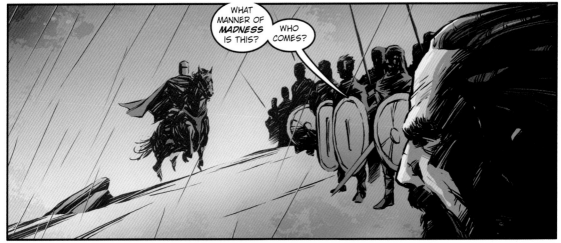

WHAT MANNER OF **MADNESS** IS THIS?

WHO COMES?

CALM, OLD FRIEND. MY MOTHER INFORMED ME OF THIS.

HE IS AN EMISSARY OF THE **UNSEELIE COURT.** HE IS AN ALLY.

MY PRINCE **MORDRED.** MY KING **ULRIC.**

GREETINGS FROM THE UNSEELIE COURT.

UNSEELIE COURT BE **DAMNED!** WHO THE BLAZES **ARE** YOU? TAKE OFF THAT HELMET!

APOLOGIES, MY KING.

NO! IT **CANNOT BE!**

I AM **LANCELOT DU LAC.** I AM THE **DARK CHAMPION** OF THE **UNSEELIE COURT.**

AND I AM HERE TO **KILL ARTHUR** FOR YOU.

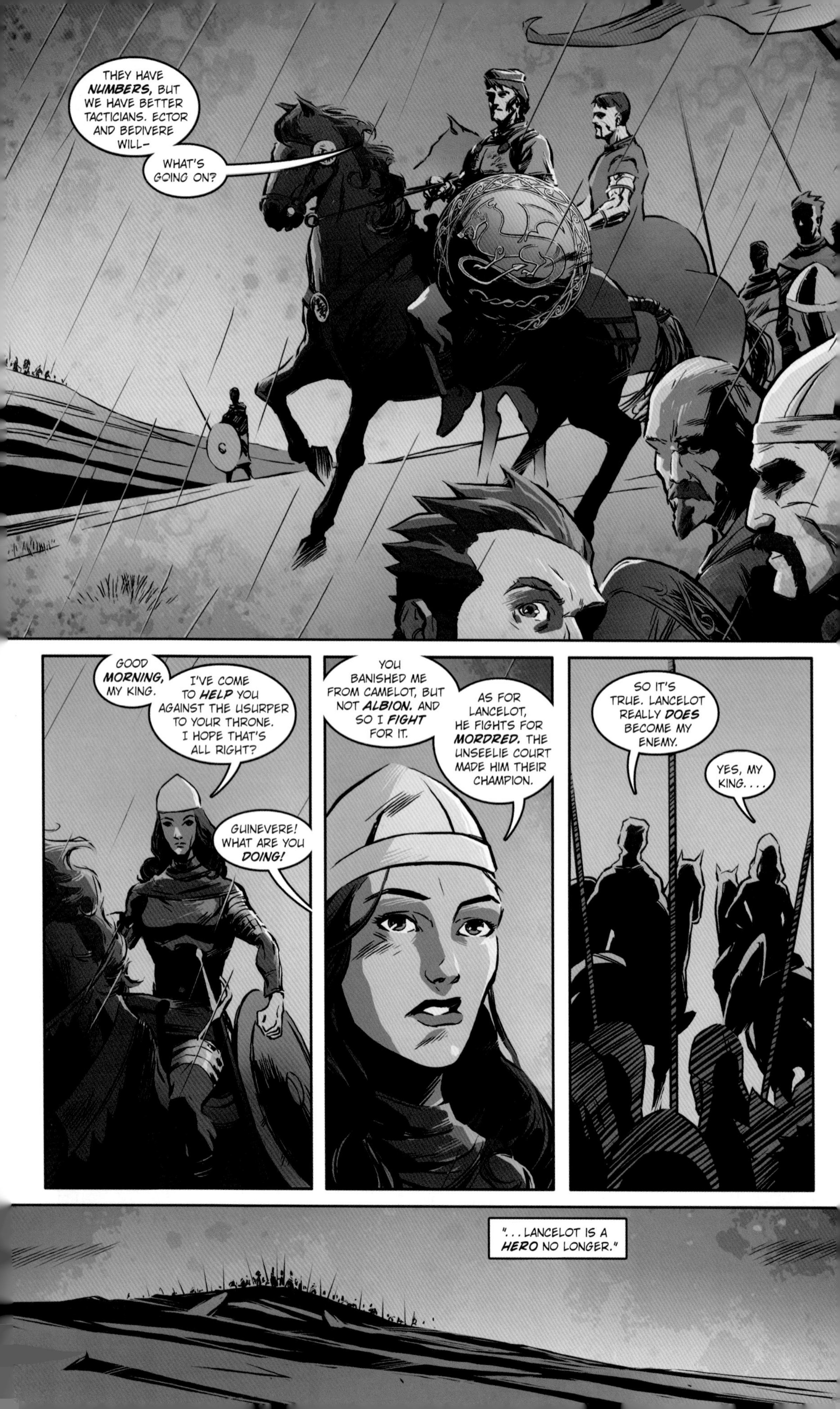
THEY HAVE NUMBERS, BUT WE HAVE BETTER TACTICIANS. ECTOR AND BEDIVERE WILL–
WHAT'S GOING ON?
GOOD MORNING, MY KING.
I'VE COME TO HELP YOU AGAINST THE USURPER TO YOUR THRONE. I HOPE THAT'S ALL RIGHT?
GUINEVERE! WHAT ARE YOU DOING!
YOU BANISHED ME FROM CAMELOT, BUT NOT ALBION. AND SO I FIGHT FOR IT.
AS FOR LANCELOT, HE FIGHTS FOR MORDRED. THE UNSEELIE COURT MADE HIM THEIR CHAMPION.
SO IT'S TRUE. LANCELOT REALLY DOES BECOME MY ENEMY.
YES, MY KING. . . .
". . . LANCELOT IS A HERO NO LONGER."

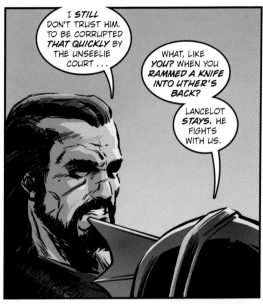

A MESSAGE FROM YOUR **MOTHER,** MY LORD. WE HAVE NEWS FROM OUR **SPIES** IN ARTHUR'S BATTLE LINE.

THE QUEEN **GUINEVERE** HAS ARRIVED – AND HAS INFORMED ARTHUR THAT LANCELOT HAS TURNED **TRAITOR** TO HIS KING.

SO HE **REALLY HAS** TURNED UNSEELIE THEN? EXCELLENT!

ALL THE SWEETER A BLOW WHEN IT COMES FROM A ONE-TIME **BROTHER,** EH, ULRIC?

I **STILL** DON'T TRUST HIM. TO BE CORRUPTED **THAT QUICKLY** BY THE UNSEELIE COURT . . .

WHAT, LIKE **YOU?** WHEN YOU **RAMMED A KNIFE INTO UTHER'S BACK?**

LANCELOT **STAYS.** HE FIGHTS WITH US.

I HAVE ONE REQUEST, MY LORDS. LET ME STRIKE THE **FIRST BLOW** OF THE BATTLE.

LET ME KILL THE KING AS IF CUTTING THE HEAD OFF A **SNAKE.**

ONE BLOW TO END THE WAR? **AMBITIOUS!** I LIKE IT!

VERY WELL. DRAW YOUR SWORD. **YOU** WILL START OUR BATTLE. AND **YOU** WILL STRIKE THE FIRST BLOW.

THANK YOU, MY PRINCE.

FOR ARTHUR!

SHUNK!

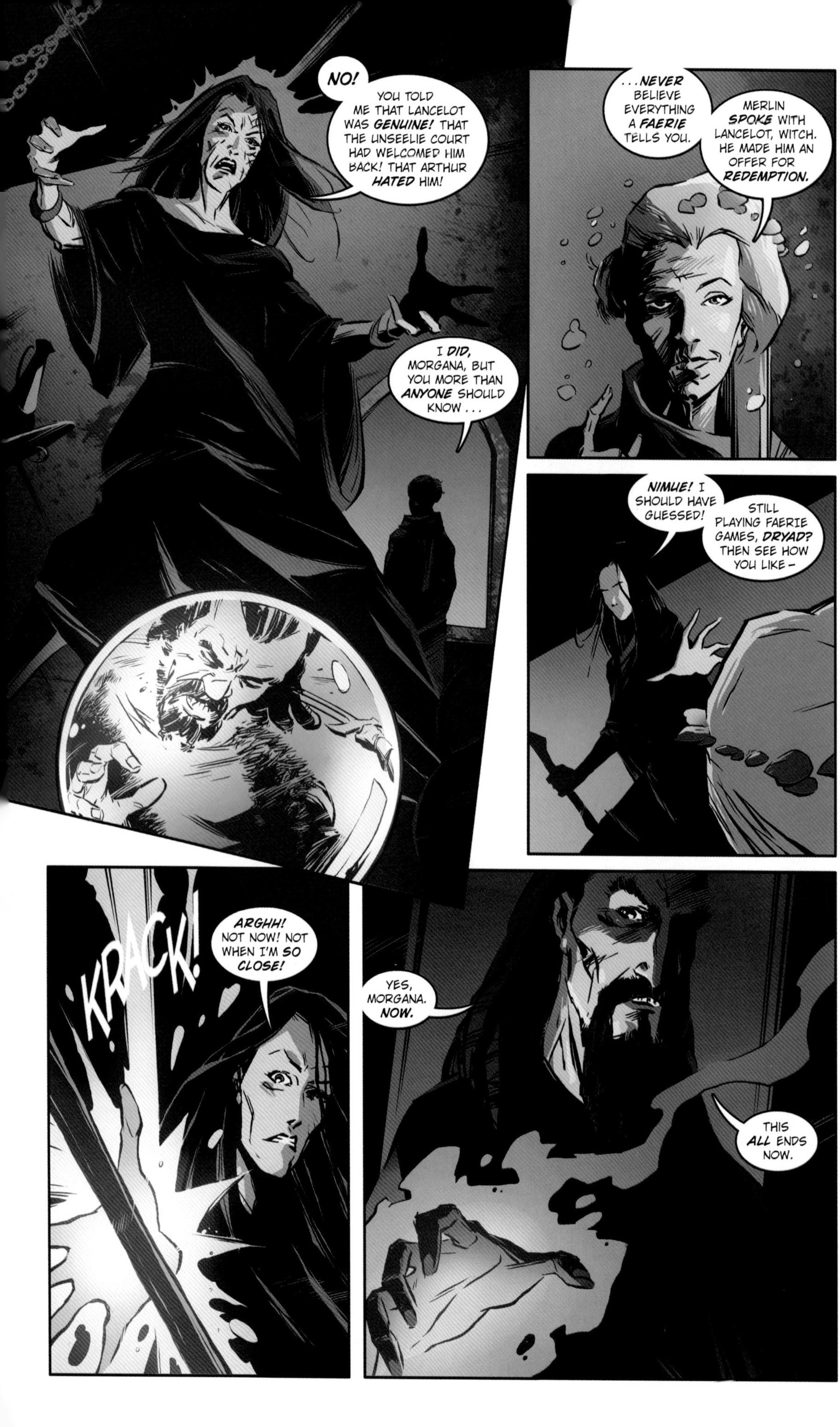
NO!
YOU TOLD ME THAT LANCELOT WAS GENUINE! THAT THE UNSEELIE COURT HAD WELCOMED HIM BACK! THAT ARTHUR HATED HIM!
I DID, MORGANA, BUT YOU MORE THAN ANYONE SHOULD KNOW . . .
. . . NEVER BELIEVE EVERYTHING A FAERIE TELLS YOU.
MERLIN SPOKE WITH LANCELOT, WITCH. HE MADE HIM AN OFFER FOR REDEMPTION.
NIMUE! I SHOULD HAVE GUESSED!
STILL PLAYING FAERIE GAMES, DRYAD? THEN SEE HOW YOU LIKE –
KRACK!
ARGHH! NOT NOW! NOT WHEN I'M SO CLOSE!
YES, MORGANA. NOW.
THIS ALL ENDS NOW.

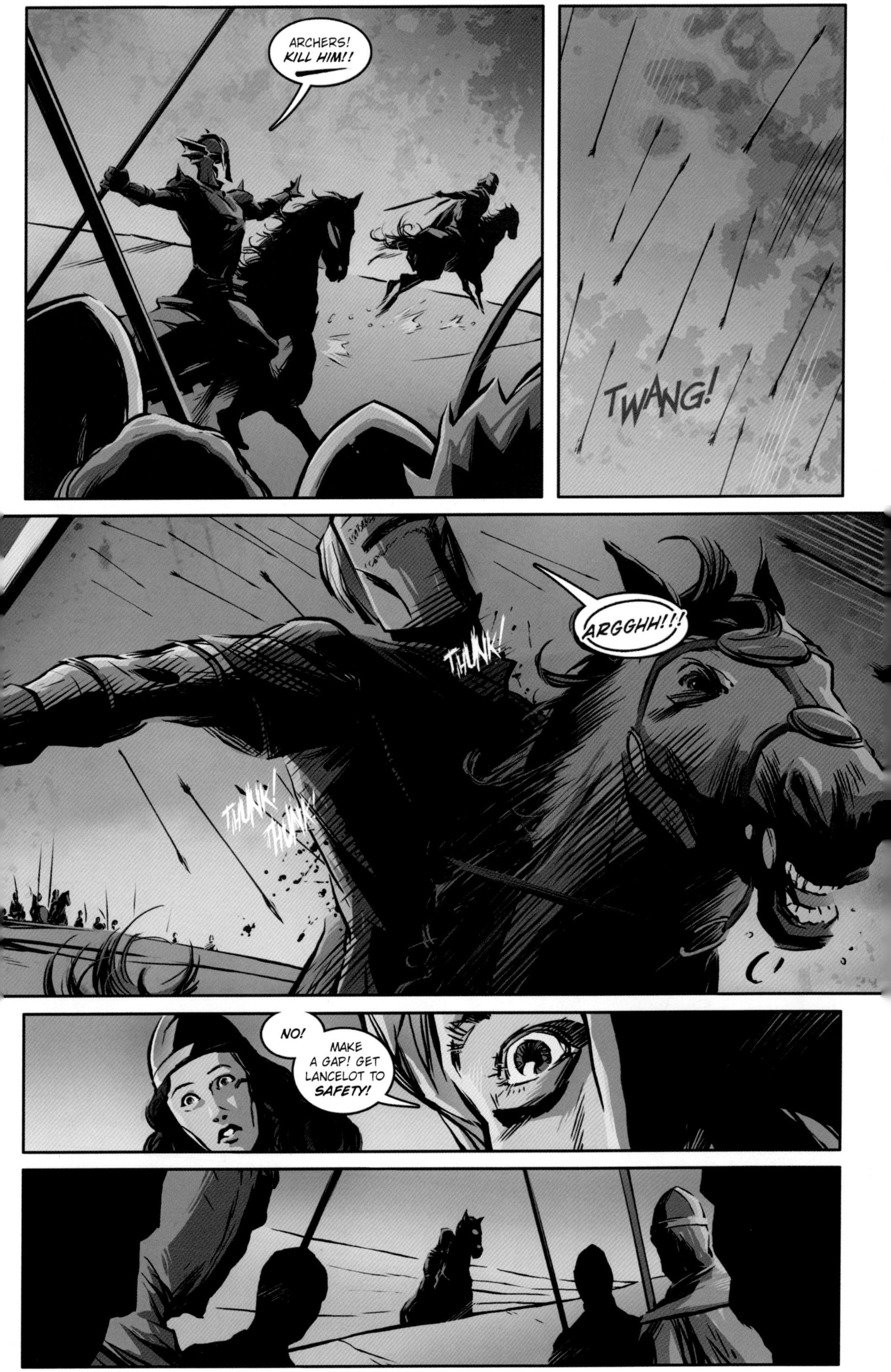

ARCHERS! KILL HIM!!
TWANG!
ARGGHH!!!
THUNK!
THUNK!
THUNK!
NO!
MAKE A GAP! GET LANCELOT TO SAFETY!

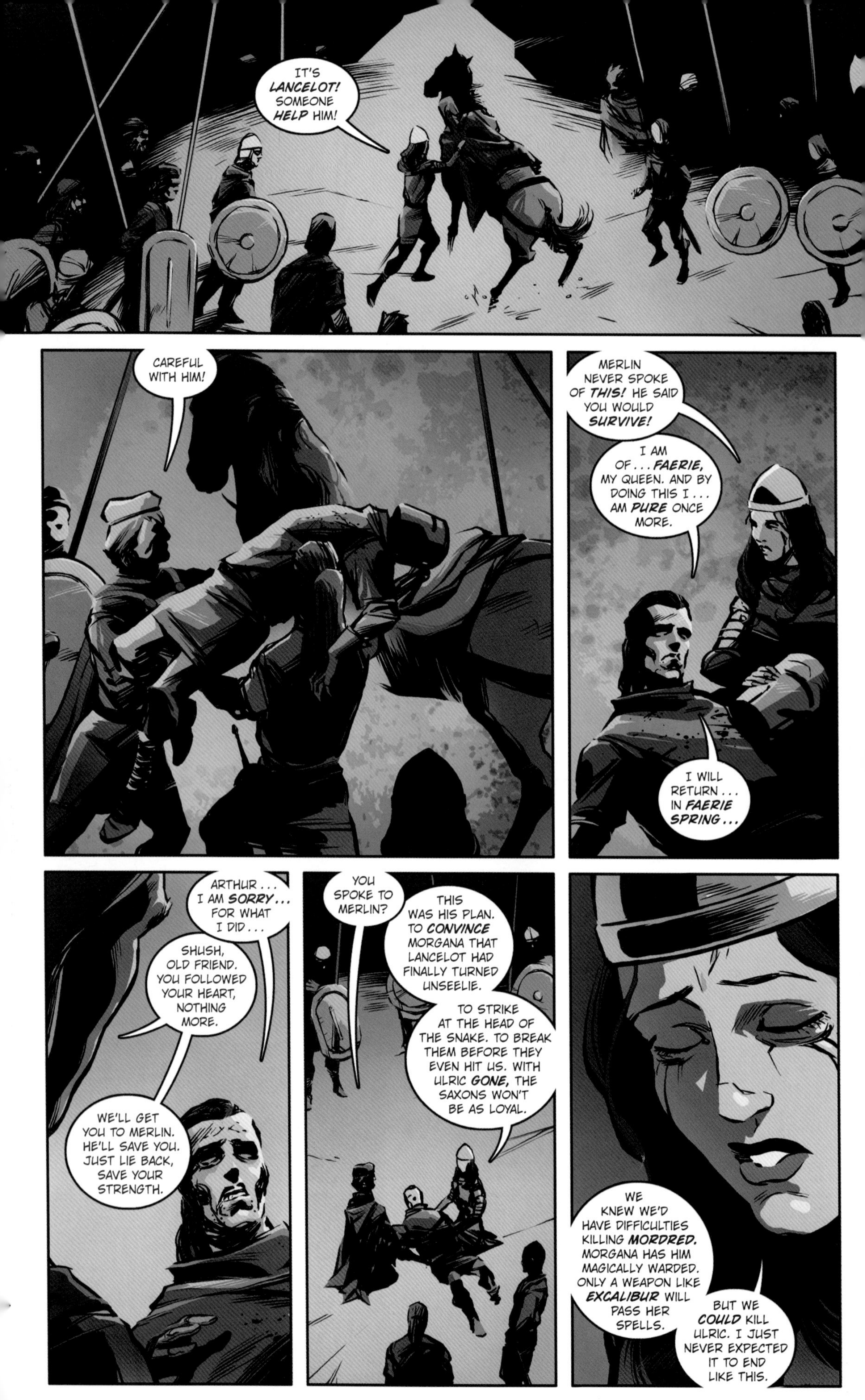
IT'S LANCELOT! SOMEONE HELP HIM!
CAREFUL WITH HIM!
MERLIN NEVER SPOKE OF THIS! HE SAID YOU WOULD SURVIVE!
I AM OF . . . FAERIE, MY QUEEN. AND BY DOING THIS I . . . AM PURE ONCE MORE.
I WILL RETURN . . . IN FAERIE SPRING . . .
ARTHUR . . . I AM SORRY . . . FOR WHAT I DID . . .
SHUSH, OLD FRIEND. YOU FOLLOWED YOUR HEART, NOTHING MORE.
WE'LL GET YOU TO MERLIN. HE'LL SAVE YOU. JUST LIE BACK, SAVE YOUR STRENGTH.
YOU SPOKE TO MERLIN?
THIS WAS HIS PLAN. TO CONVINCE MORGANA THAT LANCELOT HAD FINALLY TURNED UNSEELIE.
TO STRIKE AT THE HEAD OF THE SNAKE. TO BREAK THEM BEFORE THEY EVEN HIT US. WITH ULRIC GONE, THE SAXONS WON'T BE AS LOYAL.
WE KNEW WE'D HAVE DIFFICULTIES KILLING MORDRED. MORGANA HAS HIM MAGICALLY WARDED. ONLY A WEAPON LIKE EXCALIBUR WILL PASS HER SPELLS.
BUT WE COULD KILL ULRIC. I JUST NEVER EXPECTED IT TO END LIKE THIS.

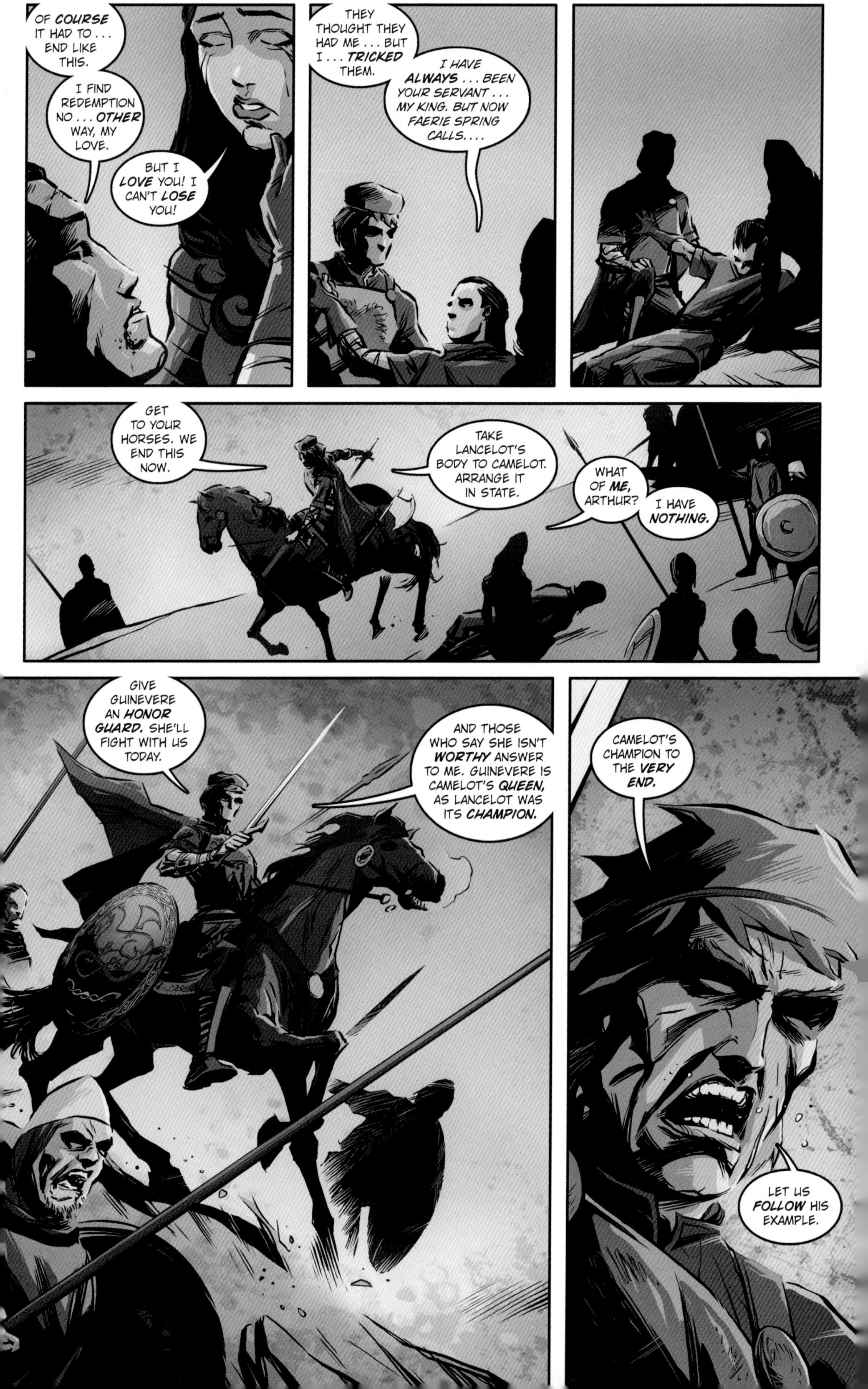

OF COURSE IT HAD TO . . . END LIKE THIS.
I FIND REDEMPTION NO . . . OTHER WAY, MY LOVE.
BUT I LOVE YOU! I CAN'T LOSE YOU!
THEY THOUGHT THEY HAD ME . . . BUT I . . . TRICKED THEM.
I HAVE ALWAYS . . . BEEN YOUR SERVANT . . . MY KING. BUT NOW FAERIE SPRING CALLS. . . .
GET TO YOUR HORSES. WE END THIS NOW.
TAKE LANCELOT'S BODY TO CAMELOT. ARRANGE IT IN STATE.
WHAT OF ME, ARTHUR?
I HAVE NOTHING.
GIVE GUINEVERE AN HONOR GUARD. SHE'LL FIGHT WITH US TODAY.
AND THOSE WHO SAY SHE ISN'T WORTHY ANSWER TO ME. GUINEVERE IS CAMELOT'S QUEEN, AS LANCELOT WAS ITS CHAMPION.
CAMELOT'S CHAMPION TO THE VERY END.
LET US FOLLOW HIS EXAMPLE.

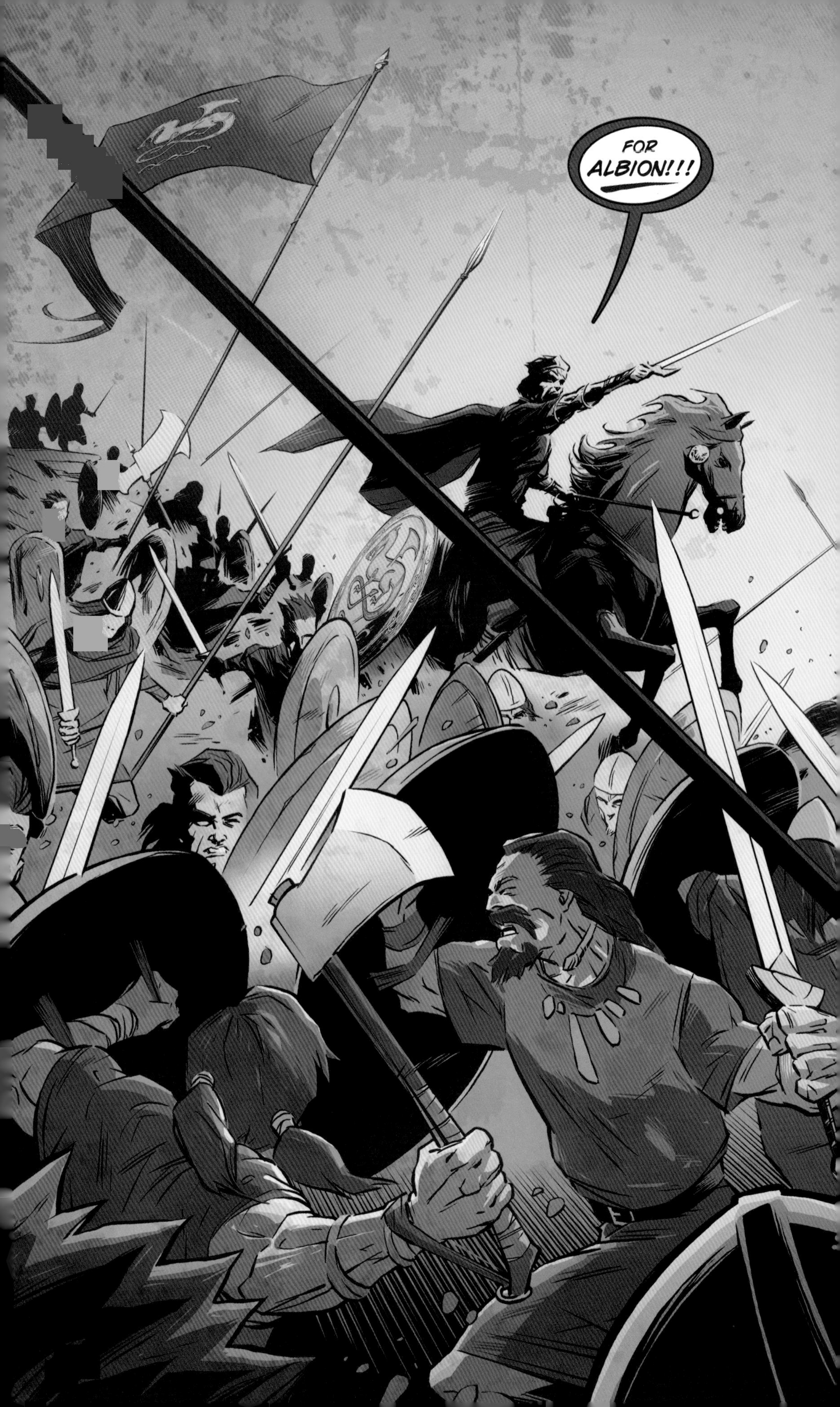
FOR ALBION!!!

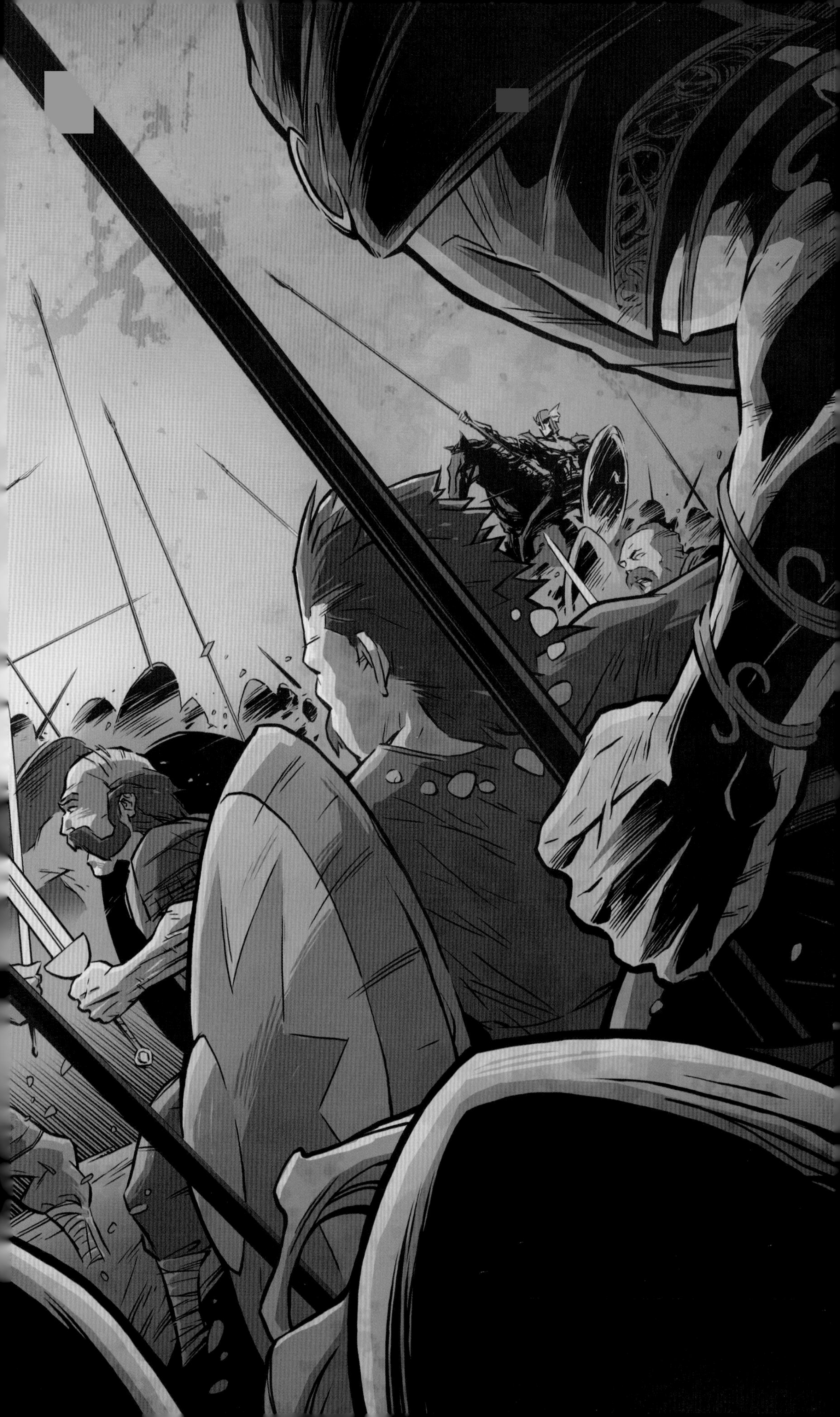

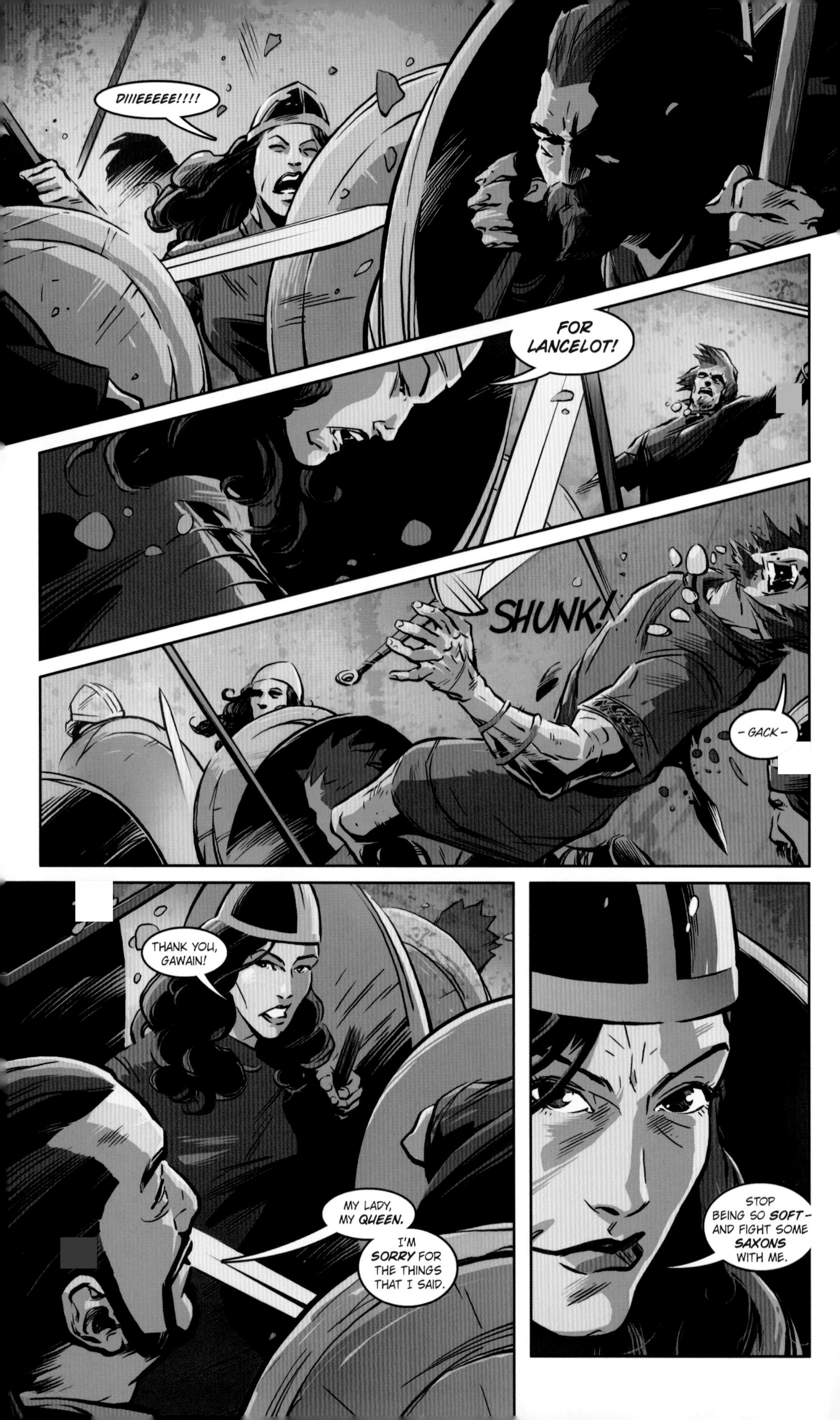
DIIIEEEEE!!!!
FOR LANCELOT!
SHUNK!
- GACK -
THANK YOU, GAWAIN!
MY LADY, MY QUEEN.
I'M SORRY FOR THE THINGS THAT I SAID.
STOP BEING SO SOFT - AND FIGHT SOME SAXONS WITH ME.

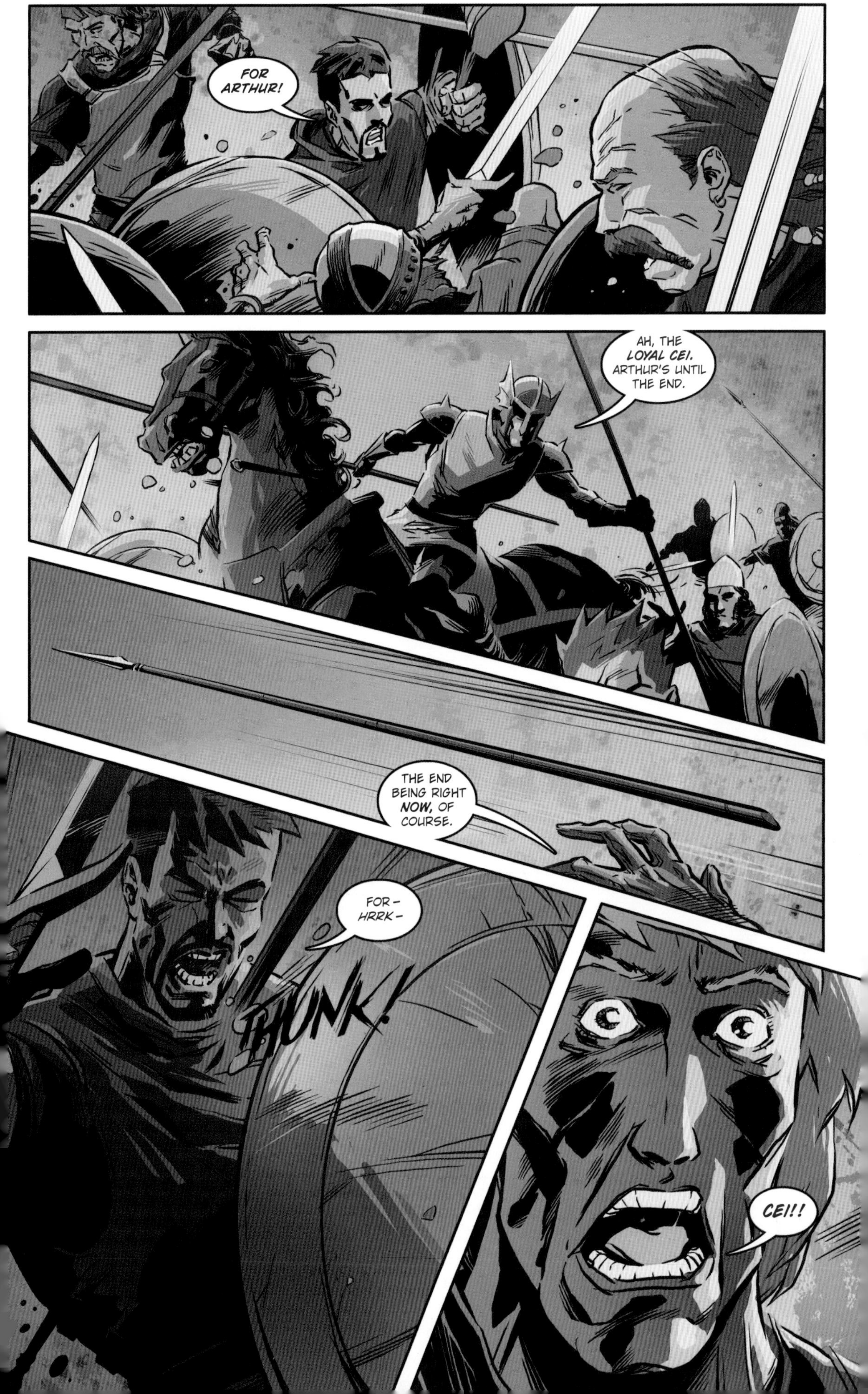

FOR ARTHUR!
AH, THE LOYAL CEI. ARTHUR'S UNTIL THE END.
THE END BEING RIGHT NOW, OF COURSE.
FOR- HRRK-
THUNK!
CEI!!

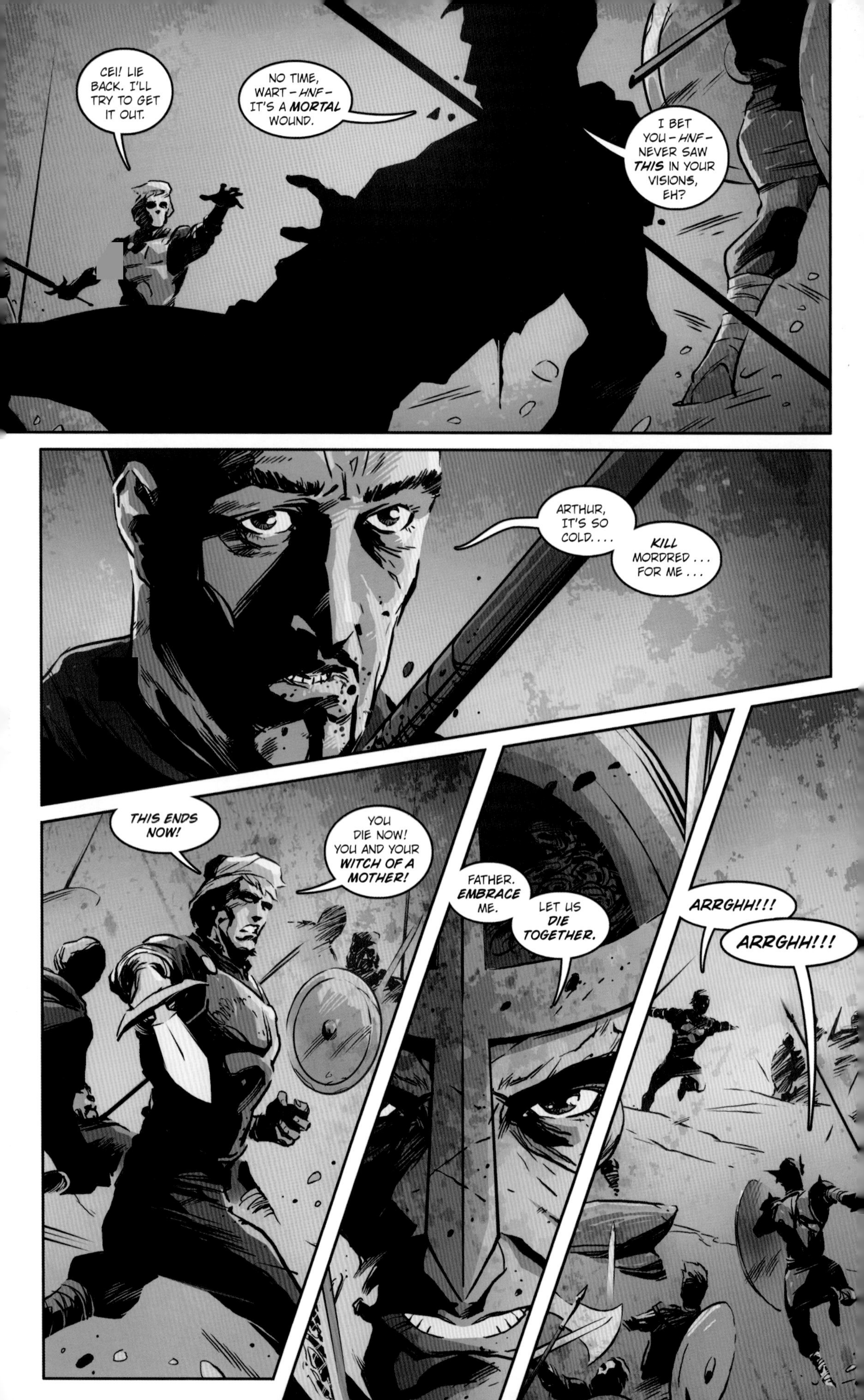
CEI! LIE BACK. I'LL TRY TO GET IT OUT.
NO TIME, WART—HNF—IT'S A MORTAL WOUND.
I BET YOU—HNF—NEVER SAW THIS IN YOUR VISIONS, EH?
ARTHUR, IT'S SO COLD. . . .
KILL MORDRED . . . FOR ME . . .
THIS ENDS NOW!
YOU DIE NOW! YOU AND YOUR WITCH OF A MOTHER!
FATHER. EMBRACE ME.
LET US DIE TOGETHER.
ARRGHH!!!
ARRGHH!!!

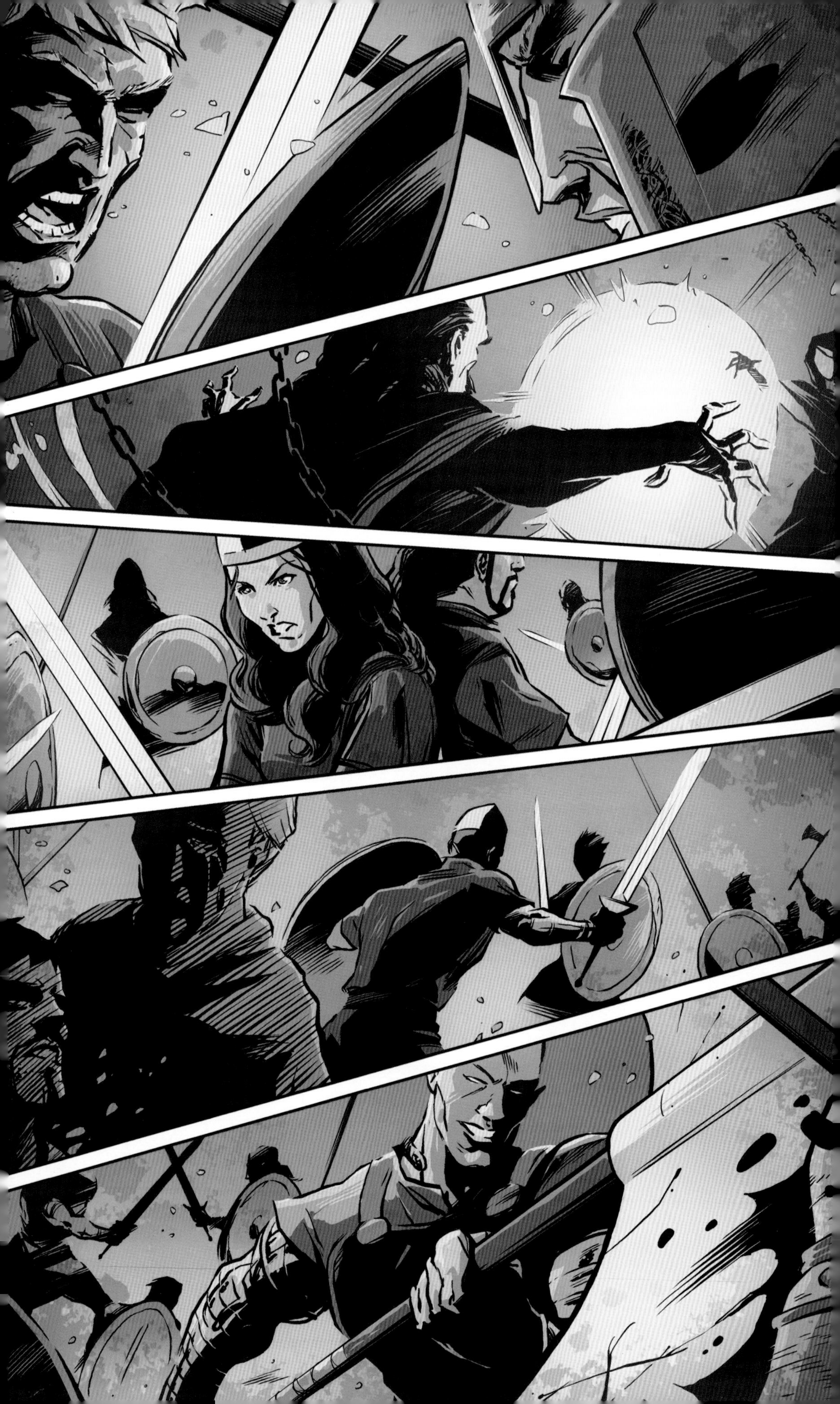

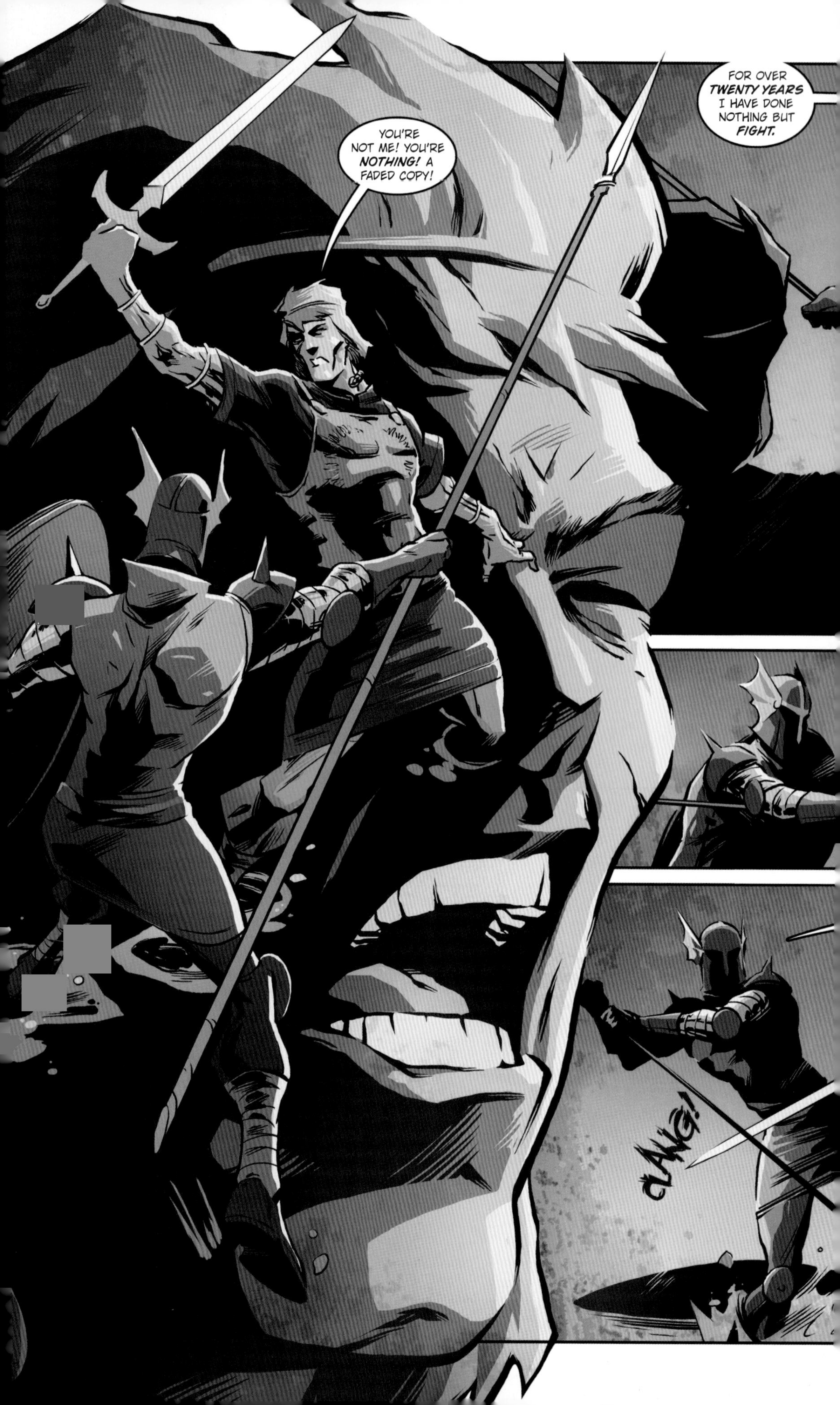
FOR OVER TWENTY YEARS I HAVE DONE NOTHING BUT FIGHT.
YOU'RE NOT ME! YOU'RE NOTHING! A FADED COPY!
CLANG!

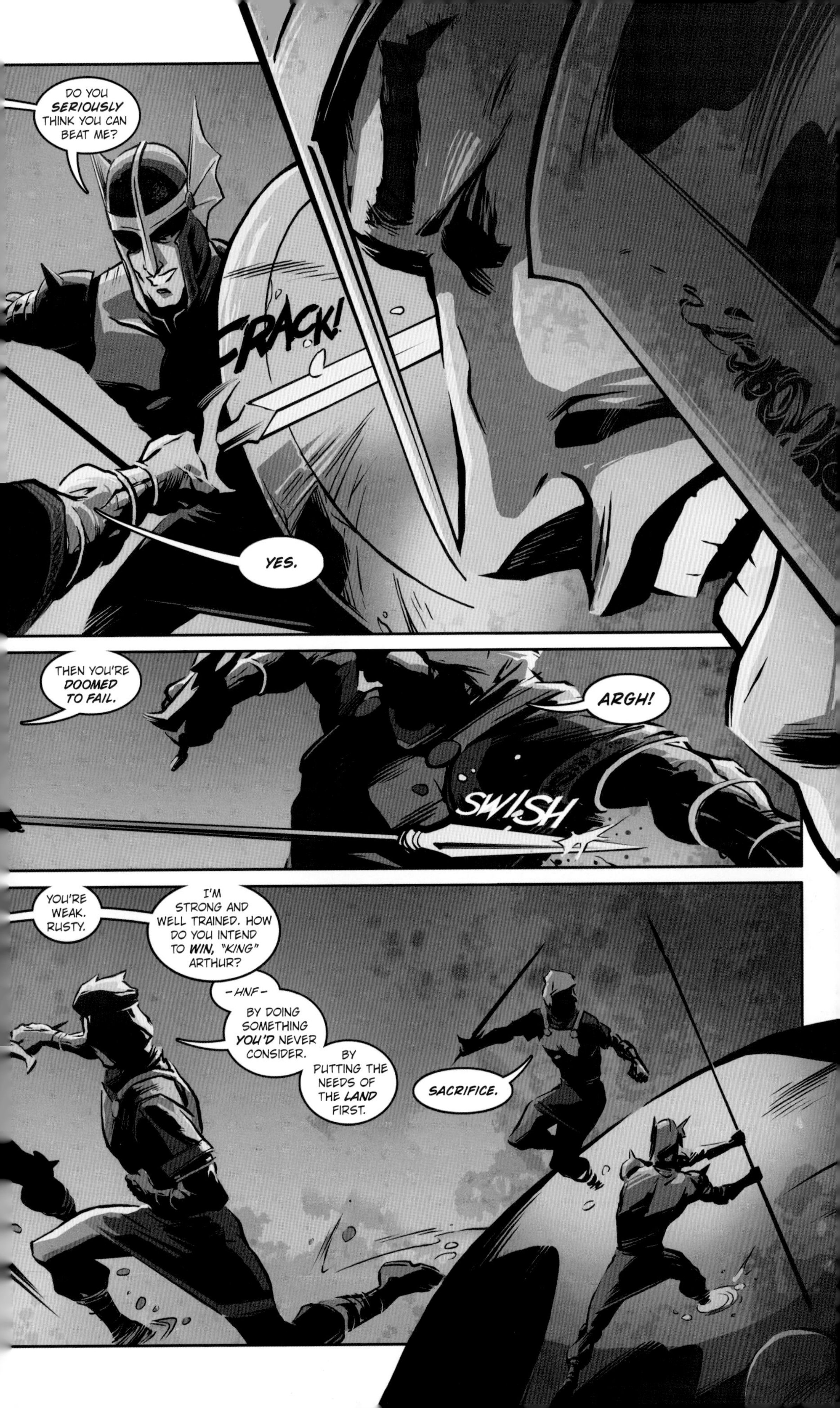
DO YOU SERIOUSLY THINK YOU CAN BEAT ME?
CRACK!
YES.
THEN YOU'RE DOOMED TO FAIL.
ARGH!
SWISH
YOU'RE WEAK. RUSTY.
I'M STRONG AND WELL TRAINED. HOW DO YOU INTEND TO WIN, "KING" ARTHUR?
-HNF-
BY DOING SOMETHING YOU'D NEVER CONSIDER.
BY PUTTING THE NEEDS OF THE LAND FIRST.
SACRIFICE.

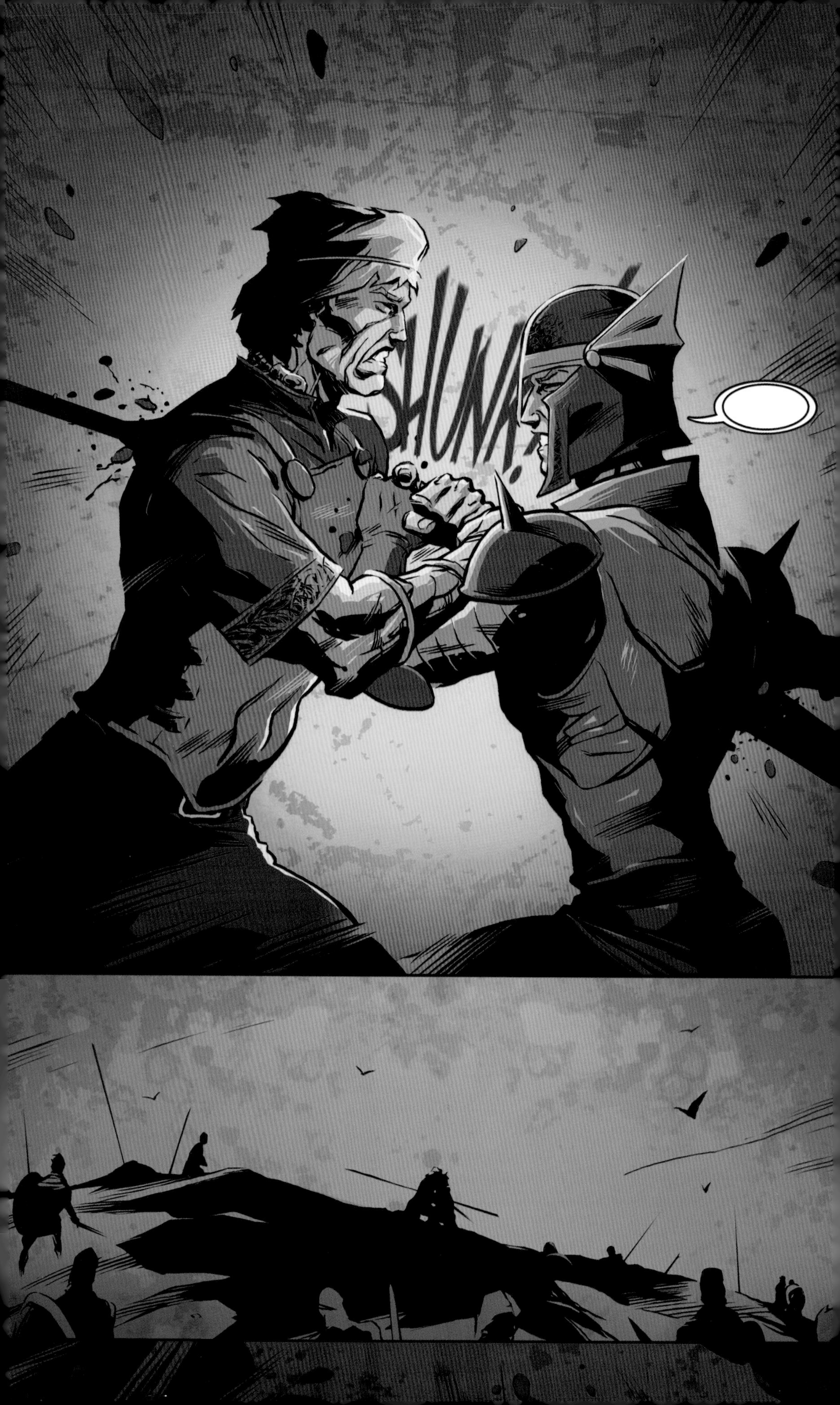

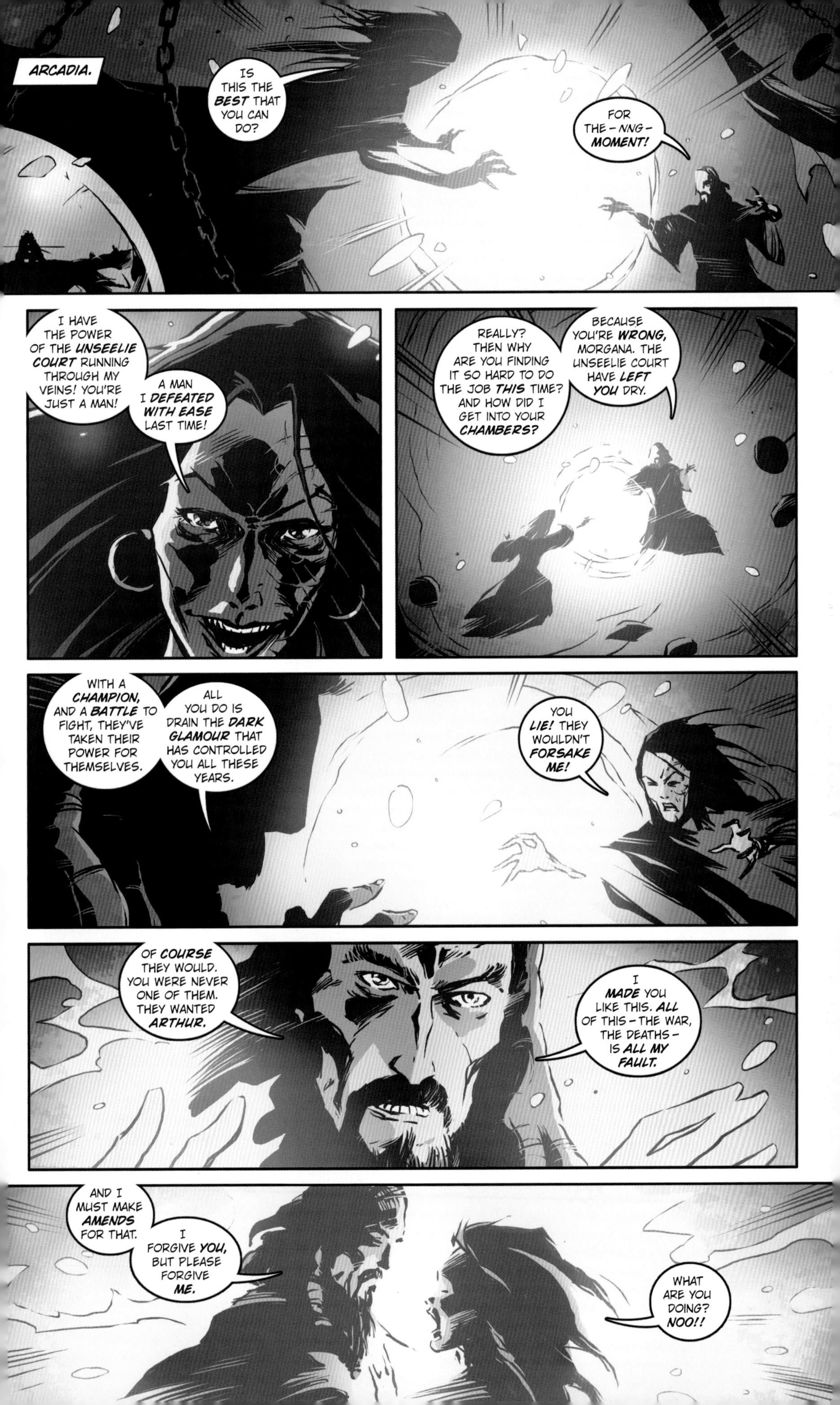
ARCADIA.
IS THIS THE BEST THAT YOU CAN DO?
FOR THE — NNG — MOMENT!
I HAVE THE POWER OF THE UNSEELIE COURT RUNNING THROUGH MY VEINS! YOU'RE JUST A MAN!
A MAN I DEFEATED WITH EASE LAST TIME!
REALLY? THEN WHY ARE YOU FINDING IT SO HARD TO DO THE JOB THIS TIME? AND HOW DID I GET INTO YOUR CHAMBERS?
BECAUSE YOU'RE WRONG, MORGANA. THE UNSEELIE COURT HAVE LEFT YOU DRY.
WITH A CHAMPION, AND A BATTLE TO FIGHT, THEY'VE TAKEN THEIR POWER FOR THEMSELVES.
ALL YOU DO IS DRAIN THE DARK GLAMOUR THAT HAS CONTROLLED YOU ALL THESE YEARS.
YOU LIE! THEY WOULDN'T FORSAKE ME!
OF COURSE THEY WOULD. YOU WERE NEVER ONE OF THEM. THEY WANTED ARTHUR.
I MADE YOU LIKE THIS. ALL OF THIS — THE WAR, THE DEATHS — IS ALL MY FAULT.
AND I MUST MAKE AMENDS FOR THAT.
I FORGIVE YOU, BUT PLEASE FORGIVE ME.
WHAT ARE YOU DOING? NOO!!

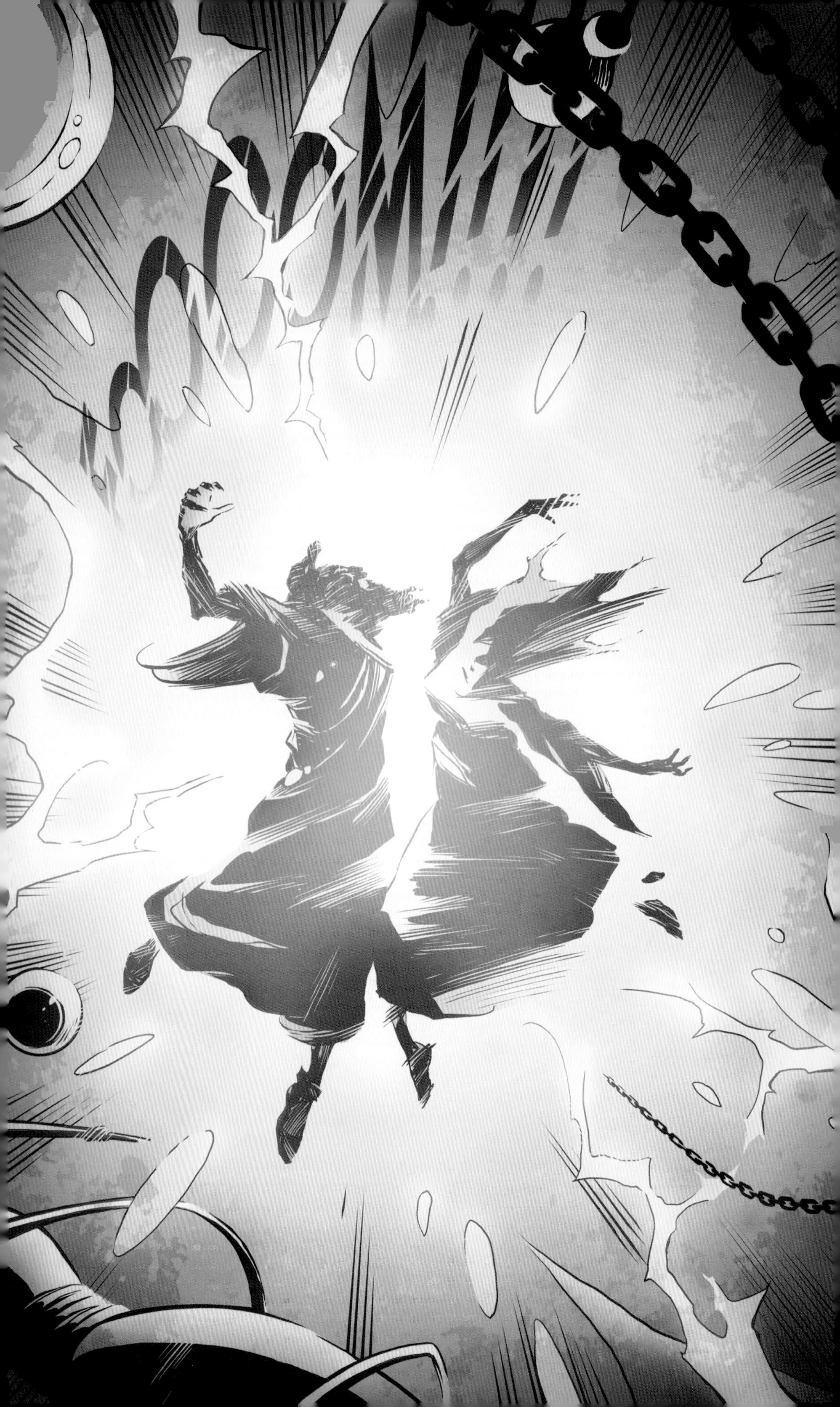

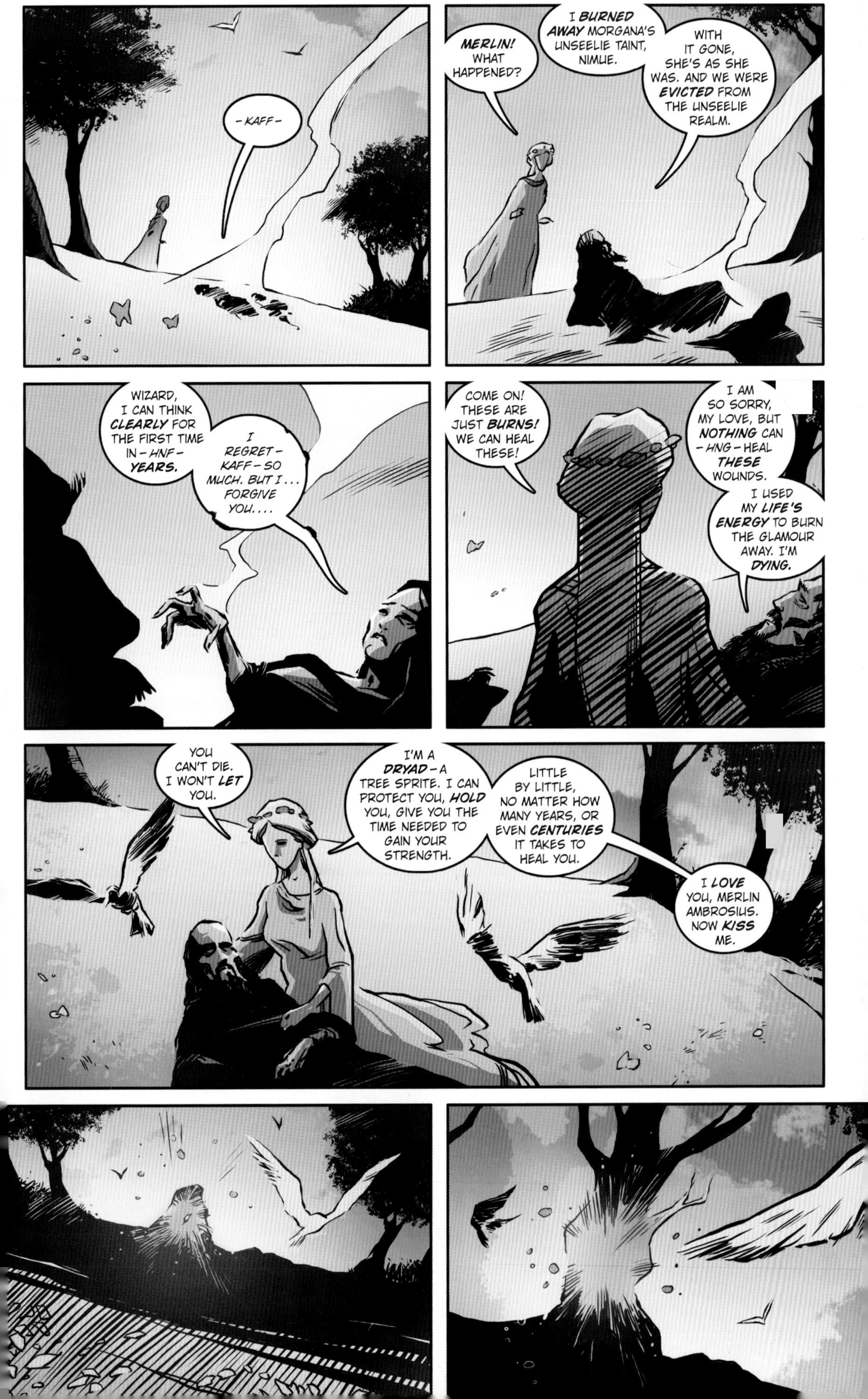
-KAFF-
MERLIN! WHAT HAPPENED?
I BURNED AWAY MORGANA'S UNSEELIE TAINT, NIMUE.
WITH IT GONE, SHE'S AS SHE WAS. AND WE WERE EVICTED FROM THE UNSEELIE REALM.
WIZARD, I CAN THINK CLEARLY FOR THE FIRST TIME IN -HNF- YEARS.
I REGRET -KAFF- SO MUCH. BUT I... FORGIVE YOU....
COME ON! THESE ARE JUST BURNS! WE CAN HEAL THESE!
I AM SO SORRY, MY LOVE, BUT NOTHING CAN -HNG- HEAL THESE WOUNDS.
I USED MY LIFE'S ENERGY TO BURN THE GLAMOUR AWAY. I'M DYING.
YOU CAN'T DIE. I WON'T LET YOU.
I'M A DRYAD -A TREE SPRITE. I CAN PROTECT YOU, HOLD YOU, GIVE YOU THE TIME NEEDED TO GAIN YOUR STRENGTH.
LITTLE BY LITTLE, NO MATTER HOW MANY YEARS, OR EVEN CENTURIES IT TAKES TO HEAL YOU.
I LOVE YOU, MERLIN AMBROSIUS. NOW KISS ME.

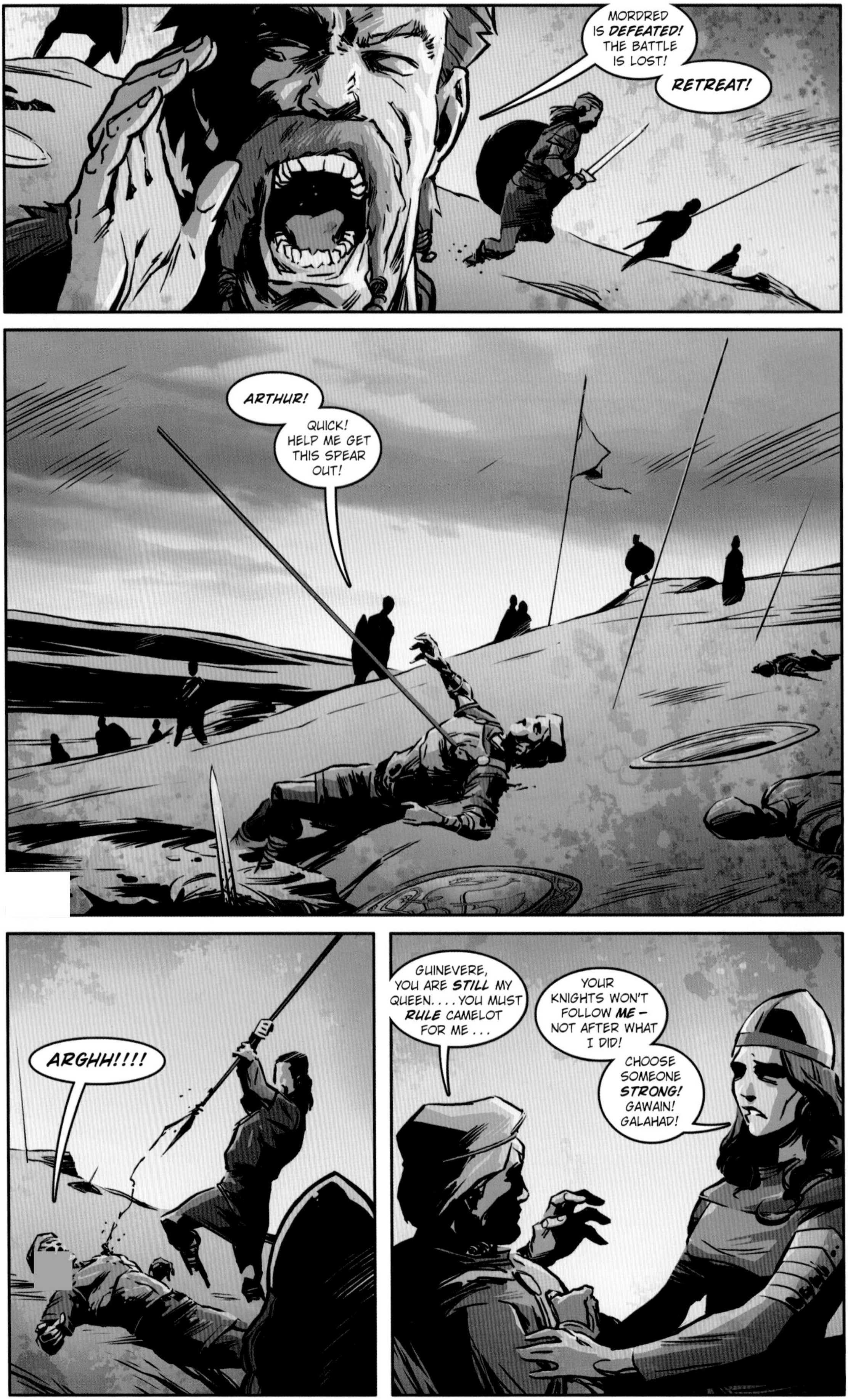
MORDRED IS DEFEATED! THE BATTLE IS LOST!
RETREAT!
ARTHUR!
QUICK! HELP ME GET THIS SPEAR OUT!
ARGHH!!!!
GUINEVERE, YOU ARE STILL MY QUEEN. . . . YOU MUST RULE CAMELOT FOR ME . . .
YOUR KNIGHTS WON'T FOLLOW ME — NOT AFTER WHAT I DID!
CHOOSE SOMEONE STRONG! GAWAIN! GALAHAD!

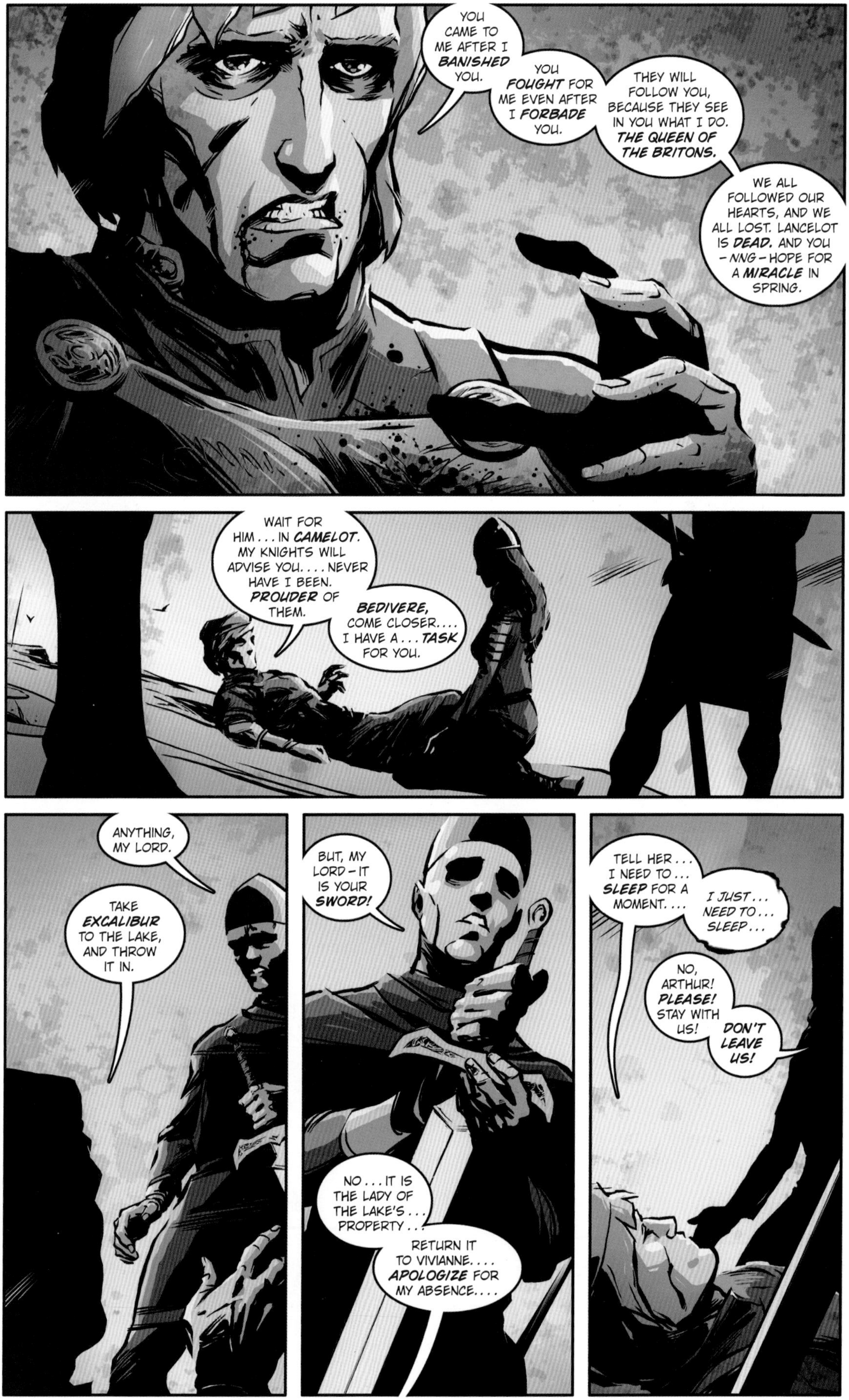
YOU CAME TO ME AFTER I BANISHED YOU.
YOU FOUGHT FOR ME EVEN AFTER I FORBADE YOU.
THEY WILL FOLLOW YOU, BECAUSE THEY SEE IN YOU WHAT I DO. THE QUEEN OF THE BRITONS.
WE ALL FOLLOWED OUR HEARTS, AND WE ALL LOST. LANCELOT IS DEAD. AND YOU –NNG– HOPE FOR A MIRACLE IN SPRING.
WAIT FOR HIM . . . IN CAMELOT. MY KNIGHTS WILL ADVISE YOU. . . . NEVER HAVE I BEEN. PROUDER OF THEM.
BEDIVERE, COME CLOSER. . . . I HAVE A . . . TASK FOR YOU.
ANYTHING, MY LORD.
TAKE EXCALIBUR TO THE LAKE, AND THROW IT IN.
BUT, MY LORD – IT IS YOUR SWORD!
NO . . . IT IS THE LADY OF THE LAKE'S PROPERTY . . .
RETURN IT TO VIVIANNE. . . . APOLOGIZE FOR MY ABSENCE. . . .
TELL HER . . . I NEED TO . . . SLEEP FOR A MOMENT. . . .
I JUST . . . NEED TO . . . SLEEP . . .
NO, ARTHUR! PLEASE! STAY WITH US!
DON'T LEAVE US!

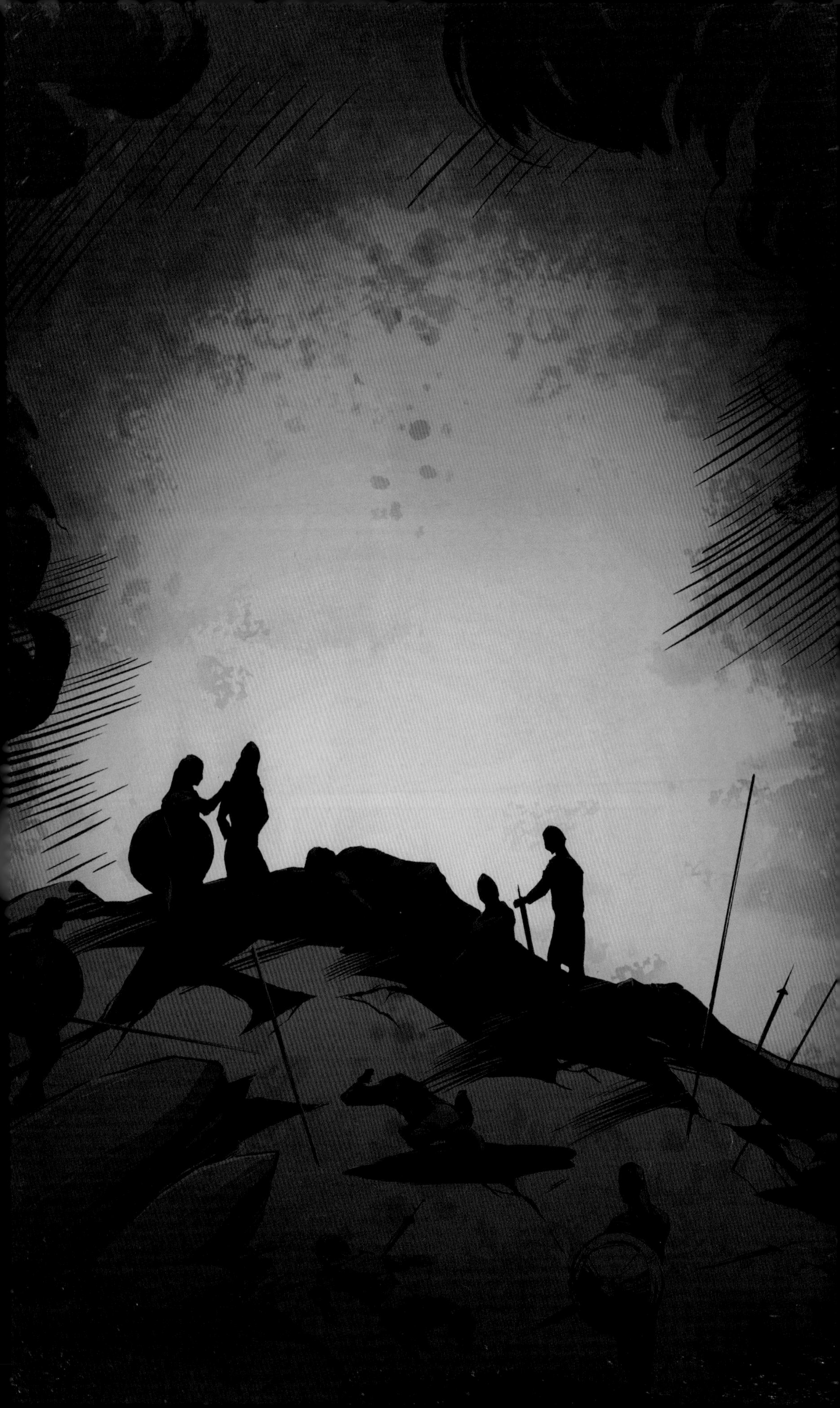

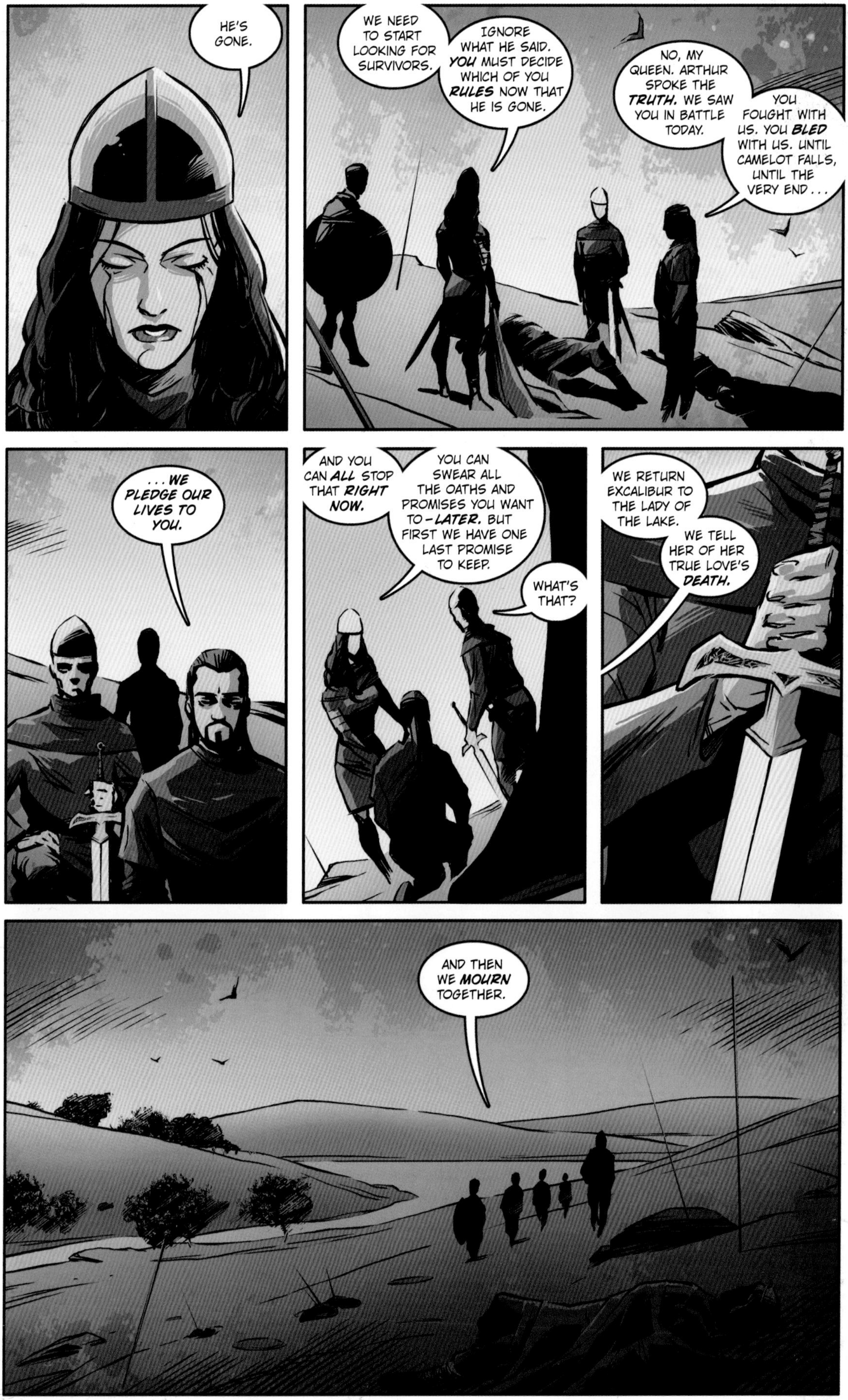

HE'S GONE.
WE NEED TO START LOOKING FOR SURVIVORS.
IGNORE WHAT HE SAID. YOU MUST DECIDE WHICH OF YOU RULES NOW THAT HE IS GONE.
NO, MY QUEEN. ARTHUR SPOKE THE TRUTH. WE SAW YOU IN BATTLE TODAY.
YOU FOUGHT WITH US. YOU BLED WITH US. UNTIL CAMELOT FALLS, UNTIL THE VERY END . . .
. . . WE PLEDGE OUR LIVES TO YOU.
AND YOU CAN ALL STOP THAT RIGHT NOW.
YOU CAN SWEAR ALL THE OATHS AND PROMISES YOU WANT TO—LATER. BUT FIRST WE HAVE ONE LAST PROMISE TO KEEP.
WHAT'S THAT?
WE RETURN EXCALIBUR TO THE LADY OF THE LAKE.
WE TELL HER OF HER TRUE LOVE'S DEATH.
AND THEN WE MOURN TOGETHER.

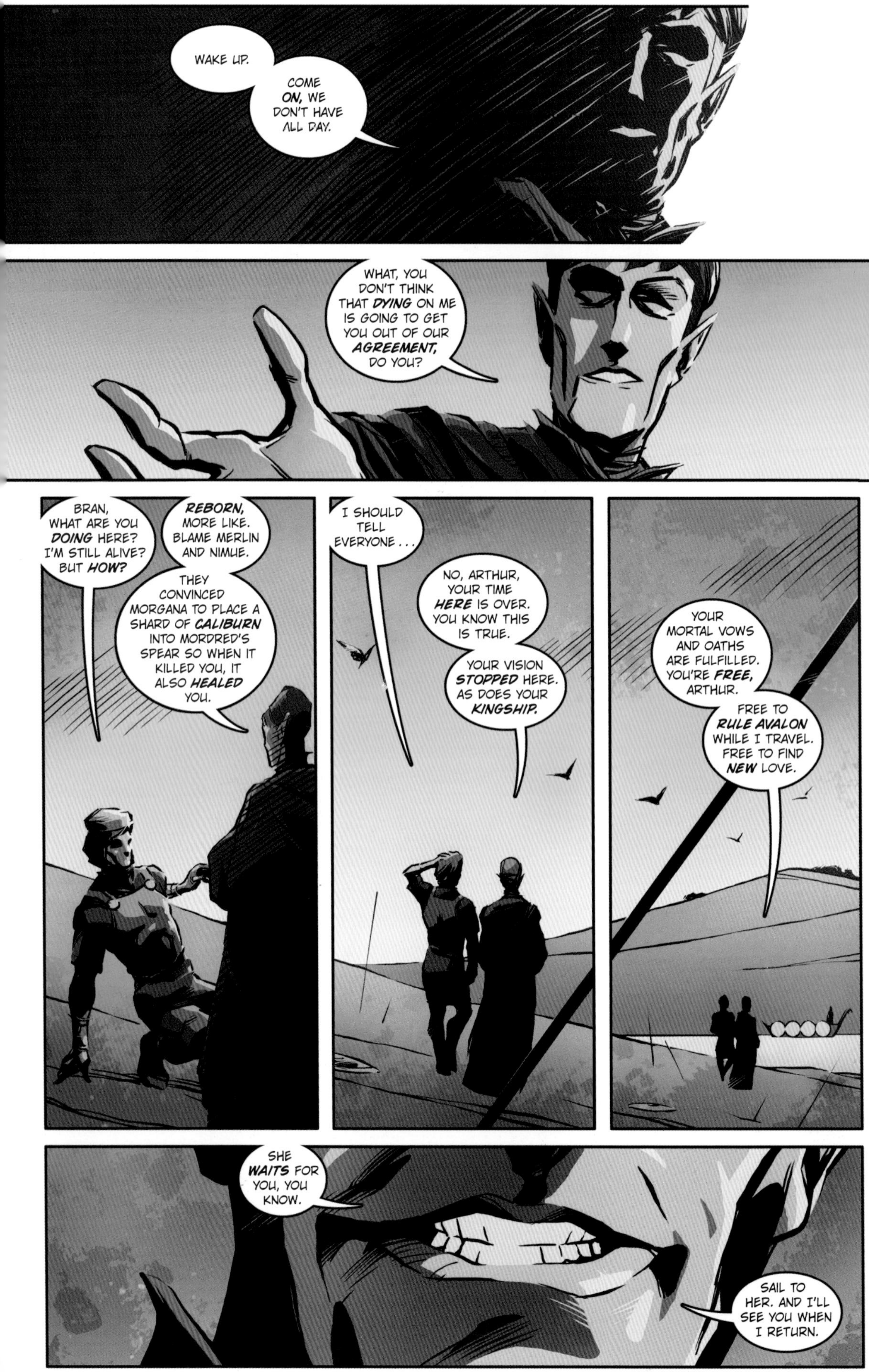
WAKE UP.
COME ON, WE DON'T HAVE ALL DAY.
WHAT, YOU DON'T THINK THAT DYING ON ME IS GOING TO GET YOU OUT OF OUR AGREEMENT, DO YOU?
BRAN, WHAT ARE YOU DOING HERE? I'M STILL ALIVE? BUT HOW?
REBORN, MORE LIKE. BLAME MERLIN AND NIMUE.
THEY CONVINCED MORGANA TO PLACE A SHARD OF CALIBURN INTO MORDRED'S SPEAR SO WHEN IT KILLED YOU, IT ALSO HEALED YOU.
I SHOULD TELL EVERYONE . . .
NO, ARTHUR, YOUR TIME HERE IS OVER. YOU KNOW THIS IS TRUE.
YOUR VISION STOPPED HERE. AS DOES YOUR KINGSHIP.
YOUR MORTAL VOWS AND OATHS ARE FULFILLED. YOU'RE FREE, ARTHUR.
FREE TO RULE AVALON WHILE I TRAVEL. FREE TO FIND NEW LOVE.
SHE WAITS FOR YOU, YOU KNOW.
SAIL TO HER. AND I'LL SEE YOU WHEN I RETURN.

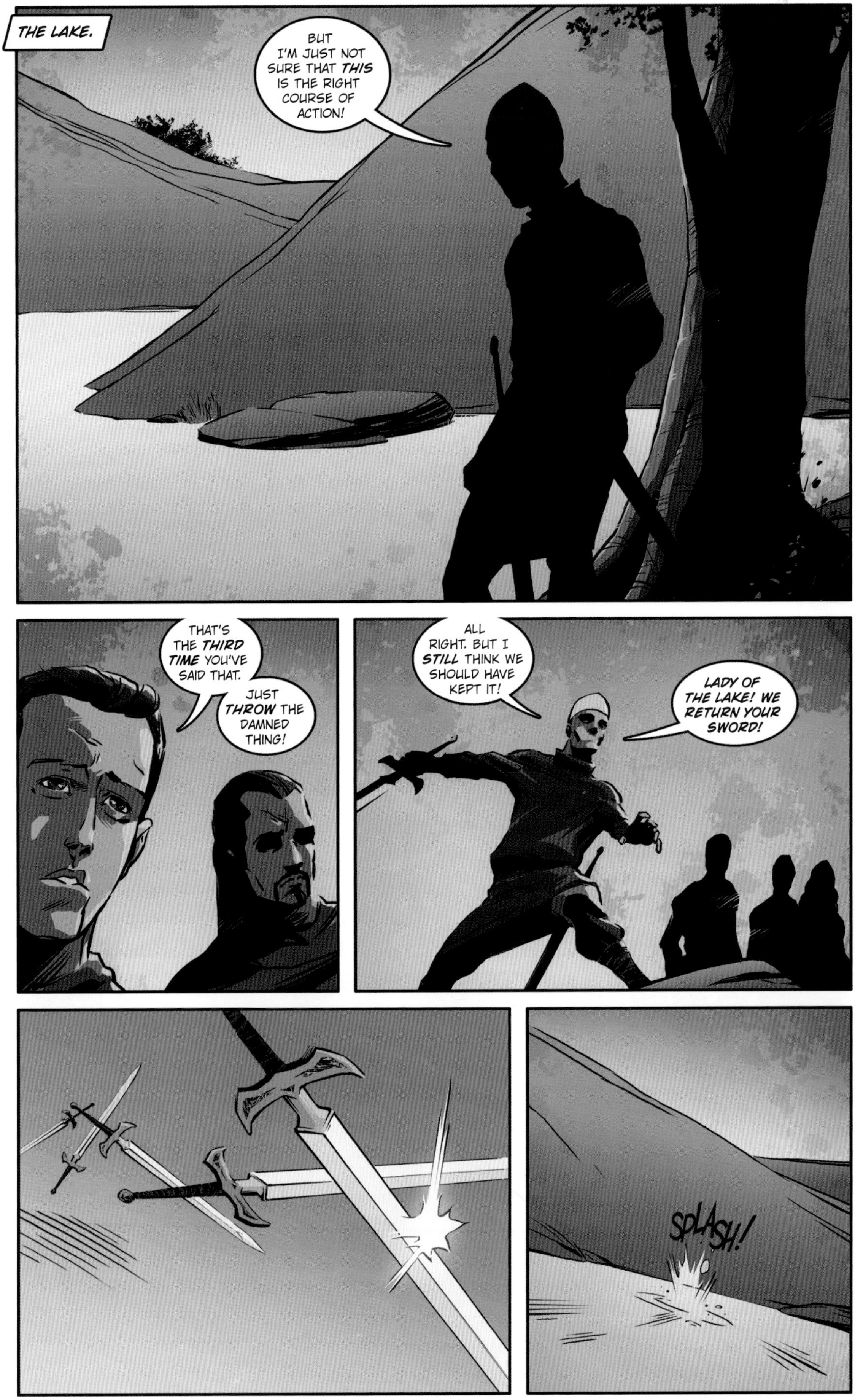
THE LAKE.
BUT I'M JUST NOT SURE THAT THIS IS THE RIGHT COURSE OF ACTION!
THAT'S THE THIRD TIME YOU'VE SAID THAT.
JUST THROW THE DAMNED THING!
ALL RIGHT. BUT I STILL THINK WE SHOULD HAVE KEPT IT!
LADY OF THE LAKE! WE RETURN YOUR SWORD!
SPLASH!

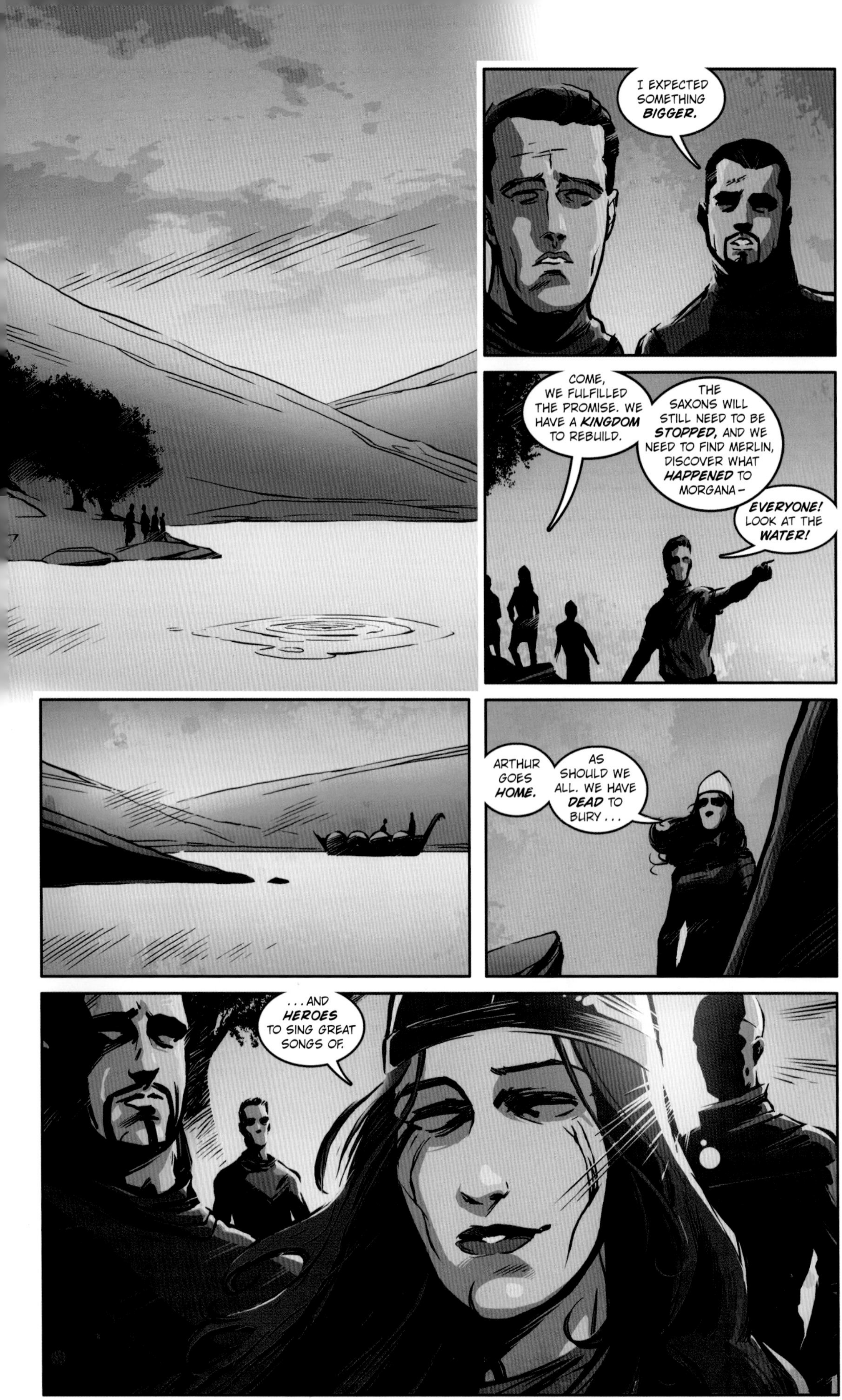
I EXPECTED SOMETHING BIGGER.
COME, WE FULFILLED THE PROMISE. WE HAVE A KINGDOM TO REBUILD.
THE SAXONS WILL STILL NEED TO BE STOPPED, AND WE NEED TO FIND MERLIN, DISCOVER WHAT HAPPENED TO MORGANA–
EVERYONE! LOOK AT THE WATER!
ARTHUR GOES HOME.
AS SHOULD WE ALL. WE HAVE DEAD TO BURY . . .
. . . AND HEROES TO SING GREAT SONGS OF.

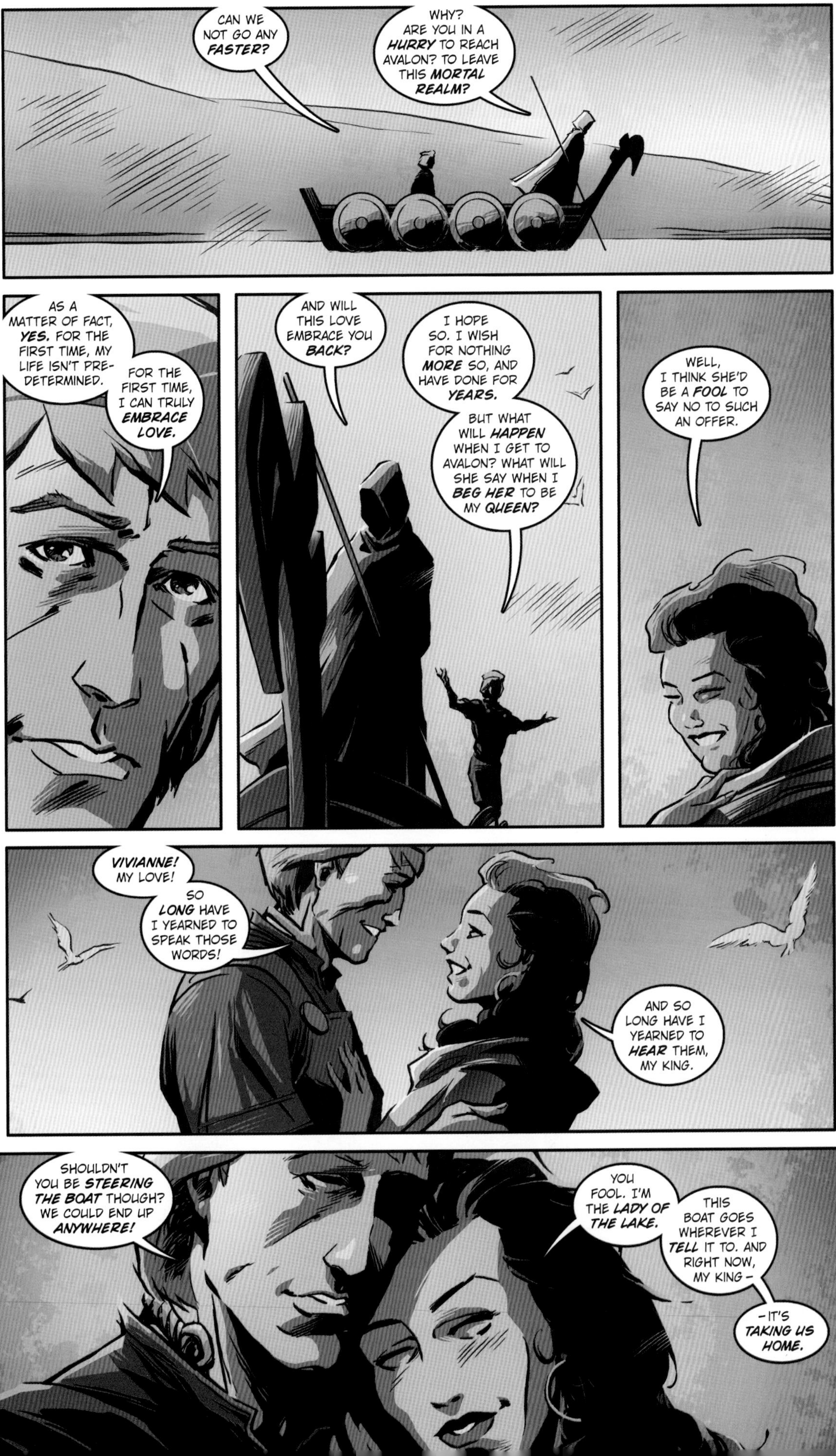
CAN WE NOT GO ANY FASTER?
WHY? ARE YOU IN A HURRY TO REACH AVALON? TO LEAVE THIS MORTAL REALM?
AS A MATTER OF FACT, YES. FOR THE FIRST TIME, MY LIFE ISN'T PRE-DETERMINED.
FOR THE FIRST TIME, I CAN TRULY EMBRACE LOVE.
AND WILL THIS LOVE EMBRACE YOU BACK?
I HOPE SO. I WISH FOR NOTHING MORE SO, AND HAVE DONE FOR YEARS.
BUT WHAT WILL HAPPEN WHEN I GET TO AVALON? WHAT WILL SHE SAY WHEN I BEG HER TO BE MY QUEEN?
WELL, I THINK SHE'D BE A FOOL TO SAY NO TO SUCH AN OFFER.
VIVIANNE! MY LOVE!
SO LONG HAVE I YEARNED TO SPEAK THOSE WORDS!
AND SO LONG HAVE I YEARNED TO HEAR THEM, MY KING.
SHOULDN'T YOU BE STEERING THE BOAT THOUGH? WE COULD END UP ANYWHERE!
YOU FOOL. I'M THE LADY OF THE LAKE.
THIS BOAT GOES WHEREVER I TELL IT TO. AND RIGHT NOW, MY KING –
– IT'S TAKING US HOME.

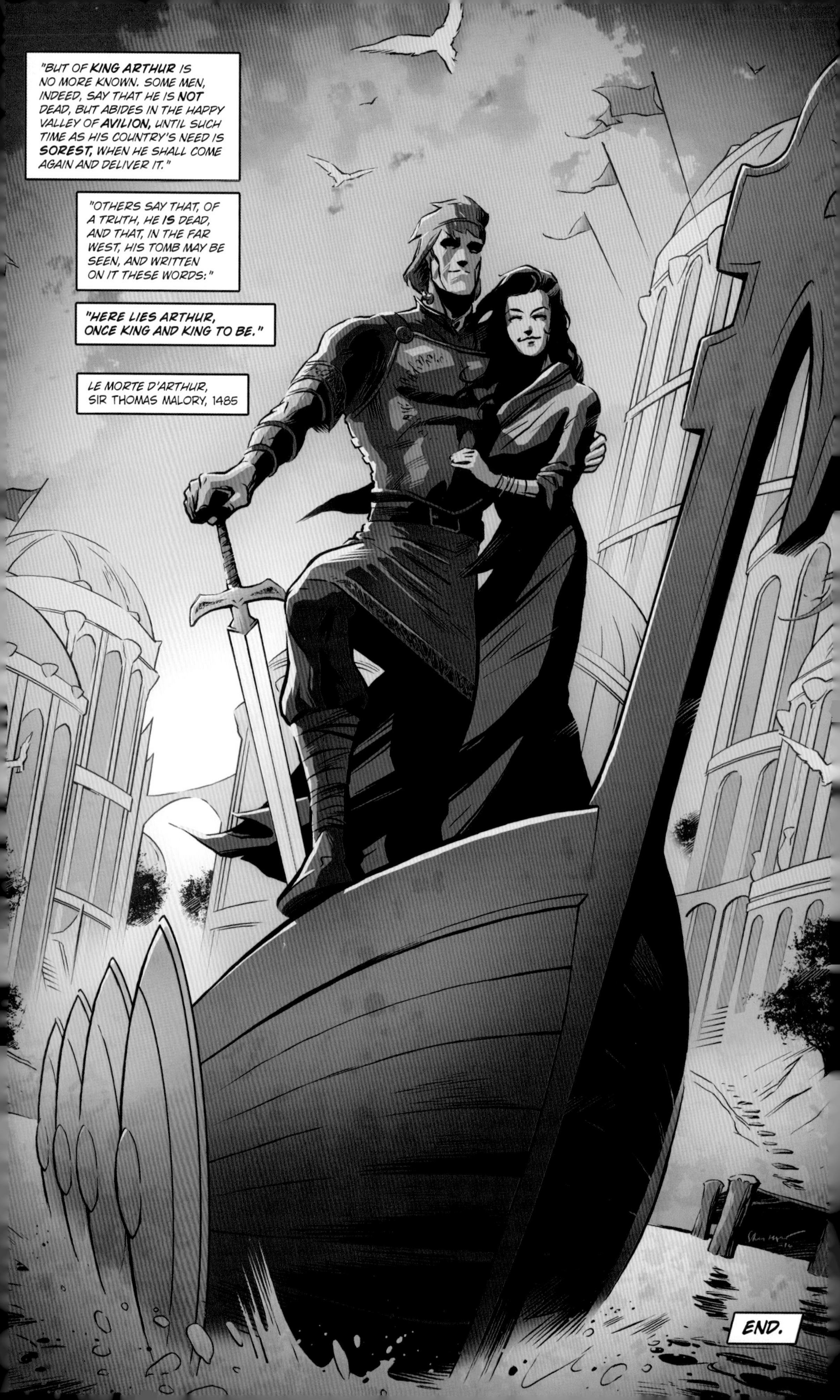
"BUT OF KING ARTHUR IS NO MORE KNOWN. SOME MEN, INDEED, SAY THAT HE IS NOT DEAD, BUT ABIDES IN THE HAPPY VALLEY OF AVILION, UNTIL SUCH TIME AS HIS COUNTRY'S NEED IS SOREST, WHEN HE SHALL COME AGAIN AND DELIVER IT."
"OTHERS SAY THAT, OF A TRUTH, HE IS DEAD, AND THAT, IN THE FAR WEST, HIS TOMB MAY BE SEEN, AND WRITTEN ON IT THESE WORDS:"
"HERE LIES ARTHUR, ONCE KING AND KING TO BE."
LE MORTE D'ARTHUR, SIR THOMAS MALORY, 1485
END.

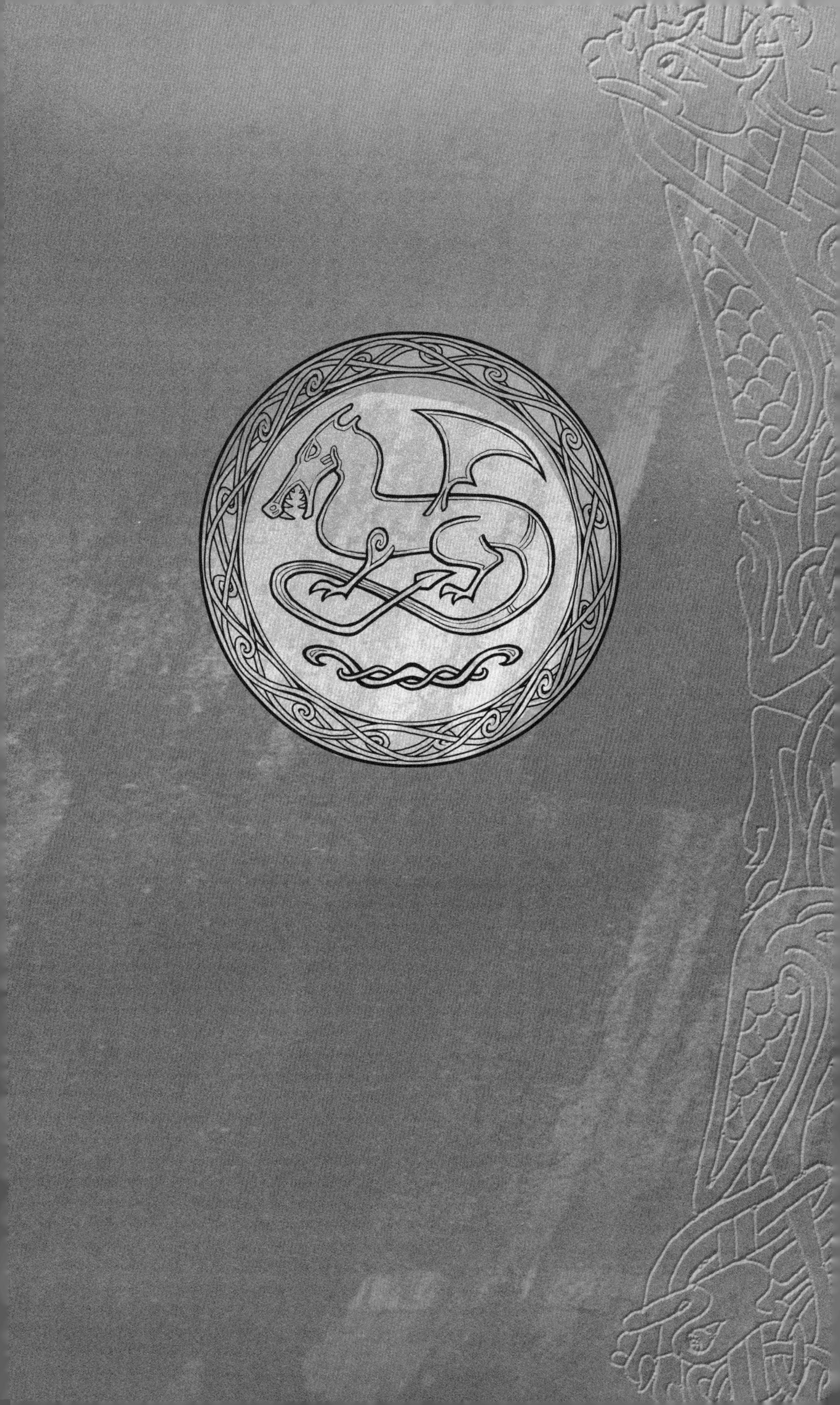

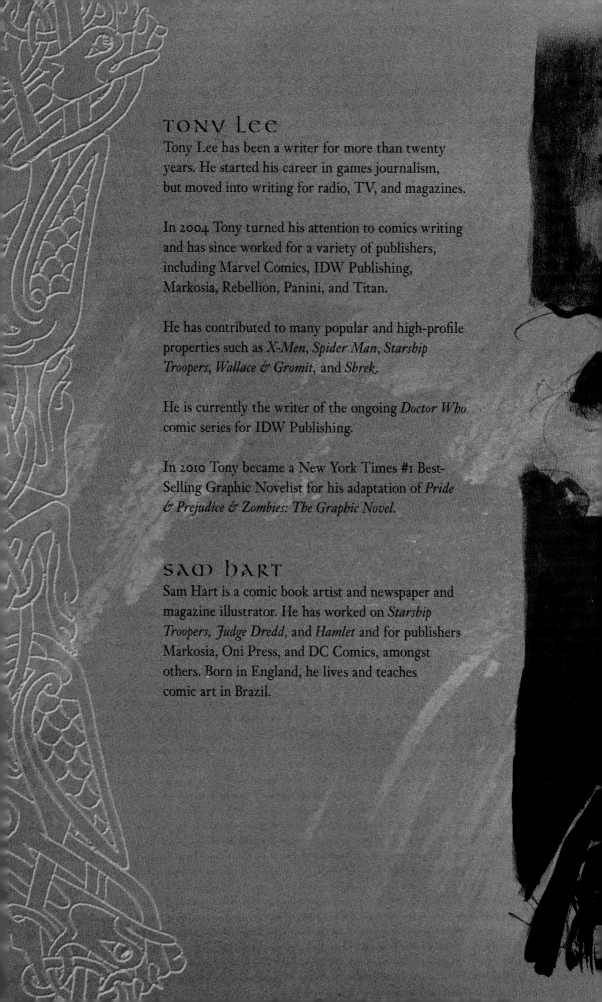

## TONY Lee

Tony Lee has been a writer for more than twenty
years. He started his career in games journalism,
but moved into writing for radio, TV, and magazines.

In 2004 Tony turned his attention to comics writing
and has since worked for a variety of publishers,
including Marvel Comics, IDW Publishing,
Markosia, Rebellion, Panini, and Titan.

He has contributed to many popular and high-profile
properties such as *X-Men*, *Spider Man*, *Starship
Troopers*, *Wallace & Gromit*, and *Shrek*.

He is currently the writer of the ongoing *Doctor Who*
comic series for IDW Publishing.

In 2010 Tony became a New York Times #1 Best-
Selling Graphic Novelist for his adaptation of *Pride
& Prejudice & Zombies: The Graphic Novel*.

## SAM HART

Sam Hart is a comic book artist and newspaper and
magazine illustrator. He has worked on *Starship
Troopers*, *Judge Dredd*, and *Hamlet* and for publishers
Markosia, Oni Press, and DC Comics, amongst
others. Born in England, he lives and teaches
comic art in Brazil.

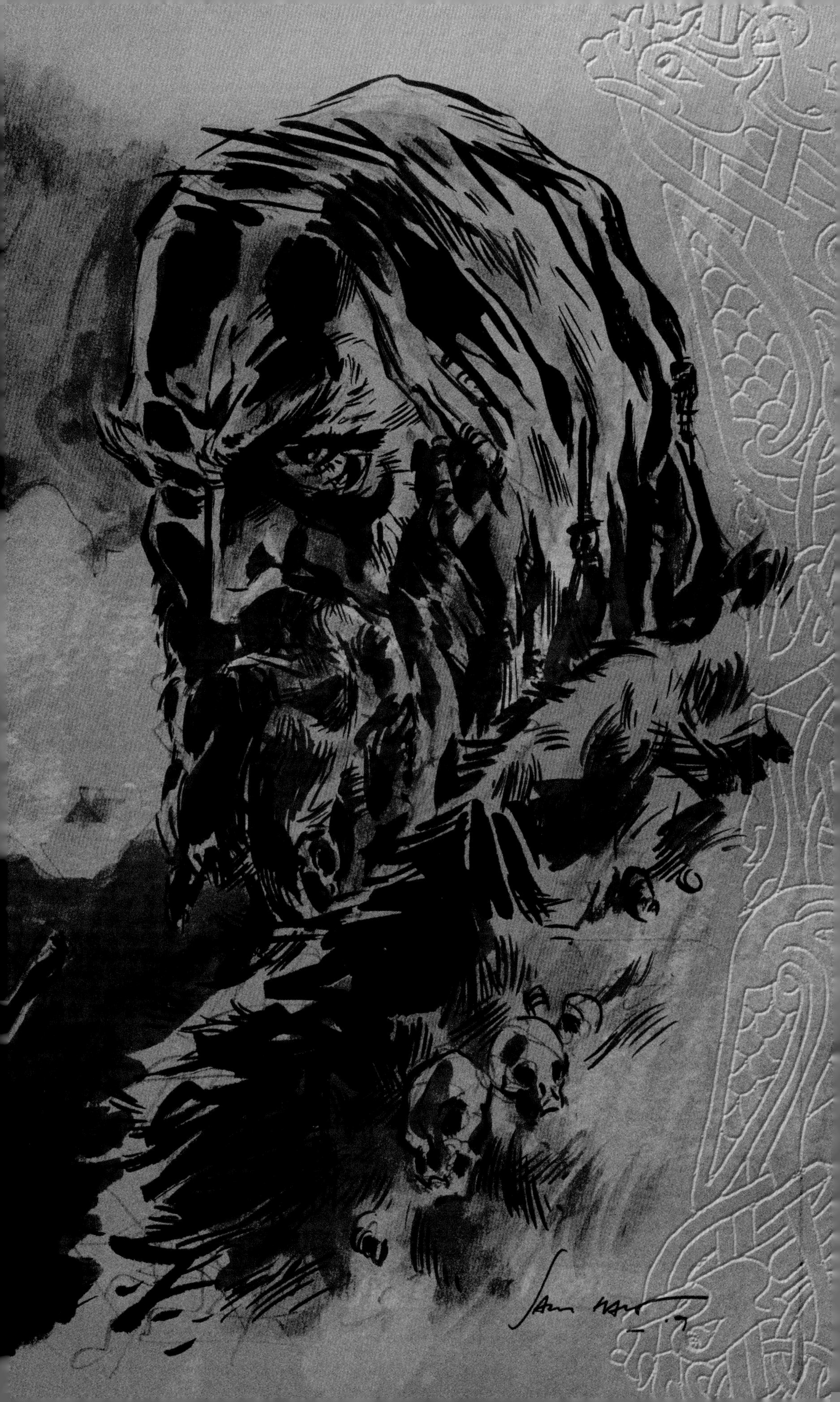

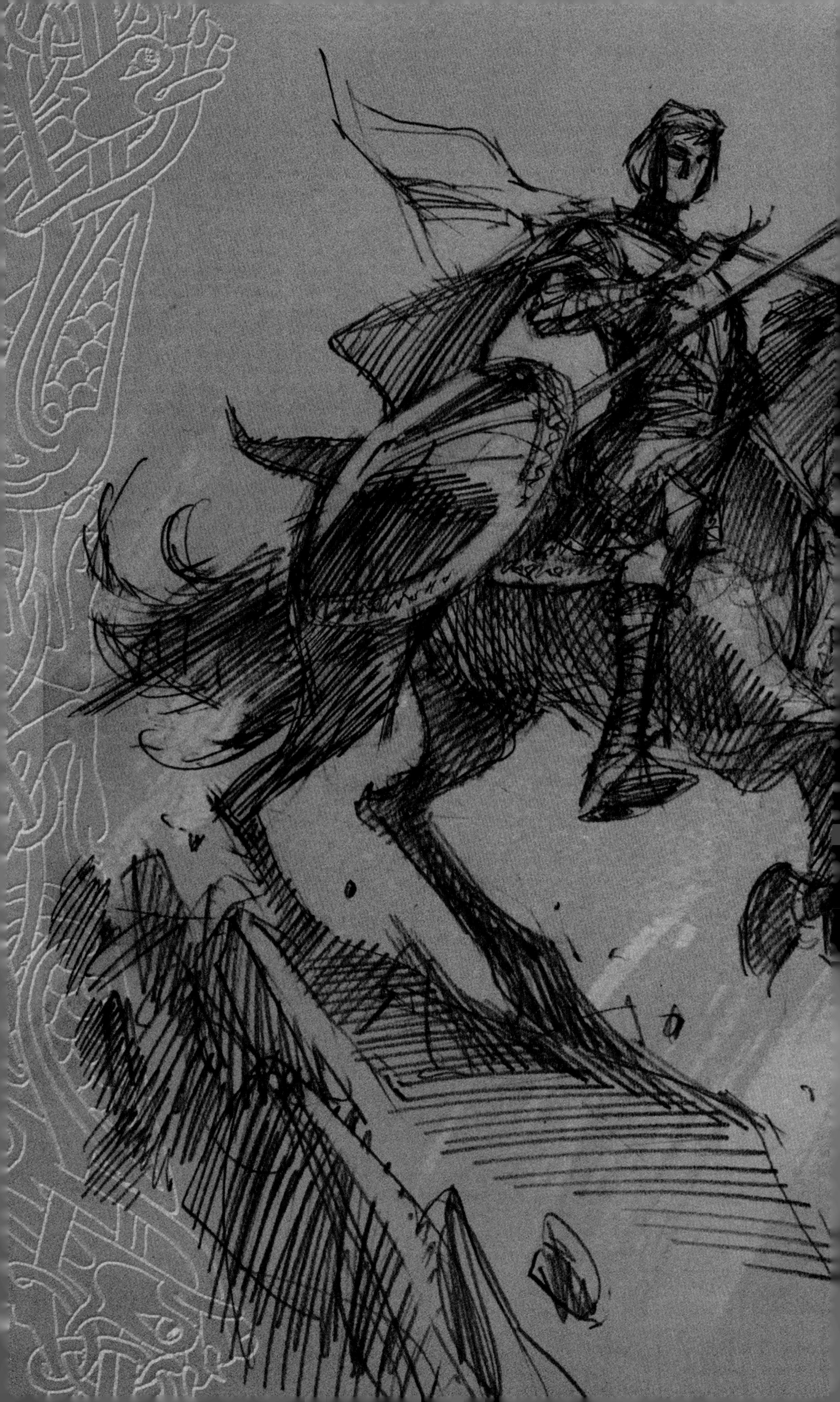

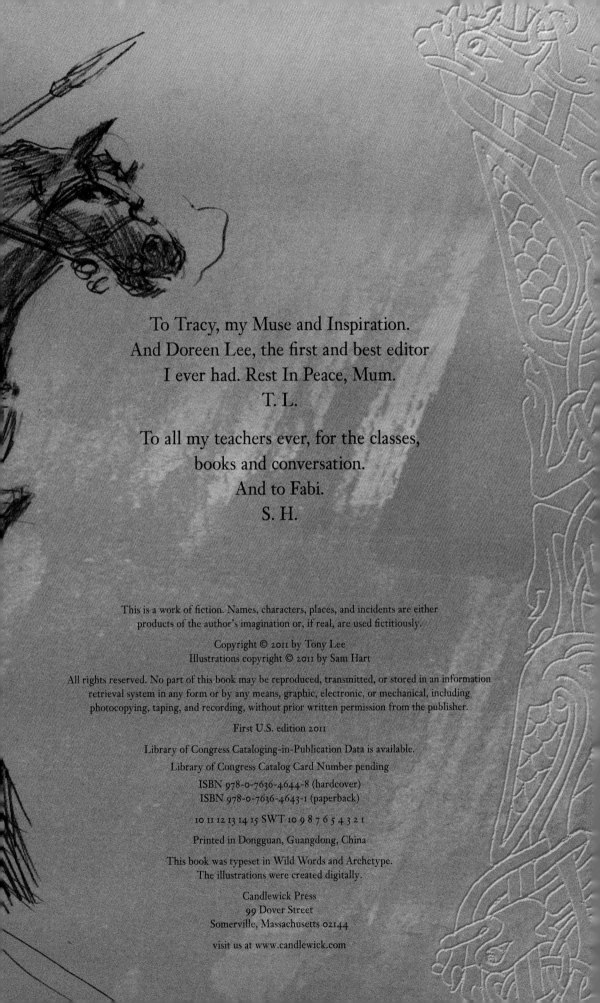

To Tracy, my Muse and Inspiration.
And Doreen Lee, the first and best editor
I ever had. Rest In Peace, Mum.
T. L.

To all my teachers ever, for the classes,
books and conversation.
And to Fabi.
S. H.

Copyright © 2011 by Tony Lee
Illustrations copyright © 2011 by Sam Hart

First U.S. edition 2011

Library of Congress Cataloging-in-Publication Data is available.

Library of Congress Catalog Card Number pending

ISBN 978-0-7636-4644-8 (hardcover)
ISBN 978-0-7636-4643-1 (paperback)

10 11 12 13 14 15 SWT 10 9 8 7 6 5 4 3 2 1

Printed in Dongguan, Guangdong, China

This book was typeset in Wild Words and Archetype.
The illustrations were created digitally.

Candlewick Press
99 Dover Street
Somerville, Massachusetts 02144

visit us at www.candlewick.com

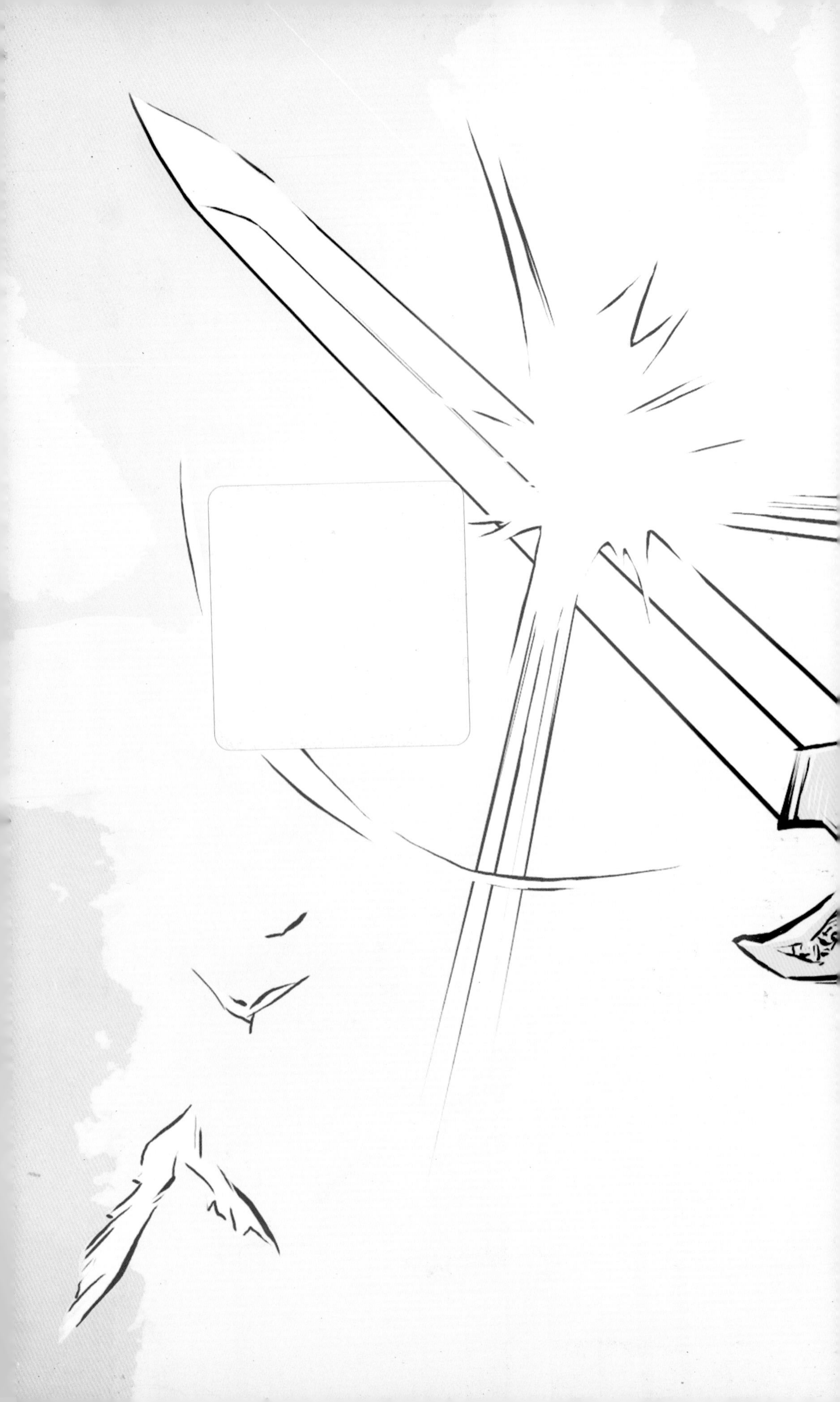